JOEL AUSTIN

RECKONING

VINCI
BOOKS

Vinci Books

vinci-books.com

Published by Vinci Books Ltd in 2026

1

A CIP catalogue record for this book is available from the British Library.
Paperback ISBN: 9781036705336
The EU GPSR authorised representative is Logos Europe, 9 rue Nicolas Poussion, 17000 La Rochelle, France contact@logoseurope.eu

To my mother—thanks for being amazing.

Chapter One

Samuel tapped the rusty thermometer with relative disinterest. It hung from a bent nail hammered into the plywood wall of his small security booth. The red line came even with one hundred and five. A record of sorts, if such a milestone was worth noting. Behind him, the refugee camp baked under a dirty haze of heat. No one dared to move too far from the shade. Samuel did not care either way, and if he had, it would not have changed the weather. He was too busy fiddling with an empty plastic sachet of water. The liquid was long gone, and so was the adolescent girl who had sold it. She wandered off down the red clay road with a basket full of goods angling precariously to one side of her head. Only the plastic wrapper remained. Dozens littered the small guard post.

Samuel folded it one way and then another, trying to get the blue mountains printed on the plastic to align. They were jagged and steep, unlike anything he had ever seen. His brother called them 'White Mountains', and Samuel was not sure if that was on account of the snow or the *obrunis* who lived nearby. A place so cold, it made him laugh. He wondered why anyone would suffer through such indignities.

Plumes of swirling dust sailed into the sky near the horizon and Samuel squinted into the distance. The day was a quiet one. Most of the Westerners were working in the primary part of the refugee camp, so traffic was sparse. A clipboard on the wall had no listings for any arrivals. He flipped through the smudged pages but saw nothing. Fourteen hours had passed since his shift started and Samuel was bleary-eyed, so he stepped out of the barren shack to get a better look.

Heat shimmered like broken glass just above the road— the churning of dirt was just distinct enough to see. Three brown lines were approaching fast from the north. Only refugees came from that cardinality. Save for the war itself. The rebels had driven south from the mountains and laid bare the crumbling facade of dictatorial rule.

Samuel grabbed the old AK-47 leaning against one of the exposed timbers. The security company he worked for had given him the gun and some training, but the bullets came out of his own pocket. Money was tight. His wife had a small vegetable stand on the side of the highway, but only the locals bought anything. Those fleeing had nothing, and the aid workers did not care for cassava or groundnuts. Such constraints left him skimping where possible, and only ten rounds were in the magazine.

A nagging sense of fear pulled at his lungs, and each breath was a little shorter. Samuel tried the radio, even though he knew the battery had died two hours earlier. The vehicles were almost in view. Sliding back the bolt, he chambered one-tenth of his ammunition and waited. The tightness in his chest had turned to jitters in his stomach. Samuel felt his bowels quiver, and the unexpected need to go was overpowering.

Across the road was a small ditch. He ran to it and barely got his trousers down before fear drained his intestines. Squatting in a small hole with his pants around his ankles, he had never felt more vulnerable.

"Not like this," he prayed.

Three Toyota trucks, scarred by age and battle, sped into view. The trucks themselves were nothing new. Throw a stone in West Africa, and it will hit a Hilux or Tacoma. Average people appreciated reliability, but there was nothing ordinary about the heavy machine guns mounted on the beds of the approaching vehicles. His gut exploded once more.

Samuel didn't own a TV—not with his meager paycheck—but his neighbor left the window open. At first, he found it irritating, like the man was showing him up, but in time, it became a ritual. Every night, after his son was asleep, Samuel would pull back the curtains and watch the news with his wife. Images of the war dominated the screen. Night after night, the news cycle contained video clips of heavily armed rebels surging south. They came not in tanks or on horseback but in the very trucks speeding in his direction.

Hisab, they called themselves—the reckoning. As if they alone were the arbiters of the end. They were extremists to some and true believers to others. For Samuel, none of the semantics mattered. He curled up like his son did when the dry crackle of lightning rolled overhead. In that slight depression, scraped from the sunbaked earth, Samuel cried —a quiet but mournful howl against all that was not. From the mistakes and missed opportunities to the future waiting just over the horizon.

A deafening roar filled the air as the lead truck shredded the guard post. Samuel clutched the red soil beneath him. It was hard and dry, but at that moment, it was all he had for comfort. Time did not slow down. There was no movie montage playing in his head. No epiphanies. The moment was nothing but fragments, sensations stitched together and masquerading as a memory.

A high-pitched whine from the engines. The deep thuds of a large-caliber weapon. Bullets the size of mango seeds. Dry crunching as plywood turned to splinters. The smell of gunpowder, exhaust, and shit. Spent casings glimmered on the ground. The rough texture of hardened soil on his face. That was what Samuel felt.

By the time he dared to breathe, they were in the camp. The small wooden gate that he so ceremoniously raised and lowered snapped like a twig. Broken pieces littered the road. Chunks of black and white stripes were everywhere, as if a zebra had exploded. He watched the men head straight for the small white tents that housed the doctors. He stood there, pants still around his ankles, unable to turn away or run.

The trucks stopped just shy of the World Health Organization office. Four men jumped out and waded into the sea of tents. Samuel pulled up his pants and was working on the buckle of his belt when gunshots echoed down the road. The men were back, dragging two people onto the trucks. Samuel knew most of the doctors, but he couldn't tell from that distance. Whoever they took did not go without a fight. One victim was unconscious. They dragged the second by the hair, the same way an abusive husband might pull his wife.

As the trucks turned around, Samuel ran into the thin brush, further away from the camp. He left the gun and his dignity behind. Neither was necessary for survival. Through the parted leaves, he saw two trucks drive back into the dusty north. They were returning to the fight, but for Samuel, the war had just arrived.

The last truck turned south.

Chapter Two

"We're close," said the copilot.

Captain Frank Sherman did not bother opening his eyes. A mental map had the small Gulfstream crossing into Ghanaian airspace ten minutes prior. That was before the dip in altitude and speed confirmed it.

He was stretching his six-foot frame across a couch built for a five-foot adolescent. It was short but made of some hard-to-find leather, and thus expensive. Given the preceding week, Sherman would have found a mound of coal comfortable. Despite the undersized accommodations, he gave Major Sanders credit. The army had confiscated a damn fine plane. Men and gear dotted the cabin, but no one dared to challenge his appropriation of the leather couch. Exhaustion took over after the first beer, and Sherman had slept for most of the 7,527-mile trip—not even a brief fuel stop woke him up.

Everyone gave him a yardstick's worth of space. Losing a friend was something they had all experienced, and people coped in unique ways. None of the men aboard questioned Sherman's bloodstained clothes or the muddy Glock lying unloaded on the floor. Trust and respect—he had earned them, and not one man second-guessed his actions.

"Wheels down in fifteen," shouted the pilot through the open cockpit door. There was no need for security measures on such a flight.

Sherman sat up and chugged a bottle of water. The dull tendrils of a headache were working their way around his temples. Opening another bottle, he used it to wash down an energy bar. When was the last time he ate? Was it twenty hours ago? He could not remember.

The extending flaps gave off a mechanical buzzing sound. The landing gear would follow. Sherman brought his attention to the present. He looked like shit. Most of his clothes were muddy, and despite a rainy night, his shirt had splatters of blood. Glancing down at the crimson stains barely brought a reaction. Sherman assumed they were from the fat man, but he was not the only person to meet a violent end that night.

Sergeant Raylan Gournsey caught his attention and tossed him a fresh pair of clothes. No camouflage—just basic civilian garb. They were not landing in a combat zone, at least not yet. Sherman stripped down where he sat. Embarrassment was not a concept shared among the passengers. Modesty did not exist in their world, where friends might get picked up piece by disfigured piece. Self-image was self-indulgent when things went wrong.

Major Sanders sat down next to Sherman as he was pulling up new socks. The two men had known each other for over a decade, but there was no doubt who gave the orders.

"We're headed straight to the embassy," informed

7

Sanders in his gravelly baritone. "The ambassador will give the briefing."

Sherman raised his eyebrows. "JSOC isn't running this?" he asked.

"We're not operational yet. The gold stars still think it's a French problem."

"It's always someone else's mess until it's yours," replied Sherman as he rubbed his head. "Who is the ambassador?"

"Chuck Franklin."

The name was familiar, and Sherman searched for the connection. It took a moment for his jet-lagged mind to catch up. "Wasn't he the South African station chief?"

Sanders nodded. "Went private after leaving the agency. Started his own little mercenary army. Recently sold the company and retired into politics."

"Must have some pull to get an ambassadorship."

"The money was ungodly," replied Sanders.

Both men laughed at the idea of a big payday. Neither of them believed they would leave the army alive, and if they made it out, it would not be to work under some fancy suits. Cashing in was never a motivator.

"You and I are going. The boys will get the gear loaded," said Sanders before his phone beeped, and he walked away to take the call.

Sergeant Gournsey ambled over and looked down at the muddy pistol. "Are you keeping that?" he asked.

The answer was no. Three murders were linked to it, but it took Sherman a few seconds to arrive at that conclusion. He handed the pistol over.

"This needs to disappear."

Gournsey nodded and picked up the weapon. It looked tiny in the massive mitts he called hands. "There's a river of shit not far from here."

"Appropriate," muttered Sherman as the sergeant handed him a new pistol. The matte black H&K .45 caliber felt much heavier than the Glock. Gournsey knew him well; for over ten years, it had been his preferred sidearm.

"Thanks," mumbled Sherman.

The sergeant smiled with a big, lopsided grin and unloaded the gear strewn about the cabin.

Sherman checked the weapon. It was loaded and chambered. He grabbed three extra magazines. They made his cargo pants bulky, but style was never his priority. Major Sanders walked down the thin metal stairs, and Sherman followed. A white Land Cruiser sat nearby. No matter where he went in the world, there was always a white Land Cruiser. The vehicle was ubiquitous.

The major got behind the wheel while he finished up his phone call. Some local embassy driver stood anxiously on the tarmac, wondering how he was going to explain a missing vehicle to his supervisor.

"You know the way?" asked Sherman, already aware that Sanders had likely memorized half the city.

"I'll wing it," joked the older man.

While the major was only ten years his senior, Sherman considered him a father figure. The man once held Sherman's rank when he ran ops from South America to Southeast Asia. He traded up for the golden oak leaf after taking a bullet in Iraq, but no one doubted his abilities. They had all seen their share of carnage. Sometimes it healed; other times, it stayed.

Sanders pulled out into traffic. The air was thick with the smell of unregulated exhaust, a by-product of a weak government and poverty. Dozens of horns blared seemingly at random, but there was an order to the chaos. Making a turn—one beep. Passing over a double yellow—two beeps.

Pissed off—lay on the horn. That part was not different from anywhere else.

They were not expecting trouble, but both men stashed their pistols between the seat and the console. Sherman had an MP7 compact submachine pistol down by his feet. Two HK416 assault rifles were stashed in the back. An arbitrary checkpoint or police stop might escalate quickly, but few locals wanted to interfere with embassy plates. It was a carte blanche for traffic violations.

"So, why are we here?" asked Sherman. The question was more practical than rhetorical. There was no doubt in his mind that someone needed killing. Sherman's team did not deploy for anything else.

"The suits want to avoid another Islamic State," answered the major with a shrug.

"Three guys and some assault rifles will not make much of a dent."

"This place is a tinderbox. *Hisab* attacked the refugee camp and kidnapped some aid workers."

"The reckoning?" asked Sherman, having translated the Arabic.

The major glanced over. "I take it you missed Anderson Cooper while you were in California?"

Sherman did not reply. Twenty-four hours earlier, he had put two bullets into a man he once trusted with his life—a former operator. The same man had killed his only friend. To say that it distracted him would be a gross understatement.

Major Sanders stopped short of apologizing. He had known Tillerman and exalted the man even though he had walked away. But they had no genuine bond, not like the one he had with Sherman. Sanders wanted to give him space to process what had happened. He also wanted distance and deniability from whatever actions the captain undertook. Knowing Sherman as he did, Sanders could only guess that the damage was significant.

Traffic flowed slower than a squalid creek. Horns were blaring, and people were yelling. Kids dashed in and out of the gridlock, hawking plastic bags of water and a random assortment of food. Sherman flagged one over and got a bag of something fried. A proper meal was what he needed, but he settled for anything over nothing.

"Doughnuts?"

"Bo-froot is what the kid called them," answered Sherman as he started on his second.

"You'll try anything."

"Beats another bag of Lays."

He had finished a half-dozen by the time Sanders pulled up to the front gate of the embassy. The whole compound was new and imposing, with three massive granite buildings separated by an immaculate sea of grass.

"So much for blending in," joked Sherman.

All vehicle traffic passed through a single-entrance building, like a garage with doors on both ends. Two large steel wedge barriers, thick enough to stop a tank, prevented any unwanted vehicles. Four-inch steel bars interspersed with concrete pillars formed the walls. Unobtrusive cameras dotted the entire place, and he knew they were being watched.

Two guards in dark blue uniforms circled about. The black and red emblem of a triangle on their shoulder looked menacing and oddly familiar to Sherman. Sanders rolled down the window halfway, and the eldest of the men leaned in with an alarmed look.

"Where is Daniel? This is his car."

The major smiled and held out his military credentials. "They needed him elsewhere."

"This is highly unusual," shouted the other man.

"Unorthodox, and a violation of protocol," concluded the older guard.

The younger one came over and knocked on Sherman's window. "Roll it down," he commanded.

Sherman tucked the pistol under his leg and lowered the glass a few inches. Smiling, he offered the guard one of the last doughnuts.

"Bo-froot?"

The man's mask of seriousness melted, and he smiled widely. He held up the treat for the older guard to see. They shared a brief laugh as the tension eased.

"Who are you here to see?" he asked.

"The ambassador," replied Sanders.

"And he's expecting you?"

"You could say that."

The man shrugged and picked up a nearby phone. Sherman couldn't hear what they said, but the guy looked apologetic as he walked back to the vehicle.

"Sorry about that, Major. Head on through. It's the big building straight ahead."

"Much obliged," said Sanders as he took back his badge.

The back barrier lowered, and they drove to a nearby parking spot.

"Doughnuts," grumbled Sanders.

"Doughnuts," repeated Sherman with a hint of glee.

As they approached the central building, the door buzzed and released a heavy locking mechanism. Sherman grabbed the handle and held it open. He guessed the door weighed a ton. Five inches of ballistic glass and steel gave the impression of security.

Once through, they entered a waiting area reminiscent of a corporate lobby. A Marine was watching them from behind a wall of bullet-resistant glass. Next to him was another massive stainless-steel door.

The soldier instinctively saluted as Sanders approached. There was something very austere and martial in how the major carried himself. He exuded a commanding presence, as the Army so happily put it.

"Major Sanders, sorry for any delay getting through the gate. I just received word you were coming."

Sanders looked the man over and replied, "It wasn't a bother, Corporal Olley."

Sherman was wandering about, and the clean-shaven Marine eyed him like a wild animal needing a wide berth. It was a fair assessment, despite the change of clothes. Sherman looked grizzled. A half-formed beard and specks of blood still clinging to his neck suggested he was someone not to be crossed.

"Captain Sherman will join me," informed Sanders.

Olley swallowed hard, "Yes, sir. Special Agent King will be down shortly. He's in charge of the ambassador's security detail."

The name rang a distant but pleasant bell in Sherman's memory. Years ago, he had known a Diplomatic Security Service agent by that name, back when JSOC still operated out of the Green Zone in Baghdad. His back was to the door when it opened, but he knew the voice without looking.

"Major Sanders, I'm Special Agent Clay King. Damn fine to meet you," said the man in a heavy West Texas drawl. A thick handlebar mustache drooped beneath his nose.

"Likewise," replied Sanders, extending the vice grip he called a hand. "This is Captain Sherman."

Agent King tilted his head in unsure amusement. "Frank—the tank—Sherman. God damn."

Sherman smiled politely, even though he hated the nickname. Surnames were enough for most interactions. First names worked if they were friendly, and rank was only for introductions.

"Kingsy. How the hell have you been?"

"Hot, sweaty, and my balls won't stop itching."

"Just like home, then," joked Sherman.

Sanders lifted an eyebrow at the exchange.

Clay smiled. "The captain and I were both stuck in the Green Zone back in the day. Shit, when was that? Twelve years ago?"

"Another lifetime," answered Sherman.

"Well, let's not dawdle. The SCIF is upstairs. Follow along."

Sherman and Sanders followed King up the stairs and through two more heavy steel doors. The major's glare made it clear he was no fan of the special agent.

"Frank the Tank?" he whispered.

"He wasn't an awful guy, and he had a good bourbon stash," replied Sherman with a shrug.

"Alright, fellas, here we are," said King. He held open the door to the SCIF—a small metal shed in the middle of what used to be a conference room. "You just can't trust these locals to build it right."

King was right not to trust local contractors with information security, but Sherman could not help but feel that the comment carried a certain misunderstanding verging on intolerance.

The ambassador sat at the head of a small metal table that belonged in a prison waiting room. It did not take more than a glance for Sherman to form his opinion of the man.

Chuck Franklin did not look up as they entered. His head was buried in artfully arranged paperwork. The gray streaks only highlighted the two-hundred-dollar price tag of his haircut. A Hublot watch, costing more than a corporal's annual salary, hung from his wrist. The blue suit was Savile Row, the pen Mont Blanc, and the brown leather shoes would not even make it through a forty-yard dash. The man had taste but no substance.

"Major Sanders," said Franklin as he slicked back an unruly strand of hair. "Welcome to Ghana."

"Thank you, Mr. Ambassador. This is Captain Sherman."

Franklin extended his hand and tried to impress Sherman with his grip. It didn't work.

"Why don't you gentlemen take a seat, and we can get started."

Sanders sat down, and Sherman followed suit. The ambassador smiled and took on a very professorial air, like someone about to explain a complicated subject to those of lesser intellect.

"As you've no doubt heard, Burkina Faso is descending into madness brought about by *Hisab*."

"Madness?" interjected Sanders. "Looks like your average civil war to me."

A smug smile rose at the corners of Franklin's mouth. "Don't be so naïve, Major. Africa is never simple. Kabore lost the trust of the generals after he threatened to institute a mandatory retirement age. Combine that with rising commodity prices and the structural inequities of his predecessor's rule, and a challenge to his power was inevitable. But that is not the actual danger here. *Hisab* is the heir to the Islamic State. They want to carve out a new caliphate in West Africa and threaten the very fabric of security in the region."

More words came out of Franklin's mouth with increasing vigor, but Sherman struggled to care. The history lesson was fine, but he already knew enough about the region to see that Franklin was bending the facts. The U.S. no longer had a diplomatic presence in Burkina Faso, so the ambassador's word carried extra weight.

Major Sanders barely blinked during the exchange. Sherman wondered how he kept a straight face with all the bullshit being bandied about. It was a solid reminder never to play poker with the man.

"I'm still unclear why you think *Hisab* is such a threat."

The ambassador sighed dramatically. "Major, were you not listening? They are the conclusion to a story decades in the making. They are worse than the Islamic State."

"And the attack on the refugee camp?"

"The first of many such attacks, I assure you."

"Let's hope not," said the major.

"Of course. I don't want further bloodshed, but we must stop them."

"I'm here to see if that's true."

Franklin's eyes narrowed, but he held his tongue.

The major stood to leave. "Thank you, Mr. Ambassador. I look forward to keeping in touch."

Franklin forced a smile. "Please let Agent King know if you need anything. He is my point man for any issues pertaining to security."

Sherman and Sanders wove their way out of the

embassy without saying a word. The guards smiled in recognition as they exited past the heavy steel barriers. Only once they pulled back out into the morass of traffic did Sherman speak.

"What kind of twisted sales pitch was that?"

"A condescending one."

"He sure took pains to demonize *Hisab*, not that they needed it," said Sherman.

"That he did," replied Sanders, scratching his chin. "Which makes the call I got earlier even more interesting."

Sherman turned in anticipation.

"An old buddy of mine at the agency called to tell me one of his assets is missing. He's been trying to run it up the flagpole but is getting nowhere."

"Odd he didn't mention that fact. Would have added fuel to the fire."

"Exactly," replied the major.

"Do you think he is hiding that fact or just willfully ignoring it?"

"I'm not sure, but someone is screwed either way."

"Should I tell the boys to stop unpacking?"

Sanders nodded. "Call those cockpit jockeys too. Wheels up in thirty."

Chapter Three

Rays of sunlight streamed through bullet holes in the cheap plywood walls. The tiny guard post was more transparent than solid. Standing inside, Sherman felt like he was inside a cheese grater. Even with the extra ventilation, the space was stifling hot. He looked around—not even a fan to ward off the heat.

"I don't see any blood," he yelled toward the major.

Sanders stooped over a shiny string of brass cartridges lying in the dirt. He held up a spent casing and shouted back, "Fifty caliber."

The radio in Sherman's ear hissed to life with Sergeant Gournsey's voice. "Captain, we've got company."

A pair of burly-looking white men were trotting in his direction. Judging by the R5 rifles slung across their chests and their clean tactical vests, Sherman knew they weren't aid workers. The hardware indicated they were South African.

"Hey, bru, what you doin' there?" shouted one man.

Sherman stepped out of the shack with his hands up.

He knew the type—killers. Fancy gear could not hide their dead eyes. The spark was long gone.

"Hey, boys. Sorry to step on your turf. We're with the U.S. Army Corps of Engineers. We saw this little mess as we passed by. Curiosity got the better of us."

He looked nothing like an engineer, but the two South Africans were not ordinary security guards either. Squinting into the bright sunlight, both groups sized each other up like all humans have done since the dawn of time.

A thin smile streaked across the guard's face. "No problem, but what do you Americans say about curiosity? It shot the cat?"

His partner laughed.

"Something like that," replied Sherman. "We'll be getting out of your way now."

The guards waited until Sherman and Sanders were back in their SUV—yet another Land Cruiser on loan from an American charity with friendly back-channel ties to the intelligence community.

"What's up with the PMCs?" asked Gournsey. A rifle lay across his lap, and Sherman knew the South Africans had been in his sights the entire time.

"Looks like they buffed up their security after the attack," observed Sanders.

Sherman added, "Funny, the ambassador also forgot to mention that."

Gournsey raised an eyebrow. "Why would he care?"

Sanders started up the vehicle. "He used to own the company."

Sherman rolled down his window and watched as the men took up positions behind a newly installed blast wall. A phone rang, and Sanders answered. Sherman was half-listening, but it did not sound good. He scratched at his slowly returning beard. It no longer itched, but there was something compulsive about the action. The smoothness of his own skin felt liberating at first since he had hidden it for a decade. That was before they killed his friend in California. Someday, he would read about the fallout, but not soon.

An adolescent girl walked by with a tub full of small plastic bags. "Water?" she asked.

"No, thanks."

"I saw you in the guard booth. It gets hot in there," she countered with a wide smile.

Sherman grabbed a few dollars and handed them over. "Do you know what happened?"

The girl's eyes gleamed as she grabbed more cash than she could earn in three days. "I didn't see, just heard the story."

"I like stories," replied Sherman.

"That was Samuel's. They said he crapped his pants when they came."

"*Hisab?*"

Her head bobbed a little. "He was nice. His wife, too."

"Do you know where I can find him?"

The girl narrowed her eyes. "Trouble?"

"No trouble. I just want to know what he saw."

She thought for a moment, deciding if she could trust a foreigner. "His wife has a market stall down the road."

Sherman gazed south, past her outstretched finger. "Does it have a name?"

"Jesus Loves Veggies."

He smiled at the audacity of such a name and handed the girl twenty more dollars. "Thanks."

The girl giggled and wandered down the road. Her

interest in selling for the rest of the day was gone. Sanders shrugged and pulled onto the dusty road.

"You think he saw something?"

"If he shat himself, I'd wager he was close enough to get a good look."

"Or he had some bad goat stew," suggested Gournsey.

Sherman laughed, "I thought you liked goat."

"I do," replied the big man. "But you gotta simmer it low and slow."

The major headed south, away from the refugee camp. Red dust swirled behind them, fading into the afternoon light.

"What was the call about?" asked Sherman.

"*Hisab* just freed one of the aid workers." Frustration drove Sanders' voice lower than his usual growl.

"Ain't that a good thing?" asked the sergeant.

"Not ours. A Jean Pierre so-and-so. Charlie McMillan is still missing."

"Makes sense," said Sherman. "*Hisab* doesn't want to piss off the French. They still treat the old colonies like their backyard."

"That leaves the American as leverage," sighed Sanders.

"Looks like they're playing the long game."

"Aren't we all?" mused the major as they pulled up next to the market.

Across the road, hidden amongst the tangle of ramshackle homes, Samuel frowned as he butchered a scrawny chicken. The bird was too small, but there was no money for anything else. It had wandered aimlessly around the streets, drinking putrid green water from the open sewers and eating whatever scraps it could find. Now it was barely a meal for his wife and son.

Their hunger was his fault. At least that was what he

kept telling himself. If he had stayed at his post, the company wouldn't have fired him. That job was the difference between three meals a day and one bowl of fried rice with a few bits of stringy chicken.

Shame lingered longer than the stench caked on his pants. Two days had passed, but everyone knew. Neighbors laughed as they passed by his small two-room cinder block house. The gun and uniform, once a source of pride, were gone too. They even took the bullets he paid for out of pocket.

"Let me finish," said Ama.

Samuel smiled at his wife, but every time she offered support, he felt more helpless.

"I can do it," he protested.

"Of course, my love, but I need your help to fetch a cassava from the shop."

"Anything for you," he replied.

In ten years of marriage, he had never said no to Ama. There was a glow in her eyes that melted any anger or frustration lingering in his heart. Unable to stay mad, Samuel choked down the sorrow left behind.

He was worth more dead than alive. Had he stayed to fight, the company would have paid out five thousand dollars for his corpse. That was almost two years' salary. More than enough for Ama to expand the tiny stall and buy goods the Westerners cared about. With their money, things would only get better.

As Samuel crossed over the concrete gutter glowing with urine and feces, a neighbor waved him down. He had no desire to chat, but the man looked insistent.

"Samuel. Some men are looking for you."

"What men?"

His neighbor shrugged. "They asked if I knew you."

"And?"

"Evil stalks their eyes. I said no."

"Evil?" asked Samuel. He knew no such men and held no debts or wealth to steal.

"Drug boys."

Samuel was further confused. He did no drugs, nor could he afford them. "Where did you see them?" he asked.

The neighbor pointed just up the road. "The silver Mercedes."

Between the corrugated tin walls of the market stalls, rusted with age, he saw a glimmer of new money.

From the street, Sherman saw it too. Two muscular men in dark tank tops and designer jeans were poking around a small stall when he and Gournsey arrived. The sergeant spotted them first—overbuilt meatheads sticking out like a sore thumb. They were milling about the market stalls, draped with gleaming gold necklaces and cruel grins. Each had a body built with too much gym time and not enough work.

"They don't look too friendly."

"Swanky ride too," added Sherman. "Not exactly locals."

Sanders nodded. "I'll stay on the Mercedes. You two see if you can round up this Samuel character."

A few months prior, *obrunis* wandering about would have caused quite a commotion. The border wasn't a tourist destination. Most foreigners flew over it if they crossed it at all. That changed with the war. First came the refugees. The rest followed. Aid workers arrived, and convoys of food flooded the markets with cheap grain. This forced local farmers to sell their crops at a loss. Crime soared with the influx of money and desperation. It happened all over the world, all in the name of saving lives.

Sherman motioned for Gournsey to take the opposite side of the road. A nod sufficed. After four tours together, the sergeant didn't need words to understand.

Handing over a few cents for some plantain chips gave Sherman a bit of cover. He looked average enough to blend in with the foreign contingent sampling the local culture or buying trinkets for family back home—a tourist on the fringes of suffering.

Chapter Four

Smoke lingered in the air. Cooking fires mingled with smoldering trash heaps—the familiar smell of everyday life that Samuel took for granted. Children were playing nearby, squealing with joy and youthful exuberance, the normal din of afternoon life. Ordinary, yet not.

With the shame of running still ringing in his ears, Samuel felt emboldened. *It must be some misunderstanding,* he thought. Why else would those thugs be looking for him?

Passing by the small plywood shack that served as his cousin's hair salon, Samuel stopped. Through the stacks of old tires and disassembled engines strewn about the neighborhood mechanic's shop, he saw two men rifling through Ama's stall.

Standing by an overturned carton of pineapple, one man blocked nearly the entire doorway. A refrigerator had less total volume. Samuel swallowed hard and took a step back. His welled-up courage popped like an overfilled balloon.

The man grabbed a passerby and asked a question

Samuel could not hear but fully understood. Whether out of fear or decency, the unlucky stranger pointed in his direction. A moment passed where both men looked at each other—past the roaming chickens, over the grease-stained tarps, and through the stacks of worn-down tires. Samuel still couldn't fathom why the other was there but had seen enough to know it portended ill. Retreat was the only option. He turned and walked away as fast as his ego allowed. The muscled malcontent followed, bounding toward Samuel with the inertia of a freight train.

Sherman watched the commotion and caught Gournsey's attention. He pointed to the second man still wreaking havoc in the small store.

"Alive," he said into the radio before chasing after the appliance-sized man.

Samuel cut across a small field of corn, hoping to put some distance between himself and his pursuer. It was not working, but he had nowhere else to go. The nearest police checkpoint was at least a mile away, and he dared not head home. Fear was taking hold again, and he felt the familiar pangs of panic in his stomach.

"Not now," he muttered to himself.

Fleeing away from the road reduced his chances of survival, but it was all he could think to do. Bystanders grew less frequent. Potential witnesses vanished as he bolted into the thin brush.

Out of breath and options, Samuel stopped by an abandoned brick maker's building, half reclaimed by nature. The business, built on a boom, had ended with a bust. Maybe it would come back with the refugee camp. Maybe not.

Samuel ducked behind a stack of sunbaked mud rectangles and waited. It wasn't for long. A thrashing noise akin to an animal running through the jungle announced the man's arrival. The Ghanaian was breathing hard. His fancy jeans were torn, and a small rivulet of blood trickled down his cheek. Sensing his prey had stopped, the man smiled and grabbed the pistol from behind his back. Like everything else about the drug smuggler, it was oversized and gaudy. The nickel-plated Desert Eagle .50 caliber hand cannon glinted brightly in the late-day sun.

"Samuel," bellowed the man. "Come out, and I'll end it quickly."

The knot in Samuel's stomach tightened. Not only did the guy have a gun—an enormous gun—but he knew his name. The old compound was small. Being discovered was inevitable. He took a deep breath and readied himself for another adrenaline-fueled dash.

"Don't shit yourself again," boomed the voice.

Samuel ran, but it was too late. An arm the size of a small tree knocked him to the ground. He coughed and wheezed, struggling to find a pain-free breath.

"You shouldn't have made me look. I was going to be nice, but now…" The man pointed the pistol at Samuel's kneecaps. "I'll have some fun."

Samuel gazed up at the barrel of the gun. The periphery disappeared, and only the chambered bullet was in focus. Everything else was dim and hazy. He did not hear Sherman slip out of the surrounding bush or close the gap. Both men were so preoccupied with the finality hurtling toward them that neither felt the American's presence.

"Weakling," spat the smuggler.

The barrel hovered inches above Samuel's head. He closed his eyes and prayed again—a last-gasp effort to all the gods. Then he cried.

"Garbage in. Garbage out," said the man.

Samuel closed his eyes and braced himself for the end. When the gunshot came, it felt like a relief. There was no pain. No black nothingness. No hell or purgatory, just a faintly sweet metallic smell. Slowly, he opened one eye, then the other. Looking around, he saw no changes, except for the body lying face-down on the ground. There was a gaping hole in his forehead. Blood mixed with the red earth to form muddy black clumps. Disbelief came before the shock.

"Samuel," said Sherman. "We'd better get going."

Wearily, he turned toward the voice. "Who are you?"

"Captain Frank Sherman. United States Army."

Samuel paused as his brain tried to catch up with the fact that he was still alive. He pointed to the dead man and asked, "And who is that?"

Sherman shrugged. "Someone who didn't want you talking."

"Talking about what?"

"We'll sort that out, but right now, we'd better get moving. Someone heard that."

The radio in Sherman's ear hissed with Gournsey's voice. "You okay, Cap?"

"Yeah. One down. I'm coming back with our friend."

"Copy that. We'll be waiting in the Mercedes."

Sherman turned back to Samuel and pointed to the body. "He wasn't alone, and he won't be the last. Let me help you."

Samuel shook his head in despair.

"Okay," coaxed Sherman. "Can you tell me about the attack?"

"You said there are more of them, right? I need to protect my family. You did that for me. Can you do that for them?"

Sherman scratched his meager beard and considered the request. For all he knew, the man had no useful information. If that was true, then he had murdered a man for some petty squabble—not that he would lose sleep over it. A misunderstanding didn't resonate as an explanation for what he had witnessed. Large-caliber pistols aren't needed for everyday disputes. The texture of the event was all wrong, which led Sherman to nod his head in agreement.

"Alright, Samuel. I'll help you, and then you'll start talking."

Samuel nodded. "Thank you."

"Save the platitudes for later. How far is your house?"

"A kilometer or less. By the petrol station."

Sherman keyed the radio. "Major, meet me by the gas station. Party of…" He turned to Samuel. "How many kids?"

"One son."

"Party of three."

"Understood," replied Sanders.

Sherman grabbed the dead man's phone and wallet before stripping the expensive pistol. He tossed a few parts in each direction as Samuel eyed the congealing carnage.

"Come on," said Sherman. "Good luck explaining this to your wife."

Ama was at the front door when they arrived. Creases of worry stretched from the corners of her eyes. When she saw Samuel, stress turned to tears, and she ran into his arms.

"What happened? You were gone so long, and then we heard the gunshot," she sobbed.

"It's okay, my love. I'm okay."

Ama saw Sherman. "Who is this?"

"A friend."

"You have *obruni* friends?"

"I do now."

"Love, what are you not telling me?" asked Ama.

Samuel sighed. "We need to leave. Maybe go and stay with your sister for a few days."

"You hate my sister. What is going on? You're scaring me."

"I'll tell you in the car. Grab Kofi and some clothes. Trust me."

Ama had always believed in Samuel and saw something special where others did not. She took a deep breath and looked at the fear smeared across his face.

"Okay," she replied.

The major pulled up as Ama and Kofi were gathering their meager belongings.

"This is a mess," said Sanders.

"It had no other ending," replied Sherman.

"I need not remind you we're not authorized to operate on Ghanaian soil."

"Yet you are reminding me."

Sanders gave Sherman a long, hard look. It was not the first time the major had glanced at him in such a way. It was a question of competency—plain and simple. The previous week had been brutal. The major knew something terrible had happened in California. He hadn't asked, nor did he want to know. But it could undo even the most solid of men.

"Guy had a Deagle to Samuel's head. My options were limited," Sherman explained.

"I don't give a shit about a body, Captain. Tillerman was a great friend. I want to make sure you have a lid on all that."

The major cut straight to the bone. Sherman appreciated the honesty. In his world, bullshit killed people.

"Airtight, sir."

"Good. Now what's this all about?"

"He'll talk but wants to keep his family safe."

"Fine. There is an NGO house on the outskirts of town. I'll send you the coordinates. Meet us there when you're done."

Sherman flashed a smile and turned to Samuel. "This is Major Sanders. He'll take you somewhere safe."

"Thank you, my friend."

Everyone piled into the SUV and disappeared into a cloud of dust. Sherman couldn't help but wonder if Samuel was lucky or cursed. Two scrapes with death and two escapes in almost as many days. Fate was toying with the man either way. Judging by the family driving away, he felt no remorse over pulling the trigger. Regret and guilt were frayed concepts, dulled and torn over the last fifteen years of war. He turned and walked back to the Mercedes.

Gournsey gave him an inquisitive look when he opened the door.

"I'm fine," replied Sherman.

"Just checking, Cap."

"He in the trunk?"

"For working out so much, the guy had a glass jaw."

"Breathing then?"

"For now."

Sherman nodded. "Okay. Let's go somewhere quiet and have ourselves a little chat."

"With pleasure."

They drove south on a road paved with neglect. Like small uneroded mountains, the rare patches of asphalt only made the ride bumpier. Vast fields of grass edged into eternity on either side of the road. Scrawny trees emerged, growing in density as the town receded. Only the occasional deserted concrete foundation revealed any signs of human presence.

The year was not that old, but that made no difference to the sun. It always drops with a certain suddenness near the equator. Gournsey opened the trunk and yanked out the smuggler like he was a piece of luggage. The man's shirt had stains of crusted crimson from a broken nose. Sherman saw a familiar look of panic in his eyes—a look he'd seen too many times during the wars. It spread from dilated pupils across the entire face until nothing but fear remained.

Sherman knelt next to the prone figure. "What's your name?"

"Prince," mumbled the man.

"Okay, Prince. We have some questions. I hope you have answers."

"And if I don't?"

Sherman nodded toward Gournsey and said, "Don't let it come to that."

One eye was swollen shut, but Prince glanced at the hulking sergeant and the pistol in his hand. His nose burned, and his face ached. There was no doubt in his mind about the outcome of not talking.

"Where is Isaac?"

"The big guy?" Sherman clarified.

Prince nodded.

"Dead."

Gournsey took a step forward, and the smuggler flinched.

"What do you want to know?"

Sherman smiled. "Wise choice. Why were you after Samuel?"

Prince shook his head in disbelief. "He be a name. We don't ask why."

"Now, Prince," growled Gournsey. "You've got to do better than that."

"Truth. I didn't know d'em. Some loose ends."

"Whose loose end?" asked Sherman.

"Kutu's."

Gournsey was losing patience. "Forgive our ignorance, but who the hell is that?"

"Hero of the north."

Sherman motioned for him to continue.

"The boss man."

The sergeant took another step in.

"A smuggler. *The* smuggler."

"Better," said Sherman. "Now, why would this Kutu want some nobody like Samuel dead?"

"He saw something."

"The attack?"

Prince nodded.

Sherman's mind started picking up the scattered dots and drawing lines. "Do you have the other aid worker?"

"I don't know. Seriously. I got the name on a piece of paper."

"Where do we find him?"

"Really, I don't know."

Sherman frowned at the man's lack of imagination. "Your boss. Where do we find your boss?"

Prince looked at both men, trying to decide which betrayal was worse: his boss or the Americans.

"Look, kid," said Sherman, "this isn't a choice. Tell us now, or we'll leave your body for the dogs and find Kutu another way."

"Tamale," blurted Prince. "He runs a garage there."

Sherman stood up. "I shouldn't need to tell you this, but it's worth underlining: don't let me see you again."

"Wait," said Prince. "You're leaving me here?"

Darkness was falling like a curtain across the flat expanse. Sunlight that had been there moments before fizzled away in a matter of seconds.

Sherman rolled down the window. "For your own sake, find another job."

Chapter Five

Charlotte McMillan was teetering on the edge of panic. She had not slept since men barged into the tent and dragged her out by the hair. Forty-eight hours had elapsed, and her nerves were fraying. A thin, cruel-looking man with a shaved head had asked her a few questions. She played dumb, but they had taken her, and that meant something. Coincidences didn't exist in her reality. Soon enough, the questions would turn to demands backed by the threat of what did not need to be said.

The tin shack serving as her prison was both dark and hot. A bottle of tap water lay nearby—an open invitation to intestinal distress. Charlotte knew it was only a matter of time before she would have to drink it. The results would leave her worse off, but it bought her time. What to do with that time was a question she couldn't answer.

Rescue was unlikely. She was more of an asset than an agent, and the United States government didn't officially negotiate with terrorists. Off the books, the CIA traded cash and drugs for many exchanges, whether people or intelligence. The problem, as Charlotte saw it, was that she had no clear value to trade. She wasn't spying on China or Russia. She didn't know the location of the ISIS leaders. At a glance, she was just an aid worker who kept her eyes and ears open, sharing information with an old friend when it seemed appropriate. Navy SEALs don't knock down doors for just anyone.

A car door slammed nearby, and her back stiffened. Sandals slapped against heels. Then came the screech of metal, and the rusty deadbolt on the outside of the shed opened. Blinding light flooded the minuscule space. Charlotte flinched as a thickset man, with rolls of fat folded up under his chin, knelt next to her. He smelled of expensive cologne and cigar smoke.

"Ms. McMillan, I apologize for your harsh treatment."

The voice was as deep and textured as a blues singer, even though the accent was British. Charlotte squinted against the sunlight, hesitant to see a face.

"My name is Kutu, and I have some questions for you." The man paused for a moment. "Perhaps that is the wrong word. Maybe 'demands' is more appropriate."

"You want to know something," replied Charlotte.

Kutu's boisterous laugh shook the tin walls. It was full of mirth, not menace, and it caught Charlotte off guard.

"You are a smart woman, Ms. McMillan, very smart indeed."

"And if I tell you this thing you are demanding to know?"

Kutu ran one of his thick hands across the top of his shaved head. "I won't lie to you, miss. Your situation is not good."

"How not good?" she asked, having left hope behind some hours before.

"I'll give you the choices, and you can decide," answered Kutu. His round face almost lit up with the small act of humanity, as if offering two terrible fates was a kindness.

Charlotte could feel her stomach twisting with panic. At the edge of a war zone, no good choices were almost worse than death. She choked out the question, "What are my options?"

Kutu nodded in thought. "We can finish our acquaintance here, or I'll sell you across the border to *Hisab*."

Death or slower death. It took a moment for Charlotte to process the statement. Only then did she grasp her mistake. In the panic of being taken, she thought they had turned right but had dismissed the thought. She was in Ghana and didn't even know it.

"I'll be honest with you, Mr. Kutu. Your choices suck."

Again, Kutu's laugh filled the hot, stale room.

"But," she continued, "I'll take my chances with the jihadists."

The colossal head bobbed solemnly. "You know their work firsthand?"

She nodded. Enough brutalized and maimed people to fill a thousand lifetimes had crossed her path. But time was time, and Kutu was offering a glimmer of hope.

"I'll take my chances."

"Very well, I'll make the arrangements for tonight. Now I really only have one question."

Charlotte nodded.

"Have you seen anything strange passing through the camp? All the specifics, if you will."

While she had never faced interrogation before, Charlotte was no fool. She still had something they wanted. From the sound of the question, it seemed like Kutu wanted assurances. For over a decade, she'd witnessed the best and worst of human proclivities. In the heart of that madness existed an economic system built around exploitation—capitalism stripped of any fancy talk about equal participants or market forces.

Under her watch, many goods exchanged hands and got smuggled into refugee camps and across borders. Charlotte wasn't sure what Kutu was fishing for, but she had a damn good idea: the same information she intended to send to Langley.

"Drugs, girls, food, medicine. But you already knew that," she answered.

"Anything else?"

"A goat," she offered with feigned ignorance.

The smuggler grinned, but she could see the wheels turning, weighing her words and facial cues. The difference between a slow death and an immediate one hung on her poker face.

Kutu slapped his knee. "It was a pleasure to meet you, Ms. McMillan. Again, I apologize for the circumstances."

"I wish I could say the same."

The door closed without another remark, plunging Charlotte into darkness. This time, her nerves didn't feel so raw. A small ember of hope burned in the deepest corner of her mind. Kutu had fanned it into a small fire with his questions and his very presence. She knew for certain something that had been only a guess when the man walked through the door: the truck had turned right. She was in Ghana.

Slumped low in the seats of an old Peugeot, Sherman and Gournsey watched the compound. Trading the Mercedes for something less conspicuous had been easier than either man had foreseen. The minor car dealer had asked no questions and required no paperwork.

Following Prince's directions led them to a dirt alley about two hundred feet from Apscom Motors. They parked in the shade of a lone palm tree and waited. Dozens of smashed cars stood stacked on one side of the compound, creating a mangled barrier. Cinder block walls topped with shards of broken glass enclosed everything else.

Sherman counted twenty-two people coming and going within the first hour. "Business is booming," he noted.

"Catering to all sorts," added Gournsey. Not only had they seen fancy suits driving Audis and BMWs, but at least three soldiers in uniform had visited.

Most of the men loitering around the perimeter were dressed in black with varying levels of bling. "At least they have a dress code," Sherman joked.

"I make at least ten on the outside."

Sherman tapped his radio button. "Major, we found the place but can't confirm the package."

"Understood. The general confirmed he could spare a nearby UAV in four hours."

"Do they need clearance from the locals?" asked Sherman.

"No. Why?"

"We've seen a handful of troops come and go. My guess is they are on the payroll."

"I'll keep it low profile," Sanders assured him.

Corrupt soldiers were unsurprising in parts of the world where criminals made a corporal's annual salary in a week. The longer Sherman watched, the more convinced he became that the hostage was inside. If Kutu had the local army and cops in his pocket, there was no need for so much manpower—unless he was protecting something of significant value.

"Does their roster seem heavy to you?" he asked Gournsey.

"Like foxes around a chicken coop. You want to look around?"

Sherman glanced around the neighborhood. "This isn't exactly expat land."

"Wait for overwatch?"

The dials on his watch said four o'clock. Sunset was only an hour away, and darkness would swiftly follow. His subconscious surfaced the little details that had kept him alive for so many years—which cars had come and gone, and the lone one that stayed.

"You remember the van that pulled in when we were arriving? Did it leave?"

Gournsey shook his head. "Nope, but they ain't exactly uncommon."

The sergeant was right. Publicly funded transportation didn't exist on any significant scale in Ghana. Six-row mini-vans plying routes across the country provided the cheapest means of getting around. With so many miles seen each day, their appearance at the mechanics was unsurprising.

"It's the only thing that stayed."

"Transport?"

"I think they're moving him."

"Or selling."

"I hope you're right. Corpses come cheap around here," replied Sherman. He tapped the transmit button. "Major, clarification: I think they are planning on moving the package soon."

"Any visual confirmation?"

"Negative."

The major paused for a moment to consider Sherman's gut feeling and the implications of operating on friendly but foreign soil. The list of signatures needed was long and time-consuming. North of the border in Burkina Faso, it was another story. Most of the intelligence community was coming around to the ambassador's argument that *Hisab* did not differ from ISIS.

"We're in murky waters here, boys. If you see him, grab him. Otherwise, we wait for overwatch."

Sherman understood the position. The major could not green-light a firefight based on his gut alone. Not then. Not in Ghana.

"Copy that."

Gournsey glanced in his direction. "Suit up?"

"Let's make it a party."

Under a blanket on the back seat lay a small arsenal. Both men slipped on tactical vests and grabbed silenced MP5s. The integrated suppressors made them a favorite among the Special Forces community. The loudest sound came from the bolt cycling back closed after each shot.

"At least this junker has tinted windows," joked the sergeant.

Sherman glanced at the slow trickle of foot traffic walking by their car and laughed. "We'd be terrible spies."

"Now, now. Don't sell yourself short, Cap. A man's got to dream."

The sergeant belonged nowhere else in life. Raylan Gournsey's retirement plan was a pine box draped in the American flag. They were howling in the wilderness of human depravity and growing hoarse by the effort. After all, humanity was built around the war cry, but it consumes all who take part. Anything less was a lie.

Neither man spoke. They waited as the horizon swallowed the sun and cast about twilight like a handful of gray confetti. Soon enough, it dissolved into the harsh glow of fluorescent bulbs. Incandescence didn't exist in West Africa. There wasn't enough power to waste. Scarcity never allowed such products to proliferate.

Gournsey broke the silence. "It ain't my place, but—"

Sherman cut him off. "I shouldn't have asked you to get rid of the Glock."

"It don't bother me."

"You just want to know what happened," said Sherman.

The sergeant gave a half-hearted shrug of his massive shoulders.

"The lieutenant had a lady."

"Tillerman found a woman?" asked Gournsey.

Sherman nodded. "A wonderful one at that."

"What happened?"

"Dumb luck," answered Sherman. "He found a bunch of meth-cooking crazies."

"Sounds like home. That got him killed?"

"No. His stubborn pursuit of principles did him in," replied Sherman. Saying it felt like throwing stones in his own glass cage. Many people would still be breathing if it were not for his own myopic pursuit of retribution.

"You can take the man out of the blood, but you can't take the blood out of the man," added the sergeant.

"Him or me?" asked Sherman.

Gournsey laughed. "You two were born in the wrong era."

"I'm not much of a revolver man, and I hate horses."

"My thought was more medieval."

Sherman unspooled the image: a time when brutality was normal. When death didn't stalk from the shadows but charged right down the line. For all his callousness, imagining a world of mud and blood without antibiotics was nothing but a dim light.

"I like my beer cold and carbonated," he concluded.

Gournsey bobbed along in agreement. Each generation looks back at the last and wonders how they managed. They judge their predecessors based on age alone, as if the past was the only true road to adulthood. The dirty truth was that nothing changed but the tools of slaughter.

"How did you leave it?"

"Empty."

The sergeant didn't need or want more details. He knew Sherman well enough. There was only one conclusion to such a story: everyone was dead.

While they were talking, a new black Tahoe with shiny chrome wheels slid through the front gate. Ghana didn't have many American-made vehicles, especially not those used by rich soccer moms and the FBI. The rarity caught their eye. As the windows rolled down, they glimpsed the back seat.

At two hundred and twenty pounds, Kutu was a conspicuous figure, but his moon-like head was unmistakable, even to those who had never seen him. The muscle with the glass jaw described it as an overripe cantaloupe. No matter the descriptor, he was the man in charge.

Sherman keyed the radio. "Major, Kutu just arrived. I think they'll move the package soon."

"Understood," replied the major. It was a stock statement that meant little, as they knew little. Intelligence was sparse. They had not confirmed whether Charlie was in the compound or still alive. The UAV was two hours away, and inspecting was too dangerous.

"Lopez, are you in position?"

"Copy that. I'm across the street on your six."

A small silver Toyota glimmered in the rearview mirror, and Sherman could just make out the diminutive corporal.

43

Raul Lopez hailed from Oaxaca and almost missed out on citizenship entirely. His mom crossed the border eight months pregnant, praying to Santa Maria with every exhausted step. They found work where they could, picking oranges in Tulare and strawberries in Oxnard. The elder Lopez did a stint in a poultry processing plant, but the working conditions were too terrible even for his standards. That was coming from a man who took jobs with no questions asked and worked for eighteen hours without breaks, let alone insurance. Raul bounced around schools until the family finally settled in the Central Valley. School was a blessing, but college was always just out of reach. He was too afraid of putting family names on government forms, even though they were for financial aid. Uncle Sam came calling on the tenth anniversary of 9/11. Lopez signed up for all the right reasons, but with few considerations. Sherman found him five years later, shackled in a dingy room at some dusty forward operating base in Afghanistan. The commanding officer had detained him for disobeying some asinine order and then breaking his nose. When Sherman found out the order involved leaving a man behind, he broke the CO's leg and filed a transfer for Lopez.

"Be ready to follow us," Sherman ordered.

"Like glue or a kite?" asked Lopez.

"Unspool some string. We don't want to look like a convoy."

"Like the overly armed Americans we are," interjected Gournsey.

"Exactly."

"Will do," replied Lopez.

"Did you pack the long gun?"

"Is the Pope Catholic?"

"Good. You're on overwatch if we stop them."

"You pick the spot and I'll put 'em down," replied Lopez.

Sherman pointed to the front gate. Two men were opening the heavy steel bars. The Tahoe exited first, followed by the van. The men closed behind them and hopped in the white Nissan van. Gournsey cracked his neck to one side and shifted into first gear.

"Kutu and the potential package are leaving. We are in pursuit," Sherman announced.

"Can you confirm?" asked Sanders.

"Negative," Sherman answered. The hour was much too late for anything but silhouettes. "We'll assess again on the road."

"Copy. Follow your gut."

Certainty didn't exist in their world. Everything was some shade of gray masquerading as truth. High-priority targets appeared and vanished with disturbing regularity. Even when they were confirmed, the margin of error was big enough to drive a tank through. Context became fact. A military-age male in a free-fire zone was a terrorist. No questions asked. In that regard, Sherman's gut was no better or worse than standard operating procedure.

Chapter Six

The stench of her own waste clung to Charlotte's nostrils. It stuck to her skin and permeated her clothes. Heat amplified its nauseating power. By the time Kutu opened the door, she was suffering from dehydration and heatstroke. Seeing his oversized head was a relief, even though it portended far worse things to come.

"Good evening, madam. It is time we left. Let us not keep our new friends waiting."

"Who paid?" she demanded.

"Patience, my dear."

"I seem to be short on time," she quipped back.

Kutu rumbled with laughter. "Ah, I love a spirited woman. You would have made a splendid wife."

"And now?"

"Gory details have never been my forte, but I think you know the outcome."

She understood all too well: rape, torture, and death. In that order if she was unlucky; death first if she hit some stroke of good fortune.

"Why me?" she asked as two men walked her towards a white van.

Kutu smiled. "Don't trouble yourself with such bureaucratic details."

Charlotte tried to reply, but the black hood being pulled over her head stifled any words. It smelled of stale sweat. She wasn't the first to be blinded by the fabric.

They threw her onto one of the many bench seats crammed into the small space. Anyone over six feet didn't fit. Most passengers scraped their knees during the ride, but Charlotte had the entire thing to herself.

"Lay down and be quiet," yelled one man.

She would have flipped him off, but her hands were zip-tied together.

Stalling was her only hope, and even that was a far-fetched dream. She wasn't on the list of those worth saving. The World Health Organization had ransom insurance, but no one made any demands. They took her for a reason, but it wasn't money. Kutu could have made more from another buyer, but he was selling her into slavery. Slaves were cheap in war zones.

She lay down. The seat had the rubbery smoothness of fake leather. It reminded her of the school bus she took in grade school. Those green Naugahyde seats stuck in her memory far more than any teacher. She kissed her first boy in the back of the bus, huddled under his beige jacket. Mrs. Kowalski and her fifth-grade class were just a faint smudge in comparison.

The van pulled away with a sudden jerk, and she struggled to stay on the seat.

"Learn how to drive," she yelled, hoping to get a rise out of her captors.

Silence was the reply. Like the eye of the hurricane,

47

Charlotte swirled in the middle of violence well beyond her control.

They headed north for about an hour. At least that was what her gut said. It was the only direction that made sense. *Hisab* wouldn't come into Ghana to buy a woman—even an American. She was contemplating stalling for a pee break when the guards became agitated. They spoke rapidly in some local language she hadn't bothered to learn.

The van sped up. There was a shout. Then she lost all sense of direction and time. Whipped by unseen forces, it launched her body against the plywood seat in front of her. She heard a crack, and her forehead exploded in bright, shiny streaks of pain. After that, the world turned blacker than the hood over her head.

The pursuit had led Sherman and his men within twenty miles of the northern border. Traffic was thick leaving the city, but only the intermittent roadside stands and random pigs hinted at the surrounding inhabitants. Gournsey was hanging half a mile back, trying not to spook the van. Lopez trailed just behind them in the silver truck.

"Major," said Sherman into the radio. "We're thirty minutes from the border. Any word on authorization?"

"Order still stands. Brass maintains we need to have a visual before interdicting."

The United States rarely recognized sovereign soil as an impediment to violence. Sherman's team had killed enemies of the state in at least thirteen countries. If they were driving in Syria or Afghanistan, shooting a bunch of military-age men wouldn't have mattered. Once over the border, it wouldn't matter much either, but Sherman didn't want it to go that far. Waiting risked many unknowns. A few guys on the highway might turn into forty armed militants. The thought made him fidget.

"Just say the word, Cap," offered Gournsey.

"What's your gut saying?"

"Something's in there," replied the sergeant.

"Is it worth murdering a couple of guys?"

Gournsey chuckled. Not once over the last six years had he heard Sherman worry about statistics. "I think it's a little late to be worried about that."

"Maybe not."

"We can wait for the exchange."

"You know that's an idiotic plan," chided Sherman.

"I do."

Sherman scratched his beard more. It had finally filled in enough to be worthy of the word. "Pit 'em."

Gournsey smiled, switched off the lights, and mashed the accelerator.

"Major, we are taking a closer look."

"Understood," replied Sanders. He'd hoped Sherman would act sooner rather than later but could not lawfully give the order.

"Lopez, go dark. I want you three hundred yards south when we get close."

"Copy."

Sherman flipped the safety off on his MP5. "Come from the right side."

They closed the gap fast on the darkened stretch of road. Ghana had no streetlights in that corner of the country. Only a few stray lights cast any illumination onto the asphalt. In a matter of seconds, hundreds of yards became a handful.

The driver must have seen them in the van's taillights because he tried to speed up. The sergeant applied an equal amount of acceleration. Amid the chaotic moment, right before impact, Sherman saw a hooded figure struggle to sit up.

"Do it," he yelled.

Gournsey cut hard and smashed the left front bumper of the compact sedan into the back right tire of the van. The result was quick and decisive. The smugglers lost traction, panicked, and slammed on the brakes. With smoking tires, the van came to a stop, facing one hundred eighty degrees from where it started. The whiplash dazed both men in the van.

Speed mattered. Fast was good. It provided untold advantages. Sherman was out of the sedan before the passenger in the van shook off his sense of dizziness. The silenced MP5 was leveled at his head.

In the thick night air, the Ghanaian could only make out a silhouette. Fear followed confusion, and he fumbled for the Uzi between his legs—a useless last act.

The glass shattered as three rounds ended his search.

Sherman was twenty feet away when he pulled the trigger. Any reservations regarding the outcome were long gone. Ambiguity only existed in those moments before the action, when it had space to breathe life into doubt.

He keyed the radio, "Passenger down."

Metallic pings and shattering glass filled the space behind him as Gournsey fired on Kutu's car. The driver of the Tahoe gunned the V8, and the SUV surged forward into the night.

The sergeant reloaded and fired another magazine for good measure. It was a vague buzz in the background of Sherman's mind. A bigger threat was right in front of him. The driver's side door was open. He ducked down, hoping to see feet or movement, but found nothing.

"Lopez," he growled.

From three hundred yards away, the sound of the

suppressed MK-17 still resembled a firecracker going off next door. The heavy 7.62 mm round was a favorite among shooters. Raul was no exception.

No sooner had Sherman spoken than two massive pops echoed down the road, and a body collapsed onto the pavement.

"Driver down," announced Lopez in a voice devoid of emotion.

Sherman swung the MP5 onto his back and threw open the side door to the van. Two rows back, he spotted the hooded figure lying on the floor. Under different circumstances, he might have said something or untied the person, but they were on the hook for murder if the cops showed up. So, Sherman just grabbed the target and hoisted them onto his shoulder.

"Gournsey," he yelled on the way back to the sedan. "Move the bodies under the van and Willie Pete the thing."

The sergeant already had a white phosphorus grenade in his hand. "Copy that."

He rolled the two dead smugglers under the van and tossed the incendiary inside. It hissed like a slashed tire on a quiet night. When the fire got going, the slag and heat would reduce the corpses to ash. Not even the fancy CSI labs could tell who died.

"Lopez, we're RTB. Hang back and make sure no one follows."

"Understood."

Sherman turned to Gournsey. "Get us away from this mess."

Chapter Seven

When Charlotte woke up, still hooded and bound, she expected to hear Arabic or French. Instead, it was English. Not some colonial holdover dialect either, but the ordinary nouns of Americans. Two men were discussing something. Nothing so trivial as sports or the weather, but nothing of great importance either. One was Appalachian, from some holler or another. The other man spoke with the familiar nondescript accent of the left coast.

A golf ball-sized bump was forming on Charlotte's forehead, and her entire skull throbbed. She gingerly touched the contusion. Was she concussed or hearing voices? The questions haunted her. She didn't want to raise false hope from a trick of the mind.

She searched for something to corroborate her ears. Running her fingers across the seat she was lying on, Charlotte felt the threadbare softness of fabric. Gone was the van's faux leather. Her chest tightened with possibility.

"Who are you?" she asked.

The talking stopped, and the car slowed to a standstill.

She struggled to sit up as the door opened and someone else got into the backseat. The cold brush of a steel blade caused her to jump as they cut the zip ties. She gasped and tried to catch her breath as they removed the hood. A man's face stared back. She blinked hard and long.

"Frank?" she cried in bewilderment.

"Charlotte?" replied Sherman.

They sat there for a moment, absorbing the absurdity of it all. Then she slapped him hard enough across the face to leave a welt.

"That's for Istanbul, you son-of-a-bitch."

Gournsey started laughing. "I like her already."

Sherman grimaced at the memory more than the fingers imprinted into his cheek.

"You're Charlie?" he asked, exasperated.

"One nickname I've picked up over the years."

"So, how do you know each other?" Gournsey asked with a snicker.

"It was years ago," Sherman dismissed.

"And yet you haven't changed at all," Charlotte snapped back.

The sergeant was enjoying their exchange, so he kept up the pressure. "You were in Turkey in 2012, right, Cap?"

Sherman gritted his teeth. He would get back at the man, eventually.

"2011," Charlotte corrected.

"Like I said, it was a lifetime ago," lied Sherman. He remembered the day and always would. It ranked as one of the best and worst days of his life. The outdoor café, the small cups of Turkish coffee, her smile in the warm air of the early summer sun, basking in the pleasure from the night before. Those things would never tarnish.

On some base level, she had known who he was. Few

soldiers sport full-length beards and speak Arabic fluently. The hardness in his eyes spoke volumes about his past. Yet Charlotte ignored those warning bells. Sherman hadn't tried to hide anything on purpose. She didn't ask, and he didn't volunteer. From the outset, they agreed it was a fling —a casual thing, nothing else. It was until it wasn't. Then it was more. It stayed that way until he killed a man with a butter knife.

Some events materialize from nowhere, like ships emerging from the mist. Pleasant afternoons can suddenly turn cold and violent. That day was no different, and had it not been for happenstance, Sherman would not have seen him at all.

The man in question was a top-tier Al Qaeda operative from Anbar province in Iraq. His name was Faraj Almasi, but most knew him only by his *nom de guerre*: Fawz. Victory in Arabic. He was a pious man who treated his wife with respect and doted on his children. Fawz also had a penchant for bombing marketplaces full of civilians and planting IEDs on American patrol routes.

At the café that day, a server dropped a glass. The shattering sound grabbed Sherman's attention. Walking past the sun-drenched, white linen-covered tables was Fawz. Charlotte knew something fundamental had changed with one look at his face. Gone were the slight crinkles around his eyes and the carefree smile. Like a flipped light switch, the man whose company she'd been enjoying vanished as if a veil had fallen or perhaps lifted. Looking back, that was the scariest part—her unanswered question. Was he a man masquerading as a killer, or was the man's face merely a façade?

Without saying a word, Sherman grabbed a butter knife from the table and walked into the crowd. A moment later, she watched him plunge the dull stainless-steel flatware into an unsuspecting man's neck. Then he walked away. Sherman didn't change his gait or run. He just strolled away and never looked back.

Eight years later, his face looked almost the same as it had that day in Istanbul. Charlotte spotted a few more gray hairs, and the creases on his forehead were a little deeper, but he smelled the same.

"Damnit," she muttered with her head in her hands. "What the hell."

Sherman rubbed her back as Charlotte let out forty-eight hours of stress and fear. She opened the mental release valve, and out it came—all the emotional pressure it took to maintain her composure in the face of imminent violence.

They were on the outskirts of Tamale when she came back into the present. Dimly lit market stalls and over-crowded *shebeens* filled with intoxicated youth were merely smears of gray in the night. She watched people go about their lives. It was comforting to see, to imagine such normal-ity, even if it would never come to pass for herself. The unwanted intrusions in her life said otherwise.

"Thanks, Frank."

Sherman smiled, and for a moment, she saw that jovial soul she had almost fallen in love with.

"How did you find me?" she asked before breathlessly adding, "Wait, why are you here?"

"Slow down, darlin'," said Gournsey.

"Don't darlin' me," she snarled.

"He didn't mean it like that," assured Sherman. "The sergeant here is merely pointing out that there are several unanswered questions floating around right now."

"Fine. Sorry for snapping. It's been a shitty few days."

Gournsey smiled in the mirror. "I didn't mean no affront. You're a damn warrior in my book."

Charlotte nodded at the compliment, even if she couldn't imagine herself as such.

"We're here for the war," added Sherman.

"Is the U.S. intervening?" she asked. The reporter in her never died, even if her days of writing had long since faded.

"Not officially, but you know how these things go. There are always boots on the ground despite what Washington says."

She was seeing the bigger picture. "So, this wasn't a rescue mission?"

"Your handler is a friend of my boss. He turned us onto your trail."

"Kutu," she spat.

"We started with some camp guard, but Kutu's men tried to leave his body for the dogs."

"Samuel?" she gasped. "Is he okay?"

"You know him?" asked Sherman.

"It's my job to know people. Sweet guy too, but he's not cut out for a fight."

"He saw which way the trucks left, including the one with you in it."

"A loose end in need of burning, as they say," added Gournsey.

"Only hicks say that," chided Sherman.

"Don't judge what you can't understand," retorted the sergeant.

Sherman shrugged. Few people visit the backwoods of Kentucky, and as far as most people thought, Sergeant Raylan Gournsey came from worlds apart. He didn't just grow up poor; his family had been poor since the Civil War.

Multigenerational poverty. Endemic. Except no one notices if everyone else sails in the same boat.

Gournsey grew up on the land, hunting, fishing, and doing anything else he could under the sun or moon. By his own admission, he'd spent more years outside than inside. High school came and went. He was lucky enough not to get his girl pregnant. Teen pregnancy didn't have a separate category in his county; it was just a pregnancy.

Prospects were dim during the boom, but then he graduated into the Great Recession. There was nothing. Even the illicit trades, moonshine and oxy, were in dire straits. Raylan was smart enough to see that life in Kentucky held nothing for him. If not coal, then the army, were his father's words.

Gournsey chafed under the discipline of basic training but got through on sheer will. That and he could bench press four hundred pounds or carry two wounded men at the same time. Size was his ally.

Sherman met him during a daft raid on the Mahdi militia in Iraq. Some one-star asshole wanted to make a name for himself in the counterinsurgency world. He thought he could force the locals to disarm. Carrying weapons was second nature to those people. Their ancestors picked up a spear thousands of years ago, and they hadn't dropped it since. What started amicably escalated into bloodshed as soon as the general made his proclamation. Gournsey's team got hit first. They holed up in some apartment building nearby, but everyone was walking wounded.

Sherman should have been somewhere else. Sanders was on point but got called in by the higher-ups. They needed someone levelheaded, so he went. The plan was shit. He knew it from word one. So, he hung back on the periphery. When the shooting started, Sherman was the only American shooting back. By the time he got into the apartment building, it looked no different from a trauma room. Blood covered everything. Wrappers of gauze littered the floor. In the middle of all that chaos, Gournsey was beating the hell out of some insurgent who had rushed through the front door, firing his AK from the hip like some action hero. The sergeant took two in the abdomen before he tackled the guy.

Given such history, the hick had a point. Rushing to judgment was a net loss. Nothing gained. Nothing learned. He understood well enough. People talk; they always do. Communication got baked into our DNA. Evolution made sure of that. Samuel was no exception.

"So, what did you see?" Sherman asked.

"What makes you sure I saw anything?" she retorted.

"It fits."

"They took others," countered Charlotte.

"Just a ruse."

"A five-dollar word for smoke screen," scoffed Gournsey. The sergeant didn't care much for fancy synonyms or men who could only spell a word one way.

"Besides, they freed the other guy," added Sherman.

Charlotte looked unfazed.

"But you already figured that one out."

She nodded.

"It makes me think you had value. At least knowledge, which gave you leverage."

"Maybe I was just unlucky."

"Maybe, but no. Kutu wanted you to talk. Why risk keeping you in Ghana? Not worth it unless he wanted to hear it from your lips in person."

"You haven't changed, Frank," she said with a crooked smile.

"More scars. Less empathy."

"Like I said."

Charlotte glanced out the window once more. The pause wasn't tactical, but it gave her a moment to consider the implications. Eventually, she would tell someone—maybe her handler, or Major Sanders, or some pencil pusher from Langley. Knowledge would get out. Plans would hatch. Her maternal side wanted to protect Sherman from those plans, but she knew him too well. He hadn't changed. Men like him never did.

"Guns," she finally said.

"You're painting with a broad brush there," said Gournsey.

"Someone was smuggling guns through the camp."

"Who?" asked Sherman.

"Don't know. They started appearing a week ago. Wooden crates. Official labels and paperwork. The whole nine yards."

"From where?"

"World Health Organization. W.H.O. was stamped in capital blue letters. Except it didn't exist in the system. No record of where it came from or how it got there."

"How did you find out?"

"Luck—good or bad. I was in the warehouse looking for something else. Got the crate number mixed up. Opened the wrong one."

Gournsey hated the suspense. "What did ya lay your eyes on?"

"Guns, but not the normal African arsenal. This wasn't ancient AKs. It was modern stuff. Things I'd read about."

Sherman motioned for her to continue.

"SCAR rifles, TAR-21s, HK416s, and even a Javelin missile. I mean, who the hell can get their hands on that?"

The list was impressive and top-of-the-line. Straight from the cutting edge of Western armies, not the second-hand stuff dumped on most African conflicts.

"What did you do?" asked Sherman with a frown.

"I closed the box and got out of there. The next day, it disappeared, and so did I."

"So, you don't know how many came through?"

"Yes and no. I don't have an exact number, but it must have been small. A half-dozen at most. This isn't Syria. We don't have thousands of crates coming through every day."

"That's a lot of work for some hardware," said Gournsey.

"We're not in Iraq. *Hisab* can't just find American military gear at every base. The Burkinabe army is shooting the same shit, they just have more soldiers."

"Other avenues?" asked Sherman.

"Maybe through the north, but fun fact about Ghana. It's a world-leading hub for cocaine distribution," said Charlotte.

Sherman's eyes widened. "They must have left that one out of the travel brochure."

"Besides, what better way through the border than on an aid convoy destined for the needy," said Charlotte.

She was right and Sherman knew it. Escaping scrutiny was easy in the face of catastrophe. No one looked twice when children were starving. Compassion and guilt overwhelmed diligence.

Gournsey nodded slowly, but something wasn't computing. "A few crates wouldn't make much of a difference. Why risk it?"

Two valid points in quick succession had Sherman thinking. He was still mentally flipping through the list of weapons when Gournsey pulled over. They had skirted the town on some battered old ring road around the lingering smog of evening rush hour. A Land Cruiser was waiting for them down some forgotten road.

"What now?" asked Charlotte, still teetering on the edge of despair.

The sergeant grabbed another white phosphorus grenade from his bag and held it up. "Good ol' Willie Pete."

"An abundance of caution," said Sherman as he transferred the gear.

Two dead locals. A road full of spent brass. Charlotte got the picture.

"You weren't sanctioned for this, were you?" she asked.

Sherman looked up and said nothing. Gournsey managed a dismissive shrug. Well-trained non-responses. Charlotte sighed, knowing she shouldn't have asked. Murder or collateral damage? It was a thin line, really nothing more than verbiage written in the office of some mid-level bureaucrat. Thirty words, maybe less, authorizing deadly force.

Charlotte realized she should be dead. The odds were never on her side. The game was rigged, yet there she was, standing in one piece with the cool night air settling on her shoulders and palm trees rustling overhead, all thanks to someone capable of killing a man with a butter knife.

They circled back three or four times until Sherman was comfortable that no one was tailing them. Another abundance of caution. The better part of two decades in combat had taught him a few things. All people are predictable, freeze-dried pizza is good, always carry extra ammo, luck exists but skill comes first, and finally, trust no one but your team. That last lesson came at a steep price—one paid out too many times over too many lives.

JOEL AUSTIN

"You guys are more cautious than spooks," said Charlotte after seeing the same cell tower for the third time.

"The captain here is a pessimistic man," said Gournsey.

"Ah, Frank, I always thought of you as a glass-half-full person," she replied.

"Funny," added Sherman. "I just assumed it was the wrong size."

They parked the Toyota out of sight behind the unassuming concrete house. The major was at the back door, arms crossed. Sherman knew something was wrong. It was in the eyes—sunken and distracted, looking twelve moves ahead but not liking the view.

62

Chapter Eight

The footage was grainy—black and white pixels from twenty thousand feet up. Good enough to see the action, but not the faces.

"When?" asked Sherman.

"Thirty minutes ago," answered the major.

"Bastards," said Lopez and Gournsey almost in unison. Anger seethed beneath their normally placid exteriors.

Charlotte could not stop watching the laptop screen. She had seen drone footage before. It all looked similar: a close-up of a vehicle or house, some small white crosshair hovering over an unsuspecting target. Then came the inevitable streak of gray and the white heat of an explosion, overwhelming the thermal camera for a moment. Finally, the aftermath—death, debris, and charred earth. Scattered fragments of what existed only moments earlier. She had seen that on CNN. What she was watching was something else altogether.

"What were they doing out there?"

The major eyed her warily. His friend had vouched for her, but Sanders looked up the records anyway. Leave no stone unturned, or in his case, leave no weapon unchecked. Risks were risks, no matter the gender or age. What he found gave him pause. It looked familiar, in the same way a carpenter might recognize someone else's framing job. Houses are all constructed the same these days, and it wasn't hard to spot a similar build. The spacing, the time-lines, the materials did not differ from what he had built—intricately woven lies meant to support a necessary false-hood. But then again, sometimes it's nothing more than lumber.

"Black ops drone base," he replied. "CIA likes to have their own toys these days."

"And the people?"

"Contractors. We outsource most of the war on terror. No one has to testify before Congress if some PMCs die. Losing a battalion of Marines is a scandal."

"Who's on point for this?" Lopez asked.

"We are," said Sherman without hesitation. "SEAL Team Eight redeployed to Yemen two days ago. That leaves them at least six hours out. The nearest forces are in Nige-ria, but that is mostly the Army Corps of Engineers."

Major Sanders nodded in agreement. "Wheels up in thirty. The colonel says he can land our Gulfstream on any strip."

"Overwatch?" wondered Gournsey.

"SAT-9 has an unimpeded view."

Lopez chimed in, "Air support?"

"The French have some Mirages in Niger, but Langley is staying silent."

"Locals?"

"It's Mali, man," chided Gournsey. "Are they gonna drive us there in a technical?"

Sherman hadn't taken his eyes off the recording. Little bells in the back of his mind were trilling. "Grab the gear. Heavy stuff too."

Gournsey and Lopez didn't need the order. They were already loading up the Toyota.

"Did *Hisab* take credit?" asked Charlotte.

"Crickets, but the UAV had enough fuel to see some trucks head back towards Burkina Faso."

"Looks like we'll get that war."

Sherman grabbed his rifle from the steel rack. "I'd say it already started."

The Gulfstream turned off the small tarmac as the Toyota sped down the dirt service road. Colonel Paulson considered the possibilities—both good and bad. Then he dropped the door as the small plume of dust dissipated into the warm night air. Sherman bounded up the steps.

"Thanks again for the lift. Hope we didn't scare you."

"Ah, your truck is too clean to be dangerous."

"Yeah, I'd try to scuff it up, but Uncle Sam would just deduct it from my pay."

Gournsey and Lopez moved past with bags in tow. The colonel took a glance at the arsenal being loaded into the back of the plane.

"No offense, Captain, but where the hell are we dropping you off?"

"About that…" said Sherman as he handed over a scrap of paper with coordinates—latitude and longitude. Nothing else.

Paulson looked at the long string of numbers and blinked for a moment. The wheels whirred away. All those thousands of hours in the cockpit translated the almost unintelligible piece of data.

"Nothing much out there."

"Not officially," said Sherman.

"Unofficially?"

"A black bag drone base."

The colonel raised an eyebrow but displayed no surprise. The war on terror had spread American interest into some strange corners of the globe: Niger, Mali, Egypt, Yemen. He'd seen plenty of places that never existed on a map.

"One more question, Captain."

Sherman glanced up from loading magazines full of 5.56mm rounds.

"Seems a little late to drop in unannounced, and you guys aren't exactly wearing party attire."

"They got blown to pieces sixty-three minutes ago."

"Shit."

"Yeah."

The colonel sealed the door and took his seat behind the controls. His copilot looked over skeptically. "Where are we headed?"

"CIA drone base in Mali just got annihilated."

"Shit."

"Yeah."

Sherman stretched out on the same leather couch he had ridden on coming into the mess. Craving the familiar, Lopez and Gournsey had retreated to their own favorite seats. It was the little reassurances that mattered. For some, it was an object or picture of family. Others had smells of home or textures from another life. Sherman had no such tether. There was no other life waiting for him stateside. Even Gournsey and Lopez, despite their commitments to duty and country, had families. They existed outside of the uniform. He hadn't for a long time, not since Istanbul.

The engines whined with activity as the small jet climbed into the darkness. The copilot, Colonel Carlman, stuck his head out of the cabin once they cleared five thousand feet.

"Captain. A word."

Sherman wandered over and took a knee.

"We're spoofing a commercial flight, but if anyone looks too hard, they'll figure it out."

The hesitation came from experience. Landing a plane used by CEOs and celebrities on an unknown, hostile runway was not standard protocol. Lots of possibilities waited in the darkness—most of them bad.

"Satellite images show nothing but bodies."

If Carlman had doubts, he didn't show it. "Okay. Any info on the strip?"

Gournsey handed the man a military-grade tablet in a thick rubber case. Carlman glanced down at a still image taken by the UAV and narrated, "Drone base. Decent condition. Maybe five thousand feet long, if we're lucky."

"And if it's not?" asked Lopez.

"This might be a one-way trip."

"Ain't that the truth every time," Gournsey quipped.

"Anything else?"

Sherman inhaled. "Head to the far side. We'll be off in two minutes. After that, get out quick and stay close. I'll call when we are ready to head back."

"We will need to refuel. It may take a while."

"Understood. I don't plan on a quick retreat."

"This really is a one-way ticket."

"So is life," quipped Sherman.

"Wheels down in forty-five minutes."

"Thanks, Colonel."

"Anytime, Captain."

With nothing else to do, Sherman wandered back to the couch and caught a quick nap. The grainy images replayed briefly in his head like an itch he just couldn't scratch. The landing gear extending woke him up. Everything was black in and on the plane. No landing lights or red flashes pulsing into the night. Sherman grabbed a sat-phone and dialed from memory.

The major answered, "Status?"

"Five minutes out. Any movement?"

"Nothing on the perimeter. There are some heat signatures coming from the mess hall."

Sherman had memorized the layout but wanted to confirm. "Building four?"

"Correct."

"Friend or foe?"

"Unknown, but likely base personnel."

Sherman felt the same way. "No sense in *Hisab* sticking around."

"Agreed, but there was no chatter leading up to the attack. NSA. CIA. They're all scrambling for answers."

"Facts are for the living. Truth is for the dead," Sherman lamented.

Sanders grunted in acknowledgment. "They'd settle for a body count."

"The count is too many."

"So it is. Try not to add any more to their column."

"Will do. Sitrep in ninety."

"Copy. Good hunting."

Sherman ended the call and pulled a set of night vision goggles over his head. Pale green rocks passed below in a blur. Closing fast, but still in the distance, was the base. A few random lights blinked along the tarmac.

"Power must be out," said Colonel Paulson. "Those are emergency lights."

"Generator took an RPG."

The colonel adjusted the throttle but said nothing of the implied danger.

"You boys might want to hold on," suggested the copilot. "This could get bumpy."

Sherman sat down in the jump seat next to the galley and waited.

The bump was hard and abrupt, but the pilot stuck the landing without a bounce. Wailing engine sounds filled the small cabin with a high-pitched frenzy. The jet decelerated with stomach-twisting brevity. A final squeak of the brakes, and the plane stopped.

Gournsey was out first with nearly two hundred pounds of gear. It might have been only twenty the way he took the stairs three at a time. Lopez followed with cases of ammo.

Sherman turned to Paulson. "I'll call when you're needed."

"Stay sharp, Captain," replied the pilot, but Sherman was already on the ground. He shrugged and powered up for the return trip. *They had been on the ground for only ninety-four seconds—a record,* he thought.

The team had most of the gear ready to use before the Gulfstream was airborne again. Sherman set them up at a small mechanical shack at the end of the runway.

"This is the Alamo. If they attack, we fall back here and hit them with the heavy stuff."

"Understood," came the replies.

"Alright. Any chance of surprise went the way of flip

phones with our grand entrance. If anyone is here, we'll know forthwith."

Five minutes of warm, humid silence passed. Only stray emergency lights revealed anything about the base. A dead dark save for the faint green glow in their goggles.

"Lopez, find a vantage point along the eastern fence line. Gournsey and I will sweep the buildings from south to north. Number four from our position has heat signatures, so someone is still alive," Sherman instructed.

The night reminded him of home more than any recent memory. It was balmy and sticky, with the sharp scent of vegetation swirling in the wind. The last fifteen years contained few such nights outside of the Euphrates Valley. No, it took him much further back—to a time when war was his father's burden. When he snuck out of the house to read by flashlight and watch the stars above. A lifetime ago. Several lifetimes.

Flat ground lay between them and the first building. Sherman and Gournsey moved quickly but methodically, their eyes glued to the ghostly green shapes in the distance.

Lopez keyed his radio, "All clear."

Silence engulfed them as they stopped outside a small metal-clad building—offices of some sort. Sherman listened but heard little. A distant fire crackled, and some birds called out their midnight activities, but not much more. The quiet veil of nowhere.

Gournsey whispered, "This place is eerie."

"Dead quiet."

"Makes sense. We're ghosts walking in a damn graveyard."

They swept the offices in under a minute. The place had an open layout, with only a few rooms having actual doors. Piles of bureaucratic refuse sat in neat stacks around the room—documentation of a secret war hidden in the sandy expanse of Mali.

"Hell of a place to hide our drones."

Sherman nodded. "North Africa is target-rich."

"Too rich," replied Gournsey, staring at a small pool of blood.

"Corporal, we're coming out," whispered Sherman into the mic, which picked up the faintest of voices.

"Copy. All clear."

Building two was more of the same—empty, abandoned in a panic during the attack.

"Moving up."

"Copy. Looks like some bodies up ahead," informed Lopez.

Sherman parted the cheap horizontal blinds and peeked out. In the green glow, it was hard to make out specifics, but he counted three shapes sprawled out in the dirt.

"Casualties," he whispered.

"Ours?" asked Gournsey.

"Who knows? I'll search. You cover."

The sergeant flashed a thumbs-up.

"Coming out," said Sherman as he approached the first shape.

Details emerged as he got closer. The clothes and size indicated male. The guy lay on his stomach, but enough of his face was visible to tell he wasn't local. Sherman didn't touch the body; he'd seen the dead multiply too many times before—grenades pinned under corpses, IEDs buried under women and children. Death begets more death.

"One of ours," he said. "Looks like any agency boy—idealistic and entitled."

"Cause?" asked Lopez.

Two exit wounds had painted a Rorschach blot on the

dead man's shirt. The fabric was ragged and torn outward. "Took two running towards the fight."

"The others?"

Sherman glanced over, but the results were the same. A pistol lay nearby. He checked the magazine; it was still full. "No different. Didn't even get a shot off."

Building three was a giant supply closet filled to the gills with whatever Americans stuck at the edge of nowhere could want. Cases of cheap beer and cheaper booze lined one wall. The rest was an assortment of hamburger buns, mac-and-cheese boxes, and Cup-o-Noodles. Amid all that, Gournsey pointed to a small wooden crate. The word "KENTUCKY" was stenciled across it in charred letters.

"It better be the good shit," replied Sherman.

The sergeant pulled out a bottle of WhistlePig and held it up. "At least someone knew how to drink," he said with a silent laugh. The bourbon went straight into his pack. Another few pounds would not slow him down.

"How are we looking?" radioed Sherman.

The corporal was moving up with them along the east fence line, leapfrogging ahead to cover the next building. The layout of the base was simple enough: a runway sandwiched between five buildings to the east and three hangars to the west. Having landed from north to south, they were edging toward the carnage.

"Nothing moving, but it ain't lookin' pretty."

"Casualties?"

"Many, and some vehicles are still smoldering by the hangars."

"Copy. Moving out."

Fifty-seven steps separated the buildings. In that time, Sherman counted no fewer than fifteen bodies. Some American, some not. The sergeant stopped near one who fell into the latter camp: an African in the early edge of his twenties. He wore the same black cotton clothing fashionable in ISIS training videos. A vintage AK-47 lay nearby, covered in fine powdery dirt. Several of his comrades had met similar fates in the same fifty-seven-step space. Based on the geometry, Gournsey reckoned they ran into each other in the darkened chaos—two armed groups shooting it out within spitting distance.

"CQB," he said.

Sherman nodded. A close-quarters battle.

Building four was the mess hall—another name for an oversized canvas tent with doors and plastic windows to keep in the air conditioning during the hottest months. In Mali, that ran from November to June.

Sherman gave the front door a gentle tug, but something caught his eye and stopped his breath. Someone had tied a thin monofilament line to the inside of the door. Adrenaline flooded his system, and he let out a short, hard exhale. In the silence, it felt like a scream.

"Cap?" whispered Gournsey.

"Claymore. Attached to the door."

They took a few steps back, and Sherman took out his knife. With a few quick strokes, he entered through the fabric siding. His hunch was right—wedged underneath a cheap folding chair was the small explosive device. Whoever left it there was smart but still in the building. A booby trap like that was protection, not an ambush.

Inside the thin walls, it smelled like a mix of combat and Hometown Buffet. Sweat, urine, and blood mingled with French fries and seared meat—the stereotypes of America distilled into a scent. Overturned tables had served as cover from the battle outside. Globules of macaroni and cheese covered the shell casings on the floor.

Scanning the room, Sherman saw few places to hide outside of the kitchen. He pointed toward the back, and Gournsey nodded. Both men took care with each step. Booby traps aside, the floor was covered with all sorts of food waiting to cause a slip. Jell-O, banana pudding, mashed potatoes, and cream of corn were all smeared across the concrete.

As kitchens go, there wasn't much to the place—just the same as any diner or local joint. Only the fridge stood out. It was a giant walk-in unit about the size of a New York City studio apartment. It must have been the sole unit for the entire base.

Sherman put his ear to the outside wall and listened, but not much made it through the insulating foam. Gournsey pointed to the handle, but Sherman raised his hand to signal him to hold tight. Gently at first, but then with more effort, he began tapping out U-S-A in Morse code on the enormous door. His knuckle rhythmically conveyed: dot-dot-dash—dot-dot-dot—dot-dash.

After three attempts, he stopped and waited. There was some commotion from inside, as if people were trying to decide if the message was genuine. Then came a muffled yell—a question needing a response.

"What makes Carolina BBQ sauce special?"

Gournsey flashed a toothy grin and yelled back, "It's the damn vinegar you boys add."

A second passed before the door cracked open. "Ain't nothin' better in this world," came a voice from inside.

"You alright?" asked Sherman. His finger was still on the trigger.

The door swung open, and out stepped the cook in his striped pants and blue Crocs. He said his name was Eugene and that he hailed from the Mississippi Delta. Gournsey asked how he came to like Carolina sauce so much, but Sherman cut him off.

"How many are in there with you?"

"Six," replied Eugene, who motioned for the others to exit the stuffy box.

The power had gone out during the attack, and things were getting pungent. They lined up in the kitchen while Gournsey gave everyone a quick pat down: three mechanics, one intel lady, two supply clerks, and the cook. Of the seven, only Eugene had a weapon, which he happily handed over to Gournsey.

"Who set the claymores?" wondered Sherman.

The intel woman raised her hand.

"Where did you learn that?"

"Did a tour with the 407th Brigade Support Battalion."

"What's your name?"

"Samantha, but everyone calls me Sam."

"Sam, I'm Captain Sherman, and this is Sergeant Gournsey."

Sherman nodded. "Give her the gun. Sam, I'm gonna need you to take them to the southern end of the runway. There's a small mechanical shed. Stay there, out of sight."

"Aren't you the cavalry?" asked Eugene.

"No, we're just the spear. The rescue team will be here in a few hours."

Samantha nodded. "Understood."

"Good. Now, tell me what the hell happened here?"

Sam took a deep breath. "Just another lazy night. Only one bird was up. No real chatter or targets. I was in the office when some locals pulled up to the gate. A bomb went off after that. Shit rolled downhill from there."

"It always does."

"I can't be sure, Captain, but I'd swear this was no jihadist undertaking."

"Why?"

"They blew up the Bradley with a missile."

"An RPG?"

"No, like an AT4 or something bigger."

"A Javelin?" asked Gournsey.

"Yeah, yeah. It went up before coming down."

Sherman and Gournsey shared a glance. Neither man liked the picture being painted.

"Thanks. Get hidden. Oh, you did well with the claymores."

Sam forced a weak smile. "If only they had gone off."

The ragtag group went out the cut side while Gournsey disarmed the explosives at each door.

"Ain't she something," said the sergeant with a smile.

"You can share the bourbon with her," offered Sherman. He could have added a qualifier about getting out alive, but that was a given. No need to give voice to such doubts.

"I don't know, but it would be a shame if such good bourbon went to waste."

Sherman couldn't help but crack a smile as he keyed the mic. "Lopez, there was a ladder next to building three. Find a clear view. We will search the hangars once you have eyes on the place."

"Copy that."

Thirty minutes had elapsed since they roared onto the tarmac. The small green Tritium dials on Sherman's watch had converged at the top. Twenty-four hundred hours. Six more to sunrise.

"In position," said Lopez. "It ain't pretty out there."

"Anything moving?"

"Nothing but the sand."

"Copy. Coming out."

Three massive hangars loomed like oversized barns in the pale viridescent gloom. Steel-clad homes for America's secret air force. Everything was there except for the pilots sitting seven thousand miles away in some air-conditioned trailer at the edge of Las Vegas. Same climate, different deserts. Same war, two vastly different experiences.

Chunks of metal clustered around the charred carcass of a Bradley Fighting Vehicle still smoldering on the other side of the runway. The armor plating was peeled back like a half-eaten pomegranate, revealing the structure underneath. The crew was nothing more than swabs of burned DNA.

"Took the hit from the top," observed Gournsey.

Sherman grunted in acknowledgment. It was the hallmark of a Javelin strike. The missile climbed a few hundred feet before coming down on the target—a $300,000 curveball.

The missile didn't surprise him. Weapons flow to where there is conflict: supply and demand. There was no shortage of the latter, but the thing he couldn't understand at that moment was a simple question of motivation. Why attack a U.S. base? All the rational reasons made no sense. Even the irrational ones felt like grasping at straws. A terrorist attack didn't serve *Hisab's* goals. They wanted to be statesmen, not pariahs.

They stopped at the outskirts of the first hangar. The giant steel doors were closed, but the service entrance was not. Without a word, they stacked up against the structure. Sherman could smell the metallic tinge of blood coming from inside. He squeezed Gournsey's shoulder, and both men entered with rifles at the ready.

With no power and the doors closed, it was pitch black inside. Even their night vision barely worked. Sherman switched on the infrared flashlight attached to his HK416. It bathed the interior with a spectrum invisible to the human eye, but everything appeared brighter in their goggles. He swallowed hard at what they found.

Stacked like a cord of wood under the plane were six bodies—Americans, men and women—a tidy pile of mortality. A message.

"Shit," uttered Gournsey upon seeing the stack.

"Sweep the perimeter and watch for IEDs. This feels like a trap," Sherman instructed.

As the sergeant checked the cavernous space, Sherman walked around the drone. Every so often, he stepped over a recently dried streak of blood—six red roads leading to the same point. Halfway around, he stopped and knelt on the concrete floor. A lone shell casing twinkled in the infrared light. He picked it up and rolled it between his fingers. The small stamp on the bottom read '6.8 SPC'. The U.S. Army designed the round, but it hadn't been adopted. It was not the standard caliber for CIA contractors.

"What d'ya find?" asked Gournsey.

"Something that shouldn't be here."

Gournsey glanced down at the brass. "Six-eight?"

"Seems so."

"The coincidences are piling up."

Sherman pointed up at the sleek metallic fuselage. There was a massive hole just before the wing on the port side, like someone opened a can with a plasma torch.

"You know I ain't much for avionics," said Gournsey, "but I believe that is the valuable bit."

"Search the other hangars. See how many they got. I need to make a call. This is going straight to the top."

Gournsey bounded out as Sherman dialed the major.

"Status?" answered the gravelly voice.

"A dozen-plus dead. Some theirs, most ours. Six survivors."

"Copy. Any sign of who?"

Sherman stood looking at the jagged hole in the drone. "No, but I have an idea of why."

"Care to elaborate, Captain?"

"They stole the brains of a Reaper drone."

The major paused for a moment. "Shit."

Chapter Nine

The general was yelling. His eyes bulged with each expletive. Ambassador Franklin was wearing a hole in his nine-hundred-dollar loafers by pacing around the room. Off to the side sat Major Sanders like a calm lake. It wasn't his mess to own. Sherman was in the back, watching the scene unfold. It did not differ from what he had imagined four hours earlier when he made the call.

"How in the flying hell did we allow this colossal shit-storm to happen?" bellowed the general.

Several talking heads appeared on the oversized television screen. Each passed the blame to the next. The CIA blamed the NSA for not sharing information, while the NSA blamed the DIA. The general's face reddened with each pass, and he denounced the shadow war in the most colorful terms. It went like that for several minutes. All the while, Sherman was certain Major Sanders never blinked. The man had a unique ability; all the bureaucratic bullshit slung around just slid right off. It convinced Sherman that his boss was destined for a gold star. The army did not have a more competent officer.

"Alright, alright. Enough of this paltry circle jerk. What do we know?"

"Nothing on SIGINT," said the NSA.

"Too soon for HUMINT," offered the CIA. "But we have feelers out. Someone will talk."

"Ambassador," said the general. "You're the regional expert. Thoughts on culpability?"

"*Hisab* is the obvious choice. They have the means, motive, and opportunity."

"That is presumptuous and premature," countered the NSA. "Your opinions regarding *Hisab* are well known."

"And correct," countered Ambassador Franklin. "Major Sanders and his team found dead *Hisab* fighters at the airfield."

"They found dead terrorists," replied the general. "Where's the link?"

"With all due respect, General, it's obvious. Based on Captain Sherman's description, the young man was clearly from the Fulani tribe in northern Burkina Faso, the homeland of *Hisab*."

"That might be proof it's shit, but not horseshit."

"It's the logical conclusion," replied Franklin.

The general grumbled some inaudible obscenity and snarled at the lackluster intelligence being presented. "If I go to the Joint Chiefs with nothing, they'll have me by the balls. Let's go with the *Hisab* angle until we have something else. Since no one can agree on who, I assume we don't know shit about where these things are."

"The UAV had them heading south," said the CIA.

"Further supporting my point," interjected Franklin.

Sherman glanced over at Sanders. The major hadn't

mentioned the smuggled weapons or the Javelin missile. For whatever reason, he was holding those cards close enough to his chest that it might smother them.

"SAT-9 has eyes on the region, but they have an eight-hour head start," added the DIA.

"Good," said the general. "SEAL Team Eight will hold the base until the CIA can plan for security. In the meantime, all assets in the region are active. That includes you, Major Sanders. The Air Force has assured me they will have birds in the air if we need those jet jockeys to take credit."

"We've contacted Layer Three Security. They will assume control in twelve hours," added the CIA.

The slightest of smiles curled from the corner of Ambassador Franklin's mouth at the sound of his old company. Sherman glanced over at the major. He was watching.

"Fine. Let's go and kill these pricks," yelled the general before the call ended.

The screens went black, and the embassy SCIF fell silent. Major Sanders slowly rose from his seat and straightened his uniform. The ambassador stood there, bathed in quiet smugness. He enjoyed being right—it stoked his shallow ego.

"Major, I presume you can see yourself out."

Sanders said nothing but nodded and moved toward the door. Sherman followed. Agent King was waiting outside.

"Franky boy, I heard you stumbled into a real pile of buzzard bait out there."

"Something like that."

"Franklin told me *Hisab* got their grubby mitts on our tech."

Sherman squinted at the comment.

"You gearing for the hunt?"

"Good to see you, King," answered Sherman as he walked away.

It took a few minutes to wind their way out of the byzantine embassy layout. Back in the SUV, Sherman turned to Sanders.

"What was that about?"

"Spit it out, Captain."

"You didn't mention the weapons."

"Neither did you."

"Not my place."

"Your sudden deference to command structure notwithstanding, what does your gut say?" asked the major.

"Someone is playing both sides," replied Sherman without hesitation.

"That's a serious accusation."

"The same one you're making but not saying."

Sanders grunted but did not reply. There was no point. Both men agreed. *Hisab* may have been involved in the attack, but something else was afoot. Like a rotting carcass in the woods, they could smell the rancid meat well before seeing it.

The Gulfstream was already on the tarmac when they arrived. Gournsey sat on the stairs like the king of small spaces.

"Which way did the shit roll?" he asked as Sherman approached.

"They spread the stink around."

"Figures," he replied with an indifferent yawn. "Who are we hunting?"

"*Hisab*."

The sergeant scoffed, "And the Javelin?"

"The topic was not broached," replied Sherman.

"No shit?"

"The ambassador made it clear who was to blame."

Gournsey's large brown eyes narrowed. "So, that's the convenient truth."

"What's your impression of Franklin?" asked Sherman.

"I ain't quite got the measure of the man, but he don't seem level."

"At least we're all on the same page."

"Hence the crickets on the guns?"

Sherman nodded and headed into the plane but stopped in the doorway. Charlotte sprawled out on the couch with an expression that said she wasn't moving.

"Oh, did I forget to mention that?" chided Gournsey. "It seemed like the safest place, you know, in case Kutu came looking."

"Your idea or hers?"

"Blame her," he said with a laugh.

Sherman took a seat across the aisle from the leather couch.

"Frank," she said.

"Charlotte."

They looked at each other for a moment that lingered past uncomfortable. A decade's worth of the unsaid rose like a swollen river. Each of them retreated from the banks for fear of getting swept downstream.

"Captain," came the major's baritone. "A word."

Sherman rose from the chair with a sigh that couldn't hide his interest. Rarely was Sanders so indirect.

"Major?"

"NSA imaging got a lead. They picked up a truck heading east along the border."

"Blow it up," replied Sherman.

"They want confirmation."

"Have the SEALs blow it up."

"They're still holding the CIA's dick."

"I bet they're just loving that."

"Layer Three is replacing them in eleven hours, and you can hold your comment on that."

Sherman understood. The major was still clutching his cards. "We are still two hours out," he replied.

"Talk with the colonels and see how close we can get," instructed Sanders.

The pilots were busy flipping switches Sherman would never understand when he ducked into the cockpit.

"Where to, Captain?" asked the copilot.

"Northern Burkina Faso."

"We're gonna start charging by the mile," joked the pilot.

"Put it on my tab."

The copilot flipped open a thick binder with maps of the region. "How far north are we talking? There are only two paved commercial runways in the country. Neither is very far north."

"Anything private?" asked Sherman, although he knew the answer was almost certainly no. It was the Sahel. Stretching from the Atlantic Ocean to the Red Sea, it was full of many things, but people were not one of them.

"None listed."

"Gravel?"

The pilots took a sideways glance at each other but kept their conclusion private.

Colonel Paulson gave a very non-technical shrug. "I'm sure the Colombians opted for the off-road package, so we can make it work."

"There is a mining camp outside of Arbinda. It lists a gravel runway," said the copilot. He held up the map so Sherman could see.

Geographically, it looked promising. It was on the southern edge of the Sahel, which was further north than most of the population cared to live. Gournsey flashed a thumbs-up.

"Then it's settled," said Sherman. "How long?"

The copilot punched in the coordinates and did some quick mental math. "An hour and forty-five if we punch it."

"I'll pay for the speeding ticket. Let's get moving."

The pilot powered up the small jet and pointed it down a small unused tarmac recently appropriated by the U.S. government under some black budget line item. A lone windsock hung limply in the late morning air. Sherman glanced at his watch and took a mental note. At touchdown, they would have five hours of daylight left.

Chapter Ten

Under the sweltering summer sun, everything north of Ghana looked two shades lighter than a UPS truck: a beige expanse dotted and slashed with green. Charlotte watched the landscape change with each passing minute. There was nothing new beneath it. Nothing she hadn't driven over, but it was still manna for her soul—the mystique of the continent.

Her fixation was palpable, and Sherman took long looks at her lithe frame draped across the couch. She possessed an old-school grace of form that he found binge-worthy. Seeing her again was bad enough, but seeing her so poised made his chest hurt. Thoughts of the past kept manifesting as wistful regret—a melancholic stroll through what never materialized.

"A penny for your thoughts," she said.

Sherman looked up from the rifle magazine he was loading and replied, "They're not worth the price."

Charlotte smiled gently. "Don't sell yourself short, Frank. A fool you are not."

"This isn't about the past then?"

"Oh, save it. Everything is about the past. You know that better than most."

Years had not changed her much. The crow's feet extending from the corners of her sage green eyes were a little longer. She also looked a little wiser, as age often confers, but little else was different. There was still that inquisitive glint in her gaze, except it had a hard edge, like the flash of a knife, and they cut just as well, past bone and into the soul.

"You're fishing for something," he said.

Charlotte shrugged. "Just curious where my ride is going."

"North."

"Pretty broad considering we were almost on the equator sixty minutes ago."

"Some acronym thinks they found one brain."

"The stolen CPUs?"

His eyes narrowed. Somehow, he'd forgotten she liked to correct him, albeit indirectly. "Yes. Those."

"Why not blow it up?"

"Distinguishing computer parts from wreckage isn't easy."

"And you are sure it is *Hisab*?"

Sherman stopped loading the magazine. The same question was running through his mind. "Care to share?"

"Not really their style," she responded.

"They seem adept at murder and mayhem."

"Sure, but it has a purpose."

"Oh," he replied as they resumed their familiar pattern of banter.

"They want the state."

"So did ISIS."

"No," she countered. "Those crazy bastards wanted a new state. *Hisab* just wants control over the existing one."

"Every rebellion needs money," suggested Sherman.

"True, but not once they're in power. Then they can just steal it like everyone else."

"So, you're saying this attack threatens what they are working towards."

"Exactly. What did the acronyms say about those guns?"

A moment passed after the question, where Sherman almost filled her in on everything. Then he started reloading the next magazine in silence.

Charlotte leaned in closer and softly said, "Are you kidding me? No one cared?"

Sherman gave no reaction.

"Oh," she gasped. "You guys didn't even mention it. That means… holy shit. Frank. There is only one reason not to share that intelligence."

Sherman looked up.

"You think someone is playing both sides."

She had not lost a step, but he maintained a blank stare.

Charlotte was practically humming with concentration as her mind raced through all the possibilities. She spoke as they came and went.

"A big meeting like that would have had all the top brass, plus the alphabet soup. It could have been one of them, but I work for them. No. Who then?" She tapped her knee, lost in thought. "Wait… it was at the embassy. You were in the SCIF. That means Franklin was there."

She leaned in even closer. Sherman could smell faint hints of perfume—the same one she wore in Istanbul. Had she never changed it, or was she wearing it for him?

"You think the ambassador is dirty."

Once again, Sherman stopped loading bullets into the

thin metal magazines. She had no outside information, yet in the space of a breath, she had pulled the same name out of a hat. Years earlier, he had found her bright, but Sherman wondered if he had sold her short back then.

"Call it a hunch," he answered.

"Now you're scaring me."

"Why?"

"I've met no one with better instincts for this shit than you."

Sherman smiled. "Maybe I'm slipping in my old age."

"Lying doesn't suit you."

"It's just a hunch."

"Crap," she said again, staring off in disbelief.

"Before this, what was your take on the man?"

"Uh," she said with a pause as if she was considering something bigger. "Sort of weasely, I guess. I mean, I only met the guy twice, but yeah, he struck me as someone who has a portrait of himself hanging on the wall."

"I never got into the office," replied Sherman, "but I don't think you're mistaken."

"Where does that leave things?"

"With us forty thousand feet up, chasing after lost time."

"You mean there's no proof," she sighed. "So, nothing changes."

Sherman stood up to stretch and gave her a gentle pat on the back. "Even if we had proof, we'd still be here. So, you're right, nothing changes."

"That doesn't make me feel any better."

He chuckled, and they shared a brief smile. Both were cynics at heart. They measured progress in slow, leaden steps across the vast desert of human history. Change was incremental.

"Fifteen minutes," called out Colonel Carlman.

The Gulfstream plunged downward as Sherman straddled the narrow cockpit opening. From their altitude, it looked no different from eastern California past the rain-catching Sierra Nevada. Dry patches of scattered humanity, except the dusty trails underneath were older than Marco Polo. Rough patches of black basalt jutted out of the ground—remnants of a violent geological past. A land for those of fortitude, humor, and sheer will. The birthplace of *Hisab*.

"We're gonna wake up the neighborhood on a steep approach like this," reminded Carlman.

"Better this than staying in Dushka range," replied Sherman. He'd seen plenty of planes downed by the venerable Soviet-era machine gun.

"This thing ain't a fighter," said Colonel Paulson. "Surprise is our only countermeasure."

The pilot pushed the nose further down, edging toward the limits of the jet's performance envelope. Such a steep angle had Sherman's stomach up by his lungs—a 525-knot rollercoaster. Gournsey howled with delight as Sherman braced himself for the sudden pull of gravity. Both pilots pulled up hard as the plane roared into a four-G turn. Sherman tried not to cringe at the force. Soldiers train for many things, but high-speed turns in a jet were not among them.

In the distance was a gray diagonal stripe sandwiched between looming chunks of black rock. As evidence of their crimes, a giant pockmark nearby showed proof of the strip mine.

"You want to do a flyover?" asked the pilot.

Sherman glanced back at Gournsey, who was reviewing the satellite images. The sergeant flashed a thumbs-up that was three-quarters of the way to vertical.

"Not unless you need it."

The pilots exchanged a brief but contemplative glance.

"No need. What could go wrong?" replied the pilot sardonically.

Everything was the answer. Everyone on the plane knew it, but a one-thousand-foot flyover would change nothing. Looking at the water doesn't tell you the temperature; sticking a foot in was the only way to know.

For hard-packed dirt and gravel, Sherman thought the runway was almost smooth. Either that or the jet had some good tires. The thought perished midway down when they were still traveling over twice the Arizona speed limit.

The pilot groaned when he saw the cable strung low across the strip—a rusty two-inch steel-braided line that impeded any travel.

"Hold on," was all he could yell before the cable shredded the front tires. The force caused the forward landing gear to buckle. Down went the nose of the plane, burrowing into the dirt as the 55,000-pound jet whined to a stop, chased by a billowing cloud of dust.

Sherman was on the floor between the two pilots, realizing why they insisted passengers stay buckled up. Other than a slight lump forming on the top of his head, the rest of him felt whole.

"Sit-rep," called out Major Sanders.

"Good," yelled Sherman, followed by Gournsey and Lopez.

"Fine, I guess," came Charlotte's reply.

"Just peachy," said Colonel Paulson.

"You ever seen that before?" asked Sherman.

"Not in seventy years," replied Carlman, who was massaging his chest. "That is an old World War Two trick."

"Great, we found the ghost of Rommel."

"Captain!" shouted Sanders.

Sherman didn't need an order. He already knew their situation was tenuous and liable to deteriorate with each passing minute.

"Gournsey, get our gear off ASAP. Lopez, find whatever vantage you can. I don't want anyone sneaking up on us."

The men nodded and went about the task at hand.

"What can I do?" asked Charlotte nervously.

"Help get the gear off and away from the plane."

Sanders already had the satellite phone out and was talking with command. It was an unusually one-sided conversation.

Having picked an outcropping of rocks as the best defensible position, Sherman was busy helping everyone move the weapons and gear. He barely noticed when the major approached.

"A word," said Sanders, motioning away from the group.

"Sir?"

"The mission is still a go. We need eyes on that truck."

There was no surprise in such news; Sherman assumed no less. "Is there a catch?" he asked.

"Two technicals are now escorting the vehicle."

"Misery loves company."

Sanders nodded towards the motley group. "We can't take them into a fight. You three pursue as planned. The rest of us will hunker down out of sight."

"Understood, sir, but I'd feel better if Lopez stayed back."

"Noted, Captain," replied Sanders, signaling the end of the conversation. There was no doubt the major could handle himself. It was the other three who had Sherman worried.

He grabbed two spare M4s and offered the weapons to the pilots. Both men looked like fish out of water, but they each took the rifle with nimble hands. There was an ease in their handling that boosted Sherman's confidence.

"I take it you can use one of these," he said.

The two men looked at him with dull yet calm smiles—glances earned through action.

"SERE grads?"

"Level C," they replied.

Sherman nodded and handed each man four extra magazines. "Sunscreen is in the med kit. You guys might want to lather up."

Charlotte was stacking like with like and trying to keep herself calm. Organizing usually defused the stress, but piling up crates of ammunition and weapons wasn't helping. She was just beginning to process the trauma of being taken by Kutu. Another near-death episode would only increase her future therapy bills.

"How are you doing?" asked Sherman.

"Like shit, but thanks for the concern."

He smiled. "Major Sanders will keep you out of trouble."

"If you hadn't noticed, trouble has a recent history of finding me."

"In that case," he replied, offering her a pistol.

Charlotte looked at the weapon blankly for a moment. With reluctance, she grabbed the gun and pulled back the slide enough to expose brass.

"Is this where you say to save one for yourself?" she asked morbidly.

Sherman gave her a quizzical look. "The Chinook will be here in three hours. Sit tight. Stay out of sight. I'll buy you a beer back in Ghana."

"You say that like we're stranded on the side of the interstate. This is *Hisab* territory. We aren't welcome."

"Ain't that the truth."

"Doesn't that bother you?" she asked.

He looked across the vast nothingness that stretched over the horizon. "Feels homey enough."

"The place or the war?" asked Charlotte.

Sherman smiled and shrugged his shoulders. The question was worth avoiding, and he needed to find some transportation.

Satellite images showed a few abandoned vehicles near the mine—leftovers from when the company pulled up stakes and ran from the armed trucks rolling south. He headed in that direction while Charlotte gazed on with narrowing eyes.

A worn dirt path connected the airstrip to the open scar hewn from the earth. The view reminded Sherman of a carton of chocolate ice cream with one giant scoop removed. Everything was still tidy. Trucks sat parked in rows, and tools were stacked neatly in piles, but a thick film of dust covered everything.

The locals, if they existed, had left the place alone. Sherman checked the first truck he came upon—an old, rickety Nissan with no rear windshield. One of the back tires was flat, and it had enough rust to sink a ship. He kept walking.

Near the principal office, Sherman found what he wanted. Three newer model Renault trucks sat lined up too neatly for a company digging up the earth quicker than a dog searching for a bone. After wiping the dust off, he peered inside. The keys were on the seat. He opened the unlocked door as the dirt tumbled off in a miniature avalanche.

Any new car smell was long gone, replaced by sweat and diesel. A charred scent that Sherman could not place wafted about the cabin. The fuel gauge showed somewhere south of half. The can strapped down in the back of the truck was drier than the ground underneath. Sherman checked all three trucks—none were fuller than the first.

Grabbing the can, he cut a length of hose from what remained of the landscaping. Sherman fed the hose down into the gas tank and started sucking hard on the other end —a simple siphon. Physics at work. When the diesel came out, he almost puked before spitting it out. His eyes burned worse than a thousand chopped onions. Gas was better; it burned, but not like that. When the can was full, he poured it into the first truck. He repeated the process until he had a full tank and a container to spare.

The drive to the tarmac was short, but the fumes only amplified the burned smell of the Renault. Images of fire raced haphazardly through his mind, triggered by an olfactory response.

Sanders and Gournsey were looking at the map when he pulled up.

"Nice ride," said the sergeant, poking his head through the window. "Kinda smells like a NASCAR barbecue in here."

"Get the gear," ordered Sherman, still a bit off-put by the siphoning.

Gournsey knew the tone and was having none of it. "Yes, sir. Captain, sir."

The insubordination cracked a smile across Sherman's face. For men like them, rank meant nothing without trust. When it all went sideways, Sherman knew the sergeant trusted him implicitly. The same was true for Major Sanders.

"Lopez," radioed Sherman. "It's time to move out."

"Understood, Cap, but we have company."

Sherman turned towards the rock outcropping over-looking the lone road into the mining area.

"Who?"

"Three technicals and a minibus."

"How far?"

"Two and a half miles, turning towards us."

Sherman glanced over at Sanders with the glint of a question in his eyes. The major nodded. All plans go to shit, often more than once. This was round two for their well-laid idea.

"What's your effective range?" asked Sherman.

"A mile and a quarter in these conditions."

"They don't come an inch further," said Sanders.

"Understood."

Sherman pulled out the extra can of gas and handed it to the major.

"In case you need to create some distance."

Sanders nodded, knowing that running might be the best option. "Good hunting."

"You as well, sir," Sherman replied with a smile.

Paulson sidled over to the major, worrying about the far-off future. "How are we gonna explain this to command?" he asked, pointing to the wreckage.

Chapter Eleven

The stark report of the rifle rolled across open ground like a muted wave breaking against some distant shore. The road into the mine was long—a straight shot in from some half-deteriorated ribbon of asphalt. They gave no thought to turns. They needed none. There was nothing to avoid until it neared the small airfield, and geology caught up with the landscape. Massive charcoal-colored rocks sprang up from the dry earth like nails through a board. Each was imposing in its own right, but Lopez lay slightly below the tallest cluster in an innocuous spot.

Snuggled among the rough surface, the corporal racked another round into the long gun. Mission requirements aside, he felt remiss for not bringing more range—something chambered for the .338 or .50 caliber. Then again, making do was just a way of life. Growing up poor in a state known for wealth, he survived no matter the circumstances. When he was fourteen, their one and only TV broke. Buying a new one was not an option—not without credit, which his parents lacked because they didn't technically exist in the country. Raul wandered the alleys of some middle-class neighborhood until he found an old Sony left for scrap in a dumpster. It took him two trips to Radio Shack, but he got it working again. Circumstances were only as bad as you made them.

"Good hit," intoned Major Sanders, peering through the spotting scope. The bullet splayed the body of a man from the lead truck out in the dirt as the other vehicles swerved to avoid his corpse.

Lopez exhaled and squeezed the trigger again. The first shot was easy—a big guy behind a machine gun, standing tall like he owned the world. Even at speed and twenty-six hundred yards away, it was a basic shot. Now they were onto him, keyed into the danger. The second round was for the driver of a truck speeding up and swerving. There was nothing basic about the ballistics of that shot. The interior exploded in red like an over-pressurized Capri Sun when the bullet struck flesh.

"Good hit," repeated Sanders. His normal baritone climbed higher with admiration.

Driverless, the truck drifted to a slow stop. Lopez fired once more into the engine block of the minivan. It sputtered to a standstill as the occupants scurried to hide in its shadow.

"Colonel Paulson," yelled Sanders. "Grab that cell jammer and flip it on. Colonel Carlman, gather up the mortar tube and a case of ammo. Ms. McMillan, you're taking my place on the spotting scope."

Charlotte spoke up as they passed on the rock, "What should I do?"

"Call out anyone you see. Lopez will do the rest."

She slid under the camo netting. The hard, porous surface was still warm, and cordite lingered in the air. Lopez did not move. Gazing through the 60x magnification scope, the distance that existed—both emotional and physical—fell away. A veil was lifted, and the carnage was revealed. Dead *Hisab* fighters lay awkwardly in the road, their bodies contorted. Arms bent under torsos and legs splayed wildly perpendicular. A dark brown stain of blood outlined the man in the roadway like a bottle of water carelessly spilled.

Shadows danced behind the van. Feet scuffed one way and then another. A head peeked out from a window. Curiosity got the better of survival.

The instinctive 'ah' that escaped her throat was drowned out by the roar of the long gun. A shudder went down her spine and ended in her toes. A mixture of surprise, fear, and awe rolled down her nerves.

"Sorry," said Lopez, his first words since she entered the hide.

"Don't be," was all she could reply.

Pressing her eye to the scope once more, Charlotte saw two holes puncturing panes of glass on either side of the van. Faint tendrils of red clung to the far window—remnants of high-velocity spatter.

Her whisper carried a faint sense of conspiracy. "I think you got him."

"I did," replied Lopez. His voice was flat and matter-of-fact, carrying no boast.

The radio crackled with Sanders's voice. "Ms. McMillan, what is the range to the van?"

Charlotte aimed the scope at the driver's side door and read the small green numbers in the scope's corner: "2,509 yards."

She looked at Lopez for some cue or reassurance, but his eyes never left the gun. A moment later, a deep thump echoed from behind them. The dry whoosh of a mortar.

She held her breath, waiting for what would follow. It came not as a jarring explosion, but as a flash and muted pop.

Lopez keyed his radio. "Ten yards left and five short."

The shadows behind the van fluttered in panic, and decisions were made or ignored.

Another whoosh, then wait, then a flash. The 60-mm round exploded in the middle of the vehicle. A cloud of debris leaped out as the windows shattered. Although Charlotte couldn't hear the screams of agony, her heart felt them.

"Fire for effect," yelled Lopez.

Uninjured from the blast, a man sprinted away from the flaming wreckage.

"Right," gasped Charlotte.

Her voice trailed off, melding with the crack of rifle fire. She watched the stranger fall flat on his face like a doll hit with an invisible bat. The effect appeared staged, as if the man would hop up moments later and take a bow for his fine acting skills. Except there were no retakes. Only one scene, one cut, one curtain call.

More thumps careened overhead. Explosions shredded the thin metal exterior of the minivan until it resembled the never-used backside of a cheese grater.

"Cease fire," said Lopez.

Sanders crawled into the hide a minute later. His presence startled Charlotte, whose ears still tingled from the gunfire.

"Ms. McMillan, do you mind helping the colonels move supplies into the truck?"

"Uh, sure," replied Charlotte. A sense of relief washed over her as she climbed down the rock. No longer did she have such a direct connection to the killing. Although she was on the CIA's payroll, she was not a traditional field agent. No, that wasn't her role.

"Status?" asked Sanders.

"Four confirmed, five probable."

"Good shooting. Be ready for a quick exfil. We may have just kicked up some real shit."

Lopez reloaded. "Yes, sir."

The muted cracks of gunfire prickled the ears of Sherman and Gournsey as they drove north across the water-starved, empty Sahel. How such a faint noise could raise the heart rate and blood pressure of healthy men was a matter of history and training. For years, they had lived at the edge of that sound, hoping the projectile wouldn't hit flesh. Now it was someone else in the suck, and that felt even worse. A sense of abandonment tugged at the corners of their souls.

Sherman radioed the team. "Major, what's your status?"

"Convoy neutralized," came the monotone reply. Nothing more.

A big howl came from the driver's seat as Gournsey drummed on the steering wheel.

"Damn, that boy can shoot."

"Copy," replied Sherman. He almost said to keep an eye out for more, but why waste the breath? With thousands of hours in the field and three wars' worth of notches, Sanders was one of the most experienced commanders in the entire army. Telling him what to do was an insult.

He looked at his watch instead. "Four hours to dusk."

Sergeant Gournsey nodded. Fifty miles of open terrain separated them from their target. Making up ground was all they could do. "I reckon they're headed for the nearest town. SAT-9 had them doing about thirty-five, like a moonshiner headed to market. We should catch them on the outskirts."

Sherman played with satellite images, zooming in and

out, getting a feel for what was coming. His mind devoured geography. It did not take more than a long glance for him to tell the best spots for an ambush or the fastest egress. The benefits of overuse. It took him a few extra hours to do his taxes, but the civilian side of his brain was underutilized.

"Five miles west is our best bet. Nice and secluded."

"God help the women in your life," crowed Gournsey with delight.

Sherman laughed. He needed a laugh, however off-key the joke. Of all the people to be speeding across the unknown with, excluding the dead, Raylan Gournsey was the best. Only missions with Tillerman were better, and he was still lying on a steel slab waiting for what could only be an FBI investigation.

They say drive easy on the way in, lest you get stuck on the dark side. This was not one of those trips. Gournsey kept the accelerator mashed to the floor. One way was the only way. Aggression above all else. Once that failed, hunker and survive became the name of the game.

The horizon felt endless as they bounced across the dusty steppe. If he squinted hard enough, Sherman could not say with certainty where they were. Iraq? Afghanistan? Syria? Most wars were shades of the same color. The drive was no different. It left him feeling circumspect, or maybe that was from seeing Charlotte again.

"How many miles have we wandered? How many bodies have we buried?"

"Feeling philosophical?" Gournsey asked.

Sherman nodded. "Something is gnawing at my gut."

There was a goat stew joke in there, but Gournsey held back. "Tillerman?" he asked.

"Maybe. Maybe more."

"Crisis of faith?"

Sherman grunted with laughter at the mention of a higher power in his muck-filled life. "Call it slowing down for speculation."

"Well, hell. You've been goin' through life as fast as a jackrabbit with his ears laid back. Passing everybody up like a freight train!" exclaimed Gournsey. "It's only right to look back at the track occasionally."

"You're a hillbilly scholar, my friend."

"My people have the wisdom."

"They got something," agreed Sherman.

"Now, Cap, I'm not one to dwell on the past, but it sounds like you need to hash some shit out."

"You hit that on the fat part of the bat. I'm dwelling in the past for sure."

"Lay it on me," replied Gournsey, mimicking the task force-mandated psychiatrists.

Baring his soul sounded liberating, but the timing was off. "If I allow myself, I'd say I feel responsible for his death."

"Mmm... hmm..."

"One day off. If I'd gotten there one day earlier, he might be breathing."

Gournsey nodded.

"He got out, and it still killed him."

"It?"

Sherman gestured around them. "This shit. It doesn't stop at the jetway home."

"You expecting to go home?"

"I expect nothing, but I'd like my occasional dream not to be messed up by some meth-dealing assholes."

"Assholes are like trucks in Kentucky."

Sherman raised an eyebrow. "Everyone's got one?"

"That, and they seem to multiply. Point being, they ain't

going away, and neither is this shit."

"So, you're saying suck it up?"

"Hell no. I'm saying wouldn't you rather be fighting the assholes on Uncle Sam's dime than deal with the same shit at some Walmart?"

"I'm more interested in a bloodless ending. Tillerman deserved as much."

"Frank," replied the sergeant in a rare use of his superior's first name. "You're a world-ender. Own it."

Sherman looked over at the younger man, almost twice his size, and could not help but smile. He suffered none of the disquiet that age creates. The creeping doubt dredged up by the long lines of the past was still years away. Youth has a way of shielding men from reality. Frank Sherman wasn't old by societal standards, but he was ancient for active combat troops. Even for Special Forces operators, who blossomed later in life, he was no spring chicken. But he was, without a doubt, a veteran.

"I'll add it to my resume," he replied, choking down the truth with jest. "Right under field stripping an M4 and applying a tourniquet."

"I'd call that attention to detail and first aid."

"Oh, written a lot of resumes, have you?"

Gournsey's chest heaved with laughter under his tactical vest. "Just keeping my options open, ya know."

The truth, as both men knew it, was that little space existed for people of their practical skill sets back home. Guns-for-hire jobs existed, but they were not motivated by money, so why leave the army? Veterans get preferential treatment, but neither saw a future in some corporate office. Life on the outside became another battle for survival, scraping together the odds and ends to make life work.

"I'll keep that in mind during your performance review," joked Sherman.

"But seriously, Cap, take care of the mental stuff. When the screws come loose, the entire thing rattles apart."

Sherman nodded, but the mission kept moving. Images continued to feed through at regular intervals: three beige smudges on a massive canvas of the same color. Mental math told Sherman the convoy was speeding up. Maybe word had reached them about the fireworks display Sanders put on, or perhaps they were anxious about the coming night. Humans are hardwired to fear the dark when the noises take on an ethereal quality and shapes grow long and jagged.

"They're speeding up."

Gournsey looked up at the cloudless sky. "I would too."

"Got another gear?"

They were already going forty across uneven terrain, swerving around unannounced boulders and skirting nearly hidden wadis.

"Sure, but our chances of getting there drop quicker than panties with tequila."

"You want to fight in or out of town?" asked Sherman, knowing full well the answer.

"I'll fight where you point me."

The truck groaned under the strain of increased speed. Each dip brought with it an ear-popping crunch as the shocks could not absorb the impact. Time hurtled by as the sun slid towards the horizon like a broken egg down a dirty window. More images popped up on the thick, chunky device. Catching up was impossible. The convoy was driving faster with each passing hour.

"Ease off," said Sherman as he massaged his battered kidneys.

"They got Earnhardt behind the wheel?"

"It's not my grandma, that's for sure."

"Now what?" asked Gournsey.

"Urban assault."

"And if they don't stop at the town?"

"We pick through a crater full of flesh and silicon."

"Sounds better than a town full of bitter locals."

Sherman shrugged. "Can you tell the difference between an obliterated motherboard and a smashed stereo?"

"They're both useless," joked Gournsey.

"Veer right ten degrees. We'll aim for the far side of town."

"Population?"

"Two or three hundred souls who would happily see our heads roll," answered Sherman.

"No different from the ATF wandering into my holler."

Governmental reach extended no further than its willingness to project power. For the U.S., that willingness to police its own ended at the mountains of Kentucky, yet extended into the wilds of West Africa, going well past the desires of the struggling Burkinabe government. An untouchable land beyond the reach of almost everyone else. Not even the French, former colonial masters as they were, had boots on the ground. Deep in the heart of the Sahel, everyone but *Hisab* was *persona non-grata*.

Sherman picked up the sat phone and called command for more information. A tersely spoken lieutenant colonel informed him they were late, and the convoy was already in the insignificant town. The opportunity was gone.

"Did they stop?" asked Sherman.

"Yes," replied the man in a monotone squeak.

"Then we are still operational."

"That's not your call to make."

Chain of command be damned, Sherman would not let some office dipshit impede his operational freedom.

"It ain't your ass on the line," he growled. "Put the general on."

"I'll end your career for this," squealed the high-pitched voice before the general cut in.

"Captain, skip the bullshit. You want to stay? Give me a reason."

"Gut feeling, sir," Sherman replied. He knew the general was a muddy boots leader who had led infantry during the First Gulf War.

There was a pause as he considered how much leeway he should give for the captain's insubordination. Not that the general cared much for the pipsqueak colonel, but he related the guy to the Secretary of Defense. This made it hard to reprimand, let alone discipline him.

"Let's hear it."

"I think they'll switch vehicles tonight. It's too risky to drive the same thing. These guys aren't dumb; they get CNN just like the rest of us. Understanding what we can do ain't hard. It wouldn't surprise me if an entire fleet of trucks left tomorrow, all headed in different directions."

The internal politics of such a mess made decisions more impactful. Some leaders were urging a strike against the entire town. Heavy-handed reactions were something the general did not endorse. As he saw it, there was no point in making a few hundred martyrs to a cause that did not yet exist.

"What's your plan?"

"The sergeant and I will infil after dark to confirm the package and vehicle if possible."

"Captain, I can't offer you more than a prayer if things go wrong."

"Understood, sir. Just keep this line available."

"Always," replied the general as he carried the phone away from the colonel's desk.

Gournsey glanced over as the conversation ended and asked, "We good?"

"We're authorized, but far from good."

"You reckon everyone in that pile of rocks is hostile?"

"I imagine we'll find out when the shooting starts," Sherman answered.

"Like flies to pig shit, the truth will show up."

Sunset was fast approaching as they parked the truck about three miles from town. Sound traveled too well across the empty landscape for anything closer. Sherman spent the time memorizing the routes in and out while Gournsey hid the extra gear.

Under the shade of an acacia tree, they divided up the silenced weapons and ammo. Sherman took the MP5. It was venerable but on the verge of being replaced by fancier weapons. It was reliable and deadly—like Sherman himself. That left Gournsey with the UMP45. Once loaded, all that remained was the waiting. War had always been a waiting game punctuated by bits of sheer terror and adrenaline.

As the stars twinkled through the fading purple light, they stood to leave—one man following the other into the many faces of darkness. Ghostly and forlorn trees danced in the distance, swept by an imperceptible breeze. Swathed in the pale green glow of night vision, everything inherited a slightly surreal quality. The trees became lithe interpretive dancers in some wild off-Broadway production.

The steady hum of life arrived before any sights. Even

the sweet smells of cooking fires drifted beyond the string of rocks cradling the village. Inhabited since humankind wandered that far west from their origins, the stone and mud structures fanned out from a rock-hewn well. Life follows water, and those who settled in the area stayed close. Over time, the village grew larger. Colonialism brought roads and power, but not without cost. Assimilation to greater France cost many their lives and mother tongues, but the locals persevered. They measured time not in years, but in generations. The French came and went in but a tiny few.

Climbing on some rocks overlooking the village, Sherman could sense the history. A well-worn past rose and fell on the nightly breeze.

"This place feels ancient," whispered Gournsey. His voice held a certain reverence for that which persisted.

"It does. Let's keep it that way."

At thirty thousand feet, pilots had no sense of the old and rooted. They pressed a button, and destruction followed. Bonds were broken, but seldom made. Not in the same way as those hugging the earth below in fear.

"Intel has the convoy pulling into a garage on the west side," said Sherman.

Gournsey looked through the infrared scope. "Lonely down there. Activity from the center out north to the road. Only a few bodies out to the west."

"Any vehicles?"

"Nothing warm."

Sherman looked down at his watch. "It's almost dinner-time. We should move as people head inside."

As if cued by the comment, the sergeant took a bite of jerky.

"Do you know what it is?" asked Sherman.

"Meat," replied Gournsey, unmoved by the question.

Sherman took the piece offered and slowly chewed on what he assumed was goat, although the potential list of livestock was long. A slow but not unpleasant burning sensation roiled his taste buds. "Got some heat," he added.

"Keeps those lids from drooping."

"Better than some pill," he agreed.

As the spice faded into memory, the men made their way down the boulders and edged into town. Sherman took point. They skirted around a few old houses built from the very rock they had just descended. Children's voices carried through open windows and into the night. A lone dog barked nearby, but no one took notice as the sound melded into the chorus of dinnertime.

A trio of buildings emerged to their right, and Sherman pointed toward the tin-clad structures. Gournsey squeezed his shoulder, and they took a knee, waiting for sounds of company. Faint streaks of fluorescent light slashed through the poorly built walls of the furthest garage. A low-wattage light for those not wanting to draw too much attention.

With two fingers pointed at the closed shed, Sherman motioned for them to move out. Gournsey gave him a pat on the helmet, and they crossed over a spate of open ground toward the first building. Calling it a garage would discredit the concept of an enclosed space. It had three walls and an opening covered by an oil-stained tarp, but it bore no resemblance to the American concept of free-standing structures with doors.

Miles from help and wrapped by the slowly cooling night, Sherman felt an almost euphoric sense of calm. All the angst over Tillerman's death ebbed away in the pale green glow. The world shrank. Only the man next to him and a handful of people ahead existed. The background noise of life fell silent. Things became simple. A rudimentary equation of survival remained—one he'd become accustomed to over the years: him or them, survival or not.

Sherman motioned for Gournsey to stay put. With practiced ease, he pulled open one end of the tarp and slid into the unlit space. A battered old truck took up most of the interior. Childlike smudges covered its original paint job of brown and tan—homemade camouflage from those accustomed to improvising. Stacks of ammo boxes lined the back wall, remnants from some Soviet-sponsored conflict or another. Nothing seemed abnormal about the gear.

Sliding out, he tapped the sergeant on the shoulder, and they moved on to the second building. Sherman repeated the process with the same results. Nothing unusual—just rusted old equipment and nearly derelict ammunition. It wasn't even worth blowing up. The continent was awash in cheap stockpiles of arms. Half the buildings in town probably contained something similar. Take one out, and *Hisab* would have it replaced by morning.

Swishing fabric caught their attention as Gournsey tapped his left hip. Two teenagers groped their way through the darkness and each other as they snuck out past the fringes of parental supervision. They waited until the young lovers were out of sight before moving up to the final garage.

Once an asset, the night vision became a liability as they prepared to enter an illuminated space. It took another few minutes for their pupils to widen. Sherman listened to the conversation inside as they waited, rapt with attention.

Four men were speaking Arabic in hushed tones. The context was missing, but there was some disagreement.

"*This blasphemy must end,*" said the first.

A second countered, "*All things that pass are the will of Allah.*"

"*I agree,*" said a third. "*Allah's hand is sometimes cloaked in foreign cloth.*"

"*We should not turn down such support,*" added the second.

"*Nonsense,*" replied the first. "*Allah does not condone it, this devil's deal we have made.*"

Sherman glanced at Gournsey, who also spoke Arabic. They shared the same quizzical look.

"*Enough,*" barked a fourth man. His voice carried the dominance of age. "*What's done is done. With or against Allah's will, it matters not. We must see this done. After that, we can wash our hands of the infidel's stench.*"

By voice alone, Sherman grasped where each person stood inside the building. Silently, he crossed to the other side of the tarp-covered opening and flashed three fingers. Each man started a silent countdown. Three, two, one, go. After so many years, their timing was identical, and with simultaneous precision, they entered the room.

The four men stood gasping at the sudden intrusion. None could quite comprehend the situation. Their superiors had warned of the threat, but it comprised bombs and missiles. No one mentioned men—a flesh-and-blood raid into the heartland of *Hisab*. In the realm of their current experience, such a thought perished. Shock was too pedestrian a description, but the terror they felt was palpable.

In the space of a deep, anxious sigh, it was all over. The Americans fired without hesitation. Sherman took down both men in front of him with a quick burst. The sounds of the brass ricocheting off the tin walls seemed louder than the shots themselves. Gournsey stitched the third man with four bullets to the side. The force of the heavy .45 caliber knocked over the whippet-thin man like a weighted boxing dummy. Except there was no popping back up. Only the oldest moved toward a weapon, but it was not enough.

Caught in the crossfire, he died reaching for a well-polished AK-74u. The shiny rosewood stock became speckled with crimson.

With an abundance of caution, Sherman fired four more methodical shots. Bullets were cheap; mistakes were not. Gournsey had opened the back of the van and was pulling off a frayed blanket covering a bulky rectangular shape.

Neither man quite knew what they were looking at, save for mangled wires and exposed circuit boards.

"Says General Atomics."

Sherman nodded. "Find the keys. I don't want to blow up a village for some binary bullshit."

The sergeant found them stuffed in the pocket of the third man and started the engine. Sherman slapped a magnetic IR strobe on the roof and pulled open the tarp. Frozen by the sudden illumination, the two illicit lovers stood planted like deer. The bulb's low wattage did little else than silhouette the American, but the couple knew he was a stranger.

"*Not a word*," growled Sherman in Arabic. His voice carried a cold menace translatable into all languages. "*Go back into the night and you'll see the morning.*"

Stifling an urge to cry out, the teenagers nodded and retreated, each step shakier than the last. Sherman's MP5 remained trained on their backs until they slid out of view. Only then did he turn off the light and hop into the van.

Gournsey watched the entire incident unfold in the rearview mirror but said nothing. He respected Sherman's restraint, and it needed neither encouragement nor admonishment. It was right until it wasn't.

Using only night vision and memory, they navigated to

the hidden gear, pausing long enough to throw the bags into the van and slash the truck's tires.

"Think they'll tell?" Sherman wondered in a moment of second-guessing.

"And risk getting caught screwing around before marriage?" laughed Gournsey. "Not a chance."

Sherman shrugged. The kids were in danger either way, but at least he didn't pull the trigger. Reaching into his bag, he grabbed the sat phone and dialed. The general answered on the first ring.

"Sitrep."

"Package in hand. Need extraction."

"Wait one," replied the older man. "Echo-Foxtrot-Two-Seven-Two."

Sherman glanced down at the code and map, then turned to Gournsey to ask, "Ninety miles?"

The sergeant looked at the fuel gauge. The orange plastic hand rested slightly north of the one-third mark. "She's thirsty, we might ride in on fumes."

"Location's good. ETA of three hours," replied Sherman, knowing the drive would be slow and arduous.

"Night-Stalker Two-Three will meet you. Twenty minutes on the ground, no more."

"Copy. Out."

"They gonna wait for us?" asked Gournsey.

"Twenty minutes of idle time."

"Alright. Bearing?"

Sherman glanced up from the map and compass in his lap. "See the big pulsar on the horizon?"

"Yup."

"Straight at it for the next hour."

"Got it."

Only the hum of the motor and Gournsey's fingers

tapping out 'You'll Never Leave Harlan Alive' were audible. Like climbers, they knew the descent was the most dangerous stretch. The creeping sense of relief that came toward the end of missions fueled many mistakes. Each man watched for threats with religious zeal.

They spoke only briefly with each course correction. Time slid with the stars in the sky until a pale orange glow appeared on the dashboard.

"Bingo on fuel," informed Gournsey.

It did not matter. The extraction lay just ahead. Two hours and fifty-two minutes of travel had elapsed as they pulled the van over on the outskirts of the well-defined open space. Both men held their breath.

Thumping chopper blades rolled across the distant air. When the Chinook landed, they had already unloaded the gear and package. The crew chief—a thickly built man with narrow eyes—shook Sherman's hand.

"Captain, someone said you boys needed a ride."

"Thanks, Chief, much obliged. Can your team secure that big gangly box first?"

The man took a tilted look at the pile of wires and circuit boards but said nothing. His job was transportation without question. He motioned, and the crew hustled the package into the deep belly of the helicopter. Even with liftoff, Sherman didn't feel relaxed until they reached Ghanaian airspace.

Chapter Twelve

The old radio crackled in the corner of the bar—a relic of an earlier era.

"Fighting in the capital of Burkina Faso continued for the third straight day as *Hisab* militants pushed into the outskirts of the city. Government forces have faced a string of defeats leading up to this battle but appear to be putting up a stiff resistance. With heavy fighting expected, thousands of civilians are fleeing south toward the refugee camp on the Ghanaian border. This is Sam Stonebridge reporting for the BBC in Ouagadougou."

Sherman tilted his head back and took another swig of cheap domestic beer. He tried the local brew wherever he went. Most were crap, but it was always cold.

"Did Tillerman ever make it on the outside?" asked Charlotte.

Sherman's right eye narrowed. "He got sober, got a life, and then got dead."

"Frank, I am sorry to hear that. Can I ask what happened?"

He shrugged. "Tried to do the right thing."

Charlotte knew that choices regarding good and bad—this fundamental dichotomy of life—were always made and not left to chance. "Who did it?"

Sherman chuckled at how quickly she concluded. "You don't miss a beat, do you?"

"No," she said, raising her bottle of beer.

"Some locals bent on keeping their ill-gotten gains."

"Gournsey said you just got back from California," she added, knowing full well where Tillerman lived.

"The sergeant talks too much."

She said nothing but did not avert her gaze either.

"I was there," he admitted.

"You set things right?"

"Depends on your definition of right."

She smiled. "Yours. Did you do right?"

Sherman couldn't help but shake his head. She had always seen right through his words to some core meaning. Such clarity made their break in Istanbul even more difficult. Had she not seen who he was? Or had she, and that was why the act stung so much?

"I buried them."

Charlotte didn't flinch or bat an eye at his admission. Her expression was flat and wide. "Did it make you feel better?"

"No," answered Sherman. "It never does."

Her eyes furrowed in a way that he once found irresistible.

"Fine," he continued. "Maybe some of it was justified."

"Tree of tyrants and all that," she paraphrased.

"Tree of meth-cooking assholes, but same sentiment."

"Feel better?"

"Telling you that?"

She smiled and gave a half-shrug. "Yeah."

"A little, but I assumed you didn't approve of such measures."

She sighed. "You think I'm mad because you killed a terrorist that day?"

Sherman held up his hands, not possessing an answer.

Charlotte went to speak, but Gournsey rushed onto the patio, upending a plastic chair. "Cap, you gotta see this."

They turned toward the intrusion and followed the sergeant out behind the bar. Major Sanders was sitting in the white Land Cruiser, staring at a small tablet screen.

Eighteen hours earlier, the Chinook had dropped them off in Accra. Since then, SEAL Team Six had destroyed a second CPU in the sands of Niger, near the Libyan border. Judging by the commotion, Sherman guessed SEAL Team Eight's mission to retrieve the third had gone awry. Tier-One operators existed in a small community, and his mind braced for losing comrades.

Major Sanders hit play without a word. Helmet-cam footage rolled by on the small screen. Heavy breathing, yells of contact, muffled pops, and the flash of gunfire filled the video. A clean mission. Sherman leaned in closer. The operator's hand reached forward and pulled off a plastic sheet covering something large. Only, there was no stolen CPU underneath.

"Shit," uttered Gournsey as the camera got closer to the boxes.

Stacked neatly in the compact space were six Stinger surface-to-air missiles. Sanders stopped the playback and looked up at the group huddled around.

"It appears we have a problem."

"Where'd they find them?" asked Sherman.

"*Hisab* stronghold to the west of Ouagadougou."

Charlotte spoke up, "Tougan?"

The major nodded.

"Any other targets?" Sherman wondered.

"Nothing viable. That should have been the third. All the intel supported it."

"Ask them suits how foot tastes," mumbled Gournsey under his breath.

"It was always a guess," Sanders continued. "The satellite feeds weren't online until after the attack."

"What's the gap?" asked Sherman.

"About an hour."

He grabbed a map of the area and spread it across the hood of the SUV. A bright red Sharpie marked the drone base's location. He measured out about sixty miles and drew a thin circle in pencil. "They must have switched the cargo somewhere in here."

The group looked at the graphite enclosure, but little existed within its confines. The clandestine base was miles from any population centers for a reason. Secrets are hard to keep when they are visible to anyone sipping coffee at the café. Three tiny dots existed to the north—villages of some delineation or another. Scraps of arable land with ancient-sounding names. The only geographic marker south of the border in Burkina Faso was a town called Havre. Sherman jabbed his finger.

"Let's start here."

"Why there?" asked Charlotte. "There are plenty of sympathetic groups to the north. *Hisab* could get help from them."

"They ain't infidels," exclaimed Gournsey.

"Sergeant. Care to explain?" demanded Sanders.

Sherman answered, "Something we overheard. They

were talking about the infidels and some bargain they had struck. Havre is French for haven."

"So, *Hisab* had help," added Lopez.

"Someone smuggled in the Javelin for them to use. It's not a gigantic leap to think it cost them something."

Sanders agreed, "Coincidences don't exist in this line of work. Let's start there. Captain, you know some French, right?"

"High school level."

Lopez and Gournsey shrugged when the major looked their way.

"*Je parle français,*" said Charlotte without hesitation.

The major grunted, took a deep breath, but nodded. "Fine. Take Lopez. Gournsey and I will pay Mr. Kutu a visit."

Sherman went to protest, but Charlotte beat him to it, just not in the form he was expecting.

"Wait," she growled. "I want to see Kutu squirm."

"Not a chance," countered Sanders. "I don't want him to draw any conclusions."

Surprised by the exchange, Sherman trotted off toward Sanders, who was heading inside to inform the general.

"Major, a word."

Sanders motioned toward a darkened corner of the empty bar. "You're questioning my call."

"Respectfully, sir."

The older man rubbed his graying temples, uncomfortable with the news he needed to share. "She's not who you think."

"Not an ex-journalist working for the WHO and moon-lighting for the CIA?"

"The first two, yes. The latter is more... complicated."

"Agent?"

"Not sure, but her security clearance is higher than mine. I found that out when I went asking around."

They read the major in on most counter-terrorism operations, so the comment caught Sherman flat-footed.

"How?" he asked.

"Don't know, but I'm digging deeper."

"But you're putting her in the field?"

"Yes, until I know more. Like I said, I don't believe in coincidences."

Sherman understood the major was playing a long game, one he did not fully comprehend, but he trusted the man, and trust was all that mattered. As for Charlotte, she piqued his curiosity. If she really was a big fish, then how long did that go back?

Questions swirled around his head. Things he could not shake. They materialized long enough to take shape but were too fleeting for any real remembrance. Phantoms of the past. He was still grasping at the half-seen when Lopez approached.

"Cap."

Sherman looked at the much younger man. It was like staring at a slightly distorted mirror. Ten years earlier, he had the same glint in his eyes—cold, hard, and filled with patriotic menace.

"Concerned?" he asked.

"You ain't?"

The corporal was right. Sherman had a whole simmering kettle of concerns, but none worth sharing.

"Don't pack light."

Lopez chuckled. "Copy that. When do we leave?"

"Dawn," replied the major as he emerged from his phone call.

"Chinook?"

"No, it's tied up with Six. Ghana is graciously loaning us their one and only Bell 412."

Sherman recognized the model—an upgraded member of the Huey family. Reliable and with enough range to get them there, assuming the pilots were good.

"Who's flying?" he wondered.

"The only decent pilots in the country."

"The colonels? This ought to be interesting."

"Licking their wounded pride, no doubt," joked Sanders.

"I'd fly anywhere with those two," added Lopez with a smile.

Sherman nodded. "Better get some sleep. It ain't gonna be a short trip."

Lopez and Sanders left him in the still-warm night air, moving on to attend to all the details still unchecked: the logistical and political needs of any military operation. Once more, Sherman stood and gazed upon the muddled stars above.

"Not quite the starkness of a desert night," said a voice he recognized as Charlotte's.

"No. Nothing comes close."

She stepped closer, putting her hand on his back. A familiar tingle ran up his neck.

"We never finished back there."

"The bar or Istanbul?" he asked.

"Both, I suppose," she said, flinging her long dark hair to one side with careless ease. It was one of those unconscious acts everyone does, but Sherman ate it up like a kid with a giant soft-serve cone.

"Tell me," he said. "I've got nothing but time."

"I wasn't disappointed that morning at the café. You did

nothing less than expected. But there was a moment of hesitation."

Sherman frowned.

"Maybe you don't remember, or you've chosen to forget, but I saw it. It took you a split second longer to grab the knife than it should have. That is what made me mad. Not that you would do such a thing, but that you would compromise for me. I knew eventually it would put you in a pine box, and I couldn't live with such thoughts."

"So, you never reached out because I was falling for you."

"It was a dereliction of purpose."

"And my purpose is murdering some guy with a dull knife?"

"Don't kid yourself, Frank. You know exactly who you are."

Sherman teetered somewhere between the heights of anger and surprise. Such surety of purpose, especially when projected onto others, gave him pause. He was a good soldier and took pride in what he did, but such a summary felt shortsighted. Even if he had no other skills. Even if he expected to die in the line of duty. He chafed at the exactness of her proclamation. No one should be so sure.

He went to say something, but she had disappeared, fading into the night and leaving him once more alone under the stars. They twinkled furiously, and for a few minutes, they left him alone with the weight of his thoughts.

Then the phone in Sherman's pocket shuddered rhythmically with an incoming call. It was being routed from his personal phone number. Caller ID did not recognize it, but the country code was American. Few people had his number. In fact, he could count them without using his toes. He answered against his better judgment.

"Yeah."

"Hey, Franky, it's Clay. Wow, I didn't think you'd still have this number."

Sherman squinted at the sound of King's voice. "I didn't think you had it either," he replied.

"Ah, the cloud… you know, it keeps all this shit. Anyway, Franklin is on my ass to get some info from you boys."

"The daily meetings aren't enough for him?"

"He wants the real dirt. Not the horseshit you boys shovel out at those circle jerks."

"Afraid I'm in the dark as much as anyone," lied Sherman.

"Oh, come on, Frank. We go way back. Think of all that bourbon. Help me out here."

"Sorry, Clay. I've got a pocket full of empty wrappers and no candy."

King sighed heavily, almost dramatically. "Fine, well, if something turns up, give me a shout."

Sherman was not about to share information with the agent or the ambassador, but he thought it prudent to ask his old friend a question.

"Your boss, what do you think of him?"

"He's slicker than a boiled onion," replied King. "But he ain't a bad man."

"I'll be in touch."

"Thanks."

Sherman slid the phone back into his pocket and stared absently into the cosmos. The oddity and timing of the call felt off. Someone was digging for information.

Chapter Thirteen

Dawn charged over the horizon like an angry dog chasing the nighttime creatures. Few vestiges of the nocturnal remained as Sherman loaded their gear onto the helicopter. He had ditched the camouflage in favor of civilian clothes, or as close as an active-duty soldier comes to such things: a dark green long-sleeved sun shirt that a fishing guide might wear and khaki pants. They baked utilitarianism into his nature. A thin ballistic vest went under the shirt. It was noticeable only with prolonged concentration. Try as he might, Sherman was still wearing his combat boots—a point Charlotte made immediately upon seeing him.

"You're not hiding much with those on."

"It's these or flip-flops. I own nothing else."

Her brow furrowed with disbelief. Every guy she knew had a pair of dress shoes hidden somewhere in their closet.

"You got the camera?" she asked, changing the subject.

Sherman held up a Nikon from a well-worn bag.

"And the press card?"

"Freshly falsified."

Charlotte did not like impersonating journalists. Call it a reticence from her former life, but it was the best cover story to emerge. Wars, however far-flung, were news. They drew all sorts to the churning waters of conflict and depravity. Two reporters showing up were less conspicuous than a soldier and a spy.

"Where's your gun?" she asked.

He pointed to a messenger bag half tucked under the seat. An MP7 with a collapsible stock was tucked inside.

"That enough?" she asked. Concern tugged at the corners of her eyes.

"This is for you," said Sherman, handing her a smaller version of the same vest.

The gesture did nothing to calm her nerves, but Charlotte stripped down to her sports bra while Sherman pretended not to look or care.

"Nothing you haven't seen before," she said with casual indifference to his feigned attempts at modesty.

"Everyone has a right to some privacy."

She laughed. "I don't know what to make of that coming from an army man."

Not knowing the truth either, all he could do was shrug and continue loading the crates. It was enough ammo and guns to fend off a small force if there was no other option. Luxury and the helicopter did not coexist. Filled from top to bottom with explosives and fuel, the whole machine was a giant bomb.

"Lady and gentlemen," boomed Colonel Carlman as he approached. "Lovely day for flying."

Colonel Paulson glanced in the back and raised his eyebrows in mock concern. "Grand day for flying a bomb. Did you boys not get the TSA announcement regarding flammable liquids?"

Still securing the crates, Lopez cracked a thin smile. He was not a fan of helicopters, particularly the models that I.C.E. used. The deportation of his family loomed over everyday life like the omnipresent stench of cattle on Highway 198. Twice his father had been sent back to Mexico. Twice he had returned, but each time the journey was more precarious and costly. Thousands of dollars were loaned and gifted to reunite his family. All that for what? His father paid taxes he would never see returned and Social Security he would never reap. Lopez never understood but had been running from the answer for years, as if joining the army would absolve the family of any patriotic deficiencies.

"All set?" asked Sherman, giving Lopez a firm squeeze on the shoulder.

"Brought everything from .50 caliber to 9mm."

"Good. Did you pick some spots?"

Lopez handed over a few sheets of satellite images and jabbed his finger at three different locations. Each was elevated yet integrated into the surrounding area. Sherman nodded in agreement. The junior man had done his homework, but he expected nothing less.

"Let's start with number two. It covers more egress options."

"Range okay?" asked Lopez.

"Fifteen hundred yards?"

Lopez nodded. The captain's mastery of geographic space never ceased to amaze him. "Fifteen-zero-three."

"Fish in a barrel, then," replied Sherman with a supportive grin before sticking his head in the cockpit. "Colonel Paulson, I believe we are ready for our sightseeing tour."

The helicopter whirred to life, and they tumbled upward

as the sun burned across the horizon like a fifty-cent piece soaked in gasoline. Beneath them flashed an irregular checkerboard of unregulated subsistence farms. Farmers carved fields of corn and cassava from the verdant bush. Smoke from hundreds of fires curled skyward and hovered over the area—a mixture of people burning trash and farmers burning dried crops or newly cleared land. The hum of normal life made Sherman smile and sigh at the same time, like greener grass always out of reach.

For hours, they sped north. The colonels were unusually chatty, dispensing pearls of aviator wisdom—a distraction from their earlier mishap. Charlotte wondered if it was for her benefit or their own. Tamale was but a smudge in the distance when they set down to refuel at a dilapidated air force base. Colonel Paulson handed the base commander a wad of cash, and they were back in the air within minutes.

"You got enough for an out and back?" asked Sherman into his headset to be heard over the noise.

"No," replied the copilot. "We're topping off at Dierma, the Burkinabe garrison south of Ouagadougou."

"And then?"

"Straight shot north... well, minus a detour around the war."

Good luck with that, thought Sherman. The country was crumbling as they flew over it. Avoiding the war was impossible, even for those running away. He stood no chance, hurtling as they were, into the chaos.

Across the border, shades of green wilted to brown with each passing mile. The conversation slowed to a trickle as tension rose. Lopez was religiously cleaning his rifle, a habit burned into his psyche at sniper school. Charlotte kept gazing out the window, lost in the land below, contemplating what the future state would be if any remained when the guns fell silent. Sherman did not care who won—a corrupt dictatorial holdover or some half-bent zealots. Neither outcome seemed good for the majority, but then again, that was how minority rule tended to play out. With time to burn, he took a nap.

Colonel Paulson's voice woke him up sometime later. It carried a heavy tinge of unease. "Okay, they cleared us to land."

"You don't sound convinced," observed Sherman.

"I'm guessing the higher-ups want our gear, and the recruits want a ride out."

"The ship is sinking," added Charlotte.

"Give me the cash," said Sherman. "I'll deal with them."

The copilot offered no argument and handed him an envelope stuffed with Franklins.

"Shit," joked Sherman, "I didn't know the price of gas was so high."

"Blame OPEC," said the pilot in jest.

The rotor wash blew away some makeshift H painted on the ground as they set down. Sherman jumped out and strode over toward two men clearly in charge of the chaotic mess. The fat men wore designer fatigues and way too many medals. Corruption and the *ancien régime* oozed from their very pores.

Sherman gave a cursory salute to break the ice, but neither man stopped glowering. "Gentlemen," he began, "I believe you have some fuel for us."

The younger of the pair stepped forward into Sherman's space and snapped, "This is Field Marshal Kadole, and you will address him with due respect." His hand hovered near a nickel-plated pistol.

"Listen, we had an agreement," continued Sherman.

"The price has gone up," crowed Kadole. "Leave whatever illicit cargo you are carrying illegally across Burkina Faso, and we have a deal."

The army had taught Sherman how to reason with warlords and bargain with arms dealers, but those two were something else. His bullshit meter was off the charts, and what patience remained spoiled quicker than milk in tropical heat.

"Ask your sidekick to take his hand off the gun, and we'll talk."

Gold-capped teeth glowed as the soldier snarled a reply, "This is our country. Our rules."

Sherman glanced around at the ragtag forces and countered, "Not for much longer."

"Screw you, American," said the soldier as he unsnapped the holster cover.

"If you draw, you won't like the ending. Just take the cash and give me the fuel."

"And the woman," added Kadole.

"Yeah, and the woman," echoed his henchman.

"Unbelievable," muttered Sherman before hitting the soldier in the neck with a quick snap of his arm.

Down he went—a lump of unconscious human waste. Upon seeing the strike, Kadole reached for the revolver dangling from his waist. The field marshal didn't clear leather before Sherman broke his nose with a sharp elbow and took the gun from his hand. Stunned by the sudden reversal of fates, Kadole fell backward onto his ass, ripping his fancy uniform.

"I'll be taking that fuel now."

Kadole motioned for his men to fulfill the request but said nothing.

"That went well," said the copilot as Sherman returned, cash tucked into his back pocket.

"I'm an expert negotiator."

"God help any used car salesman you meet."

"He's usually quite pleasant," noted Charlotte. "Did they cause you some affront?"

Sherman took his seat. "They wanted something no man can demand."

"Frank," she exclaimed coyly. "Did you just defend my honor?"

He chuckled to himself. "I came to the defense of common decency and standard pricing."

As the helicopter lifted off again, Kadole was still sitting in the dust, his deflated pride swelling into anger. The side door was open, and Sherman stared gravely in his direction as Lopez sat with a rifle in hand. The message was simple, even if the field marshal did not want to accept it.

Colonel Paulson kept the Huey under one thousand feet for the next hour. A stark landscape of baked red earth and patchworks of green undulated below them. It reminded Lopez of the National Geographic specials he borrowed from the library as a kid. Those long helicopter shots zooming over some nearly alien terrain inspired such a sense of freedom in his young landlocked heart—a spark of hope for something besides long, scorching days in the fields picking oranges.

"We're going hedge hopping," informed the copilot as they descended.

Charlotte gave Sherman a quizzical look but soon understood what that meant. On the flat sections, Colonel Paulson kept the bird fifty feet off the ground. Spindly trees and boulders the size of buses whizzed by at one hundred and eighty miles per hour. Her stomach leaped up into her abdomen with each twist and turn. They dipped into shallow ravines and followed old water flows from long-gone storms.

For what felt like hours, Charlotte held tight to her seat, hoping she would not puke across the bare metal interior. Then it all slowed down. Even the whine of the engine and thump of the rotor blades seemed quieter.

"Your spot is a few miles ahead," said the copilot.

Sherman already knew. He had seen the hills looming against the otherwise flat horizon. His eyes comprehended before his mind could process. He handed the copilot a map marked with three red circles. Each had a Greek name written above in all caps. They were listed in order of volatility—Apollo, Athena, and Ares. First came the easy extraction: everything went well, and it was time to go have a beer. The second had more urgency and was closer to town: things were not going great, but it was not yet a shootout. Ares fell into the category of shitstorm. It was the closest defensible position—one that Lopez could reach in a hurry.

Colonel Carlman looked over the map and nodded. "How far out do you want us?"

Sherman pointed to a low point on the map, some ten miles away—a dried-out pond or some other quasi-depression in the earth.

"That'll put us about five minutes out from your hot zone."

"Don't dawdle if that gets called," added Sherman for emphasis.

"Perish the thought."

Perishing was exactly what Sherman wanted to avoid. A landing zone full of bullets and shrapnel was pure madness, where the world seemed to slide past all reason and hope. He had already seen enough of that for several lifetimes.

The helicopter stayed low and slow as the pilot tried to minimize noise on their final approach. For ten thousand pounds of machinery, the colonels set it down gentler than Grandma's best china. Lopez took off at a jog before the skids hit the sand. What cover story they possessed would be burned if someone saw them walk in with an American sniper.

As the last thump faded into the late afternoon air, Charlotte felt her chest tighten with unease. It was not her first stroll into the unknown. Years earlier, and another career ago, she covered the disintegration of Sierra Leone for Reuters. Back then, walking anywhere was dangerous, yet she interviewed warlords, played soccer with child soldiers, and drank wine with priests protecting civilians in half-ruined churches. Looking back, it all seemed surreal—a mad time for a headstrong woman bent on making a name for herself and changing the world. That was long before she realized the world does not change.

Sherman turned and waited for her to catch up. "You doing alright?"

"This reminds me of all the crazy stuff I did straight out of college."

"You weren't far from here, right? Liberia, was it?"

"Sierra Leone."

"Dark times," he replied, the last syllable trailing off with some old memory.

"Were you there?"

Sherman almost made a remark about her security clearance and finding out for herself but held back. "Officially, no."

"And unofficially?"

"We ran an op or two. I was really green back then. I hadn't been with the unit for more than one tour. The brass pulled us out of Iraq for a week when things got extra barbaric."

"You never told me," she said, a bit disappointed in the missed connection.

"You never asked."

"There were a lot of things left unsaid back then."

"Youth has a way of suppressing the pursuit of wisdom."

"That's a very poetic way of saying it was all about the sex," she added.

Sherman stopped so abruptly that she almost ran into him. A small horned viper sat coiled below the rock in front of them. Agitated, the snake moved its anvil-shaped head in small circles in the air. With casual indifference, Sherman grabbed a nearby stick and flung the serpent into the distant sand.

Charlotte held her breath until it was out of rock-throwing range. The exhale was long.

"Not a fan?" he asked.

"Irrationally so. You're not?"

"Call it a robust fear."

"Spiders or scorpions—no problem. Snakes—no thanks," she said.

"I'm more worried about the tiny things that'll kill you, not so much the bigger ones."

She gave the comment some thought. It made sense. Frank had been on the fringes of death for fifteen years. His sense of danger was undoubtedly overdeveloped, like some prehistoric man accustomed to running from saber-toothed tigers and other creatures going bump in the night. "An abundance of caution?"

He laughed gently. "There are some things you don't change."

"Sage advice for someone living on the edge of a catastrophe."

"I have my moments," replied Sherman with a certain level of resignation. There was a truth to her words he had always known—not regarding his profession, but in himself. A volatility or propensity born not of anger, but indifference. Part of the darkness we all keep bottled up, hidden behind platitudes and common goals.

The ground rose around a singular gash in the earth. A ravine emerged with small tendrils of green. Damp dirt covered the bottom, and they started walking along a well-worn trail.

"What is this place?" asked Charlotte.

"A shard of the past."

"Colonial?" she asked while ducking under a low-hanging acacia branch.

"Sort of. Part French, part mixed, but not assimilated. Old, yet new."

"That sounds like the future, not the past."

"I hear their politics say otherwise."

She tilted her head with interest. "Like the AWB?"

Sherman remembered a book he had read about the far-right fringes of the Afrikaner movement. They fizzled in the aftermath of South African democracy, but their ilk always made an eventual resurgence. "Something like that," he answered.

"How'd they get out here?" she asked, gesturing toward the endless views of nothing behind them.

"Water."

"Of course," she murmured. Of all the wars fought in

human history, few had been over water. It convinced Charlotte that this would change in the next fifty years.

"This place has been a no-go zone for the government since independence."

"So, angry white neo-colonialists on the edge of the desert?"

Sherman threw his hands high into the air and looked toward the ridgeline ahead. "You forgot the heavily armed part."

Chapter Fourteen

Mistrust ran deeper than the red soil beneath their feet. Strangers and hospitality were incompatible concepts in Havre. The farmer's eyes burned with suspicion. Existentially under threat, they were people living on the edge of all their fears—an entire town dedicated to an ideology that had failed fifty-some years earlier.

"*Bonjour,*" said Charlotte, both hands held halfway to the sky.

Two men capable of throwing a refrigerator overhead stood uphill. Their deeply tanned features bore the marks of hardship. Sherman could see they shared a kinship of violence. A woman perched off to the side, a wide-brimmed hat shading her eyes, held no maternal gaze.

"*What do you want?*" she shouted in French.

"*Some water to drink, if you can spare it,*" answered Charlotte in her cleanest French.

The woman was in her early thirties but had the eyes of an elder, filled with hostility. "*Water is for friends. Who are you?*"

Charlotte slowly held up the forged press pass hanging around her neck. "*Journalists from the BBC.*"

"*We're covering the fighting near here, but the helicopter we chartered… well, they didn't want to go that far,*" added Sherman.

Charlotte glanced over. His French was much better than high school level, and the accent was almost Parisian. *Liar,* she thought.

The men had no interest in letting them come any further, but the woman shifted her weight as if considering the request.

"*Just you two, out here, all alone?*"

"*Afraid so,*" replied Charlotte. "*Look, I don't want to be a burden, but we could use a little help.*"

A small, almost invisible earpiece crackled to life, and Sherman could hear Lopez.

"Cap, you've got two more flanking around at your three o'clock."

Sherman turned enough to catch a streak of blue through the green bushes.

"*We'd be happy to pay for supplies,*" he offered, hoping to reward their acceptance.

After a prolonged silence, the woman replied, "*We have little and at great cost.*"

"*Thank you,*" said Charlotte, genuinely pleased at not being shot on the spot.

"*Follow Emmanuel, he'll take you to the store,*" instructed the woman.

"*Much appreciated,*" said Sherman. "*My name is Francois, and this is Lottie.*"

The woman nodded as if she had received unwanted news that needed a response. "*Eloise.*"

"*Thanks, Eloise,*" replied Sherman with a smile.

"All clear, Cap," Lopez informed as they followed their escort over the ridge and into town.

Emmanuel was a few inches under six feet but had the width of a door frame. The FN-FAL rifle he carried looked almost childish in his hands, as if it might break if he played roughly with it. There was no doubt he possessed an intimate knowledge of the weapon and its primary purpose. Sherman knew killers, and Emmanuel was one.

"If they wanted to shoot us, they'd have done it back there, right?" whispered Charlotte.

Sherman nodded. "Unless they're cruel. In which case, we might be lambs to the slaughter."

"You have a heartless sense of humor, playing on my fears like that."

"Would you rather I lie?"

She frowned. "Obviously not."

"Okay then. You've got to take in the good truth with the bad."

"*Emmanuel,*" called out Charlotte cheerfully. "*Who is your friend?*" She pointed to the other man still talking with Eloise.

"*My brother.*"

"*Ah. And his name?*"

"*Jacque,*" came the reply in two terse syllables.

Emerging from the bush, they walked down the major boulevard of the town. Along the dirt road, everything looked more Old West than Paris, but the buildings had a French flair. Mansard roofs and balconies with French doors lined the streetscape.

"*Emmanuel, are you worried about the war?*" asked Charlotte.

The rotund farmer stopped as if considering her request required all his concentration. "*What war?*" he wondered.

Unable to help herself, Charlotte dug into his response. "*The one on your doorstep.*"

He waved the comment off dismissively. "*Those macaca never stop killing each other.*"

The racist slur hung in the air like sour milk. Having put his cards on the table, Emmanuel turned to continue down the road.

"*Are you not worried about the state falling apart?*"

He shrugged his thick shoulders and answered, "*What state? Their state is no state of mine. One day we'll—*"

"*Emmanuel,*" shouted Eloise, cutting him off before he could finish his thought. "*Our guests need not hear your opinions.*"

"*It's fine,*" said Charlotte.

Eloise smiled a thin, cruel smile and pointed to a low-slung building. "*Let's get your supplies.*"

As Charlotte wandered down the three-aisle store like it was a Costco full of things to explore, Sherman stood outside surveying the town. Eloise stopped, and her eyes narrowed as she glanced down at his combat boots.

"*Where did you learn French?*" she asked. The question stung with skepticism.

Sherman lied. "*Montreal.*" Truthfully, the army had taught him in between classes on improvised explosives.

"*Canadian?*"

"*Guilty.*"

Her brow furrowed with thought, and Sherman knew his story was under scrutiny. "*Where did you serve?*"

He tried to act surprised, like the observation was a lucky guess that no one had bothered to ask. "*Afghanistan. Years ago.*" Looking down at his boots, he added, "*Got so used to them, I wear nothing else.*"

"*For a photographer, I haven't seen you take any photos,*" said Eloise, changing the subject.

"*For a farmer, you ask lots of questions,*" he countered.

"*We're not exactly a tourist spot. Outsiders don't come through here too often.*"

"*Oh,*" replied Sherman casually. "*Anybody else of interest? Don't tell me Le Monde was here first?*"

"*No one like that,*" she said. Then ended with, "*No one else.*"

Sherman could see Charlotte listening through the open window and pressed their luck, hoping she could change the subject if things went sideways. "*Well, between us, we got a good tip about some fighting close to here. Near the border. Something big went down, but our source wouldn't say what.*"

A momentary flash of recognition danced across her blue eyes, but Eloise shut it down. "*We stay out of politics.*"

Charlotte opened the door with a bang and walked out. "*Sorry, did I just hear that you stay out of politics?*"

Eloise turned at the sound. A quick, compact movement learned through years of awareness. Sherman knew it well.

"*We're farmers who want to be left alone. Nothing more.*"

"*Hard to stay out of war all around you,*" continued Charlotte.

Eloise raised her hands to the surrounding land, "*Governments come and go. We remain.*"

Homing in on some unseen fact, Charlotte asked, "*At what cost?*"

The question unsettled Eloise, and the corners of her mouth curved down in personal disapproval. She glanced towards the horizon and the orangish sun sliding down. "*You're headed north, right?*"

Sherman nodded.

"*Well, you better stay the night. It's not safe to travel after dark.*"

"*Much appreciated,*" replied Charlotte. "*I'll see if we can get another helicopter chartered by then.*" She walked off and dialed

Major Sanders on a satellite phone, pretending it was the BBC office in Nigeria.

Sherman smiled at Eloise. "*Thanks for the hospitality.*"

She returned the formality but looked him over with renewed interest. Crossing her arms, she added, "*Somehow, I don't think you need safekeeping.*"

"*That was a lifetime ago.*"

"*We do not forget some things.*"

Charlotte interrupted, "*Fantastic news. Another helicopter will be here around ten tomorrow morning.*"

"*You can stay with my family tonight. Father is a news connoisseur. I'm sure you'll have plenty to discuss over dinner,*" offered Eloise.

Something in her voice left Sherman doubting there would be much in common. Eloise turned to walk down the dirt boulevard and motioned for them to follow.

"Cap," radioed Lopez, "I have eyes to the end of the street. No further."

As casually as possible, Sherman asked, "Can you see the gigantic house at the end?"

"Copy."

"That's where we are going."

"Understood."

"How do you know?" whispered Charlotte.

"Who else would have the clout to invite journalists in and let them stay the night?"

"But the head honcho," she concluded.

"Exactly."

"So, they're on the level?"

"No," he answered. "I'm pretty sure they mean to murder us tonight."

Fury rose in Charlotte's voice as she asked, "And yet we're staying?"

"Oh, they're holding something, and I aim to find out what."

"At the risk of getting our throats slashed in the night?"

"Don't fall asleep, and you'll be fine."

"Damnit," she muttered. "I should have kept my mouth shut."

Sherman smiled. "Where's the fun in that?"

As the sun set, Eloise showed them to a bedroom on the second story of the mansion Sherman pointed out. It had a certain rustic elegance in both construction and décor.

Charlotte sat down at the end of the bed, on top of the mosquito net, but could not look away from the lion's head affixed to the wall. The eyes seemed to follow her gaze in a most unsettling way. Other than the mounted trophy, it was a typical tropical bedroom—netting, a ceiling fan, slot windows, and a balcony. Sherman poked around, looking for anything obvious, like a camera or a bomb, but the room was too sparse to hide such things.

She set her bag down, but Sherman shook his head.

"We're not staying that long," he whispered.

They waited for Eloise to announce dinner, which, in typical French fashion, was running late. He gave the small balcony doors a nudge, and they opened with a weary creak. A cooling breeze rolled across the town, tumbling off the nearby lakes and bringing a pleasant riparian smell to the night.

Gently, he keyed the microphone hidden under his shirt and asked, "Good view?"

"Copy that. Good down to the… uh, veranda," replied Lopez. "Looks like they're prepping for a feast."

"I'm afraid we're the main course."

"Just say the word."

Sherman knew the corporal would put holes where he

asked, but what happened after that had him worried. Escape meant making it out of town. His mind churned through the possibilities.

"Keep it tight. We might run if the conversation turns sour."

"Always," replied Lopez from just under a mile away.

A knock at the door drew Sherman inside as Charlotte rose to answer. Eloise stood smiling on the other side. The thinly veiled hostility of earlier was all but replaced by her ebullient attitude and attire. Gone was the farming outfit, replaced by a simple but flattering dress. It hugged her body in all the feminine places, and she looked much younger than Sherman remembered.

"*Dinner is ready,*" she said in her accented French, which sounded phonetically closer to Tangiers than Paris.

"*I feel underdressed,*" replied Charlotte as she eyed the other woman's ensemble.

"*I'm sure I have something you could squeeze into.*"

Charlotte feigned gratitude at the grating remark, "*Oh, I don't want to be a bother, but you look lovely.*"

"*Follow me.*"

Sherman grabbed his camera bag and headed for the door.

"*There's no need for that,*" added Eloise.

"*Sorry, but it goes where I go. Call it a professional curse.*"

Consternation creased her brow, but Eloise relented. "*Of course.*"

Winding down the stairs encased by a well-worn banister, they followed Eloise out onto the screened-in veranda. High columns ringed around the edge and a giant dining table commanded the center. Fit for a king, the massive wooden table sat at least a dozen, some of which were milling about the space.

Eloise glided over to Sherman and nodded toward Emmanuel and Jacque. *"You already met my brothers, but I apologize for any offense they spoke."*

Sherman could sense a question or desire lingering in the back of her throat as if she wanted to see his reaction to her apology before saying more.

"None taken," he said. *"To each his own."*

A few more guests entered, and Eloise dutifully introduced them to the two BBC reporters she was hosting. Sherman and Charlotte smiled politely, which came easier to the latter than the former, and made small talk with Havre's high society. Those families lucky enough to have made something of themselves or to have taken it from the original inhabitants of the area. Wine flowed, and they took small sips as people regaled them with stories of yore.

Some minutes later, the doors opened again, and in sauntered a thick, gnarled man dressed in a freshly pressed shirt and slacks.

Eloise motioned them over. *"I'd like you to meet my father, Danton Martel."*

Sherman extended a hand. *"Mr. Martel, it's a pleasure to meet you."*

Danton took it and squeezed with the force of a crocodile snapping at prey. It was the strongest grip he had felt, which was impressive given the company he kept.

The patriarch pointed to some empty seats near the head of the table. *"Please, sit down."*

In the candlelight, Sherman guessed the man was in his early fifties, but he had the vigor of his distant past. Danton's jaw was square enough to define a right angle, and his shoulders were double the width of the chair underneath. Years under the African sun had left his skin as pliable as well-worn leather. Those coppery hues stood in contrast to his light, almost pastel-blue eyes—the sort that mesmerizes those gazing upon them.

"*I hope the boys didn't scare you this afternoon. Most of our visitors these days aim to cause trouble.*"

Charlotte smiled, and Sherman could see she was applying her considerable charm. "*It's alright. We've run into much worse lately.*"

Danton grunted and gave an understanding nod.

"*The country is coming undone at the seams,*" continued Charlotte. "*Hisab seems bent on remaking the state in their twisted image.*"

A brief flicker of pleasure crossed Danton's eyes. It was the sort of hidden pleasure one might get from knowing a secret and reveling in the obscurity.

"*A shame. My daughter tells me you're covering this conflict.*" The last word hung over the table like an unsaid joke.

Sherman nodded with the enthusiasm of a little kid waiting to unwrap a present. "*Yes, it's quite the story.*"

If Danton knew more, his face gave nothing away. "*Well, you've come to a dangerous area. If I can help, please let me know.*"

"*Much thanks,*" answered Charlotte, "*but you've already done enough.*"

A look of disappointment or regret crossed Danton's face. He was someone who enjoyed giving help to others, as it reinforced his own position of power. "*I'm sure you'll find a story of one sort or another.*"

"*Oh, there's always something worth reporting,*" noted Sherman.

A young African woman entered with dinner as they spoke. Danton looked proudly upon the meal but did not acknowledge the cook. He waved her away once the massive tray was on the table.

"*Nile Perch,*" announced the patriarch with clear pride. "*From our bountiful lakes.*"

The fish looked prehistoric with bulging eyes and a massive mouth, and had scales akin to razor blades. It could have been a dinosaur for all Sherman knew, but it smelled good.

They passed bread around the table and poured wine. Then, with great fanfare, Danton served the perch. Charlotte and Eloise received petite chunks, while the men's portions were heartier. The slight eluded neither of the women, but only Eloise looked resigned to her fate. Not willing to be passively put in any place, Charlotte held up her plate and smiled until Danton added more with a reluctant grunt.

The conversation felt abnormally tame to Sherman—small-town gossip and talk about the weather. Farming topics came and went, but no one mentioned the state unraveling around them. Politics, it seemed, was a taboo subject in the company of strangers.

Danton's words held substantial weight among the group, like a king in his court. Questions and disagreements filtered his way for adjudication. Most were common quibbles over which fertilizer brand worked best or the difference between Bordeaux vintages. Sherman and Charlotte watched the dynamic closely. Their unspoken conclusions were the same: all power and decisions came through Danton. He was the nexus of Havre.

By the time dinner wound down, Sherman knew the Martel family, if not the entire town, was involved. The details of the arrangement eluded him, but they were hiding something worth killing over. He could see the malevolence lurking behind their smiles, secretly gloating over his impending doom. All except for Eloise, whose finery was dulled by some unseen shadow darkening her mood.

Any actual threat of violence remained in the future. Civilized people, which Danton very much considered himself, did not murder others at dinner. That much was clear to Sherman. Whatever fate awaited them would come well after dessert and espresso.

He slid the strap of his camera bag over his knee and waited.

"*Tell me, Francois, what brought you this far north? Surely the war is more accessible by the capital,*" asked Danton.

The old man had taken his time to get to the question. Sherman set down his fork and wiped his mouth in a show of false manners.

"*A source told us something unusual happened near the border?*"

"*This source… he or she is reliable?*"

Memories of dead Americans stacked like broken pallets rolled through Sherman's mind like a gruesome highlight reel. "*Very,*" he answered.

Danton nodded with increased interest. "*But you don't know what this 'event' was?*"

Sherman shrugged with added flair and waved his arms around at the unseen battle waging all around them. "*Good enough for us to miss the fighting down south. Something of the secret variety.*"

"*Not much to hide around here,*" said Danton.

"*I'm sure you have your share of secrets,*" added Charlotte.

The old man's eyes lowered slightly as he answered back, "*What, pray tell, do you think we're hiding?*"

Charlotte could have given some innocent laugh or joking gesture, but she pressed on over a plate of half-eaten fish. "*Mr. Martel, over all these years, don't tell me this place has no skeletons under the sand. How long have you fought off the winds of change? Building your walls, filling your stores, and stockpiling your weapons.*"

The last word caught Sherman's attention and ignited a spark at the fringes of his memory. Why hadn't he seen it earlier? Emmanuel carried an old rifle, but Jacque had something new and shiny.

He gently keyed the radio. "*You have quite an armory for farmers. Some looked quite new.*"

On the other side of the radio, Lopez paused and struggled to translate the French. It was close to Spanish, but not that close. Even though Sherman had been closer to the action, he had a better view.

"MTAR," he said after connecting the hazy dots of the afternoon.

Sherman smiled as Danton offered an excuse about living in a dangerous place. The Israeli assault rifle was the same model that Charlotte had discovered being smuggled through the refugee camp. It was not something sold on the open market and not for civilian use. The major's adage about coincidences not existing rang true. He looked at Charlotte, hoping she saw the same truth. Her eyes sparkled with adrenaline.

"*I can imagine your neighbors aren't onboard with your particular strain of nationalism,*" quipped Sherman.

The table fell silent as all eyes turned, waiting for the response.

Danton gave a shallow laugh and smiled thinly at the much younger man. His voice rose as he spoke, "*Let me be clear, Francois, in case there has been some mistake. You are a guest in my house. My house that has stood on this land for more than a hundred years. You, who is a stranger to this country and this continent, cannot pass judgement upon those who were born to lead its next evolution.*"

Such blatant idiocy made Sherman snicker with incredulity. *"Cut the shit. You and yours have no place in the future of Africa. You cannot turn the clock back a hundred years and become petty tyrants once more. That ship sailed long ago. I don't care how much you prance about pretending to be the logical conclusion to what ails this place."*

The room reverberated with Danton's fist as he slammed it down on the table. *"Get out!"* he screamed. *"I will not tolerate such insolence."*

Sherman grabbed Charlotte by the elbow and pulled her towards the screen door. The entire room stood gawking as they left under a tirade of insults from the owner. The complete affair may have been demeaning, but for Sherman, it was going well. They were leaving, and he knew there was another layer to the onion. Mission accomplished. Then Lopez cut in.

"Cap, you've got company on your six. The daughter and two more followers are gearing up."

They were halfway down the boulevard when Eloise caught up. *"Wait,"* she yelled. *"My father is a decent man, but some things are just bred into you."*

Sherman turned around. Caught in the sliver of moonlight, her face looked pale and distraught. His words were plain and direct. *"This is a moment of choice. The old or the new. But know this… if your brothers come any further, you'll be the last of your name."*

Eloise stopped for a moment. Never had she heard such sincerity before—not in all those lessons her father had instilled or the books he forced her to read. She knew her brothers were behind her, gathering weapons in the dark. Their goal was obvious: a replication of their father's will. No survivors.

"What would you have me do?" she asked.

"*Who else was here? Who came from the north?*"

Her mouth curled down in the corners and it was obvious their cover story was nothing more than a laminated card. "*Who are you?*"

"*You already know what I am. Does 'who' really matter?*"

"*No,*" she said with a sigh, her shoulders slumping down like willow trees. "*I don't know their names, but they were white. They switched cars and headed south.*"

A spark of understanding burned brightly in Sherman's mind. They were not local. Those *Hisab* fighters were not talking about the nationalists of Havre, but the men who helped them in the attack itself.

"*What were they wearing?*" he asked.

"*Camouflage, I guess.*"

"*Any flags or emblems?*" added Charlotte.

Eloise looked up and into the past, "*A strange triangle, I think.*"

"*Thank you,*" said Sherman. "*Get yourself out of here. Find something else.*"

Her voice sank, "*Where else can I go?*"

"*France. Canada. Anywhere,*" suggested Charlotte, but it seemed obvious Eloise would never leave Africa. Leaving that place, the land, her home, was beyond what she could overcome.

Sherman nodded in understanding at her dilemma. "*Tell your brothers not to follow.*"

Eloise understood what he meant, yet minutes later, she said nothing as they passed, rifles in tow, chasing after strangers in the night. Havre was all she knew, but that did not mean it was all she wanted.

Sherman and Charlotte were jogging near the end of town when the radio hissed back to life. Gone was the camera. The submachine gun swung around his neck.

"Two tangos on your six. Three hundred feet back and running fast," said Lopez.

"The big boys?"

"Affirmative."

"Anyone else?"

A moment passed as Lopez scanned the rest of the town. "No one."

"Bury them."

A muffled crack echoed up the ravine as Lopez took the first shot.

In the distance, they heard a man scream in French, *"L'intrus."*

Then another crack, and nothing else sounded but the gentle buzz of insects in the dark.

Lopez spoke with a monotone distance, "Two down."

"Colonel, how copy?" asked Sherman.

"Good copy. Engines are hot. Where to?"

"Athena," replied Sherman. Their extraction was compromised, but no one was shooting. Yet.

"On our way."

"Lopez, any movement in town?"

"A few ran over to the woman."

"And?"

Over the hill, Eloise stood with her neighbors, her friends, and lied to their faces. No, she had heard nothing. No screams. It must have been animals.

"They're walking away."

"Copy that."

By the time the helicopter roared into the landing zone, there was nothing for Danton and the people of Havre to do but listen as the vague thumping drifted away in the thick black air.

Chapter Fifteen

"Who do you trust?" asked Sherman.

Major Sanders looked at the captain with a straight face. There was no element of surprise in his expression. The helicopter had landed minutes before, and these were the first words from his second in command.

"Above me?" asked Sanders.

"Yes," answered Sherman.

"The general."

"Anyone else in the agencies?"

"No."

"We have a problem."

Sanders was a man short of verbiage. "No shit."

The unusual use of an expletive made Sherman tilt his head with interest. "I guess we both have tales to tell."

Major Sanders pointed to an empty seat on the newly acquired Learjet C-21A—the smallest transport plane in the Air Force. It was a stripped-down competitor to the Gulfstream they had crashed.

"Have a seat," he said.

Sherman slid onto some cheap, generic blue fabric while Sanders mirrored him across the aisle.

"Go ahead," said the major, already aware of where his news ranked in the threat index.

Sherman leaned in to close the gap, aware that his information carried a significant risk. "Layer Three was involved in the attack on the drone base. One resident of Havre saw them come and go that night."

"Ambassador Franklin is not someone to be underestimated. He punches beyond our reach. Do you trust this source?"

"It involved her family. They're a bunch of crazy secessionists who want to recreate colonial France, but she had no reason to lie."

"What did she see?"

"White soldiers came from the north, switched cars, and headed south."

"Why help them?"

"Guns," answered Sherman. "They gave the farmers the high-end weapons smuggled through the refugee camp."

Sanders digested the information. It was making sense. All the disparate pieces gave Layer Three plausible deniability. The weapons crossed the border separately from the men and never left the area. *Hisab* led the attack and took responsibility. It all fit together.

"And you think it involves Franklin?"

"Above my pay grade. It involved those mercenaries. Anything outside of that is a leap. But, sir, I'd say you've already made it."

"I'll grant you, I jumped there quickly, maybe too quickly."

"If you think the worst of people, then you're right."

"And if I'm wrong?"

"Then you'll destroy his reputation or your career, if he has the sway you think."

Sanders appreciated the lack of bullshit. The captain always spoke clearly when the waters were murky. "You're right. We need more evidence, which leads to my tale."

The major motioned for Gournsey to have a seat, and the three of them huddled in the aisle like some special forces pow-wow.

"Kutu?" asked Sherman.

"In the wind," replied Sanders.

"Like a sack of coal dust," Gournsey added.

"His shop?"

"Burned to the ground."

"The operation was gone. We asked around, but the locals weren't too keen to talk," explained the major.

"Does the CIA know anything?"

"Nothing they care to share, which, in this case, is nothing."

"Could be someone cleaning house," Sherman offered.

Gournsey gave a determined head shake. "He doesn't strike me as a man so easily undone. I reckon he's hiding out like a raccoon from the hound."

"You run to what you know. That is where I'd head," said Sherman as he looked to the major for a clue.

"Kumasi."

"Hometown?"

"Affirmative."

"We should get in touch with Samuel. They are staying there with Ama's family."

"You look like a dog with a bone," observed the sergeant.

"The attack involved Layer Three."

Gournsey rubbed his chin, eyes narrowing with thought. "That explains the blood."

"What blood?" asked Sanders.

"At the airfield. There was blood, but no bodies. Struck me as odd, but dead mercs would crack that facade."

The remark brought Sherman back to that night. A corpse was proof of the culprits—an unwanted fact that needed to disappear. He considered the possibility it still existed somewhere, rotting in the heat. A putrid needle in the haystack.

"You think they'd send the body home?" he asked.

"Those boys are ruthless. I doubt they give two shits about families back home. Hell, I doubt anyone on that mission has a family."

The sergeant was right. Sherman would have done the same. Family men, even those in the private sector, have different motivations and values. They will fight and die for a greater good, but secrets such as that are best entrusted to greed, not patriotism.

Major Sanders returned to his seat, phone still in hand. "The general is not pleased with our current line of inquiry."

"But?" asked Sherman. There was always a qualifier of sorts when dealing with the brass.

"The man doesn't like being played for a fool. So, we have some rope to hang ourselves. His words, not mine."

"This Franklin character got some juice or what?" asked Gournsey.

"More than I thought," admitted Sanders.

"We could take him," Gournsey said jokingly.

Such was Sherman's state of mind that he had already considered the option. Franklin was an asshole and unlikely to be missed. At least that was his internal justification for abducting and interrogating an ambassador of the United States. The thought gave him no pause, and that sent a shiver of regret down his neck. At least Gournsey was mostly joking.

"It may come to that, but not yet," added Sanders.

Miles of red tape lay in the way, maybe even a presidential order. But Sherman found some relief in knowing his thoughts were not so alone.

Gournsey shrugged with genuine disappointment. "No point in pissing into the wind. Are we hunting?"

The major stood to talk with the colonels, who, even after flying all night, were eager to take the sticks from some uppity National Guard captain hailing from upstate New York. The thought of letting some young gun fly their team around was unconscionable.

Despite the ruckus up front, Sherman found some empty cargo space calling his name. His brain needed sleep, and so did his soul. Two blankets were enough to cover the cold metal floor, and he was asleep before the plane cleared Tamale airspace.

Charlotte had given up trying to connect with Sherman, who was attempting to sleep off the invisible pull of trauma. Sergeant Gournsey flashed a smile in her direction—an unspoken nod to still being alive.

"How is he doing?" asked Charlotte, nodding in Sherman's direction.

"The captain?"

"Yeah. I'm worried about him."

"Over what?"

"He seems a little long in the face."

"Losing a friend may cause a man to reflect upon the course of his life," replied Gournsey.

"And what do you suppose he sees?"

"I ain't rightfully sure, but I wouldn't worry. The man has a disposition suited for seeing the uglier facets of human ingenuity."

"I've seen his handiwork," added Charlotte ruefully.

"I heard talk you were there that day."

"Maybe," she said coyly.

"So, you've seen half of the man," said Gournsey.

"You're telling me there's a soft side to Frank Sherman?"

Gournsey's shoulders shook as he laughed. "I'm sure you've seen something of that sort."

She shrugged. "Who knows?"

"Well, a diamond would break trying to scratch him. No, there ain't much soft to speak of. But that don't mean he's got no empathy."

"How so?"

"Let me spin a yarn for you," Gournsey said with a smile.

Charlotte nodded.

"This was about six months ago. Stateside. Some salty bar in a sand pit in Florida. We were rotating there for training, staying off base with the locals. In walks one such resident... he was a sizable man. A head taller than average, with shoulders as broad as his ego. Couple that with Hollywood looks, and he was the guy who struts more than walks —a man who expects rather than earns and demands over asks."

Charlotte nodded at the type.

"Well, Sherman just saw an asshole. The asshole had a name, but such pleasantries were not exchanged. He took umbrage at Sherman's attempt to order a beer. The captain was a regular by then, and the waitress fancied him a little. This asshole didn't find it amusing when she skipped him over for the bearded guy down the bar. It should have ended there—maybe an exasperated look or a sideways glance—but that didn't even occur to the man. Life had laid down too many splendors too easily for him to think the world worked any other way. He marched right up to Sherman like Achilles before the walls of Sparta and demanded reparations."

A smile of recognition spread across Charlotte's face.

"So, the guy said, 'You're drinking my beer.' Sherman looked him over from atop the bar stool and replied, 'I guess you're paying then.' Well, those words put the man's nose out of joint. Shit like that didn't happen to him. It took him a moment to respond; then he leaned in and growled, 'Oh, somebody's gonna pay, but it ain't me.' Or some other cliché. Then he pulled back that gym-sculpted right arm and tried to put his fist through Frank's face."

A wince of recognition passed across her face.

"Poor guy never saw it coming. The punch caught nothing but the stench of stale beer. Sherman hit the guy's carotid with the edge of his hand, and down he went. The dude was out for like ten seconds before he stumbled back to his feet, too dumb to know better. Frank was back on the stool, drinking his beer like nothing had happened. Maybe it was to save face, or maybe he was just full of himself, but the asshole gave it another go. He reared back again, but Frank just smiled and slid a beer in his direction. It completely defused the situation. The guy ended up buying the round."

"He didn't have to hit him in the first place," suggested Charlotte.

"True, but he also didn't hit him a second time."

"So, you're saying he's a good guy?"

Gournsey's laugh rumbled from somewhere deep in his

chest. "Shit. Ain't nobody claiming goodness in this line of work."

"Restraint then?"

"Maybe. Or perhaps he thought the guy deserved a second chance."

"For what? Standing up?"

Gournsey just shrugged as if the ending justified Sherman's actions.

"Out of curiosity," said Charlotte, "what would you have done?"

Taking the question seriously, he scratched his chin and contemplated for a moment.

"I would have broken his humerus. Let him try to hit the gym with that."

Charlotte was unsurprised. "And Lopez?"

Gournsey chuckled. "The guy would have drooled into a cup for the rest of his days."

"Point taken," she replied. "But that's not what happened in California."

"Oh," said Gournsey with a level of suspicion. "Some things are best left underneath the rock and not brought into the harsh light of day."

"He told me as much, and, well, maybe I looked up the news," she admitted.

"Did everyone and their family die?"

"A dozen. Mostly criminal types, according to the article."

"Well then, I'd say his restraint was intact."

"Don't you worry about that?"

"About what?" growled the sergeant. "Murder? No. I don't worry about what he did or did not do. Everyone draws this line between here and there. I say, 'What line?' It doesn't exist. Never has. Never will. Just some lawyer speak that allows Uncle Sam to do what he pleases. So, no, I don't worry that the captain did exactly what they trained him to do."

Such an empathetic response surprised Charlotte, and she demurred to the rising anger of the moment.

The fire in Gournsey's gut quickly faded, and he smiled awkwardly in her presence. "Like I said, some things should stay under the rock."

"I'm sorry I pried," she responded.

"Don't apologize. Ain't no bother."

Mild turbulence buffeted the wings as the Learjet descended through a bank of thick cumulus clouds. The shaking stirred Sherman's internal compass, and he drifted back to consciousness with the speed of a dandelion clinging to a slow summer breeze.

"Kumasi?" he asked no one in particular.

Charlotte glanced over at his inert frame hidden among crates of weapons and said, "Landing soon."

"Shame, I was having a glorious dream."

"Oh," she said, sliding toward the cargo-stuffed rear. "Do tell."

He sat up on one elbow and smiled, "Well, I was frolicking through a field of wildflowers. The sun was warm like a fleece blanket and—"

Charlotte interrupted, "Bullshit."

"Fine, fine. There was sex and fried chicken."

"That sounds more up your alley."

Sherman grimaced at how easily she had called him out and how plain his desires had become.

"Maybe there were wildflowers too."

"Frank, name one wildflower."

"California poppy, lupine, bluebells, black-eyed Susan, larkspur."

"Fine, fine," she said with exasperation. "I get your point."

Sherman had not known he was making one, but the relaxed banter with her brought back pleasant memories, even if they left a thick film of regret on his tongue.

"Frank," she said in a serious tone. "How did you know Eloise would break?"

"The way she stood... like she doubted her lot in life."

"Something you recognized?"

There was an undercurrent in her voice that made him think she was more than just prying. "Your point being?"

"Nothing, nothing," she answered, recoiling from the exchange. "I'm just checking that you're okay."

"Fine," replied Sherman. "Thanks for checking, but if you want the psyche eval, just ask the unit shrink."

Charlotte walked back to the front of the plane without another word. Her head hung regretfully low.

"Harsh," said Gournsey as Sherman took a seat.

"Maybe," he offered. "But she's been inquiring about my mental state. A lot."

"She still cares."

"Agreed, but I'm worried about it."

Gournsey felt confused about their different levels of understanding. Her affection appeared genuine from where he sat, but there was a chapter missing from the story—one that generated animosity or distrust. He considered probing the mystery, but he had no reason beyond his own pleasure. Besides, Charlotte might have a point about the captain's mental state. After Tillerman's death, he could see a reason to give space to her doubts.

"Wheels down in five," shouted the copilot.

Landing a military plane at a civilian airport was a sensitive affair. Unwanted attention was hard to avoid, even in the most discreet locations. Kumasi was anything but discreet. After languishing for years with the title of international airport but lacking adequate facilities, the place was bustling with recent construction. Workers were crawling all over the terminals and tarmac. Besides the extra eyes, there was little land left unsettled around the perimeter, and the density was increasing.

Colonel Paulson took his cues from Sanders and taxied toward an old hangar at the far end of the airport. Other than peeling paint, the structure looked intact.

"This used to be an old air force base," announced the major after sensing Sherman's unease. "They sold it off, save for one hangar."

"How much is the rent?"

"For Uncle Sam? Shoe money. For us? More than you'll ever make. But it came from our budget," continued Sanders, preempting the younger man's suspicion. "The embassy was not made aware of our arrival."

The itch got scratched, and Sherman nodded at his superior's meticulous work. For all the formality of rank and hierarchy in the army, Major Sanders appreciated subordinates who thought for themselves and weren't afraid to second-guess. It was only a matter of time before Sherman took his place as they both moved up the chain of command—assuming, and he realized it was a tenuous assumption, they were alive to see it.

"I reached out to Samuel. He'll meet you at Paddy's Pub after dark."

The name meant nothing to Sherman, but he assumed it was some lonely watering hole filled with expats. "Alone, I presume?"

Sanders nodded.

"Good. I'll take Gournsey for support."

The major nodded again. Despite his size, the sergeant could disappear into any crowd or darkened alley.

They set off as dusk folded down its sudden embrace, that brief period between light and dark before the teeming energy of night filled the city. The major obtained a gently used sedan of some Korean brand Sherman recognized but couldn't name. In the noise and exhaust-filled streets of central Kumasi, it blended in with hundreds of others.

As it turned out, Paddy's Pub was a local place that attracted both locals and expats. It occupied a middle tier of restaurants—not the cheapest, but not top-shelf either. A place where a white guy eating would not draw attention.

Gournsey was behind the wheel as they circled around the block, eyes peeled to every nook and corner, watching all the passing faces. They parked a fair distance down the street—close enough for Gournsey to lay down fire and Sherman to sprint back. It seemed reasonable that Samuel was spooked. He had gone there to hide, only to find out it was no longer safe. The abundance of caution Sherman took was as much for Samuel's sake as it was for his own.

"You think he'll help?" wondered Gournsey.

"Would you?" countered Sherman.

"No."

"What if you had something to prove to yourself and your family?"

"Going that angle, are we?"

"I think he wants to help. He seems like that sort of guy. He just needs some motivation."

"I hope we don't get him killed."

Sherman holstered the pistol under his shirt. "Me too," he agreed.

Flat white light filled the restaurant, which was mostly outdoors but surrounded by a head-high concrete wall. The tin roofing gave it an undulating look, as if the gray barrier were rippling. Sherman took his time entering, just as he did in every other room he ever entered. At the back table, Samuel was fidgeting with a Fanta. He stood, almost knocked over his drink, and resigned himself to sitting.

"Thanks for meeting me," Sherman said, extending his hand.

It hung there for a second before Samuel returned the gesture, wary of the outcome.

"Major Sanders said it was urgent."

Sherman sat down with his back to the wall and ordered a Coke—the authentic sugar kind that came in reused bottles, some of which looked battered from too many bottle openers.

"I'll be blunt, Samuel. We need your help."

The man's shoulders rose at the invocation of useful-ness. "Name it."

"Finding Kutu."

Deflated by the name, his once-excited shoulders sank in fear and frustration. "You can't be serious."

"I'm afraid so, but it gets worse."

As his eyes widened, Samuel took a long sip of Fanta, hoping to delay the news that came next.

"He's in Kumasi," continued Sherman. "Or so we think."

"What? No. Really?" The confusion was palpable as Samuel spoke. His gut tightened as fear washed down with the fizzy soda.

"I know. Not what you wanted to hear, but he is on the run. His garage in Tamale is a smoking ruin. The big man is scared."

The news gave Samuel a modicum of courage, and he asked, "What do you want me to do?"

"Ask around. You have family here. See what they know. See what the neighbors know."

Although he nodded, fear escaped with each exhale. Samuel had every reason to be afraid of the man who ordered his execution. What he didn't know or didn't consider, Sherman papered over with a smile and some choice words. He was bait but did not know it.

"Thanks, Samuel. I know this is more than I should ask of you, but we really need your expertise."

As Samuel gazed down at the half-spent Fanta, he grew and shrank with each breath. His body rocked between denial and acceptance as he summoned courage amidst the fear.

Sherman honored the silence hanging between them like a damp blanket. After a minute, he slid a prepaid phone across the table. "My number is in there. Call if you find out anything."

It took a moment for Samuel to come to terms with the phone and the risk it represented, but he finally slid it into his pocket and nodded. Nothing more needed to be said, and Sherman stood up to leave.

The sedan was idling in the darkness as he slid into the passenger seat. Gournsey gave a glance that asked all he needed to know. They waited, covered by the dark, until Samuel stumbled out, drunk with the weight of knowledge. Paranoia crept through his mind, and his eyes darted around with little awareness of what he was seeing. So lost in thought was Samuel that he walked right past his car before doubling back.

"Not exactly spy material," noted Gournsey.

"Keep on him for another few minutes."

They followed the suspecting but unaware man for a mile or so until Sherman was certain no one else was doing the same. Somewhere halfway back to the market, they turned off and headed toward the airport.

Back at the hangar, Sherman gave the major a debriefing. It was short, and Sanders asked no questions but nodded for the younger man to follow. They stepped out the side door, away from any prying eyes that might be lingering.

"I found out more. Do you know who she is?" asked Sanders.

"Given your look, I'm going to hazard a no."

"And the agency wants to keep it that way."

Sherman drew in a deep breath. "So, not just a source."

"That implies passive surveillance. She is an influencer —a mole in an international organization. They want her to craft policy."

"She's certainly persuasive."

"Beyond that. She is on the rise. She is regional director now, soon to be director general. That's not nothing."

"And you're telling me this why? Opsec?"

"Don't be shortsighted, Captain. She has a higher security clearance than both of us. I am telling you she is a zealot—a staunch believer in the cause of American supremacy."

Sherman had never heard the major talk so openly. Such honesty made the hairs on the back of his neck stand on end.

"She wouldn't be the first not to have my best interests at heart. Hell, it's your job to sacrifice me for the mission if needed."

"True, but she'll sacrifice the mission for the cause. And that is something to tread lightly over for fear of falling off a deep cliff."

The news, while surprising, did not unsettle Sherman to

the depths that some secrets can dredge up long-dormant muck. His understanding of Charlotte was neither clear nor turbid. It remained like a river after the storm, with the churned-up sand slowly settling to the bottom as light filters through. Had he learned the same back in Istanbul, it would have changed little. Major Sander's tone made it clear he felt differently.

"What's your plan?" asked Sherman.

"Before we get to that, let me ask you something else."

Sherman knew where the major was heading. "Was she involved?"

"So, you've given it some thought."

"Not explicitly, but it's hard to ignore."

"And?"

"The jury is still out."

Tiny cracks of a frown edged out from the major's eyes. "You gonna deliberate for a while?"

Sussing out motives was not Sherman's primary skill set. Sometimes the situation called for delicacy and tact. When it came, he did not shrink from the work, but that was not his role. Often, he lay on one side of the equation—the sum of all fears.

"All things in due time," answered Sherman.

Sanders could have called bullshit or demanded an answer. He had the rank and the credibility. Instead, he chose silence. Patience, he realized, often brought about results quicker than demands. The captain already knew the truth; he just needed to dig around until it was unearthed.

With nothing left to say, each man drifted away toward the impromptu command center created in the hangar. Sanders had check-ins with command—important meetings to discuss the trivial progress they had made. Sherman found a small room, not much bigger than a closet, toward the far end of the massive space. It had four walls, a door, and a ceiling, which constituted complete privacy in his world. He pulled a cot into the darkened space and was out within minutes.

Somewhere in the stillness of the night, on the cusp of unconsciousness, he heard the door open. Backlit by the hangar lights was a woman's figure. Sherman didn't think twice and laid his head back down. Privacy, when he could find it, was always fleeting.

"Charlotte," he said with his eyes still closed.

"Shut up," she replied softly before climbing on top of him.

A jolt of pleasure shot up his spine as she kissed him on the neck. Their past swirled around his half-asleep mind. The intimate moments reappeared first, surging forward into the present like heavy rain spreading across desert sand. They funneled into a singular memory, churning up the past quicker than sediment along a stream. Beneath it all was a night in Istanbul—an upscale hotel he had paid for with cash confiscated from some Afghani warlord. It was the night before everything crumbled apart: facade, walls, and foundation. Twelve hours later, a man lay bleeding to death in a crowded square, and Sherman was in the wind. None of that was known, as most of life cannot be seen coming. They spent nearly all their time naked, sweating on top of the sheets between bottles of champagne and moments of ecstasy. Lust at its basest form.

Everything about her felt familiar. Ten years separated them, but she was still the same: same skin, same curves, same silky spot on her inner thigh. Maybe there were a few more scars, a few more miles walked, but it made Sherman appreciate her even more. She pulled off his shirt and pushed him down onto the cot. He too had his share of new wounds—a history of the war etched in tissue. Those stories were told not with words but with outcomes: the silent reminder of what lurks at the edge of life.

It did not take them long to find their old rhythm. Sherman spent most of it floating between the past and the present, enjoying every push and pull. When they were both satisfied, Charlotte rolled off and disappeared like a wraith into the mist, leaving him questioning reality versus imagination. Only when Sherman awoke naked did he believe the hazy memory.

No sooner had he put his pants on than Gournsey opened the door. The room reeked of sex, and the sergeant shook his head in comic disbelief.

"One more time around the block for old time's sake?"

"She found me."

"Smells consensual."

Sherman couldn't help but roll his eyes. "What do you want?"

Gournsey paused for a moment, as if he had forgotten what had brought him to the doorway. "The general called in a favor last night. We just got word of the results."

"That's vague," replied Sherman as he finished getting dressed.

"And I almost feel bad for you," the sergeant said in jest.

Major Sanders was leaning over a folding table when they arrived. An almost invisible crinkle formed on his forehead as he saw Sherman's satisfied glow and connected the dots. Charlotte was curled up in the corner with a cup of coffee, and Sherman followed the major's gaze all the way to her relaxed form.

"Captain," he began. The invocation of rank was a not-so-subtle reminder of his duties. "We have a situation forming."

"Sir."

"The general called in a discreet favor for me last night."

Sherman glanced down at the stack of papers. They were passenger lists.

"Who's flying?"

"Four contractors."

"Are they linked to Layer Three?"

"Conjecture," answered Sanders. "But they are the best-paying gig at the moment."

"What unit?"

"Zimbabwe special forces. Most of them left after the Second Congo War. They probably saw all the money on the table."

"Are they any good?" asked Gournsey.

"Fought off the Rwandans in Kinshasa. Stopped an entire tank column," answered Sanders, as if the deed were proof enough.

"Are they here for Kutu?"

"More conjecture, but I doubt it's for sightseeing."

"When do they land?"

"Thirty minutes."

"Welcome party or kite?"

"Let them unspool. I want to see which way the wind is blowing."

"Understood," replied Sherman as he twirled his finger above his head.

Gournsey and Lopez followed him over to the small arsenal unloaded from the plane. Without a word, each man began sorting gear and guns. Within minutes, they loaded up for a minor war in the middle of the city. Rifles went into the back seat. Pistols and PDWs stayed close.

Even though they wore civilian clothes, only the most casual observer would mistake them for tourists.

Sanders ambled over to the sedan with a mischievous smile, like every other previous mission. He would have made a brilliant football coach in another life. "Good hunting, boys. Remember to give 'em enough rope to hang themselves."

All three men flashed a thumbs-up before driving out of an employee-only exit. They circled around the airport back toward the main terminal, careful to check for anyone willing to follow. Sherman handed Lopez a WHO hat he had stolen from Charlotte.

"Radio when you see them. We'll pick you up and follow," he instructed.

Lopez nodded and adjusted the hat to fit his head. He had few similarities to an aid worker, save for the eyes. Little distinction exists between those who have seen too much death and those who have caused it. The line is so fine as to be a mere blurring of two similar shapes.

Once more, they circled around, this time parking at the very beginning of the passenger arrival area. In fact, the airport was so small that there was no difference between arrivals and departures. It all funneled into a single, slow, chaotic lane of people coming and going. A few police and guards tried to enforce order, but it was an unwinnable battle. However, they were so far down the line and not taking up prime real estate that no one immediately cared.

It took twenty minutes for a guard to make her way down the road. Her actions held no malice, but her voice rose when Gournsey refused to move the car. The entire scene was distracting, so Sherman rolled down his window and handed the woman twenty *cedis*.

She scowled, not at the bribe itself, but at the amount

offered. A car full of *obrunis* could surely afford over twenty. Not wanting any escalation, Sherman doubled down, and the woman walked away with a smile. Some places call it bribery; others say fees or taxes. It all comes down to the same transaction, whatever the word.

"Our boys have arrived," radioed Lopez. "They picked up a local and are heading to the exit."

"Any luggage?" asked Sherman.

"Just a personal item. Maybe Layer Three doesn't cover checked bags."

The car rumbled as Gournsey bellowed out a laugh. Ignoring the joke, Sherman asked for a description.

"T-shirts, jeans, sunglasses, and shiny black boots."

"How long?"

"Walking out in five."

Sherman mentally counted out the seconds until the sliding glass doors parted, and five men strode out into the humid morning. Their gait was unmistakable: long, sure steps with straight backs and heads on swivels. All except for the local fixer, who kept his head down, as if being noticed meant being a target.

The motley crew entered a large silver Nissan SUV—one of the newer model offerings—and pulled out into the snarling traffic. Gournsey followed, slowing only long enough for Lopez to jump into the back seat. Horns blared rhythmically as they struggled to get out of the airport. By the time they reached the first traffic circle, movement had slowed to a crawl. Some politician was heading to work, and police were blocking off roads as if he were POTUS. The sergeant kept their sedan in a blind spot as they inched forward.

"You think the guns are in the truck?" asked Lopez.

With tinted windows, they could only see outlines, so the

question was pertinent at that moment. The corporal was asking for the odds of a shootout.

"Doubt it," replied Sherman. "The risk of getting searched there is too high. I'd put my money on the hotel."

"I say they stop on the way," countered Gournsey.

"Care to wager?"

"You have something in mind?"

"That bottle of bourbon you found," Sherman suggested.

"And when I win?"

Sherman scratched his beard, thinking of something. "Steak dinner?"

"You're on, brother," replied Gournsey with a laugh.

In the back, Lopez was incredulous. His gut said the guns were in the SUV, but he had no desire to get involved in the betting. Too many people back home relied on his paycheck. Any reckless financial behavior would leave someone wanting.

The Nissan snaked its way out of the airport and toward the rolling urban hills of Kumasi. They passed roadside stalls selling concrete bricks and freshly made wooden furniture still seeping sap. A shantytown clung to the meandering edges of a small creek with sickly gray-green water. On the corner, just past a house made of plywood and chicken wire, Sherman glimpsed a woman clothed only in a collage of black plastic garbage bags. She was stooping to fish something out of the brackish liquid. His heart sank at the sheer poverty of her situation.

"Wait for it," said Gournsey, pointing toward a man carrying a duffle bag.

The Nissan edged off the pavement and slowed. Children selling food and drinks flocked to the SUV, but only the bag went inside.

"I'll have the porterhouse," noted Gournsey with satisfaction.

Despite being wrong, Sherman's ego was unbruised. He could not say the same for his wallet. Then he remembered something.

"You sneaky bastard," he chided. "The Israelis did the same thing, with you in the car no less."

Gournsey shrugged innocently. "So what?"

The memory made Sherman laugh. The sergeant was crammed into a car full of Mossad agents speeding across the desert to avoid the border police. "Where was that?" he asked.

"Jordan."

"If they only knew…" Sherman said before trailing off.

"I heard there's a half-decent place in Accra," Gournsey continued.

"Really?" asked Lopez. From the emaciated cows he had observed, a good steak seemed far-fetched.

"Yeah, some South African joint. Beef ain't exactly a dinner around here."

"Fine," agreed Sherman. "My treat for both of you."

The two men smiled at the thought of a big steak and a cold beer. Simple comforts could do a lot to bring them back from the brink to a normal life, if such a thing still existed.

From then until the mercenaries reached their hotel, talk in the sedan consisted entirely of meat. The best cut. Gas or briquettes. Sauce or rub. Wet or dry. Lopez and Gournsey went back and forth while Sherman sat on the sidelines of the growing conflict. Not that he was uninterested, but the process did not evoke such passions. Buy the steak, cook the steak. That was all there was to it in his mind. Just don't burn it, being the only caveat.

The SUV stopped in front of a mid-range hotel, a gray four-story structure that blended with the other newer buildings in the area. Not fancy, but not cheap. Number fifteen on a list of places to look if someone was searching for foreigners.

"Decent spot," said Gournsey. He admired the anonymity of the choice. Lots of foreigners, both African and not, were used to the place. Middle management types, the kind that did not ask questions and went where directed.

Like most of Ghana, the hotel had a gate, and after a pause, the steel barrier slid open for the Nissan to enter. Gournsey kept driving for a few blocks before turning around. They parked across the street just in time to see the four men enter the lobby.

Sherman keyed the radio. "Major, we're at their hotel and setting up overwatch. All four are inside."

"Copy. Be prepared for a wait."

"Understood," replied Sherman. He handed Lopez a wad of local currency. "Round up some food. Your choice. I'll take first watch. We'll rotate every three hours."

Everyone nodded in agreement. Nothing needed further explanation. It was not their first ambush, even if they delayed the shooting.

Chapter Sixteen

"Cap. Cap."

The words drew Sherman out of a strange, colorless dream and back into consciousness. Night was upon them, no different from the dream, and it took him a few seconds to focus on reality.

"Sitrep," he said.

"Our boys just got in the SUV again," said Lopez.

Awareness flooded back, and Sherman sat up fully awake. "All of them?" he asked, focusing his attention on the silver Nissan.

"Yup. Four plus the local."

He nudged Gournsey, who was in the back seat, and keyed the radio. "Major, they are on the move. In pursuit."

"Copy that. Don't engage unless needed."

"Understood."

Not wanting to draw any attention, Lopez waited until the mercenaries were down the block before he started the car. They eased onto the narrow road and followed.

Teeming sidewalks crowded with lively colors and open

gutters soon gave way to barren patches of brown soil and empty lots overrun with vegetation. The din of the city subsided, replaced by the consistent hum of sprawl. Dots of light spread across a vast swathe of land. Houses of various sizes and materials extended for miles in every direction.

Without warning, the SUV turned down a thin dirt road. Sherman could see brake lights in the distance, and he motioned for Lopez to go past. The Nissan idled a few houses down. Traffic was still steady, so he was not worried about being the only car pulling off the road. They stopped a hundred feet past, next to a shack selling Coke and imported snacks.

"This is out of the way," said Gournsey.

Lopez sniffed the air, as if that would give him some extra information. "Something's off," he said.

Sherman almost slid out of the car when backup lights illuminated the driveway. They watched as the silver SUV pulled back into traffic and continued down the road.

"What the hell was that?" asked Gournsey.

"I don't think they know where they're going," said Sherman.

"Some hit squad," joked Lopez.

"Kutu is a slippery bastard," admitted the sergeant. "Maybe they have a list of potential spots."

The fixer kept going, leading the Zimbabweans from one house to another. Each stop was brief. The group would smash through the front door of an empty house and leave within minutes, empty-handed.

After the third such attempt, Gournsey laughed. "I like this Kutu fella. How many houses does he own?"

By the fourth house, it was becoming clear they were in for an interminable night. Once again, the contractors kicked down the door and stormed into the unlit building. A few seconds later, muted pops caught Sherman's attention.

"Shit," he muttered.

"Sounds suppressed," said Gournsey. "Maybe 9mm."

The men came running out and jumped into the SUV. They looked agitated, as if something had gone wrong. Sherman debated for a moment and then motioned for Lopez to follow.

"You think that was Kutu in there?" asked Lopez.

"No," replied Sherman. Their body language was familiar: hunched shoulders and hurried steps, more like shame than victory. "Reminds me of Third Group."

Gournsey grunted in agreement.

"What happened to them?" asked Lopez.

"This was back before you joined— a few years after they fished Saddam out of his hidey-hole. All the groups were up, and we were doing nightly raids, sometimes three or four per team. It was open season on Baathist leaders. Shit was happening fast. There was lots of pressure from above to keep up the tempo."

"Kill or capture?" asked Lopez.

"Capture, mostly, but they green-lit shooting when we met resistance. The problem was that the missions were so hectic, sometimes the intel didn't always get vetted."

"A lot of grudges and bad blood," added Gournsey.

"Yeah," continued Sherman. "And sometimes we were the axe. Third Group got unlucky that night. Someone wanted a bigger place or a promotion, so they reported their neighbor as a regime loyalist. Poor guy thought they were robbers and tried to defend his family. It ended up a mess."

"The same look those Layer Three contractors just had walking out of that house," Gournsey noted.

"Fog of war," added Lopez.

"Fog of war," replied Gournsey and Sherman in unison.

With each subsequent house, the neighborhood got poorer and poorer. The mercenaries were slowly circling back toward town as they went down their list. Number six was part of a sprawling area of wooden shacks and small cinder block homes. Most were no bigger than the average American bedroom but housed an entire family. There were no streets cutting through, no neat alleys providing access. Roads were not an issue because no one living there could afford a car. Everything was haphazard. There was no planning department. Officially, the area did not exist. On city maps, it was marked as open space—empty land. Except there was nothing vacant about the five thousand-plus people who called it home.

The Nissan went as far as it could, about a dozen yards off the paved road. By then, it was nothing but a walking path. All four men hopped out and started talking with the fixer. He pointed out a direction, but the conversation got heated quickly. The leader of the group threw up his hands in disgust and grabbed the Ghanaian by the shirt collar. He motioned for one of the men to stay put before disappearing into the maze of metal and concrete.

"Lopez, stay on the guy by the car. Gournsey, come with me," ordered Sherman.

Neither soldier questioned the decision. There was something in the air—an assured feeling that said it was the place. For a smuggler born into nothing, there was no better place to hide. A hundred people could disappear in that chaotic mess of humanity without a trace.

Sherman and Gournsey entered about seventy yards up the road from the group and tried to remain on a parallel path. Every so often, they would catch a glimpse of the men stalking their prey.

A few children shouted *obruni* and squealed with delight as they pushed forward. Others were pulled inside by their parents, aware that danger lurked nearby. Armed men stalking about in the night never ended well. Although colonialism had receded some sixty years earlier, there was still a collective, almost genetic, sense of trauma. Armed white men engendered an awfully specific fight-or-flight response.

The Zimbabweans turned down a darkened dirt path lined with stalks of green grass and roving chickens. The clucking melded into a growing racket of communal noise —a chorus of life after day when the heat subsided and vibrancy resumed.

Hurrying down the narrow path, Gournsey and Sherman caught up to the crew as they entered a bland concrete compound. The walls were a shade browner than the red dirt and topped with broken glass cemented in place.

The mercenaries were skilled. They picked the security gate lock with practiced ease before stacking up outside the front door. The owner had used a steel-stiffened ballistic door and matching frame. Even from the shadows across the street, Sherman recognized the significance. Only those with means and a craving for security used such doors. He had only seen them with governments and NGOs—never on a residence.

Emboldened by the heightened security, the lead man pulled a shaped breaching charge from his backpack. He placed it near the lock, primed the detonator, and backed around the corner. Such an explosion would attract attention, but they had a task, and the inconvenience of local law enforcement would not dissuade them.

"This ain't no interrogation," whispered Gournsey.

"And if he's not in there?"

"He's sure as shit dead if he is."

Sherman agreed. There was no doubt Layer Three wanted Kutu dead. If he was worth killing, then he knew something worth hearing.

"Lopez, we're engaging. I'd like a prisoner if possible."

"Understood."

When the detonation came, it sounded more like gunfire than dynamite. They had top-tier gear—no unnecessary booms, just enough high explosives to cut away the lock and allow entry.

The crew was through the door while smoke still hung in the air. Outside the gate, crouched down with fingers in his ears, the fixer watched with mixed emotions. The footsteps did not register as he was too preoccupied. The pain of Gournsey's elbow smashing against the base of his skull did, even if only for a moment before unconsciousness.

Sherman crossed the street so quickly he was practically the fifth man in the stack. The house layout was basic: a living room straight past the front entrance, a kitchen through a door on the right, and a hallway straight ahead that ended in a T. At the end was a bathroom, with bedrooms to the left and right. Nothing fancy—no frills or extravagance.

The second man through the door cleared right and then stepped into the kitchen while the other two advanced down the hall. Using a flashlight attached to the silenced MP9, he scanned the small, tidy space. Light bounced off the pastel paint, giving the room a pleasant glow.

By the time he switched off the light, satisfied that no one was hiding, Sherman was upon him. The mercenary felt his presence too late, like a shadow in the corner of his eye. Sherman covered the man's mouth with his left hand. His right held the knife flat and parallel to the floor. A single strike between the second and third ribs hit the liver. All effective motor functions fizzled out as pain overwhelmed the brain.

Gournsey grabbed the guy's shirt and helped lower the body to the floor. It squished a little on the gray tile, which turned a peculiar shade of red. Sherman wiped the viscous fluid from his hand against his pants and leaned out toward the hall.

Unaware of their comrade's fate, the two remaining men were getting ready to kick down the bedroom doors. Forgetting the rules of situational awareness, neither operator bothered to look back toward the front door. Sherman and Gournsey did not hesitate. After five years in combat together, they did not need to ask. Sherman shot left; Gournsey shot right.

The door to the left bedroom crashed open just before Sherman's bullet splashed gore and splinters across the wall. Dull thumps reverberated down the hall while two shell casings settled next to an old leather chair in the living room.

Silence hung long enough for Sherman to doubt his decision. Then the sound of a third body hitting the floor caught his attention. There was a weight and liveliness to the thud, unlike that of the dead mercenaries.

Sherman took a few steps forward while Gournsey covered his six.

"Mr. Kutu," he yelled. "I'd like to have a word with you."

Silence was the only reply, besides Gournsey's measured breaths.

"Mr. Kutu, I'm with the U.S. Army. I want to talk."

"Unlike those Layer Three bastards," added the sergeant.

Another moment of silence passed before a resonant voice spoke up. "Do I have a choice?"

Sherman smiled briefly before replying, "Unless you have a presidential pardon in your back pocket, I'm going to say no."

The floor in the bedroom creaked under the strain of someone heavy standing up.

"I'm coming out; please refrain from shooting."

"Hands first," instructed Sherman. His finger still rested on the trigger.

Big, round hands with thick, stubby fingers extended through the doorway. On the wrist was a gold Rolex and the start of a pinstripe suit.

"Slowly," reminded Sherman.

The rest of the man followed—watermelon-sized head and all.

"Mr. Kutu," said Sherman definitively. "You're a hard man to find."

Bits of brain and shattered cranium clung to his face, stronger than day-old leftovers on an unwashed plate. Globules of blood slowly soaked through his bespoke suit as it dawned on Kutu just how deep the pile of shit he found himself in was.

"I see you are not alone in looking," he quipped.

Sherman motioned for Kutu to keep his arms up, and he quickly patted the man down. Satisfied that the smuggler was hiding nothing but a flask and a phone, he motioned for him to follow Gournsey.

"Since you don't know me yet, if you try anything, I'll blow off your kneecaps."

Violence was a familiar form of currency, and Kutu

nodded in understanding at someone who also traded in such wares.

"Corporal," radioed Sherman. "We have the package. Headed your way. I don't think we need any other passengers."

Drawn by the noise, a crowd was gathering. Sherman zip-tied Kutu's wrists and placed a black bag over his head. It took time and some threatening, but they worked their way back towards the car. When they arrived, Lopez had it running with the trunk open. It gave Sherman options, and however much he wanted to stuff the smuggler in a compact space, he wanted to hear a story worth killing over. He shut the trunk and pushed Kutu inside. In the pale glow of the taillights, Sherman saw the last mercenary lying in the dirt. A single hole was visible just above the eyebrow. He held the gaze for a moment, but no remorse surfaced.

"Let's go," he said, hopping into the back.

Lopez eased back onto the pavement. Just another cheap imported car on a still crowded road. Beneath the hood, city lights passed by as nothing more than bright but blurry pinpricks. Sherman considered removing the bag from Kutu's head but decided the man deserved it. Eye for an eye. The smuggler had put Charlotte in a similar situation with full knowledge of her terrible fate. Discomfort was the least he could suffer.

"May I ask what you want with me?" asked Kutu in his Oxford-accented English.

"No," replied Sherman flatly. "You may answer when spoken to and nothing more."

"Surely this violates the Geneva Accords for the humane treatment of prisoners."

Scarcely had the words escaped his mouth before Sherman's elbow crashed into his stomach. Kutu bent forward in pain, his face slamming into the back of the driver's seat. Nausea surged, and bile rose in the back of his throat.

"Apologies," said Sherman, "for leading you to believe there are rights to be had. Let me snuff out that notion here and now. You no longer exist. The world will think you died back there. The United States government has officially designated you as an enemy combatant."

Kutu was unaccustomed to such direct threats. The days of rivalry were deep in his past. Having been at the zenith for so long, he had forgotten the genuine power of fear. It was a long way back down.

Gulping back the sour taste, he spoke, "But you said you only wanted to talk."

Sherman drew in a deep breath. Interrogation and causing pain brought him no pleasure, even though he thought the smuggler deserved it. There was too much gray in that world. All deceptions and half-truths, carrots and sticks, with cracks so wide you could lose yourself in them forever. His reality already comprised enough blurred lines; he did not need more.

"The ground rules needed to be reiterated," he replied. "We question, you answer."

"Indeed."

"Good. You will have this conversation more than once, but let's start now."

Kutu nodded his massive head, unable to see if anyone was watching.

"How do you know Layer Three?"

"I don't."

Sherman held the silence, then shifted audibly in his seat—a trick he picked up from an old-school spook. Fearing further pain, Kutu rushed to fill the gap.

"At least not directly," continued the smuggler. "I know their reputation."

"Yet you weren't surprised to find them knocking on your door."

"My list of enemies has grown long over the years."

"So, you didn't smuggle guns through the refugee camps for them?"

Sensing an opportunity to be useful, Kutu elaborated, "No, not for them. An *obruni* paid me. A local."

"His name?"

"I built my business on discretion. Names are not important, but he was a thick man—rooted like a baobab tree. Deep tan. Calloused hands."

"French accent and pale blue eyes?" asked Sherman.

"Accent, yes, but his eyes were green."

The description confused Sherman. It sounded like Danton Martel, but not quite.

"Are you sure about his green eyes?"

"Yes," confirmed Kutu. "They sparkled green like an emerald."

"What else did you do for him?"

"The American woman, but you already knew about that."

"She sends her regards."

A deep rumble of laughter erupted from Kutu's chest, only to be stifled by the hood.

"I admire her—what do you say… spunk."

Sherman grew impatient. He wanted something concrete, but the story ran in well-worn ruts. "Anything else?" he asked.

"We drove a van south over the border."

"When?"

"Five days ago. After you shot up my Tahoe."

For being in a stressful position, the smuggler did not miss a beat. Sherman had to give him that; the guy was calm under pressure.

"That was the sergeant. I killed your men."

Kutu paused as if collecting himself, then scornfully added, "They were honorable men. Friends."

"Not good enough."

"So it would seem."

"What was in the van?"

"A box."

"How big?"

"Maybe the size of an oven?"

"What was in the box?"

"I don't know and didn't ask. Discretion is part of the business model."

Sherman caught Gournsey's eye. He could tell they were wandering down the same road.

"Where did you take it?"

"South," was all Kutu said before the rear windshield shattered. The crack of a high-velocity bullet filled the compact interior space. Sherman's ears were ringing, and his face felt wet and sticky. A ragged hole through the black hood told him why.

"Turn," he yelled.

Lopez grunted and cranked the wheel hard to the right. The sedan skidded around the corner, almost striking a stray dog scavenging for an evening meal.

"Damnit," groaned the corporal. "I'm hit."

"Lean forward. Gournsey, check his vest," Sherman ordered. A brain overexposed to such situations compartmentalized away panic. His voice was logical and calm.

Gournsey pulled up the corporal's shirt and searched for a hole. He found one a few inches from the bottom of the vest. Reaching under, he searched for blood, but his hand was dry.

"You're lucky that guy had an enormous head. The bullet slowed enough to stick in your vest."

Lopez grimaced. "Still cracked my rib."

"You good to drive?" asked Sherman. He was still aiming a rifle out the back window, looking for anyone foolish enough to follow them.

"Yeah."

"Good. Circle north towards the airport. I want to be sure no one is on our tail."

"Did you see the shooter?" asked Gournsey.

"No, but that was a damn fine shot. Sounded over four hundred yards."

"Four hundred and fifty," corrected Lopez.

"We went under a pedestrian bridge," noted Gournsey.

The location rang a vague bell in Sherman's memory. A flash of metal passing overhead while he questioned Kutu—nothing more than a blur at the edges of his vision and recollection. "Someone was watching us then," he concluded.

Gournsey guessed, "The Frenchman?"

"Maybe… or intel missed another contractor." Sherman wiped the blood splatter off his face, then keyed the radio. "Major, we're in contact. Package is KIA. We are evading and then RTB. How copy?"

The radio hissed as Sanders held the button down before replying, "Good copy. Keep your heads down and take out the trash before coming home."

The dead smuggler hunched forward against the seat. Blood, lots of it, was pooling at his feet. It filled the indents of a rubber mat on the floor before spilling over onto the carpet. Sherman pushed the body upright and watched up ahead. A darkened stretch of road loomed in the distance.

"Lopez, pull over on the left side."

The corporal slowed down the car, and Sherman opened the passenger door. Bracing himself against the headrests, he gave Kutu's body a heavy kick, sending the corpse tumbling out of the still-moving car. The sound of flesh striking concrete reached his ears, and he tried to push out the image forming in his mind.

"Get us out of here," he said.

Chapter Seventeen

Smoke billowed from the smoldering sedan. The acrid fumes mingled with all the other trash burning in the predawn morning. People were going about their lives, disposing of a few boxes and the ubiquitous black plastic bags. Garbage trucks did not exist, at least not in that part of town. Burning had become the solution to an infrastructure problem. In the distance, roosters crowed as Sherman watched the evidence of the night burn down to a metal frame.

Gournsey had offered to do it, but he wanted the space —a little room to breathe and think. Decompression time. He had taken a perch on a slight mound of recycled electronics, the kind Americans discard with good intentions but which end up a world away, melted down for whatever milligrams of precious metal remain.

The locals were keeping their distance. Two men had given him long looks when he pulled up but eventually accepted that they shared a certain affinity with the strange *obruni*. After all, few people show up to burn a car and wait for the results. The local men respected that level of dedication. Somehow, they also knew to give him space. Maybe it was the look in Sherman's eyes, his bloodstained clothing, or the fact that he was burning a working car. Instinct told them he was a man best avoided.

The first tendrils of light were crawling over the bland horizon when he stood to leave—a bloodstained man alone atop the discarded past of consumption. Fire had done its job. It had charred any trace of them or Kutu. Both locals stood up from their smelting operations. Sherman smiled in their direction and placed two one-hundred-dollar bills under an old Apple keyboard.

"For your silence."

The men nodded and watched him saunter away. He meandered past mounds of debris and trash over twenty feet tall—mountains compared to the flat field they inhabited. Thousands of tons, with no end in sight.

Taking out a burner phone—a small rectangle with no features other than a keypad—he dialed a number from memory. Gournsey answered.

"I'm done," he said and then hung up.

The sergeant knew where to find him.

Thirty minutes later, he was back in the hangar, drifting toward unconsciousness on a leather couch crammed into some old office. A squadron commander once called it home, but that was before Ghana started leasing out the space. Still, it maintained a nostalgic feel for a bygone era. Pictures of prop planes and old British aviators lined the cream-colored walls—a twisted salute to a complicated past.

Shadows existed at a rakish angle when Sherman awoke. He glanced at his watch, registered the hour, and rubbed the exhaustion from his eyes. The stench of dried blood and gasoline lingered in the creases of his hands.

Sherman made his way to the shower with a pair of clean clothes tucked under his arm. He turned the handle to hot, stood there, and let the scalding water wash away the previous night. Red streaks swirled around the drain at his feet, interrupted by the occasional soapy bubble. He did not leave until the water ran clear.

Charlotte was standing in the doorway when he stepped out. "You still look like shit," she said.

Sherman glanced down at his naked body and knew she was not talking about anything physical. Fatigue roamed behind his eyes, settling into the furrows forming on his forehead. The feeling was familiar, like well-worn shoes—molded and comfortable, yet also thin and lacking support.

"I'm fine," he replied.

"You're not even fooling yourself with that line."

Sherman slipped on some underwear to ease the strange power dynamic he felt without clothes and took a seat in the adjoining locker room. She followed.

"Suppose you're right. What good comes from acknowledging it?"

"You can get help."

"I tried that a few weeks ago, and someone killed my best friend."

"Running away isn't a solution," added Charlotte.

"It worked for us," he shot back.

Charlotte wanted to roll her eyes and throw it all back in his direction but stopped herself. Such plans never worked. "Look, I'm no saint, but there are ways to support yourself."

"If you're suggesting therapy, I've already tried that on the orders of Uncle Sam."

"There are support groups."

"I can't imagine that going well. 'Hi, my name is Frank,

and I kill people for a living.' And why the hell are you so concerned about my mental well-being?"

"Because we need you."

There was something about the way she said "we" that twisted a core layer of suspicion deep within his mind. He wondered just how many people the pronoun covered and how far up the chain they went.

"Who's 'we'?"

"Never mind," she replied and cast her eyes to the floor —a sure sign of guilt. "Just take care of yourself. That's all I'm saying."

Sherman went to put on a clean shirt, and she was gone before the fabric pulled past his eyes. "What the hell," he muttered to himself.

Replaying the conversation in his mind made nothing clearer. He needed a break—a proper one. She was not wrong in saying so. Yet the way she kept going on about it threw him off. And who the hell was "we" in her story? The question irritated his subconscious like a foxtail poking through a sock.

The major was waiting for him by a desk cluttered with intel files and satellite photos. It was an old steel piece of furniture—heavy, cold, and bureaucratic—something from the late fifties. Judging from the scars and scratches, someone had used it well. Standing above the wooden top, Sanders looked tired. Not just sleepy, but worn down like an overused crayon after a frenzy of scribbling. Dusty foot-prints on the concrete showed that he had been pacing, waiting to debrief the captain. Gournsey and Lopez had retold the events, but Sanders wanted to hear it from the source.

"I'm ready," said Sherman.

Sanders pointed to two cheap plastic deck chairs in the

corner. For Sherman, it almost felt like the confessional, or at least his imagined version of it.

"Start from the beginning."

So, Sherman began at the hotel and briskly recounted the previous night up to the capture of Kutu. The major remained silent, absorbed in a story he already knew. Then he spoke.

"Who were you asking Kutu about?"

"With blue eyes?"

The major nodded. "Yes. Gournsey and Lopez didn't know."

"His description sounded like Danton Martel. He has blue eyes, but Kutu described a man with green eyes."

Sanders stood without a word and retrieved a manila folder from the desk. It was thin, not like the ISIS intel reports fished out of some acronym's database. Inside were a few pages sparse on details and one picture. He handed it to Sherman.

The faces were familiar—a family photo from Havre taken some years back. Eloise looked just past her teenage years, the fading embers of youth still clinging to her smile, but the brothers were just as gloomy. It was the man next to Danton that stood out: similar height, weight, and sheer presence, save for the eye color.

"He has a brother," concluded Sherman.

"It appears so."

"Where did you get that?"

"The keyboard overlords found it archived on a now-defunct message board."

"Advocating for?" asked Sherman. Those sorts of things always tilted toward an extreme.

"The reinstatement of French dominion over West Africa."

"Oh, is that all?"

"Fringe shit mostly," added Sanders.

"So was ISIS."

"Exactly."

"Do we have any intel on—"

"Hugo Martel."

"Do we have any intel on Hugo Martel?"

"Other than he's alive and, as of last night, in Kumasi?"

Sherman nodded.

"No," answered the major.

"He's an expert shot," Sherman offered.

Sanders furrowed his brow and nodded methodically. "Alive, local, and dangerous. I'll phone Langley and the NSA. Maybe we can grab a call to his brother."

For a man existing in the shadows, Sherman doubted Hugo would make such an obvious mistake. If he was anything like his brother, then the operation would be orderly.

"But if he's anything like his brother…" Sherman said aloud, not finishing the thought.

"What?" asked Sanders.

"An idea. A long shot."

Sherman grabbed the picture and his pistol. Then he wandered off to find Charlotte.

"You want to grab some brunch?" he asked after finding her reading an Economist article in a drab corner.

She raised an eyebrow and waited for the catch. There was always a catch.

"Danton Martel has a brother in town."

"We're having French then. You should have led with that," she replied with a devious smile—one that Sherman had not seen since they went skinny dipping in the Black Sea. It was full of energy and life.

"Alright. Let's grab Gournsey."

Although Charlotte was disappointed at the prospect of a third wheel, she grabbed her stuff and followed the soldiers out to a tired-looking pickup truck. The paint that was once called green was more rust than color, and it sagged at the edges like a hound dog. The prospect of spending more time with Sherman had distracted her from noticing that he had changed clothes.

"Shorts and flip-flops? Are we going to the beach?" she asked. When was the last time she had seen him in shorts? Istanbul? For a moment, she drifted back. It was a warm summer day—not hot, not yet. She could see the white linen tablecloths and feel the pleasant sea breeze playing with her hair. He looked so content and alive, at home in his skin with a pale Guayabera shirt and brown shorts. Just another holiday seeker soaking up the sun.

"I figured Hugo might spot the boots," replied Sherman.

They drove away from the city center with Gournsey behind the wheel. Crowded streets thinned as the number of gated homes rose. They were not mansions but stately homes—upper middle class to nouveau riche. Manicured medians proliferated, ostentatious to the point of being gaudy. Gournsey pulled over after nearing a small commercial district of new buildings: monoliths of glass burnished with stainless steel, shops below, apartments above.

"Leg it," suggested Gournsey. "We stick out like a dog's balls in this beater."

Sherman agreed. The neighborhood was too upscale. Automotive ruins worked in many places, but not there. "Ham and cheese croissant?" he asked.

"You know it," replied Gournsey. "Unless it looks like bush meat, then chocolate."

Camouflage did not stop with fancy patterns. Blending was key. Act the part, become the part. Sherman rolled up his long sleeves like he belonged in some expat enclave. He and Charlotte slid out and walked toward the cluster of shops on the bottom floor. The area was pleasant in a transplanted Western way that ignored local history and culture: new buildings, fresh paint, sidewalks with covered gutters, and lots of fancy cars.

"Odd place," said Charlotte. "I feel like I'm in L.A. but without the grunge."

"Someone's done a good job of ignoring geography."

An old-world-style sign hung over the door of a corner unit. Big and blue with a gold script that seemed impossibly curly, it was out of place among the harsh modern decor of the other shops, where everything was designed to be minimal. Less signage, fewer lines, less value. The Francophile lettering spelled out 'Pâtisserie'. By smell alone, they knew it was good. Yeasty aromas of freshly baked bread seeped out like steam from a Russian banya, mixing with the sharpness of melted cheese and the sweetness of caramelized onions.

Brunch was in full swing. A lengthy line of expats and well-to-do locals snaked nearly out the door. People came for the food, but also to flaunt the fact that they could afford it—an edible sign of wealth. Even the stamp on the paper to-go bags looked couture.

Sherman turned his back to the counter to see both inside and out. An old habit. A good habit. One that would never go away.

"Reminds me of that place in Tel Aviv. Remember? They had the best macarons," said Charlotte with a smile.

He remembered—a small shop with a red awning and ten feet of glass cases filled with pastries. He recalled that she skipped all that rich, buttery goodness to order sweets that were neither fully crunchy nor chewy, as if they could not decide on a texture.

"I do, but macarons are an overrated cookie."

Charlotte playfully punched him in the arm. Sherman couldn't tell if it was genuine or just for show. He was hoping, or even entertaining the idea that it was the former.

"What can I get you?" asked the woman behind the counter. She spoke English with a heavy French accent—not Parisian, but something more colloquial. Maybe southern France. Marsais, perhaps.

He glanced back and smiled—a polite smile, a smile of belonging. "*Deux croissants aux amandes et deux au jambon et suisse, s'il vous plaît.*"

The woman smiled back, pleased to hear her native tongue. She took tongs and retrieved the requested orders, placing them in the desirable bag.

"*Et des macarons,*" he added.

Charlotte elbowed him again. *Surely the former,* he thought.

"*Café?*" asked the shopkeeper as she slid the bag across the old oak counter—another import, no doubt, just like the owner and the ingredients.

"*S'il vous plaît,*" he replied and held up two fingers.

After gathering up brunch, they headed for a two-top table in the far corner of the bakery. It faced the door and the glass storefront. Sherman sat with his back to the wall. He did not know any other way. Old habits. Good habits.

Charlotte sat opposite him and split an almond croissant. She passed half back his way and repeated the process with a savory one—an almost intimate gesture between partners. *Surely the former.*

Sherman radioed out to Gournsey, "No sign of our man."

200

"Don't eat all the food," replied the sergeant.

They worked through both pastries with an ease that bordered on sloth. Only a tiny, cold drop of Sherman's coffee remained when the brunch rush ended. The woman at the counter was recovering and tallying her remaining supply. She hollered back to the kitchen, and a man replied. They exchanged a few rounds of this and that. Sherman peered around Charlotte to get a glimpse. He doubted Hugo would be back there, but stranger things happen every day. The double doors swung open briefly, and a thin, wiry man walked past, holding a five-gallon bucket labeled "sugar."

"Not him?" asked Charlotte, who was watching Sherman watch the man. His expression told her everything, but she confirmed, testing to see if she could still read his tiny facial twitches.

"Unless he's a pastry chef who went on a diet and lost a hundred pounds."

"The Martel family doesn't strike me as the dieting type."

"No, they don't. All sauce and butter."

Charlotte nodded and stood when Sherman headed for the counter. She grabbed the bag of extras and worked her way toward the door.

Sherman stopped in front of the glass case. His stomach was full, but his brain struggled to overcome the biological fact. He thanked the woman and complimented her on the entire meal.

"*My friend, Hugo, insisted we stop by,*" he said in French.

"*Mr. Martel?*" she asked in French.

"*Yes.*"

"*He is one of my regulars. In fact, you just missed him. An early riser today.*"

"*Oh*," said Sherman, leaving space for clarification. Conversation abhors silence, and people will always do what they can to fill it in.

"*Big day, he said. Meeting with an ambassador. Hugo is so good for our community and is always trying to help businesses.*"

"*Yes*," replied Sherman. "*A generous man.*"

The woman smiled, content knowing that she was not alone in her view of Hugo Martel. Sherman waved once more as he and Charlotte strolled away, arm in arm. Just another couple enjoying brunch.

"What did she say?"

"Hugo is a regular. A pillar of the community."

"And?"

"He's meeting an ambassador today."

"Which one?"

"She didn't say, but it wasn't '*the*' ambassador. It was '*an*' ambassador."

"So, presumably not the French one."

"That was my assumption."

"Franklin?" she asked, stating the obvious.

Sherman shrugged, not knowing the answer but having a gut feeling in the affirmative. He called the major as Gournsey noisily munched on the remaining pastries. He got to the macarons, took a bite, and chewed it back and forth.

"A little underbaked," he announced.

The truck was small, and Charlotte suppressed a giggle. Sherman was relaying information mere inches to her right, which meant she was sandwiched between the men. One was criticizing the execution of a classic French cookie while the other received orders on a potential traitor within the U.S. government. Within the realm of surreal, it ranked near the pinnacle.

Gournsey handed her one, and she took a petite bite. He frowned, and she took another to compensate for the underwhelming size of the first. Charlotte did not want to admit it, but the sergeant had a point—or maybe it was confirmation bias. She shrugged and bobbed her head from side to side. Maybe yes, maybe no, but mostly yes.

"I told you so," he replied.

The call ended, and Sherman put the phone back in his pocket.

"Well?" asked Charlotte.

"Ambassador Franklin is out touring new American-made turbines at Akosombo Dam."

"How far is that?" asked Gournsey. He dropped the paper bag on the floor and unfolded a laminated map. An old-school novelty from some German company, but some-times technology was better left turned off.

"Six hours."

"And Hugo was in early today," Charlotte stated, more reciting the fact than anything else.

"Maybe a four-hour head start," confirmed Sherman.

"Helicopter?" asked the sergeant.

"The colonels are fueling something right now. Wheels up as soon as we get back."

Gournsey dropped the map, mashed the manual trans-mission into first, and made an abrupt U-turn. The crum-bling truck groaned as he raced through traffic. Charlotte tightened the waist buckle and held onto Sherman's leg. *Surely the former,* he concluded.

Chapter Eighteen

Sweat rolled down Sherman's back. One bead, then another. Time under the afternoon sun slowly increased their frequency. Heat was nothing new. Iraq had plenty of it; so did Afghanistan and Syria. Humidity, however, was something beyond the pale for those places. He was enjoying this newfound discomfort.

The helicopter journey was brief—ninety minutes from wheels up to wheels down... except the thing had no wheels. Landing was too generous a word for what Colonel Paulson managed. On a ridge between one tiny village forgotten by time and the town of Akosombo, he jammed a skid into the side of a hill while the other floated in the air. The pilot held this awkward pose, half-attached and half not, for twenty quick seconds while the trio of operators jumped out. Then the helicopter floated away like a leaf in the wind. Nothing new or amiss. Suddenly, it was there and then gone. The villagers saw it. Who wouldn't have come outside to gawk? They would have thought it crashed at first, but not after it drifted away. A strange occurrence to talk about over a meal or beer, but that was it. No one posted a video on social media. Nothing went viral. The moment came and passed, and nothing remained except for the three Americans.

Ground truth was something organizations strived for in countries like Ghana. Intelligence organizations wanted sources—people to be used and manipulated to protect national security. NGOs wanted data—hard facts that would support budget line items and further grants. They wanted proof of success, however marginal and incremental. Sherman found the truth to be grass over seven feet tall, well over his own head. Thick, verdant, and green, but not sharp. Not elephant grass. This minor victory lifted his spirits and underscored a central mantra of his survival: it could always get worse.

Gournsey took it upon himself to clear the way. If he cut a path, then the other two would fit through the hole. The going was slow until it was not. From the wilderness of grass, they came upon a small trail. Nothing fancy—just a thin ribbon of red dirt across swaying fields of green. Sherman eyed it and nodded for the sergeant to proceed. Ghana was not Vietnam, and they were forty years removed from that mess. There was no need to crawl inch by inch looking for tripwires or booby traps.

The trail crossed the ridge from east to west, providing a straightforward way for villagers to travel from one side to the other. As the crow flies, it was ten miles shorter than the road that traveled west, then south, before turning back east and finally north. A fifteen-minute walk or a one-hour drive —a choice made easy. Easier still if you had no car.

Smoke drifted through the blades of grass and settled like a fog on either side of the trail. Sherman tracked the thickness of the gray fumes. Too much meant an enormous fire, which entailed a quick exit. Less meant a small fire—maybe a burning trash heap or someone cooking lunch. Near the top of the ridge, they found neither.

A lone palm tree lay off to the side of a small clearing. Felled by an axe, it rested almost parallel to the ground, with green leaves swaying against the dirt like a broom. Next to the tree was an assortment of stainless-steel kettles and equipment. Gournsey recognized it immediately. Such a sight was once common in the hills of Kentucky.

"Moonshine," he said reverently.

A spigot hammered into the tree was dripping into a large bucket. The bucket was then fermented into palm wine, a relatively quick process that produced a mildly intoxicating beverage of limited legality. That was distilled into something altogether different. The local who tended the fire boiling the palm wine looked up as they approached. No fear haunted his eyes. The ATF did not exist in his world. No one came to confiscate his booze or trash the equipment.

"What are you making?" asked Gournsey, a wide smile creasing his face.

"Akpeteshie."

The sergeant wandered over and stopped near the boiling vats and thin coils of salvaged steel that protruded from the top of the kettle. Sizing up the operation with the eye of an expert, he gave the man a pat on the back. The wrinkled old-timer offered Gournsey a small cup with a few drops of the liquid. With a slurp, Gournsey tasted the liquor and let out a strained gasp. His facial muscles clenched and slackened with the power of the stuff.

"Damn, that is some good hooch. Cap, try this."

Sherman was not in the mood for drinking unregulated liquor. Not yet, at least. He raised his hand to decline and motioned for the men to continue. "Get a bottle on the way back."

Obliging the suggestion early was irresistible, and Gournsey threw the guy some money and grabbed an old water bottle filled with the liquor. It still had the Nestlé label on the outside of the plastic, but it was holding stronger stuff. Another example of tax revenue escaping the government. One of many.

More trail meandered ahead. Visibility was a hundred feet or fewer. The hill sloped upward, but the grass was tall and getting taller. Somewhere up ahead was the top; further on was the dam. Sherman pushed on at a jogging pace, enjoying the thickness of the heat. Some kids came and went; others disappeared onto small side paths that vanished into the dense vegetation. A hundred people could have been zigzagging through the area, and they would have never known. It was the sort of place that brought out a certain level of dread in the military mindset: limited line of sight and lots of places to hide.

Cresting the top revealed a view worth the effort. On the right was the Volta River, a thick brown line snaking through endless green, all the way to the ocean. To the left was Lake Volta, a sparkling swathe of water running almost two hundred miles north, almost back to Tamale. Ferries plied the waters, delivering people and goods to thousands of tiny villages clinging to the fickle water levels. Below was the dam itself, a three hundred-plus foot tall pile of earth and rocks holding back some hundred million acre-feet of water. The largest man-made body of water, by surface area, on Earth. It was big, but not imposing—not like the Hoover Dam or some other thin arch of concrete holding back the impossible.

Two hundred yards further downhill, Sherman found

the ideal vantage point. He had seen it in the satellite photo: an odd rock outcrop that jutted into the space below as if it would slide down the slope at any moment. Lopez took out the spotting scope and centered it on the facility below. Then he removed an M24 sniper rifle from its padded case —a precaution of sorts in case Hugo tried anything or Sherman decided he did not want to ask him questions after all. Gournsey turned and planted himself a dozen yards back, where a small offshoot of bare dirt led to the rocks. Security duty. So narrow was the trail that his shoulders bridged the gap in the grass. No one would bother trying to get past him.

Most of the country operated on African time, a laissez-faire approach to punctuality that varied by hours or more. Diplomats such as Ambassador Franklin did not fall into that category. People waited for him, not the opposite. This was exactly what Sherman saw through the high-power spotting scope: ministers of the central and local governments gathered near the visitor's entrance, milling about, getting anxious, and sweating in their suits. Important men, as they considered themselves, were also not used to waiting.

There was an arbitrary ribbon draped off to the side next to a podium. The ambassador would cut it after some speech about cooperation between the two governments and the private sector. Sherman thought Franklin would be sure to extol the latter, given his mid-career switch to Layer Three. A photo op would follow, with some more hand-shakes and smug smiles. Maybe a side deal or two would be discussed.

Sherman and Lopez lay down to wait. Overhead, the sun hung large and hot in the afternoon sky, but it was not yet stifling. Both men were used to waiting and watching. Sherman let his mind wander across the valley, down the

Reckoning

river, and back up the lake. Questions were often answered when there was no search for connections.

The corporal did no such thing. Patience and focus flowed forth like an underground spring in his mind. It reminded Sherman of his own father's ability to lie in one spot for days—no boredom or listless movements. Time evaporated, leaving only the mission, the long gun, and the target.

"Convoy arriving," Lopez informed Sherman, seeing his gaze further upriver.

The convoy of black SUVs arrived at speed with a police escort. *A lot of fanfare and unwarranted attention for one man*, thought Sherman. He watched as the ambassador got out and immediately started shaking hands.

"Smug bastard," Sherman growled.

The gaggle of politicians and aides entered the facility. A waiting game began. The sun arced higher into the cloudless sky as the mercury rose. Sherman scanned the crowd slowly gathering near the podium. Most of the people looked local. Dressed in their Sunday best, they were colorful and joyous. Women chatted and bounced babies sleeping on their backs, held in place by long wraps of fabric. The men joked with each other and wiped the sweat off their brows with handmade handkerchiefs. A few older kids walked around with big plastic bowls filled with slowly warming sachets of water. All around, there was a festive mood.

"Unknown male. Southern edge of the lot. Silver truck," said Lopez in a dry voice.

Sherman swiveled back and focused on the vehicle—a French import with tinted windows and a professional off-road setup. The driver's side window was cracked slightly, enough for the smoke to escape. In the gap, he could see a white man from nose to chin. Zooming in further, Sherman tried to visualize the rest of the face but failed. As the cigarette turned to ash, a hand emerged and flicked out the butt. A flash of lively green, almost aquamarine, flickered across the scope as Sherman saw the man's eyes.

"That's him."

Lopez shifted his aim. "Copy. Shot is open and ready."

"Hold for now. He and I need to chat," Sherman ordered. Then he opened the sat phone and dialed from memory.

"Sit rep?" answered Sanders.

"We have eyes on the target. Looks like he is waiting for someone. The ambassador is in the facility now with a speech to follow."

"Understood. Don't lose the target," reminded Sanders.

The last part was superfluous. Sherman knew the stakes and the outcome if Hugo escaped. Their only link to Kutu and the missing drone equipment would vanish. The Frenchman was taking a risk with such a public showing, which meant whatever he had to say was important.

"I'm going down there. Keep overwatch. Radio the colonel for exfil; he'll be close by."

"Copy that. Good hunting," replied Lopez.

Sherman eased his way off the rock and back to Gournsey. The sergeant nodded as his captain repeated the orders once more. It was a familiar plan—one they had executed many times before in places such as Iraq.

"Copy that. See you on the other side," he replied as Sherman slid by and made his way down the path.

He wore no uniform. No insignia adorned his sleeve. His clothes came off the rack of some imposter REI. To passersby, he was an eccentric *obruni* out for a hike, whatever that meant. A lone man with a backpack, nothing more.

Anonymity was not exactly new to Sherman. Often, he passed for a local in the larger cities of Iraq. Good Arabic, a thick beard, and a decent tan meant few people gave him a second glance. That changed in the countryside, where strangers rarely ventured, and most people knew their neighbors. Ghana was different. People glanced, the kids giggled, but there was no hostility—curiosity without malice.

Near the bottom of the hill, he stopped in a thicket of low-hanging vines crawling up a gnarled tree. Combined with the chest-height grass, he was almost invisible. The silver truck sat parked across an empty field, dried up under a boiling sun. One window remained open, and exhaust plumed out of the tailpipe. Around the corner, the podium was just out of view.

"I have eyes on the target," radioed Sherman. "Where is the speechmaker?"

"Still inside, but people are stirring," answered Lopez.

Sherman settled into a well-worn mindset of waiting. Knees bent, half-leaning against the tree, eyes scanning back and forth, ears open. Only the occasional puff of smoke emerged from the truck. More locals appeared on the road, walking toward the growing crowd. Food vendors came. The speech was turning into a party—a shrewd political move.

Some minutes later, Lopez radioed, "People are exiting."

From around the bend, Sherman could hear voices over loudspeakers. The buildup started with a politician speaking a local language—something sing-song that Sherman didn't understand but sounded pleasant. It rose in volume, and the crowd chanted along. A good political speech.

"Okay, here comes our man," informed Lopez.

A familiar voice greeted the gathering. Ambassador Franklin gave the standard platitudes and expressed gratitude, thanking the locals and the corporations. Rounds of applause followed. Then, unsurprisingly, he dove into a speech that bordered on a lecture—similar in tone to the one Sherman and Sanders received at the embassy. It droned on. The crowd was quiet, more out of boredom than deference.

A spent cigarette came flying out of the truck as Franklin reached his monotone crescendo. Then the door opened. Out stepped a reflection of Danton Martel, only with green eyes. Hugo was thick from shoulders to shins, like a rectangle with shoes. A shade taller than his brother, he was softer from less manual labor and more pastries. He walked with purpose and short, compact, but powerful steps. From one glance, Sherman knew enough to categorize him as a serious threat—a two hundred-plus pound killer.

Sherman thought back to the file on the major's desk. There were scant records of Hugo Martel: one birth record, no evidence of formal education, and then he joined the French Foreign Legion. Nothing after that, save for a family photo and one mention on a radical message board. The gaps were too big to ignore—long years without a trace. It all pointed to something hidden: a life lived in the shadows.

Wading into the crowd, Hugo Martel made his way toward the podium. Sherman lost sight of him around the bend.

"Target heading toward the speech. Do you have a visual?"

"Copy that, eyes on."

"Give me the play-by-play. I'm finding a ride," said Sherman.

"Target is standing off to the side, waiting."

As he slung the backpack over his shoulder, Sherman considered the obvious question: Hugo had something to say. The unknown was to whom he would speak.

Down the street was a small paved driveway with a white sign reading "Employee Parking Only." Sherman followed the road for a hundred yards as it snaked back up the hill, further downriver, away from the dam. Capturing Hugo was the goal, and that could be accomplished in one of two ways. The difference lay in the location.

Option one was then and there. It was the simplest solution, but it came with an obvious downside. Such a brazen attempt would be in full view of the crowd and, potentially, Hugo's accomplices. The coon would be out of the bag, as Gournsey phrased it.

Option two was the same strategy, just further down the road to Kumasi. Since time was short, they rode in on the helicopter and, as a result, had no ground transportation or means to follow Hugo. Such was the deficiency Sherman aimed to overcome.

The parking lot had a guard, like most things of value in Ghana. He lived in a small booth once painted white near the entrance, which was also the exit: one way in, one way out. A radio played some high-life tunes—a gregarious and catchy song. Sherman liked the beat. He could see the top of a hat and boots propped up on the windowsill of the shack. He kept walking closer. Soon, the hat and boots were connected to a sleeping guard, napping through the midday heat.

Not wanting to wake him, Sherman veered off into the underbrush and steered clear of the booth. He emerged at the far end of the lot and surveyed the options. A few cars were parked in prominent spots, with signs proclaiming their owners' importance. He skipped those—too important and too new. Older vehicles had less security, making them ideal for thieves without excess time to spend bypassing all that technology. Sherman had neither the time, the gear, nor the skills. Uncle Sam had taught him the basics, so he needed to find a basic car; otherwise, it would become round peg in a square hole syndrome. An older model sedan was his usual choice—no frills. White or silver were best. Common colors blended better.

Toward the back, he found just that—a late nineties Toyota Corolla. White, with signs of rust creeping around the bottom of the doors. He pulled a slim-jim from the bag. It was not standard army issue, but the government had paid for it just the same. Army-sanctioned car theft. Once inside, he cracked open the steering column and went to work stripping the ignition wires. Three minutes later, he got the thing started. The odometer read over three hundred thousand miles, but the engine idled fine—another benefit of less technology. Things lasted longer.

"The oration is over," radioed Lopez. "Target is moving towards the front."

Sherman eased the sedan out of the parking spot and toward the exit. Not wanting to wake the guard, he gave it enough gas to coast down the hill before shifting into neutral. The car crept by the small shack at a walking pace. The radio muffled the crunch of stray gravel.

"Target is now at the front."

"Copy. I have wheels," Sherman replied once he was down the hill.

Near the road, he circled back and parked a hundred yards further down from Hugo's truck. To leave, he would have to pass by the sedan.

"We have contact," said Lopez, his voice rising slightly

with suspense. "Target approaching the ambassador. DSS is intercepting. He is talking with one of them and gesturing out back."

"Is he tall and thin with a mustache?"

"To a tee."

"That is Agent King. Maybe he'll direct the target away."

"It looks heated. Wait. Nope. The ambassador spotted them and is heading over. King is searching Hugo for weapons. Uh, negative there. Now they have stepped to the side and are talking."

"What's the mood?"

"Light. They shook hands. Target is putting on a show —real friendly-like. Wait… they are leaning in closer. Target is whispering something. The ambassador is laughing, and that's all she wrote. Target is moving back."

Something made Sherman's gut churn quicker than spoiled milk. All that risk for a twenty-second conversation. There were other means of communication—cloak-and-dagger stuff that Hugo knew well.

"Anything change hands?" he asked.

"Can't say. They shook long and hard, but I saw nothing from this distance."

"Understood. Monitor the ambassador. I want to know if he shifts anything from one pocket to another," added Sherman. Looking in the mirror, he saw Hugo enter the silver truck. "I have eyes on the target. Get the colonel on the line."

Gournsey's voice cut in, "On it."

Hugo Martel made a lazy U-turn and headed down the hill into Akosombo. Sherman leaned low in the driver's seat as he passed. The backpack lay empty on the floor as he slipped the tactical vest over his head and Velcroed the sides. The MP7 stayed within reach, and he jammed a pistol between the seat and center console. Following someone was an art. There were some rules and guidelines, but it all came down to gut feelings. Sherman had plenty of those.

For the first few miles, Sherman stayed close. Traffic was heavy with people leaving the political speeches, and his was not the only old Toyota on the road. As expected, Hugo Martel took the scenic route. It was an old trick: take the path less traveled, and anyone following you was easier to spot. Normally, that worked, but the traffic didn't thin out. He was not the only one heading home.

Tiny villages streaked by in the blink of an eye. A few small stalls sold calling cards, beer, and snacks, maybe some stray pigs and chickens. Then came a series of coffin makers—rows upon rows of wooden rectangles arranged neatly for inspection. An army of the yet-to-be-dead. Some were colorful, painted in thick, bright strokes; others were plain wood, with no lacquer or sealant to prevent their return to the earth. Most would find their inhabitants from the HIV epidemic in the area. Victims of the cruel, traveling disease were evident on major thoroughfares across the continent.

At the N6 junction, Hugo turned west towards Kumasi. There was no need to be close anymore, and Sherman fell back as traffic thinned. On the map, it was labeled as a highway. There were similarities—pavement, speed limits, street signs—but it was not much more than a two-lane road wide enough for one and a half cars. Trucks buzzed by at unnerving distances, and Sherman thought he might get clipped at any moment.

A few miles later, his earpiece buzzed to life with Lopez's voice. "This is Delta-Two-Five, arriving on station."

"Welcome to the party."

"Gournsey recommends two miles past Frimposo. Good coverage to the north and little population density."

Sherman looked down at the small map, neatly folded into quadrants. The name existed in the smallest of font sizes. The legend indicated fewer than one hundred people. A village, maybe a hamlet. It was a solid spot.

"I concur," replied Sherman. Quick mental math told him they were getting close. "Target is twenty minutes out at current speed. I will give you the go one mile past."

"Understood. Tires or engine?"

"Engine. I don't want him flipping over."

"Party time in twenty. Out."

Sherman put the map down and hooked the MP7 onto the sling already over his shoulder. The vertical magazine protruded from the bottom of the handle and rested between his legs. He pointed it to the left, making it easy to access with his right hand. Removing the H&K from its wedged position, he placed it in a black nylon holster attached to his leg. Everything was loaded, and the bullets were chambered. There was no need to check; such preparation was second nature and came from an overdeveloped muscle memory.

About a mile up the road, Sherman could see the silver truck shimmering in the tropical heat. The gap was a concern. He was going sixty miles per hour—one full minute away. A lot could happen in a minute. He pressed down on the accelerator, and the old Toyota gained a few hundred yards. Forty-five seconds away, maybe less. No mileage signs or indications of how far it was to the next town existed; such conveniences had not made it to central Ghana. Frimposo, he reckoned, was less than five minutes away. Not far at all. The tachometer hovered around the five-thousand mark. The sedan groaned under the increased

RPMs, unhappy with the stress of high speeds. *Just a little longer,* thought Sherman, hoping the car would last.

The village passed quickly—a blur of mud and concrete. Some muted colors poked through the encroaching green from which the land had cleared, a slow but inevitable reclamation by nature. Sherman counted out a minute in his head.

"One mile out," he confirmed.

"We are inbound hot," replied Lopez.

The gap between Sherman and Hugo Martel was seven hundred yards—twenty seconds at his rate of speed. Not long for a car chase, but an eternity for a football game or combat. The MP7 in his lap cycled at 950 rounds per minute. Notwithstanding magazine size, it was time for three hundred-plus bullets—more than enough to kill everyone in the village and surrounding area. Twenty seconds was a short eternity.

Sherman did not see the helicopter; he felt it. Thumping rotor blades, roaring jet turbines—the air pressure spiked. Rising from behind a ridge, it materialized as if from the ground itself. Colonel Paulson was good—better than most helicopter pilots Sherman had served with in Iraq and Afghanistan, and they were top-notch.

It all happened in seconds, like some strange highlight reel or movie scene. The helicopter flew parallel to the road next to the truck. The side door was open. Sherman could see Lopez kneeling inside the aircraft, rifle in hand, bracing his elbow on his knee. From the shape, he knew it was a McMillan Tac rifle, a .338 Lapua variety—big enough to bring down the largest of mammals or a French-made V6 engine. Lopez put two rounds through the hood and into the cylinders. Decompression followed. The engine sputtered out as fuel and oil sprayed everywhere, but the truck did not stop—not immediately. Inertia made sure of that.

"Showtime," radioed Gournsey.

Sherman pumped the brakes as he hurtled closer to the truck. The seatbelt was long gone, and he had one hand on the door handle. A hundred yards turned to fifty, then twenty. At ten, he slammed on the brakes as far as the pedal would go. The Toyota squealed in protest. A cloud of red dirt swirled around both vehicles. The smell of gas and burned oil clung to his nostrils.

Rotating to the side and aiming a weapon backward is hard to do in a vehicle. Approaching from the front or side might get you shot. Coming from the back improves the odds. Sherman approached from behind. The tinted windows were the first thing to go. He smashed the driver's side window with a tire iron he found in the Corolla. His other hand remained on the submachine gun.

What he found was Hugo Martel lying across the seats. His phone was in one hand, and he was reaching for a large thermos of water that had rolled away into the passenger footwell. A quick and dirty way to ruin a phone. Not permanently, but recovering data takes time. Frying the device would buy time for whoever had been on the other end. Sherman put three rounds through the container. Bits of wet plastic bounced about, and the floor got soaked, ending whatever hopes Hugo still entertained.

"That's quite enough," Sherman growled.

Hugo held up his hands and looked back at the voice just before Sherman dragged him out by his ankles. The sizeable man hit the dirt with a sloshing thud. His eyes searched wildly for something, anything that might get him out of the situation. All he saw was the barrel of the MP7 aimed at his head and Gournsey's hulking figure approaching from the road.

"Nice catch," greeted the sergeant as he jogged over.

Despite being twenty years older, Hugo was still powerfully built and in no mood to be taken in without a fight. It was just his nature. He met threats with violence. Preemptive was best. Reactive would do. Neither mattered to Gournsey. He bent the man's arms back like young saplings and zip-tied them together. The same went for the legs. The sergeant grabbed the latter and started dragging Hugo back toward the helicopter, which had landed in a clearing near the road.

"Got to hell," yelled Hugo, his accent sticking on the first vowel.

"You'll be wishing for something so simple," chided Gournsey.

The sergeant heaved the Frenchman into the helicopter the same way a disgruntled baggage handler moves an overweight suitcase. Hugo's face came to rest on the cold steel floor. It was the last thing he saw before a black hood smothered his vision. Industrial-strength earmuffs followed. His world shrank to almost nothing: a mild buzzing in the darkness, the slowly warming steel beneath his face, and the weight of a boot on his spine. Fear flooded in from the corners of his mind as he struggled to breathe.

Chapter Nineteen

"Mr. Martel."

The voice roared in Hugo's suddenly uncovered ears. Until then, he had heard nothing for what felt like hours, but time blurred without context. No sight. No sound. Only the smell of his own breath circulating beneath the hood. Sweat slid down his arms from fear and heat. A searing pain crept up his back from sitting on some cheap plastic chair. The material was not a foregone conclusion, but there was a smooth feel when he rubbed his fingertips over it. Knowledge of his surroundings ended there.

"Hugo Martel."

This time, the voice had characteristics. His ears were adjusting. It belonged to a man of average timbre—neither high nor low. The accent was American, but plain and crisp. No long vowels or gnarled consonants. Likely West Coast.

"*Qu'est-ce que tu veux de moi,*" he replied.

"What do we want with you?"

Boots thumped closer, then the hood came off. Hugo

blinked in the harsh fluorescent light burning brightly over-head. It came from a single bulb, but it was too powerful for the space. The voice stood in front of him—average height, average weight, muscled and confident but not cocky. A hard-earned ease. But it was the eyes that conveyed the story. A predatory swirl of green and orange. The same eyes that pulled him from the truck.

Sherman smiled and gave an amused laugh. "We can drop this pretense of mystery regarding your situation."

"*Je ne comprends pas.*"

"You can also drop the French. I know you speak English. Quite well, from what I've heard."

Hugo said nothing.

"I also know this situation is nothing new," continued Sherman, gesturing around the room. "The Foreign Legion has a class on interrogation—an excellent one, from what I recall. Although it focused heavily on torture. Why is that?"

Hugo said nothing.

"A holdover from the colonial days? Perhaps your former subjects took a penchant for the techniques you used. They say it's an art after all, and don't you French love art?"

"*Aller en enfer, serpent salope!*"

"Go to hell, snake slut? It certainly loses something in translation with that one," joked Sherman.

A voice behind Hugo laughed, deep and guttural. He struggled to see, but the restraints made it too hard to turn around.

"Look, Hugo, I have no intention of hurting you. We both know torture works but doesn't produce results. It's the nature of the beast. You'll tell me something, anything, to make the pain stop. A man with your training might play it out for a while, letting me think you've broken, buying some time for someone to find you or for someone to escape. Why waste the time?"

Hugo growled, low and menacing, "I will kill you."

Sherman rubbed his hands together. It sounded like dueling sheets of sandpaper. "I know you will try. Maybe you will even succeed, but that changes nothing at this moment. I only have one question."

"What?" he scoffed.

"Simple, really. Do you want to be there for the funeral of your nephews?"

The question took Hugo by surprise. There were many things he expected to hear—offers of immunity or cooperation—but that was not one of them. Even trained minds react to the unforeseen. Human nature cannot contain surprises; it is in our genes. Such a response formed in the corners of Hugo's eyes. They bunched together with creases that radiated back toward his ears.

"I see no one told you about that," replied Sherman.

"Empty words hold no water."

"You could be a philosopher, Mr. Martel, truly. But those are not just words; they are facts."

"You Americans and your truths. It must be nice to write the history books, to tell your embellished one-sided story without consequences. You do not understand truth, only your glorious outcome. As if your success justified the cause."

Sherman could see they shared a certain strain of nihilism—an uneasiness with noble adventures in the name of glory or patriotism. It made Hugo's choice of causes even more peculiar. The message board was about the return of the grand ideal of Greater France and its colonial empire.

"Odd to hear you denigrate such unconditional goals.

The Martels I met in Havre dreamed of a time when you controlled a continent."

Mention of his hometown deepened Hugo's consternation. His eyes darted around the room, trying to understand his situation. "You don't understand what you've not yet lost."

"Tell me," replied Sherman with genuine curiosity.

"Your empire still stands. My abduction is proof of that."

"Abduction? Is that what you think has happened? We are just having a conversation, Mr. Martel."

"At the barrel of a gun."

Sherman shrugged. "Many conversations happen under the stick's shadow. It's odd that the carrot doesn't motivate people nearly as well. Besides, I'm unarmed."

Hugo scoffed loudly. The man was a weapon, armed or not. His eyes said as much. "What do you know of my family?"

"Some."

Hugo narrowed his gaze but said nothing.

"Your brother is Danton Martel, a luminary of Havre. King of his castle at the end of the street, the one with a mansard roof. Likes to look down upon the servants and pompously serve fish on a silver tray. An asshole, if you ask me. Your niece is Eloise. She is a decent woman, if a little conflicted. Between you and me, I do not think she buys into this entire empire round two bullshit. And then there are Emmanuel and Jacque. I should say were. Neither is still breathing."

A knot tightened in Hugo's stomach. Too much truth had tumbled out for a lie, even a cleverly constructed one. The memory of his father handing down the silver to

Danton still stung. He sighed, feeling a spreading sadness and regret.

"What happened?" he asked.

"Mistakes."

"Theirs or yours?"

"They tried to bury us."

"So, you killed them?"

"I gave the order."

Hugo swallowed hard, but it did not clear the guilt stuck in his throat. "And the rest of them?"

"Look, they came after me. I just wanted a word. No different than with you."

"More words," he trailed off.

"More than Mr. Kutu can say," countered Sherman.

Mention of the smuggler pulled Hugo back from drifting through the past. He blinked against the glaring light and sharpened his focus.

"The name isn't familiar."

"Hero of the North, whatever the hell that means. Smuggler by trade. Big guy. Giant head. You put a bullet through it from four hundred and fifty yards. A damn fine piece of shooting."

"I couldn't say."

"Well, he and I were having a conversation about something he brought over the border. It fit the description of something taken from the U.S. government—something of considerable value, or so I've been told."

"I hope you find it."

"Who says I haven't already?" said Sherman with a smile. He watched Hugo's pupils narrow with recognition, yet his face remained the same. The man was well-trained. Not CIA, but something close.

"None of my business either way."

"See, now that is where you're wrong. It is your business because Kutu gave it to you."

"Captain," Hugo began, "forgive me; I assume you're a captain. High enough rank to question someone but not pull the strings. Someone still in the field at your age. Well, the rank seems right, but you have me confused with someone else."

"And who might you be?"

"An entrepreneur. I sell cacao and palm oil."

"So, you have no information regarding this valuable artifact I mentioned?"

"None."

"That's a shame for you," replied Sherman as he opened the door. "We're remanding you to the custody of the Central Intelligence Agency."

Two menacing-looking men entered with a hood of their own. Hugo eyed them warily. If the captain looked like a killer, those two looked like they enjoyed it. He had seen renditions before. They never ended well—people just disappeared into the ether. There one day, gone the next.

"I'm innocent," pleaded Hugo.

"I don't give a shit," replied Sherman. "Your guilt or innocence matters not. Value isn't held in words, and you stopped having any by telling your lies."

The two men closed in. Hugo felt their hands digging into his shoulders and watched the fluorescent light disappear behind the thick black canvas hood. It smelled of vomit, sweat, and fear.

"Wait!" he yelled, gasping for fresher air.

"Why?" asked Sherman. "So you can tell another lie and waste my time?"

"I have information."

"Tell it to the waterboarding crew. I already have what I need."

"What?" groaned Hugo as the men dragged him down a long hallway.

Sherman watched him disappear into the darkened cabin of an unmarked executive jet—the personal air force of America's rendition program. Hugo Martel would never see the light of day again unless Congress got off their asses and decided they wanted to change something about the War on Terror. The odds of such an outcome were zero.

"That was intense," said Gournsey.

"He had it coming for shooting Lopez."

"You think he had something worth saying?" asked the sergeant.

"Maybe, maybe not. His phone said plenty."

"Technology scares me."

"You're not alone."

Major Sanders beckoned them over to his desk with a brisk nod. "Anything useful?" he asked.

"Family is important, but he harbors some animosity towards his brother. He is well-trained—top tier or someone who used to work for them. And the package is still in the country."

"Good to confirm."

"Does the CIA have a hard-on already? Probably drooling over this interrogation," joked Gournsey.

The major nodded as if to agree. "We tracked the number he texted. SAT-9 has coverage. SEAL Team Eight is gearing up now. They offered you a seat."

"Professional courtesy?"

"I suppose."

Sherman almost turned down the offer out of habit. Riding along with other outfits felt like being a third wheel on a date with two oversexed teenagers. He did not want to get in the way, but curiosity pushed him past that trepidation.

"Ticket for one?"

Sanders nodded.

"Fine, as long as they don't bring up my swimming."

Chapter Twenty

Eight men gathered around a portable whiteboard on wheels. It was an older model, bought from some office supply company contracted with the government and flown in from the States. They sat on unpainted metal folding chairs, looking serious and attentive. Sherman knew some by name, others by face. Commander Morris was their leader. They had met before in Iraq, Afghanistan, and other barren spaces. Too much of a pretty face was Sherman's first impression, but the commander was no joke. He was a disciplined and adaptive leader who led his team down-range in some of the most dangerous areas in the world. If Sherman had friends, Morris might count among them.

"Alright, boys," said the commander as Sherman approached. "This here is Captain Sherman from Delta. You'll remember him from lovely vacation spots such as the Korengal Valley and Basrah. His team did the legwork on this op. He's here to give us the briefing and will ride along."

The men nodded in recognition as Sherman stepped up

to the whiteboard, which was dotted with printouts and a hand-drawn map.

"As you all know, *Hisab* and persons unknown attacked an agency base in Mali. They took three hunks of silicon that Uncle Sam wants back. You all recovered one. Sergeant Gournsey and I took back a second. The third remains at large. However, during our recovery operation, we gained intel that *Hisab* was working with some outsiders. This led us to a small town south of the base called Havre. A local there saw a truck and armed men pass through. The leader of the town is Danton Martel. Now, what was left out of your previous intelligence briefing is this."

The men looked on with some surprise.

"Days before the attack, they smuggled weapons through the Efie refugee camp. They used those weapons in the assault and ended up in Havre. A local going by the name Kutu smuggled the arms north. That same local also took something south."

"Something?" asked one of the SEALs.

"Mr. Kutu was killed before he could reveal anything else. We believe the shooter was Hugo Martel, brother of Danton Martel, the leader in Havre. Four hours ago, we captured Hugo. During the raid, he attempted to send a text to this number. The portable scrambler blocked it, but Hugo doesn't know. We traced the number to this compound."

Sherman pointed to a satellite image and the hand-drawn map.

"A van fitting the description from Kutu is sitting outside. There is a small contingent of armed hostiles guarding the building. I have no idea what is inside, but it is not kosher. Questions?"

"How many?"

"Twelve confirmed, with more potentially inside."

"Weapons?"

"Modern. Mid to high-caliber. Explosives."

"Who are they?"

The name of the contractors crossed Sherman's mind, but his tongue held fast. Neither he nor the major was ready to turn over that card. "Unknown, but assume well-trained operators. This is a precise operation with significant funding. Expect stiff resistance. Commander Morris will go over the plan."

"Thank you, Captain Sherman."

The commander stepped forward and started outlining the attack. Sherman moved to the back next to Gournsey. The sergeant was not happy with the mission allocation.

"We should do this," he said in a low, guttural voice.

"Too many of them," replied Sherman.

Gournsey shot him a hard glance. Twelve was more than three, but they had seen longer odds. Nights of suppressed terror, just beyond the fringes of the present, and the absolute clarity it allowed. Days filled with sandy gusts, waves of heat, and the snapping hiss of an unseen bullet.

"A surplus of something," he retorted.

Bureaucracy exists within all organizations of significant size, but its roots went deep in the military. Even the word itself was old and confusing, borrowing from both French and Greek. From the former, it took the word for desk, and from the latter, a suffix denoting a kind of government. The sergeant adamantly opposed anyone bound to an office chair, no matter how mighty the pen they wielded.

"Glory is for assholes, remember that," chided Sherman.

"Wasn't that in your fortune cookie?"

"Yeah, along with my favorite nugget of wisdom. The shortest point from A to B is always under construction."

Gournsey chuckled as the planning unfolded. Morris eyed the men momentarily but said nothing. Results demanded respect, and Sherman's team was known for nothing less.

"Keep the truck running, just in case," Sherman added.

"You think it'll go sideways?"

"Something feels off."

"Sounds like a real slender idea."

"Maybe, but see if you follow me—Hugo was no joke. We can agree on that."

Gournsey nodded.

"My guess is that he took his skill set to the open market after leaving the Foreign Legion. Someone scooped him up. He disappeared from the grid for almost ten years."

"I'm tracking."

"The way he carries himself reminds me of those spooks in Kabul."

"The ones with aviators?" asked Gournsey.

"Yeah," replied Sherman with a nod.

"They had that squint, like the world might reach out and slap them at any moment."

"Exactly," said Sherman. "Hugo had that same walk. Plus, he was trying to douse the phone when I caught him. The whole action felt very rough. Too rough for such a polished operator."

"I was right; this is very slender. No one plays such a long con. Dude is probably halfway to Kazakhstan for waterboarding."

"True."

"But…"

"Exactly, I can't shake it."

"My advice," added Gournsey, "don't be the first one through the door."

"Thanks, I don't think that will be a problem."

"Assholes and glory?" asked the sergeant.

"Exactly."

The briefing wrapped up, and the SEALs moved toward the few nondescript cars parked at the far end of the hangar. Each man carried enough ammo for a sustained fight—hundreds of rounds. Morris motioned for Sherman to join him near the whiteboard.

"Captain, I see some hesitancy written on that bearded face of yours."

"You're not wrong."

"Shit. I was hoping for the opposite. Being wrong will get you killed."

"Just be careful out there," Sherman advised. "Beyond normal."

Morris leaned in and spoke softly, "Frank, if you have something, I need to know."

The commander had a point. They were about to jump into the line of fire. Hearsay, coincidences, or gossip… any information was valuable if it saved his men.

"I got this sour taste in my mouth, and it's not washing out, no matter how much sugar coating they apply."

"This is your intel. What aren't you saying?"

"My gut says it's a trap."

Morris knew Sherman well enough to trust his gut the same way he did with his own. There was no point in asking why. Some people just know things that cannot be explained in common discourse or mission briefings. It bubbles up from some hidden well, slowly percolating information to the frontal cortex. Mostly, it comes in snippets—knee-jerk reactions to sounds or smells. Other times, the body itself tries to show the mind, be it a buzzing noise, a flash of light, or a sour taste.

"Suggestions?"

"Secure the perimeter but hold your team back. Let me inspect. If something changes, you order the assault."

The commander stood there for a moment, considering the request. He was not one to change well-laid plans before implementation. Once in motion, he understood that all excellent things eventually tilted. No plan stays exactly on track. For another person, he would have said no, but the suggestion did not come from some ordinary officer.

"Okay. We will sweep first and then cover. If it goes south, we're coming in hard."

Sherman extended his hand, and Morris accepted. "Thanks. For all our sakes, I hope I'm wrong."

Chapter Twenty-One

Only fourteen miles separated the airport hangar from the compound. Still, it took the team almost an hour to get there. Traffic and poor infrastructure were to blame, although the order of magnitude was up for debate. The government paved most of the roads until the last two miles. Whatever semblance of transportation existed ended there. It went from asphalt to a rutted donkey cart trail in a single turn. The SEAL team exited a little further down and walked the last miles. The going was difficult. A thick belt of grass and vines extended in every direction—thick stuff. Not great for mobility, but it masked their approach, so it was not without merit.

Sherman was near the back. He slipped forward through the clotted undergrowth, taking care with each step. The last two miles took another hour, but by then, they had the compound surrounded. From the satellite image, it looked like some colonial holdover—a villa of old, built back when the empire looked indomitable. An unassailable force for progress on the dark continent. All that was malarkey, but the people who built the place believed it. No one else would attempt something so grandiose and yet so trite.

Old wrought iron fencing ringed a giant rectangular plot of land. The jungle had reclaimed some of what it lost, and plants grew right up to the walls, but the building still stood tall. Plaster peeled off at the corners, and the wooden windowsills were all but mold, yet the house carried on, imbued with mystery—a rotting corpse of history.

It was a giant U-shaped building, two stories high, with a central courtyard modeled after some favorite English architectural masterpiece. Decades earlier, it would have made a grand impression on visitors. Once independence came, that truth faded quicker than the paint. The empire fell, the sun set, and anyone with sense fled into the ensuing night.

Parked out front in the courtyard was the van. Not exactly hidden, but no one would find it without intention. The place was too far from anywhere for strangers to come knocking. Sherman circled around the back, careful to stay concealed in a sea of green. The radio buzzed in his ear.

"Two x-rays approaching at three o'clock."

The muted sound of footsteps on half-covered gravel reached his ears. He stopped and pushed himself down toward the ground. A few seconds passed. Soft crunches receded into the distance.

"All clear," relayed the SEAL.

Sherman moved over the wall and into the compound proper. A landscape architect had assiduously planned the grounds. They took pains to incorporate local plants without losing the Englishness of the place. That meant there were quite a few things growing beyond their original allotment of space. What had once been proportional and tidy had become unsightly and overgrown. Perfect cover for moving in closer.

He slid against the plaster wall. Pieces flaked off as he passed. There was a small window. Some years ago, it held a pane of glass, back when the owners had status and money. Nothing of the sort existed anymore. All that remained was rotting wood. Sherman raised his head and glanced inside the room on the other side. Bedroom-sized for most people, it looked like an old closet filled with moldering boxes. Nothing to see. He moved forward.

Once he reached the edge of the building, Sherman stopped. The small courtyard was to his left. It was open ground—nothing to hide behind, no more overgrown vegetation. Only gravel and the van. He glanced back toward the vehicle once more and froze. His mind whirred with hidden activity, buried in all the neural pathways that made up human memory. It was searching for something he did not yet know—an unknown known. He felt an uneasy sensation in his stomach: the gut reaction.

He peeked around the corner once more—nothing but gravel and the van. Then the epiphany struck. It made the neural connections. Someone had trashed the van. The tires were flat—not recently deflated, but old enough to have cracked in place after so many years in one position. Rust crept around the frame and up toward the doors. No one had used it for years. It made sense. The road ended miles before, and nothing but a small trail remained. Sherman kicked himself for not seeing that sooner. This was not Kutu's van. This was not Kutu's place. The back of his throat felt dry.

"We're barking up the wrong tree," Sherman radioed.

"Say that again?" replied Morris.

"The van is a heap. No way it drove in here."

237

"I still see targets."

Sherman crawled back and braced himself near the window. Morris had a mission. It was clear. Search the premises. Kill anyone in the way. A crisp line as far as operations went—no gray area at all.

"Understood," was all Sherman could offer in reply.

"Alpha, move in on the rear," ordered Morris. "Bravo, you are cleared to engage any targets outside."

The shooting started almost immediately. Silenced pops echoed off the compound, only to be engulfed by the jungle. The radio buzzed with chatter—Tango down here and there. The list of dead grew by the second. Sherman counted six, which left at least six more on the inside.

"Alpha is breaching the rear door," came the call.

Sherman slid through the open window and readied the silenced MP5. "Delta Three-Six is inside on the southeast corner."

"Copy," came the reply.

A dull but substantial thud rumbled through the walls, followed by splinters. The breaching charge was at work. Sherman visualized the men entering through the destroyed door, sweeping left and right. He stepped toward the hall. A curtain served as the demarcation between the two spaces. Hinges still existed, but whatever had hung there was long gone. Footsteps slapped on the smooth tile to his right. Not the SEAL team—wrong direction.

Two sets of footsteps. One heavier than the other. They were moving down a set of stairs and closing in fast. Men were coming down a stairwell at the end of the hall. The layout made sense in Sherman's mind. He waited another second. The slaps grew louder—hurried quick strides like those needed to descend stairs. Then the sound paused for a

"Anything?" asked Sherman.

The SEAL shook his head. "Nothing."

"Let's search it."

He nodded and radioed out, "Alpha team starting a search."

"Negative," Morris replied. "We have local military assets inbound. Exfil now."

The news tugged at the corners of possibility. They had been operating under the radar, or at least on the fringes of acceptability. Sherman was sure the CIA was influencing the Ghanaian government, pressuring them to look the other way. It had worked. Or perhaps not. Maybe they had gone too far and pushed the boundaries to a breaking point. Maybe it was as simple as a local seeing nearly a dozen armed men entering the bush.

The men exited quietly, with an efficient pace that belied what they had just done. The bodies lay where they had fallen, and Sherman glanced down at the results of Hugo's mistake. If it had been a mistake. For he was still unsure. They made it to the vehicles and sped back onto the major road. Sirens blared in the distance, and they pulled over obediently as the special police trucks sped past.

"Is that what you were expecting?" asked Morris from the front passenger seat.

"No. I figured we'd be blown to bits."

Morris shook his head with a tired chuckle. "Glad your batting average sucks today."

"Oh for two," replied Sherman.

"Intel looked solid," replied Morris. Lots of missions missed by hours or minutes. It was the nature of the game, and he knew it. "They might have moved on."

Sherman nodded. The commander had a point—a good one—but it still felt off. The consequence of failure was no better. They had no other leads. It would be up to the CIA to extract more information from Hugo. Sherman had a good enough imagination, along with his firsthand knowledge, to conjure up how Hugo Martel was spending his time. It was not pleasant or moral, but he accepted the necessity.

Chapter Twenty-Two

The satellite phone in Sherman's pocket vibrated with animated interest. He slid open the antenna and jabbed the green button. Technology had miniaturized many things, but geosynchronous communication was not one of them.

"Go for Delta-Three-Six," he answered—a quick way of confirming he was not dead.

"Captain," replied Gournsey. "Meet me at Paddy's Pub."

"What happened?"

"I'll explain later."

"Okay."

Sherman tapped Morris on the shoulder and said, "Change of plans. Drop me off at Paddy's Pub."

"Serious?" asked the commander.

"He didn't say, but when did you ever get a call just to chat?"

"Fair point."

The driver slowed as they neared the location. "You want me to pass by and double back?"

Sherman shook his head. "No need. See the shitty truck up ahead?"

"Yeah."

"Pull up close. I'll switch over."

"Budget cuts?" asked the driver with a smirk.

"Something like that."

The armored SUV nosed off the shoulder of the road and into the parking lot. It pulled up next to the truck, which was pointing in the opposite direction. Sherman grabbed his gear and opened the door. Gournsey reached across and did the same with the passenger door. Two seconds later, Sherman was in the cab of the worn-down truck, still dressed in full kit. The SEALs pulled out moments later.

Gournsey could smell the cordite and blood on him. He stank of combat—the indirect olfactory link to death.

"Nothing, huh?" he asked.

Sherman shook his head slowly. "Not a damn thing."

"So, not a trap?"

"I suppose not."

"That's good," suggested Gournsey.

"Not for my ego," said Sherman.

"It was a good guess. Plausible."

"So I thought."

"And now?"

"What's before square one?"

"I see."

"Care to tell me why I'm sitting with you?" asked Sherman.

"Samuel."

"Samuel?" Sherman clarified.

"He is missing," Gournsey elaborated.

"Shit."

"Yup."

"Are we headed to his house?" asked Sherman.

"Yup."

"Shit."

Sherman stripped off the Kevlar vest and the pistol strapped to his leg. There was no uniform to remove, as he wore none, but he swapped out his shirt for a fresh one that the sergeant had brought.

The house in question was on the edge of the city. Not suburban, but lacking the flavor of central Kumasi. It was a middle-class home with concrete walls. A steel gate at the front guarded the entrance, and there were air conditioning units on the roof, flanked by two satellite dishes. Samuel's wife, Ama, met them out front and led them into the house, a cozy two-bedroom space that could sleep at least six people.

"Thank you for coming."

Sherman smiled. He liked Ama. She had a warm cloud of sincerity that enveloped everyone she interacted with; it was contagious. "Tell me what happened," he said.

Her face dropped like a stone, and worry crept into the corners of her eyes. "I don't know. Samuel went out last night and never came home."

Sherman motioned for her to sit down on the well-worn couch. An older flat-screen TV was playing some Nigerian movie that infringed upon the Rambo copyright.

"Start from the beginning."

Ama took a breath to steady herself and began. "Samuel was asking around about Kutu, like you asked. No one had said much—mostly rumors, stories from the past. Then, a day ago, an old man in the neighborhood mentioned a place."

"What place?"

"Some tunnels out east."

"Did Samuel say where?"

"No, not really. I told him not to go, to stay home, but he didn't listen."

"Can you tell me anything else to go on besides tunnels out east?"

Ama held her head with thin but calloused fingers—the kind of hands used to hard work. "I don't know. He said something about a place rotting in the bush."

Sherman's eyes widened, and a cold wave of recognition ran down the back of his neck. He knew exactly where Samuel had gone snooping. Not sixty minutes prior, he had stood in its hallways.

The change in his posture did not elude Gournsey, nor did Ama's description. "Thanks, Ama. We'll do our best to find Samuel."

"We surely will," echoed Sherman.

"Thank you, thank you," she replied, her eyes peeking out between outstretched fingers. "I am worried. Too worried."

"I understand. Do you know where this neighbor lives?" Sherman asked.

Ama nodded. "He is down the street, behind the mobile phone shop. Ask for Joseph." Then she looked at Gournsey, noting his sheer size, and told Sherman, "Maybe you should go alone."

They showed themselves out of the house and past the gate. It was four in the afternoon, and about an hour of daylight remained. Gournsey hopped in the truck and started it up, content to sit this one out.

Following her directions, Sherman turned right toward the prepaid phone card kiosk. A bright yellow umbrella advertised the place, making it hard to miss. The house behind it was another story. A small one-room shack with a tin roof sat covered in leaves and vines, nearly disappearing into the surrounding thickets of grass. After finding the only door—front or otherwise—he gave a mild knock. Not too loud, lest he begin with intimidation.

"Hold on," came a shallow voice.

The door creaked open slightly, and a thin man with sagging skin peeked out. He was in his eighties and showed his age with humble abandon.

"Who are you?"

"Joseph, my name is Frank Sherman. I'm a friend of your neighbor—Samuel."

"So?"

"Well, his wife thinks he's in trouble. I'd like to help."

"Don't surprise me. Asking around about Kutu will do that to a man. You should stop too."

"Afraid I can't do that, but I'd like to know what you said to Samuel about the tunnels."

"I don't know you, *obruni*."

"No, you don't."

The old man had nothing to gain from helping Sherman. The math was plain to see. Betting against Kutu netted zero. The worst-case scenario was six feet under.

"Kutu won't find out," added Sherman.

"Deeds travel faster than words in this town. He'll know."

"He's dead."

The statement made Joseph scrunch his eyebrows in suspicion. He would have heard such a story—the talk of the town.

"Don't insult me, young man."

"I don't intend to. What I said is true. He died two days ago—a bullet through the face. Probably why no one has figured it out yet. That watermelon head of his is gone."

The description gave the old man pause, like a sweet trickle of truth amidst the bitter swill of skepticism. He scratched his head and considered the request in a fresh light.

"The British used them back when they claimed sovereignty over this place."

"For what?"

"What things need to stay hidden?"

"That which runs afoul of your purported morals."

Joseph nodded. "They took dissidents there. They did not return."

"To the old house in the bush?"

"Nearby. The Brits never dirtied their own carpets."

"How close?"

"They built something to the west. Closed it off before independence. I heard Kutu found it years ago. The ghosts kept most people away, but not him."

"How do I find it?"

"Look for the lions," replied the man before shutting his door abruptly.

Sherman stood there for a moment, contemplating the cryptic clue. Then he retraced his steps and found Gournsey in the idling truck.

"Did he give it up?" asked the sergeant.

"It's to the west of the house. 'Look for the lions,' he said."

"You know I'm allergic to cats."

"I'm allergic to big claws, so let's hope he means something else."

Gournsey wrestled the truck into gear and slipped back onto the major road heading west.

"Maybe you weren't wrong," said the sergeant after entrenching into a thick row of traffic.

"It feels worse, like I was doubly wrong."

"Did you search the house?"

"No. The local police got word of the raid. We had to skip out before they arrived."

"So, he could still be there?"

"You mean his body?" asked Sherman.

Gournsey frowned and then sighed. There was little chance Samuel had survived the night. He knew it. Sherman knew it. Even Ama knew it, somewhere beneath all the hope and fear.

"Should I get the SEALs to pull a U-turn?"

"No. Too many of them," Sherman answered.

"I'm guessing the opposite isn't true?"

The sound of silenced gunshots and radio callouts echoed in Sherman's ears. "Nobody left breathing, that I saw."

"Okay then."

Sherman nodded and opened his phone again. "Does the major know?" he asked.

Gournsey nodded. "Up to what Joseph just told us."

A gravelly baritone answered.

"Major, we have news."

"Go ahead," said Sanders.

"Samuel found something."

"Where?" asked Sanders.

"At the compound we just left. Some tunnels near there."

"Shit," replied the major.

"Yeah."

"Should I have Lopez meet you there?"

"No. Gournsey and I will handle whoever is left."

"Understood. The police are still there, so use caution. We are on thin ice already. Franklin is getting pressure to kick us out of the country."

"Shit," said Sherman.

"Yeah."

"We'll keep it ghostly."

"Good hunting."

They drove the few miles left in silence. Sherman was in no mood to talk. Guilt and shame bounced around his mind like a couple of sugar-fed toddlers. His gut knew something was off, but his brain did not complete the picture. It missed a crucial step. Mistakes happen; he knew that, but it felt like he was slipping. Fifteen years was an eternity to live at the spear's tip. Most officers average eleven years in the service. Yet, there he was, driving into the thick of it again.

They stopped short of the narrow path into the bush. Police roadblocks were everywhere. Armed men were searching all the cars they stopped. Gournsey turned left onto a dirt road about two hundred yards earlier. It banked away from the compound, meandering between palm trees and piles of trash. A few muddy ruts traversed the road, but traffic was light.

"Looks like we're taking a detour," muttered Gournsey.

Sherman recognized the brown gash from satellite photos. It was not on any official maps, but neither was much of Ghana. Some farmers made it years ago to access land that was not theirs to farm. An illegal operation only on paper. Using anything available was just a matter of daily existence.

The muddy road had several recent tire tracks leading in or out. Ruts of various sizes, but of little discernible value. It was impossible to tell the make of the vehicle as everything ran together.

"How far?" asked Gournsey.

"The man didn't say."

Distance, like time, had a distinct quality in Africa. Soon could mean hours. Nearby might be miles. Sherman had no way of knowing what the old man designated as close. The further they drove, the darker it got. Trees angled over the road and blocked out what little light remained. A pale gray gloom enveloped the space around them as smoke from nearby fires clung to the ground below. Each man watched out the window, looking for anything.

"Stop," said Sherman.

The truck paused, and he pointed out past the trees and into the fading sunlight. A lone statue sat half-covered in vines, still regal in bearing.

"A lion," confirmed Gournsey.

"You bring night vision?"

"Do dogs eat shit?"

Having grown up on military bases, Sherman looked at the sergeant with narrowed eyes. "I never doubted you."

Gournsey pulled a black case out from a duffle bag stowed in the back and handed it over. The men slid on their vests and went through their mental checklist, patting down each location on their body where things belonged. Satisfied that everything was in order, they gave a mutual nod and slipped into the smoky bush.

The sun was falling like a fiery rock as they reached the lion statue. Deep divots gazed out from white stone pockmarked with age. The edifice reached Sherman's waist and must have weighed a ton. A family crest was carved on the creature's chest, but the details had eroded away.

"Fancy," said Gournsey.

"The Brits like their pomp and circumstance."

"That marble?"

"It ain't concrete," answered Sherman.

"It would look nice in my parents' yard."

"They have a yard?"

"There's a space... ain't nothing in it. I'd call that a yard."

"Is it filled with broken-down trucks?"

"That's the driveway, asshole."

Sherman laughed from deep down in his stomach. It worked to ease his tension and assuage the guilt. If Samuel was alive, that would do even more. It was a possibility, a small one, but Sherman wanted to hold on to that hope.

Police sirens still trilled softly in the distance. They could not see any lights, but out there somewhere in the bush were friendly forces. With the proper introductions, the Ghanaians were allies, but bumping into them in the dark would only lead to bloodshed. Operational security meant very few people knew they were on the ground. No locals outside of Samuel's family were in on that secret. "Need to know" was the excuse. The truth was no government would allow foreign forces with executive authority to run free.

The world turned to shades of green as Sherman pulled down the night vision goggles. Infrared lasers on their weapons danced across the leaves and vines. Unlike Mali, where the trees danced a duet with the rocks, the branches seemed to intertwine with the grass into a solid mass. Sherman struggled to see more than a dozen feet in any direction. The monotone glow instilled a uniformity of texture. It all blended.

Minutes passed in crowded tension, their necks craning with each sound, each swish of the wind. Never had open nature felt more claustrophobic. Then Gournsey squeezed his shoulder and pointed to Sherman's left. Through a small opening, past the grass and trees, were two more lions.

A clearing appeared as they broke through the last of the overgrown spinney. It was no bigger than a suburban lot —half an acre at most—back when someone fought against the tide of nature. The statues stood astride an ancient wrought-iron gate whose hinges had rusted in place, leaving it permanently open. The walls on either side were crumbling, the local brick returning to the soil of its creation.

Beyond the open gate and dilapidated walls stood headstones: rows and rows of stone tablets. Once neatly chiseled names were fading with the passage of time. At the center was a small structure, perhaps a crypt or mausoleum, but Sherman did not know the difference. It was a ten by tenfoot building of some delineation and purpose.

"Bit creepy for my taste," said Gournsey in hushed tones.

"The old man mentioned ghosts."

"And tunnels."

"Maybe the center building?"

"The mausoleum," answered Gournsey, certain of his word choice.

"Sweep and clear."

The sergeant nodded, and they moved toward the cemetery. Near the gate, there were signs of recent activity. The grass was trampled and bent. A small path led back toward their truck. Sherman figured if they had driven further, it would have been visible. It did not take more than a high step to clear the wall.

He pointed right. That was enough for Gournsey to understand. A single gesture distilled the entire plan. Sweep and clear. The sergeant went right, and Sherman went left. They circled around the entire clearing or coppice, weaving between old grave markers with stereotypical British-sounding names.

A Mr. and Mrs. Wilson, born in the 1850s in some Welsh-sounding place, died in 1922. Thirty-five years before, someone abandoned their ultimate resting place to the winds of change that brought independence. There were soldiers too, ranks engraved above their names. Most were young, and many names felt familiar, but they never really changed—Smith, Laswell, Martin, Evans, Williams, Davies, Taylor, Brown, Jones. The list went on.

They joined up at the mausoleum, satisfied they were the only living bodies above ground. Years ago, the building had a door, but not anymore. Sherman peered inside. A small wooden bench sat near one wall, and rows of urns filled two adjacent walls. All the ashes had names etched on small copper nameplates, neatly attached underneath.

Save for those forgotten souls, the room was empty. Sherman stood in the center and glanced around. The entire place was no bigger than an area rug placed in a living room, neither of which he possessed. It took a few minutes to find what he knew was hiding in plain sight. The trail leading in indicated as much. So did the footprints on the worn stone floor. People were coming and going, but not to honor the dead.

He started with the walls but hurried on. The structure was too small and of equal proportions inside and out. Crouching down, he checked the floor. The old, smooth stones looked unmoved since they were laid one hundred years before—cold, hard, and heavy. Too difficult to move. Sherman discarded that theory. Only the small bench remained unchecked. He sat down on it, but only for a moment. It bowed under his weight—not the wooden slats of the seat themselves, but the floor below bent. Running his hand over the material took Sherman by surprise. It looked like the rest, but it was plastic. He hissed for Gournsey to come inside.

The sergeant stood watch as Sherman pulled up on the bench. The whole seat and fake floor came up in a single heave. It weighed less than twenty pounds—easy enough to move. In the space below was a thin metal ladder leading down into the darkness. Gournsey started toward the ladder, but Sherman shook his head and took point. He never ordered his men to do what he would not. No point in starting then.

A whoosh of cool air swelled up and out as they descended. It smelled of cold earth and stale oxygen. Tunnels often felt the same. Afghanistan had many that were not so different. Sherman used to chase the Taliban into caves and through hand-dug tunnel complexes that would have made coal miners claustrophobic. No matter where or how, a familiar feeling remained. A sense of entrapment stayed with him until fresh air once again touched his lungs. But it was not confining, not in a panic-inducing way. No, there was an ethereal quality to the dread, like you were already dead and buried.

The ladder went down some fifteen feet before their boots hit solid ground. Stones lined most of the walls, but the ceiling was wood—relatively new by the look of it. Replacement meant active use, and active use meant they were on the right track.

Having entered at the start or end of the tunnel system, there was only one way to go. The space itself was cramped, six feet tall and three feet wide. Sherman had to duck a little to fit. Gournsey stooped over like an old man weighed down by age and a lifetime of burdens. His six-foot-five-inch frame was not engineered for confined spaces.

"You look like the hunchback of Notre Dame," hissed Sherman.

"Who?"

Sherman shook his head. "Never mind."

The first stretch ran straight for fifty yards before coming to a junction. Faint strands of light indicated their direction. A lone bulb shimmered in the distance. They moved forward. The light grew brighter. Sherman stopped short, flipped up his night vision, and considered his options. To the left was a medium-sized room; to the right was more tunnel. He chose left. Sweep and clear.

Gournsey tapped his shoulder, and they moved forward in unison, taking small, uniform steps. Guns up. Eyes and ears open. There was no door—only the excavated space that formed an opening into the room. He cleared left while the sergeant looked right.

Nothing but poorly lit boxes occupied the space. Gournsey turned and kept watch as Sherman searched the area. Wooden crates stood stacked like cordwood against the walls. Bland black stenciled letters detailed a litany of potential crimes.

"Got more guns here than in your closet," said Sherman.

"Anything worth taking?"

He lifted an open lid. Dark, well-oiled wooden stocks shone back—instantly recognizable.

"Mr. Kalashnikov."

"Real deal?" asked Gournsey. He was a collector of sorts; some people collected stamps or coins, while he collected variants of the Avtomat Kalashnikova Model 1947.

The stamp was in Cyrillic—close to Russian, but not

quite. Sherman had seen it before, hundreds of times in many countries, all of them conflict zones.

"Bulgarian."

"Already have one of those."

Sherman shrugged and keyed the radio. "Delta-Three-Six has weapons in the tunnels."

"Copy that," replied the major, unsure of how he would communicate that to their Ghanaian peers.

"Moving up," whispered Sherman.

The right-hand turn quickly jogged left and led them down another long corridor that snaked back and forth like an elongated S. For reasons unknown, the builder could not keep the tunnel straight. Even the floor tilted slightly to one side, as if it were an understated NASCAR track. This shortened the lines of sight and distorted everything else. Light bounced around, and several voices churned back and forth like a river.

Sherman and Gournsey stopped at the edge of a shadow cast by the low-wattage bulbs affixed to the wooden ceiling. They waited and watched. Three men moved around a decent-sized room, piling the right side high with boxes and crates. Guns leaned against the wall—some neatly, others haphazardly. Closer to them was a sturdy wooden chair bolted to a concrete slab. Black stains covered the floor—some old, some new, and some ancient. They knew at a glance the purpose of such a fixture. A grizzly confessional left unchanged by time.

Five narrow metal doors lined the left side of the room —a neat row of potential victims. They were solid, floor-to-ceiling, save for a food slot halfway up. A ring of thick iron keys lay on a centrally placed table. The whole setup was from a bygone era, older than Sherman, his father, or his father's father. A history of violence and torture, blood and suffering, was captured in a single room. Sherman could feel it in his bones.

"Set the charges over there," said one man with a Russian accent. He was thick around the chest and wore a *telnyashka*—the blue-striped shirt of the Russian armed services—underneath his tactical vest. He slung a newer model AK across his back.

"How long?" asked a second man. He was younger and thinner, also Eastern European, but not Russian.

"Twenty minutes. Boss-man wants us back soon."

The younger man nodded, and the buttons on the electronic detonator beeped in acknowledgment. A third man started opening cell doors. The tattoo on his arm suggested South African Special Forces. Grey hair around the temples and deep creases on his forehead indicated he was around fifty—old enough to have fought for Apartheid.

Upon opening the cells, he began dragging bodies into the center of the room, close to the explosives. Cleaning house. By the third door, it was clear the men had been busy torturing and murdering the local population.

As the South African went to open the fourth door, Sherman raised his hand and pointed. Gournsey implicitly understood. The two men rose in unison. It was over before the first shell casings hit the stone floor.

Sherman stood slightly to the right of the sergeant and targeted the two Europeans. The younger man was further away and took the first bullet from the MP5. Busy working on the charges, he never saw it coming. A few steps closer was the big Russian. He saw the shadows move and a tiny flash of light, no bigger than a spark from a Zippo. It was the last thing his brain registered. The 9mm ended any chance of further thought.

The South African fared no better. Gournsey's shot was

further, but the ballistics remained simple. At under thirty feet, the round had no deviation at all. He placed the small red dot at the center of the sight on the sadistic bastard's skull and squeezed the trigger. Physics did the rest.

They swept through the room and kicked the guns into the corner. No one was getting up, but some habits were best kept intact. Gournsey posted up around the next corner, guarding against anyone else coming down the tunnel. Sherman flipped over the dead man with his boot and started searching for anything worth keeping. The Slavs had phones, but nothing else. The South African had a phone and cash. He took the cash and used the keys on the table to open the last cells.

Door number four held another corpse, a few days old judging by the decomposition. Not that Sherman was a coroner, but he had seen more dead bodies than most medical examiners would in a career. Door number five presented the same scene, with one difference—he knew the name of the man lying dead on the floor.

"Crap," he muttered.

"Samuel?" asked Gournsey.

"Yeah."

"Bastards," hissed the sergeant.

Sherman stepped into the cell and bent down. The Ghanaian was recently deceased. Maybe only a few hours ago, he had been alive. They had missed their chance to save the man.

"Still warm."

"Not your problem, Cap."

Sherman pushed the thought of blame aside, burying it in his mental box. It held many such feelings of pain and remorse—too many to count, too many to handle if it ever broke.

"I'm stopping the timer," he replied, moving to cancel the countdown.

"We might run into friendlies if we push much further," added Gournsey.

"Agreed, but I want to take one of them alive if possible."

"I think that boat sank."

"Take point."

The sergeant stood up and moved towards the end of the tunnel. All the lights were turned off, likely by the mercenaries hoping to avoid detection. The Americans moved quietly across the old stones, worn smooth by years of boots. A green glow enveloped their eyes, but only more tunnel unfolded in front of them. It snaked back and forth with little regard for the shortest route between two points.

Somewhere around one hundred yards past the cells, Gournsey stopped. The man had a sixth sense for prey. Sherman smelled it too. Someone was around the corner, hidden in the dark. The fear was palpable, riding on the stale breeze blowing down from some unseen entrance. The sergeant leaned his head around the corner and held up one finger. Some poor soul left behind for guard duty—the lowest man in the pecking order. Shit duty, not literally, but much in the same vein.

Sherman shifted out and could just see a thin form cowering in a small alcove in front of another steel ladder. The man was armed and likely paranoid from being in the dark for so long. Only the occasional flashlight from the cops above filtered through the wooden slats of the trap-door. Sneaking up was not an option. His ears were wide open, the only sense working. Even the tiniest scuffle would set him off, but Sherman had one advantage. The merce-nary thought his friends were still alive.

"Hey, bru," he hissed in his best Afrikaans accent.

The man twitched at the sound, and Sherman could see him looking into the darkness.

"You done?" he whispered. The tone was soft and lilting —a southern boy.

"Ja," replied Sherman.

The southerner stood quietly and groped his way towards Sherman and Gournsey. Sherman kept walking around the corner, making himself heard as he moved away. The sergeant stayed at the corner and waited.

As the mercenary reached Gournsey, it all ended quickly. His mind registered some mass in front of him. Maybe the Russian, maybe not. Adrenaline should have spiked in his bloodstream, but Sherman's ploy had worked. There was no underlying sense of fear or foreboding lurking at the edges. He was happy to be coming out of the dark. A vicious right hook ensured he stayed there longer.

When the darkness finally faded, he found himself zip-tied to a thick wooden chair. Then the pain raced front and center into his consciousness. It burst across the bridge of his nose and washed around his cheeks. Having been in enough fights during his tender years, the man knew they had broken his nose. The blood oozing and puddling on his shirt confirmed as much. Everything else was hazy, but the bells of panic were ringing loud and clear.

Sherman stooped down and looked the Southerner in the eyes, waiting for some inkling of recognition. He smiled when fear showed up.

"What's your name?"

The man squinted back, still trying to wrap his head around the situation. "Go to hell," he replied.

It was a stock response to unwarranted aggression. Sherman had seen it before. He nodded toward the three other mercenaries, the man's co-workers, lying dead on the stone floor.

"Name?"

The answer jumbled out of the man's mouth as if his tongue tripped over itself, trying to spit out the words as quickly as possible. "Noah. Noah Sims."

"Well, Mr. Sims, it seems we have a situation here. I have questions needing answers, and time is short."

Noah's gaze danced over the three corpses, men he once emulated and looked up to. Strong, violent, remorseless men who did not take shit from anyone. They had a fiendish quality that made him feel at home. Now they were dead, and someone far more dangerous was standing in front of him.

"Who are you?" he asked.

"Oh, I think you know," replied Sherman. He reached under the collar of Noah's shirt and pulled out a pair of dog tags hanging around his neck. "Private First-Class Noah Sims."

"You killed my friends up there," said Noah, nodding towards the house above them.

"Some of them."

"What do you want?"

"Answers."

Noah sucked in a ragged breath as if an unseen weight had suddenly fallen on his chest. "Then ask your damn questions."

"I'll start easy. Who do you work for?"

"Myself."

"Yourself?"

"Yeah, you know… American dream and all."

Sherman rubbed the bridge of his nose. He was tired. Tired from lack of sleep. Tired from the war and the blood.

Tired of death and stupidity. Tired of the continual cycle of violence. Tired of the incompetence. But at that moment, he was fed up with the malignant strain of self-righteousness being espoused by the PFC.

Gournsey moved his hulking presence in from the perimeter and glared down at the younger man. "The captain here is trying to be nice—downright polite if you ask me. Question. Answer. Simple, really. But you are trying the man's patience. Do that again, and I'll shatter your tibia."

"Who do you work for?" repeated Sherman.

Noah looked at him and then back up at Gournsey. "They paid in cash. Upfront. Three-month contract."

"They?"

"Don't know any names. They didn't offer, and I didn't ask."

"This tale of yours better have legs—and soon," growled the sergeant.

"Corporate types. Suits and ties. Came and found me. Offered me more than I made in a year at those big-box stores."

"How did they find you?" asked Sherman.

"I don't know, but they knew my service record."

"Dishonorable discharge."

"How did you know?"

Sherman shook his head again. "It ain't rocket science, Noah."

"Anyway, they flew me out here. Been doing jack shit until a few days ago. Then I started guarding this place. That's it."

With a nod, Sherman pointed towards Samuel's body in the cell. "And him?"

Noah struggled to turn his head that far. "Some local.

Came snooping about. We had orders. No witnesses. I... I had nothing to do with it."

"You ever heard of Layer Three?" asked Sherman.

"Sure, I ain't livin' under a rock. I applied for them after the army kicked me out."

"And?"

"I wouldn't be working some shit job if they'd hired me."

Sherman stood up. The conversation was over. He had heard enough. There was only one question left, and the answer was his alone. Noah saw it too and started squirming about, hemming and hawing about the value of his life.

Sherman pulled out a smoke grenade from his vest and walked around the corner towards the hidden entrance. Pulling out the pin, he tossed it at the base of the ladder and headed back. Noah was staring fearfully at Gournsey.

"Grab Samuel. We owe it to his wife," said Sherman.

The sergeant nodded and gingerly picked up the body, slinging it over his shoulder.

"Mr. Sims, this goes without saying, but I find the words coming out more often than I'd like. If you somehow get out of this mess—and I truly hope that will not happen—don't let me see you again. I'll shoot you on the spot. Over here or back home."

Noah swallowed hard as white smoke slowly wafted down the tunnel and into the room. He watched until the two men disappeared. Then he wept.

Chapter Twenty-Three

Tears streamed down Ama's face well before Sherman said a word. She could read it on his face—sorrow carved into the corners of his eyes. It pulled down towards his shoulders, still slumped and defeated. He tried to smile but only quivered his lip to one side.

He walked over to where she stood before speaking. Such news was not meant for yelling. It was not meant for empty space, but for the sincerity of quiet words. There was always room afterward. When grief flowed like torrential rain across the desert sand, scouring all that stood alone, it threatened to pull out those shallow roots, leaving those left clinging with nails deep in the soil.

"I'm sorry. We were too late," Sherman began.

Anger, resentment, or hate were the emotions he had expected. Ama had no such luxury. There was too much at stake. She could only think about her son and held no ill will toward the American.

"You saved him once. For those extra moments, I am grateful."

"We got the men who—" Sherman said before she cut him off.

"I don't care for their blood. It changes nothing."

Sherman nodded, knowing she was right but also knowing he could not walk such a line. Not recently. Not with Tillerman. He tore that town apart, put bodies in the ground, all for the blood. A twisted sense of friendship or responsibility girded his actions. Letting it go was never an option, just as keeping that hate was not for Ama.

"Is there somewhere we can bring him?"

"You have... I mean, he's here?"

He pointed back toward Gournsey, who was standing watch by the truck.

"I need to see him."

They walked around to the back, and Sherman lifted the emergency blanket they had used as a makeshift cover. As if pulled by guilt, he stepped back. The moment was too personal to witness, too tender to overhear.

The soldiers stood at a respectable distance—far enough not to eavesdrop, but close enough to provide support if needed. They looked at each other, then at the ground, but said nothing. For Sherman, it was personal. A gnawing guilt sat on his chest like an overly friendly pet. Gournsey was in the same boat, but not for the Ghanaian. He had liked the man well enough, yet the responsibility did not hang around his neck like a chain. Life was life. No point in making it harder. He was concerned for his friend, the one taking it all too personally, the one still hurting over losing a brother two weeks prior.

Minutes passed in silence before Ama walked over to the truck. Her eyes were red and blurred with tears, yet her expression exuded resolve.

"Can you drive him to the undertaker?"

The men nodded.

"He's on the way out of town," she added, pointing to the east.

"Do you want to come?" asked Sherman.

The newly minted widow shook her head. "No, I need to tell my son and my sister. Start preparing for the funeral."

"If we can help, please say so."

Ama looked at one man, then the other. She took in their anguished looks, said nothing, then turned away and disappeared into the house.

Gournsey pulled the crinkly foil back over Samuel's body, then started the truck.

"Strong woman," he said.

"I don't think she has much of a choice," Sherman replied.

"Diminishes nothing."

"True."

"I assume we're paying for this?"

"That goes without saying, if she'll take it."

"I don't think she has much of a choice."

"True."

The funeral home was just that—a small two-room house: office and morgue, nothing else. They found the proprietor out back, hammering together a few sheets of plywood into a cheap casket. The lone fluorescent bulb hanging above only highlighted the paucity of the container. Nicer options lay nearby, but everything was handmade.

Dressed in a black suit despite the heat, the man had a youthful face but grey hair. He looked up as they approached.

"Can I help you, sirs?"

"We lost a friend today," said Sherman.

"Condolences."

"His wife asked that he be brought here."

The undertaker raised an eyebrow. Few *obrunis* stepped foot on his property, and fewer had patronized his services. Even fewer had dropped off a local.

"Okay," he said, and followed Sherman over to the truck. The undertaker lifted the blanket and sighed.

"You know him?" asked Sherman.

"Yes. I knew him."

"And his wife?" asked Sherman.

"Yes, and his wife and her father."

Sherman looked around and pointed toward the fanciest casket in sight. At least it looked the part—all velvet and shiny wood. Not that he knew any better.

"How much for that one?" he asked.

The man followed his gaze. "One thousand cedis."

With a one-to-one exchange rate with the dollar, it required no math.

"And the rest of it?"

"Three hundred more."

Presented with the option, normally Sherman would have haggled. There was something about the process, the fluidity of it all, that he enjoyed. But this was not the time. Reaching into his pocket, he pulled out a wad of one-hundred-dollar bills—blood money from Tillerman. He had earmarked it for his retirement fund, but that felt farfetched. The odds of reaching retirement age were one in ten, he thought. Or worse.

The undertaker took the money and nodded. It was not his place to judge, but the *obruni* reeked of guilt for handing out money like that.

"You do this?" he asked.

"Indirectly," answered Sherman.

"Is there a difference?"

"Not really."

The older man nodded as if the answer was sufficiently weighted and replied, "I'll see to it."

"Thank you."

The undertaker nodded again and slid Samuel's body onto a wooden cart worn smooth through the years. It wobbled as he moved back inside. There was nothing else to say, let alone ask.

Back at the truck, Gournsey was already behind the wheel with the engine running. He was not a man to rush about, but daylight was long gone, and they were at an impasse. Kutu was dead, and Hugo was at some black site getting waterboarded.

"Itching to go?" asked Sherman.

"The fat needs chewing."

"Time to call up Hugo."

"I'm sure he's nice and chatty."

"Talking with us keeps him off the slab."

"I don't know. It might be worse. You're not much of a conversationalist."

Sherman laughed. "I'll leave that to the major."

"Even worse for Hugo," chided Gournsey. Then, as an afterthought, he added, "Say, how much does a funeral here cost?"

"Fifteen hundred."

"Damn. Did you bury him in a gold casket?"

"The British called Ghana the Gold Coast."

"No shit," replied Gournsey with a low whistle.

"He deserved better."

"So do we all."

Sherman didn't reply but agreed with the sentiment.

Chapter Twenty-Four

As they drove back to the airport, his thoughts stewed in remorse. Samuel's death picked at a raw tendon of regret, still swollen and angry from California. The casket was compensation for his guilt, as if fancy wood and a polished shine could assuage the pain. Local assets come and go. He had fought with many over the years. Mostly, they were on the same side. Sometimes that changed. The prevailing winds of alliances were often fickle. Either way, the locals endured the war, as they had in all wars.

Major Sanders stood behind his desk as they entered the hangar. The surface was tellingly bare as all their leads had dried up. The clutter of a hunt, those endless piles of intelligence, coalesced into a single thin pile in the top corner.

"I'm sorry to hear about Samuel."

Sherman dropped the dead mercenary's phones on the empty surface. He almost made a crack about sending condolences to Ama but stopped short. The major was not to blame, and he sounded sincere. Still, the potential outburst of anger caught him off guard. He wondered if the lid, that thick emotional armor on top of all the horrors he had seen, was loose. There was certainly a leak of some sort.

"Thanks," was all he managed to say in reply.

The major turned over one phone and wiped off a few flecks of half-dried blood. He was already in possession of the rough outline of events and asked, "Care to fill me in?"

"We didn't have a chance to ask them questions, but we found one, PFC Noah Sims, amenable to conversation."

Sanders typed the name into some database on his laptop and opened the related file. A picture of Noah and his service record popped up. High school dropout. GED. Iraq veteran. History of insubordination. Petty theft. General nuisance. All-around asshole.

"And what did Mr. Sims have to say?"

"Little of material value. Paid cash in advance by persons unknown. Suits, by the sound of it."

"Anything else?"

"He applied to Layer Three but got rejected. Then someone showed up with an envelope of cash and a plane ticket to Ghana."

"Was he involved in the attack?"

Sherman rubbed his beard in contemplation. "I don't think so. He was pulling guard duty, shaking in the dark. The skill set isn't there unless his record says otherwise."

"No, you've painted most of the picture."

"Well then, any chatter from the NSA?" asked Sherman.

"Crickets."

"Time to call up Hugo?" asked Sanders.

"I'm thinking we released him prematurely."

"Agreed."

"I'll make the call. Lopez, start on the phones."

Sherman nodded and picked up the devices. He set them down on a workbench in the corner of the hangar. Lopez glanced at them for a brief second but asked no questions. Instead, he hooked them up to a small black box and hit a few keys on a laptop. Proprietary software from a company most people had never heard of began cracking the passwords.

The couch was calling, and Sherman stretched out on the threadbare material. He had barely closed his eyes when footsteps approached. They were light but purposeful. Only one person in the hangar sounded like that.

"Charlotte," he said without opening his eyes.

"Frank," she replied before pushing his legs aside to make room. "Any luck?"

"Depends on your perspective, but I'd say 'no' was the prevailing outcome."

"Samuel?"

"Him especially."

"Shit. I'm sorry to hear that."

"Thanks."

"Not for you. For his wife and child."

Point taken, thought Sherman, but he said nothing.

"You know, this self-pity wallow-fest isn't very becoming."

"I see we're cutting to the chase."

"Would you rather have me dance around the bullshit?"

Memories of her no-nonsense mentality looped through his mind. He had appreciated the directness back then. Age, it seemed, wove a web over the simplicity of his recollections. Charlotte was ripping it down.

"And if I said yes?" he asked.

"I'd say hang up your gun and dust off your resume."

"Oh, a man can't have a conscience?"

She shook her head and sucked in air between her teeth in the same way his mother did when he did not live up to her demanding standards.

"Frank. People die all the time. I know you two were friendly, and that hits hard."

It was clear to Sherman they had moved beyond Samuel. Lying down, as he was, it felt like some Freudian therapy session.

Charlotte continued, "Maybe you're even seeing a premonition of the future, and you're no spring chicken."

"Don't hold back."

"Not a chance. You need a hard slap in the face, but I doubt the pain would get through. Shit, you would probably think you deserved it. Had it coming, or some other self-deprecating claptrap."

The thick sludge of despair pooling like used motor oil in his chest stirred.

"In fact," she added, her voice rising an octave, "if you keep this farcical pity parade up any longer, you're likely to get someone else killed. Maybe Raul or Raylan. Shit, maybe even me or you."

Thoughts of another friend on an icy steel slab cut through the melancholy sloshing around. Charlotte was right; he knew it, but getting unstuck was hard. The heart was like one of those seabirds after an oil spill, all covered in the sticky substance, unable to fly, incapable of escape without detergent. That was Charlotte—a harsh chemical cleaner, washing away his self-imposed sins. The genuine ones were still there, singed deep, but those he accepted, owned, and incorporated.

Sherman sat up, grabbed her by the shoulders, and kissed her hard on the lips. "Thanks for that."

Charlotte sat there, somewhat stunned at her own success, hoping it was for real. "You're welcome, I think."

He smiled his old smile, one she knew from years before, and ambled off toward the major. Gournsey waited and then took a seat next to her.

"That worked," he said.

"Or he's good at faking it," she replied.

"You ever known Frank to be insincere?"

"No, but he's full of surprises."

The sergeant stood up slowly and started toward his superiors. "Aren't we all?"

The phones sat in single file across the major's desk like a third-rate reseller. Little bits of information were written on index cards in Lopez's clean script. He underlined one number on each piece of paper—the same number.

"Common denominator?" asked Sherman. The pattern was clear enough.

"All had calls from the same number."

"Burner?"

"Activated three weeks ago. We are analyzing the metadata now, but it is sparse."

"Last location?"

"Accra."

"Central?"

"Roughly. It hit all the downtown towers, so it's hard to say more than that."

Neither man said it, but the embassy lay within the area. However, that piece of data meant little. Africa was awash in cheap phones; it was the only reliable means of communication. Getting a landline required a hefty down payment, a substantial wait to get it installed, and then it only worked a few days per week. Even the power company was more reliable, which set an impossibly low bar.

"So, the pool of suspects is a million?" asked Sherman.

"Better than downtown Lagos or Mumbai."

Gournsey walked over with a scowl and added, "Tell me we're not going to Nigeria."

The sergeant was fond of Nigerian staples, and Sherman asked, "Had enough, *moi-moi*?"

"No, but it's not worth braving Lagos traffic for some bean pudding."

"We're sticking to Ghana for the time being."

"Find a target?" asked Gournsey.

"Possibly," answered Sanders.

"And Hugo?"

"My next call. He was being transferred to another facility."

"Complain about the food, did he?"

"Security issues."

"He's in a prison that doesn't officially exist. What issues could they possibly have?"

The question was rhetorical, and Sanders did not answer. He was busy dialing a number that would do the same until someone with enough security clearance transferred the call. The major knew of a lot of skeletons in a lot of closets, but for this one, ignorance was bliss. Some secrets were better off unheard.

Sanders stood, phone cradled between his neck and shoulder, scribbling details on a sheet of paper. When the writing suddenly stopped, Sherman glanced up at his face. The placid expression turned sour, as if puckered by a lemon. His jaw tightened and pulled to one side. When the major set down the receiver, it did not crash with angry contempt; it fell with resignation and angled off to one side.

"What happened?" asked Sherman.

"Hugo's dead."

The news itself did not seem so odd or distressing. Sherman had no connection with the man. His death was nothing more than another unfortunate statistic in the war on terror. Only the timing was terrible.

"Did they get anything out of him?"

"Never had a chance."

"What?"

Confusion ran through Sherman's tone. Prisoners die during interrogation, especially with those enhanced techniques the U.S. does not admit to using in public. Dying before any of the cruelty that human ingenuity could unleash was odd.

"They transferred him to a different site almost immediately upon arrival. Took him to solitary to sweat him. Two hours later, he died. Arms slashed from wrist to elbow."

"With what?"

"A spare razor blade from a box cutter."

"We searched him. He didn't have one."

"The agent was adamant they performed all the necessary searches but stopped short of placing blame."

Details got stuck in Sherman's mind—pieces that did not process cleanly.

"No one cuts that far. Not even the most devoted of followers."

"I know," replied the major. He had come to the same sticking point.

"And the agent was clear on that fact?"

"Emphatically so."

"So, they killed him," concluded Sherman.

"It appears so."

"What's the detail you left out? The one you stopped writing?" asked Sherman.

Sanders looked over his shoulder to see who was in

earshot. Their team was small, but the American presence in Kumasi was growing. More and more departments were making use of the hangar. Sherman and Gournsey watched the increased paranoia with keen interest. Secrecy in public was one thing; furtiveness within the group was profane. The entire thing worked on trust. It was sacrosanct.

"It's the location," said Sanders.

"Where did they transfer him?"

"A new facility run by Layer Three."

"Ugh," whispered Gournsey. "We've outsourced our torture too."

"Been that way for a long time," said Sanders.

"On whose authority was he moved?" asked Sherman.

"The agent couldn't say."

"Couldn't or wouldn't?"

"You and I both know it doesn't make a bit of difference."

"Our only lead just died in a prison owned by Franklin's old company, after he was mysteriously transferred there."

The major could only nod at the facts at hand. Then he thrust the sheet of notes into the shredder. Thin ribbons of innuendo and culpability floated into the can below.

Gournsey motioned for Lopez, and the four of them leaned on the major's desk. Sherman filled the corporal in on what had just happened. Conclusions were made but floated about unsaid.

It was Sanders who spoke first. "This isn't a democracy, but I want to put it up for a vote."

"What's on the ballot?" asked Sherman.

"Franklin's guilt."

"I'd say there are a lot of miles between us and certainty," added Gournsey.

"Agreed," replied Sanders. "But I smell something rotten in his house."

Sherman chimed in. "The stench started with the guns. We know Kutu smuggled them north, and he worked for Hugo. Layer Three showed up in Havre, home of Hugo's older brother, Danton."

"We also know someone else helped *Hisab* attack the base," added Gournsey. The memory was still fresh in his mind.

"I still don't see the motive," remarked Lopez.

Gournsey nodded. "He's right. I see means and opportunity, but why risk it all? Franklin must know he'll only see the bottom of a deep, dark hole if caught."

"Money," guessed Lopez.

"The man is already rich. I've seen the price tag on his watch," observed Sanders.

"It is money or power," asserted Sherman. "I just feel like he has both."

"There is one way to find out," said Sanders. "We go and ask the man. Who is in?"

All four men raised their hands.

"It's settled then. We are having a chat with the ambassador. Wheels up in sixty. I need to make some arrangements. Captain, can you call that DSS agent and inform him we will arrive in a few hours?"

"Are you sure, Major? That gives away any element of surprise."

"We must maintain decorum. If we show up unannounced, it will set off more warning bells than a zeppelin over London. Besides, we owe him a briefing."

Sherman shrugged, but the conversation was over. The major disappeared into the old office.

Gournsey spoke up after he left. "Arrangements sounded ominous."

"I imagine he's making sure we don't end up swinging from the gallows for treason," Sherman replied.

"Always the optimist."

"Somebody needs to see the rainbow."

The comment left Gournsey and Lopez rolling with laughter.

"Gear up," ordered Sherman. "And, Lopez, bring something armor-piercing."

The two men were still recovering from the thought of Sherman only seeing rainbows and unicorns but waved an acknowledgment.

Upon seeing the gathering break up, Charlotte approached the desk where Sherman was sitting. "That looked serious."

"Heading to Accra."

"Great. I need a ride to the airport."

Sherman cocked his head to one side and tried to decide if she was serious. "Tired of our Batcave?"

"It's time to move on."

"From…"

"Work called. I got a promotion. Probably a pity promotion, but screw it, I could use the money."

"Congrats. Where to?"

"HQ."

"Rome?"

"The Eternal City."

"I don't recall you speaking Italian."

"Like that ever mattered."

Sherman laughed pensively. "We can do that."

"Thanks," she replied and started walking away.

"Wait," added Sherman. "You said you met Ambassador Franklin, right?"

"Yeah, a few times. You guys still think he was involved in this?"

"We are going to have a chat with him."

"Frank, when was the last time you had a chat that ended well?"

"We haven't come to blows yet," he joked. "Anyway, you said he was weasely. Anything else?"

"Do you mean is he a treasonous asshole?"

"More or less."

"No. He struck me as a narcissistic asshole, but a patriotic one."

"Lots of those in government."

"That it?" she asked.

"Unless you're hiding a secret black box in your backpack, I think so."

"See you on the plane."

"Sixty minutes."

Charlotte waved her hand as she walked away. He liked to watch her walk away. It was the coming back part that he was unsure about. The attraction was undeniable, but where she went, trouble followed, and he already created enough trouble on his own.

With nothing else to do, Sherman called the embassy switchboard and asked for Agent King. His old acquaintance answered on the third ring.

"Frank the Tank, to what do I owe the pleasure?"

Sherman cringed at the nickname. "We are headed back to Accra. I wanted to give the ambassador an update on the situation."

"Alright, when should we be expecting you?"

"Wheels up in sixty."

"Well, shit. That old boy won't be in the office until morning. Why don't y'all stay at one of the guesthouses near the embassy? I'll let him know and make the arrangements."

"I don't think my boss will like it."

"Well, mine will throw a right hissy fit if he doesn't get his beauty sleep."

"Fine."

"Great. Let's get a bourbon sometime soon."

"You're buying."

"I always do."

Sherman shook his head and ended the call. Then he went off to inform Sanders that their chat was going to be delayed.

Chapter Twenty-Five

The high-pitched whine of turbine engines greeted the Americans as they walked across the tarmac. Both colonels were in the cockpit, strapped in and ready to go. Sherman flashed them an affable grin as he climbed aboard the Air Force jet, and they smiled back. Neither man knew the intentions behind the trip or the trouble they would find on the other side if things went badly. Neither cared.

The pilots chatted about barometric pressure, wind speed, altitudes, and whiskey bars. Sherman half-listened to the mundane back and forth. He would have envied the simplicity of it all had he not known there was nothing simple about their job. They were well-trained soldiers, just like him, doing a job, just like him.

With no couch to speak of on Uncle Sam's dime, Sherman headed toward a pair of overstuffed chairs. The space was not spartan, but it did not resemble the confiscated luxury of a Colombian's plane. He set his mind to the task ahead of him: the awkward and potentially treacherous conversation waiting over the horizon. It spun up in his imagination before Charlotte sat down next to him.

"What time is your meeting?"

Sherman looked out at the red light blinking into the darkness. "Morning. What time is your flight?"

"Late morning."

"Hotel?"

She laughed at the idea. "I was hoping you had a place to crash."

He shrugged. "Some guest house near the embassy. You're welcome to whatever we find."

"Thanks."

"Don't thank me yet. Gournsey snores. Bad. Like an out-of-control chainsaw."

"I'll take my chances." She paused for a moment, considering her words. "Are you still thinking... uh, it involves him?"

"Franklin? Do you have any other ideas?"

There was another pause—long enough to bridge a river.

"Charlotte. What are you not saying?"

"Nothing."

"Nothing that you can reveal?"

She eyed him cautiously, wondering what he knew and was not saying. "Just that I don't see him stooping so low."

"Treason, you mean?"

"Yeah, that."

"I'll keep that in mind."

"You don't believe me?"

"I do, but that train has left the station."

Without warning, the engines throttled up, and the city center shrank below them. Only the occasional pinpricks of light shone up from the blanket of darkness. Those above would be forgiven for thinking the place was empty of human life, but it was mostly bereft of electricity.

The quiet buzz of flying lured Sherman to sleep. He leaned back in the chair and let it take him. Somewhere after the initial descent, his mind spun back up like a hard drive retrieving information. Charlotte cast a glance his way. She looked worried or preoccupied, but he could not tell the difference.

"You alright?"

Her nose crinkled to one side, then another. "Stay safe, Frank."

"I do my best," he replied truthfully. He did his best, but there were circumstances beyond his control, and she knew that. Something was missing from her sentiment—an idea went unsaid.

Colonel Carlman stuck his head through the open cockpit door and announced, "Welcome to Accra. Local temp is still hot."

They stood up. Sherman wanted to ask Charlotte for the rest of the story, but he could see from her pained expression that it was a secret she could not reveal. He grabbed his gear and walked down the stairs into the humid night air, smelling of smoke and unfiltered exhaust. A Tahoe sent from the embassy was parked nearby. They piled inside. Major Sanders took the wheel. The third row was full of weapons, so Charlotte was sandwiched between Lopez and Gournsey in the back seat. Sherman slid on his tactical vest and jammed the pistol between the seat and console. Good habits do not stop.

"Where did the embassy put us up?" asked Gournsey.

"Cantonments," replied Sherman.

The sergeant grumbled something inaudible. He did not

like the area. The housing was fine, but it was on the outskirts of anything worth eating.

Sanders took it slow. Even at night, the traffic still snarled into a long ribbon of steel. Kids plied the stalled cars, selling water, soda, and snacks. Gournsey looked longingly at a bag of chips and tapped the window, testing to see if it was bullet-resistant glass.

"This thing ain't armored," he said before rolling down the window and handing a sleepy girl some change. She returned with a gigantic bag of potato chips featuring Chinese writing.

"What flavor?" asked Lopez.

"Little Tomato," Gournsey answered, confusion evident in his voice.

"I like the French Chicken better."

"You two are ridiculous," Charlotte added, stuck in between the bickering.

The noisy back-and-forth of crunching filled the SUV for most of the drive. Flavors were debated and criticized. They reached little consensus, save that BBQ was preferable to plain. Sanders pulled off the pavement and onto a series of dirt side roads. Even in the capital's heart, not everything had asphalt.

They rounded the corner into a quiet neighborhood. Red and blue lights flashed gently in the distance.

"Roadblock," Sanders informed them.

Sherman slid the pistol under his leg and kicked the floor mat over his MP5. A late-night encounter with the police was not how he wanted to end the day. He held his hand back, and Gournsey passed him a dark blue windbreaker. It covered enough of his vest to make him look overweight.

"Easy, boys," Sanders ordered. "Probably just keeping out the riff-raff."

"So, us?" joked Lopez.

The Tahoe carried diplomatic plates. Passing through would be easy if the police were sober. That was never a guarantee, though. Sanders edged forward, and one cop waved at him to stop in front of two wooden barricades, not much more than two-by-fours hammered together and painted blue. Two more leaned against a wall with AK-47s slung across their backs, glaring at the Tahoe with practiced disinterest.

A flashlight danced across the black exterior before the cop used it to knock on the driver's side window. Sanders rolled it down a few inches and smiled.

"Can I help you, officer?" His tone was plain and polite.

"Late night?"

"Delayed flight."

"Where are you headed?"

"Just down the road."

One of the other cops moved toward the back of the SUV. Sherman followed him in the mirror.

"Can I see some identification?"

"We have diplomatic plates."

"Procedure," the officer said with a shrug.

The third cop yawned and wandered over to Sherman's side of the Tahoe. The SUV had tinted windows, and he placed his hands against the glass, trying to peer inside. He moved further down the car, attempting the same pointless gesture.

The head officer took the passport Sanders carried for such occasions and shone his light on the document. He thumbed through the pages, making a great to-do of the process.

"He should work at the airport," grumbled Gournsey.

All the while, Sanders sat there looking calm and collected. There were enough guns in the back seat to start a coup, and his primary goal was to prevent them from opening the rear door. That meant being polite and non-threatening.

A fourth officer joined from around the corner where the police car was parked. She was older than the other three and carried a look of authority. Walking over to the first cop, she too examined the passport. They chatted in hushed tones for a minute or two. Then she walked over to Sanders.

"Can you roll down the window so we can talk?"

Reluctantly, the major complied and brought the window down halfway.

"Your passport. It's no good."

The other two cops circled back to Sherman's side of the SUV and stood back, just off the road. No longer leaning against the wall, they were alert and attentive.

"How so?" asked Sanders.

"No entry stamps."

Given their entry into the country and the nature of a clandestine intervention in the affairs of an ally, the officer was correct. There was no record of the team's entry into Ghana. Nor would they pass through customs on the way out. They did not exist on any register or hold a visa.

"Frank," whispered Charlotte from the back seat.

"Now is not a good time," said Sherman. Their situation was taking a turn for the worse, and he knew it.

"Frank," she hissed.

The tone in her voice made him lean back like a child in trouble. "What?"

"I know that woman."

He pivoted in his seat as she leaned forward. Lopez and Gournsey did the same, while the major kept on smiling.

"The cop?"

"She's not a cop."

The tiny buzz present in the back of his head grew louder than a bandsaw. He had been eyeing the two cops since they stopped. Their disinterest felt too overt, too complacent.

"Who is she?"

"I don't know, but I saw her the day they delivered the guns to the camp. She was driving the truck."

"How sure are you?"

"I'd recognize the father of my high school boyfriend, and that was fifteen years ago. I sure as shit recognize her."

Sanders wasted no time in deciding. Neither did the cops.

"Do it," he ordered.

The woman looked toward the two men standing on the side of the road and lifted her hat. It was the sign they had been waiting for impatiently. Money had changed hands, and they wanted it over with. Killing people was nothing new. This was not the first time someone had died at their roadblock. Mostly, they did it for money. Sometimes for sport. But never with foreigners. It was bad for business. Dead *obrunis* meant questions. Questions that had no answers, so that night was supposed to be their last job.

The men reached back to swing around the rifles slung across their backs. Usually, they kept them in hand, but the woman had not wanted to raise any suspicions. Weapons at the ready did that. Ambushes work best if the target does not see it coming. The men understood that. They accepted the order. After all, she was paying a decade's worth of income in cash.

Unslinging a rifle from the back takes practice and time. The body twists a certain way to bring the weapon around to the front. Sherman and Gournsey knew the motion well. They had trained Iraqi soldiers to avoid it at all costs. No experienced operator slings the weapon onto their back. "Hold it in your hand or not at all" was the motto they taught. It reinforced the idea that if you are not holding the gun, you can't shoot back. Although most of the team used a two-point sling when operational, but that was different.

Neither Sherman nor Gournsey bothered to open the door. It was a waste of time. The SUV was not armored, and no bullet-resistant glass existed between them and the cops. They drew their pistols and fired right through the window. Tinted glass shattered everywhere, and dirt rose in plumes from rifles being reflexively fired into the ground. The noise was excruciating. Charlotte instinctively covered her ears and made herself as small as possible. The corrupt police officers crumpled to the ground with more combined holes than a golf course.

Lopez did not have the luxury of a perpendicular target, but he was quick and precise in a way that the first cop—the one with the flashlight—was not. As the gunfire erupted, the officer reached for his revolver, but Lopez cracked open the passenger door and put two rounds right through his face before he cleared leather.

Once the gunfire ceased and the cordite cleared, only the woman was left standing. Her contorted face was etched with fear and speckled with blood splatter from the body lying at her feet. Sanders stepped out from behind the wheel.

"Who do you work for?"

Shock was setting in, and the woman sputtered some nonsense.

"Who do you work for?" repeated Sanders. His voice was calm yet terrifying.

The lady regained some composure and cracked a wry smile—the kind that comes not from prolonged exposure to the worst of human deeds but from true zealotry. Only fanaticism produced smiles like that. Sanders had seen it before: the face of a suicide bomber moments before pushing the button, the cruel facial twist of an ISIS soldier moments before gunning down civilians. It was a look he wished to never see again.

"I guess that's a no," he said.

"You're losing," said the woman.

"So it seems," replied the major. Then he pulled the trigger. He stood there for a moment, contemplating the actions that had led him to this point, standing over two corpses. Two deep breaths later, he bent over, removed the woman's phone, and used her thumb to unlock the device. Only then did he walk over to Sherman's side of the SUV.

"Captain, you drive. I need to make some calls."

Sherman slid across to the driver's seat and pulled the shifter down into reverse. The Tahoe squealed in protest as he gunned the big V8, sending the car careening back down the street. A few lights popped on, and the sound of sirens echoed in the distance. He jerked the wheel hard, spun the heavy SUV around, and sped off into the night. Taking the major road, he headed away from the sirens, not knowing any better route.

"What the... hell was that?" muttered Charlotte some minutes later. She was panting, but not uncontrollably, and her panic was subsiding.

"Ambush," replied Gournsey. The way he said it sounded so matter-of-fact, as if it were more common than a red light or rush hour traffic.

"No shit, but why?"

"Rats," replied the sergeant.

She stared back at him with a perplexed expression.

Sherman translated, "Inside job."

"You can't be serious."

"Who else knew where we were staying? The embassy set it up. They knew the location, the route, and the timing."

"Maybe they got lucky?" she offered.

"They? You're the one who picked her out. It involved them from the start."

Charlotte knew he was right but could not jump to the conclusion her mind screamed out. "Okay. Now what?"

Sherman turned towards the major, who was busy talking with someone on his phone while simultaneously searching through the dead woman's device. Sensing a question hanging in the air, Sanders held the phone against his shoulder and relayed directions to a safe house north of the city.

"There you go," replied Sherman. "We lie low."

Charlotte let out a deep exhale and sank back into the seat. Air from the shattered windows buffeted her face and hair, whipping the latter around like angry streamers. No one spoke, save for Major Sanders. He chatted for another ten minutes, then hung up but said nothing. Something sparked a fire of memory, and he reached under the dashboard to rip out the GPS tracking unit. It went out the window. The rest of the ride passed in silence.

The safe house was on the outskirts of Accra, near where the city melts into sporadic clumps of walled-in villas and wooden shacks selling phone cards. They turned down a nondescript dirt road and stopped in front of a peach-colored gate. Sanders got out and typed a code into a small panel hidden underneath one stone that formed a barrier around the house. Once inside, Gournsey and Lopez swept the perimeter while Sherman checked the house.

"All clear," said Sherman after a few minutes inside.

Sanders pulled them aside. "Lopez, find a way onto the roof. You and Gournsey take first watch. The captain and I will relieve you in two hours."

The two men nodded and disappeared into the darkness. Sherman moved the gear inside.

"Can I help?" asked Charlotte.

He nodded.

They shuttled bags of guns and ammo from the Tahoe to the house. After the last trip, Charlotte slumped onto a leather couch while Sherman searched through the cabinets.

"What are you rooting around for?" she asked.

"This," he replied triumphantly, holding up a bottle of brown liquor.

"Bourbon?"

"Scotch," he corrected.

"That'll do."

Sherman poured a finger into two glasses and sat down next to her.

"Frank," she said, but trailed off before continuing. "If they found us once…"

"I doubt they, whoever they are, know about this place."

"Why?"

"This is an MI-5 safe house."

She looked confused at the mention of the British spy agency.

"The scotch, a cupboard full of tea, and the gun hidden under the knife drawer gave it away. Sig Sauer 228. A favorite of the SAS."

"Wow. Sanders has that kind of pull?"

"I imagine he just burned many favors, but there's no time like the present."

She rubbed her eyes. They ached with dull tendrils of pain.

"Get some sleep," said Sherman. "It will be an interminable day tomorrow."

"Are you still going to meet Franklin?"

"I don't see another way. Do you?"

Charlotte could, but she couldn't say. She held her tongue and worried about what the next twenty-four hours would bring.

"Thanks for the scotch," was all she could come up with in reply.

Sanders stood nearby and motioned to Sherman after Charlotte left to find a bed.

"Major," he said, then offered the bottle.

"Another time."

"What did the Brits have to say?"

The ease with which the captain determined who he was talking with did not surprise Sanders. Years in the pit of vipers known as the Middle East had sharpened Sherman's wits, not to mention leaving a fair share of scars.

"Other than claiming my firstborn? They had no intel."

"You don't seem surprised."

"Are you?"

Sherman shook his head.

"The list of people who knew where we were going is slim. Ten people?"

"Maybe less, but I get your point. So, where does that leave us with Franklin?"

"If he's surprised to see us alive, I guess we'll know."

"Charlotte seems to think he's not involved," Sherman divulged.

"She give a reason?" asked Sanders.

"Nothing concrete."

"You think she's right?"

Sherman rolled his shoulders into a prolonged shrug. "Hasn't been wrong so far."

"Well, it's someone on the inside, but I think we can get to him alone. It will take some doing, though."

"What's the plan?" asked Sherman. It piqued his interest.

"He has an unofficial residence. A fancy, modern steel box on the water. Likes to entertain some local women. A source saw him there last night. If we get there early enough, it will just be us."

"Security?"

"One marine."

"That's good. You know him?"

"We've met."

"Alright then. What time?"

"Zero Five Hundred."

"Okay, I'm gonna relieve them."

"I'll do it. Get some rest first. Tomorrow will be shit."

Sherman nodded and went off to find something soft to lie on. The timer on his watch counted down from two hours. It was better than nothing.

Chapter Twenty-Six

"You look good in blue."

Charlotte was admiring the color of a button-down shirt Sherman had borrowed from the safe house closet. It was a sentiment he did not share.

"I should've joined the Air Force then."

She laughed with a softness that felt contagious. "When was the last time you wore something other than an earth tone?" she asked.

"I feel like some mid-tier insurance salesman," he answered while avoiding the question.

"Trust me," she joked, "that shirt is top-tier material. Like Allstate or that lizard character."

It was his turn to laugh, and his mind sank back years to their time by the sea. A candlelit dinner. Him feeling out of place with a tie on, and her looking stunning in a black dress. An outrageous bill and not a care in the world.

The memory did not help his situation. Their normal fatigues were on the plane, which was back in Kumasi. That left them with no choice but to raid the British wardrobe.

Sanders insisted they show up looking smart, which forced Sherman to take a shower. The drain looked rusty when he was done, with reddish-brown streaks covering the surface —a blend of blood and mud.

He was more comfortable in the body armor that fit under the fancy collared shirt. At least it had a function. *What good were buttons,* he thought, *other than looking pretentious?* The major was wearing something similar, but the clothes suited the man, adding to an air of dignity. Sherman just felt like he should sit behind some desk, typing out reports and sipping overpriced coffee. Caffeinated beverages made him think of the cabinet filled with tea. He stifled a groan.

"You ready, Captain?"

"Yes, sir."

"Gournsey, you're watching Ms. McMillan," ordered Sanders.

The sergeant's eyes narrowed at being excluded from the action, but he did not voice that displeasure.

"Lopez. Load up the long gun. You're coming with the captain and myself."

"Copy that."

"I don't need a chaperone," protested Charlotte.

"I agree," replied Sanders. "But that doesn't change a damn thing."

"Come on, let's see if these Brits have anything worth eating," Gournsey coaxed.

Charlotte had faced down her share of terrible situations. Had it not been for Sherman, she would have already caught a cab to the airport. Years earlier, she had cut ties to protect him from the dangers of caring for someone else. Staying safe with Gournsey would have the same effect, so she followed the sergeant, albeit reluctantly.

The three Americans loaded into a silver Range Rover

parked in the garage. It was two decades old and nothing James Bond would drive, but it gurgled to life without issue. They exited the safe house and headed south toward the city. It was a few minutes past four in the morning. Crossing town and getting to the beach took time, even in the wee hours before dawn.

"Did she say any more about Franklin?" asked Sanders as they crawled through the fringes of traffic.

"No, but she knows something. Did your friend say anything more about her?"

"No. Spooks don't share about their own."

"You think she is actively working on something?" Sherman asked.

"Probably, I just don't know what. Is that going to be a problem?" countered Sanders.

"Not unless you want me to shoot her."

"Not unless it comes to that."

"Fair point."

In the predawn darkness, the ocean finally came into view—an inky swathe of nothing dotted with the occasional oil rig flaring excess gas into the night. The giant plumes of industry burned brightly. A few years earlier, there had been nothing but lone pinpricks of light from fishing boats. Offshore drilling changed all that.

"Cap, this reminds me of Libya," interjected Lopez.

A warm sea breeze swelled in Sherman's memory. Along with it came the stench of rotting seaweed and people. It was the height of the civil war. Some Islamic State-affiliated group was operating in the east. They had taken a few adrenaline-seeking Americans hostage. The fools wanted to see war up close. They got an unvarnished view of guts, bombs, torture, and fanaticism—the complete package. Enough to fill a lifetime.

Sherman's team was just down the beach in Tunisia, so they were tapped for the mission. Ten hours later, they found them crawling through the sand, trying to reach an old oceanfront villa. Some imperial-minded Italians built it a hundred years earlier, back when the country was not a country, but a colony of Italy. Time had not been kind, and the place moldered in the Mediterranean sun. The roof was sagging, the front porch no longer existed, windows had rusted shut, and the door was merely the absence of anything solid.

The plan went fine until first contact. A sentry went to piss and saw one man. He screamed like a child being chased by dogs. More men came out, and bullet holes pock-marked the building when they finished.

By the time they got inside, it had all gone very wrong. Bodies were strewn about. Some mattered; others did not. None of the hostages made it out. They had been killed days before. The terrorists fared no better, but that did not make anyone on the Armed Services Committee happier.

"I hope this ends better," said Sherman.

"Do you?" asked Lopez.

With everyone dead inside and only a mess to clean up, it was not a bad ending for Franklin. Lopez had a point.

"With him dead, yeah, it would be easier. I'll give you that one."

A mile short of Franklin's house, Sanders brought the SUV to a stop. Lopez jumped out with a long gun slung across his back and headed for a construction site. Another modern mansion was rising from the sand above the surrounding poverty. It was not an ideal sniper hide, but the workers were hours away from starting.

After finding a suitable spot, he radioed, "I can cover

the front entrance, but that's about it. I can't see the beach at all."

"Understood. Anyone home?" asked Sherman.

"No lights in the principal building, but there is some poor bastard in the guardhouse."

"A marine?"

"Affirmative."

"Copy. Two minutes out."

The Land Rover slowed as Sanders eased off the accelerator. They were closing in on the gleaming structure. Even at night, with nothing but security lights for illumination, the steel siding shone like tinsel on Christmas morning. Except it had none of the warm feelings bestowed by a holiday—just a cold steel box waiting for rising sea levels to swallow it whole. A fancy shell, just like the owner—nice and crisp on the outside, yet devoid of substance on the inside.

The guardhouse was bigger than the average Ghanaian's home and stood two hundred feet forward from the house. It was next to the road, adjacent to a large metal gate and surrounded by ten-foot-tall plain concrete walls. The effect was modern and intentional, but it reminded Sherman more of the Green Zone in Baghdad than a home.

Motion-triggered lights flooded the road with a harsh glare as they approached. The major kept it at an even fifteen miles per hour, trying to convey that he had no intention of ramming the gate.

The marine was standing with his phone in hand as they came into view. Sherman recognized the face from their initial visit to the embassy.

"Corporal Olley."

"At least we have some luck," added Sanders.

The major was right. As soldiers went, Olley seemed like one to stay within the box—someone who respected rank, orders, and rules.

"Major Sanders," said the corporal as they exited the SUV. "I apologize. No one informed me you were coming."

Sanders approached the heavily fortified structure with a gentle wave, an almost fatherly gesture of goodwill. But when he spoke, there was no room for disagreement.

"I thought the ambassador might have forgotten. We have some news for his ears only. I think you know the kind."

The corporal considered the request and the orders from his boss, which explicitly forbade intrusions. He respected the rank rather than the job.

"Understood. But fair warning, he might be cranky at this hour of the morning."

"Thanks, Corporal Olley. Also, Captain Sherman will join me."

"Sir. Please come through the gate, and I will get you signed in. Do you want me to inform the ambassador?"

"That would be best," replied Sanders.

A smaller gate buzzed open, and the men stepped inside the compound. Olley was busy writing out their names in an official logbook. Sanders signed and handed the pen to Sherman.

"Sorry I didn't recognize you before," added the corporal.

Sherman looked up from the paper with a bemused smile. He liked anonymity; it was crucial to his survival.

"I have a buddy in MARSOC. He mentioned your name a few times—mostly over beers, but the stories are good."

"A Raider? Shit, tell him thanks. They saved our ass in the Korengal Valley."

Olley looked surprised. "The way he tells it... well, it sounded the other way around."

"Probably just being polite. Anyway, have a good morning, Corporal."

The junior man saluted as they walked toward the house. With another buzz, the front door opened, and they let themselves into a darkened room. Sherman guessed it was the living room—if a space that large could be labeled as something so humble. In terms of volume, it was bigger than most of the Army housing he had lived in as a kid.

He inhaled sharply and said, "This looks cozy."

Sanders did not respond. He was looking for a light switch nearby but found none. A moment later, a dim glow seemed to emanate from the walls themselves. It grew brighter until the room resembled the beach just before sunrise.

"Fancy."

"A switch would be fine with me," grumbled Sanders.

Shouting echoed around the gigantic space. It came from upstairs. The ambassador was dressing down Corporal Olley with some rather descriptive language involving the junior man's mother. Sanders motioned toward the stairs, and Sherman followed.

"Ambassador," shouted the major.

"Up here, damnit."

He met them at the top of the stairs, dressed in a silk nightgown of some sort. It struck Sherman as something Hugh Hefner would wear—probably cost as much. Judging by the exhaustion swirling around Franklin's face, the two men could see they had caught him after a late night. He looked surprised to see them, but not surprised they were alive. More like a host when some guests arrive hours too early. He was upset, but not angry at their arrival.

"Major. Captain. To what do I owe your appearance at this most early hour?"

"You were told we were coming, correct?" asked Sanders.

"Yes, but not until later this morning. Much later."

"Well, our timetable got pushed up."

"Right, Olley mentioned something for my ears only. I assume you have a new lead on the stolen CPUs."

"No," Sanders said.

Franklin looked cross. Exhaustion was mixing with exasperation and building into hostility. "Fine then, Major. Why are you here? I feel like I am playing twenty questions. Get to the point."

"Our SUV was ambushed a few hours ago while heading to an embassy guest house."

It was a moment of truth, and both men looked closely as the ambassador absorbed the news.

"What!" he exclaimed. "Is everyone alright? Why was I not informed?"

"We're fine. They're not."

"Who are they?"

"Local police," answered Sherman. "At least they were wearing police uniforms."

"You killed some local cops!" Franklin started pacing around the room. "Shit. Shit. Shit. Why did you open fire?"

"Simple," said Sherman. "They were planning on killing us."

"Wait. How do you know that?"

"They drew first."

"This isn't the Wild West. You can't go around shooting people."

Sherman glanced over at the major. The line was complete nonsense. Shooting people may not have been their only job, but if it was part of the mission, then people got shot.

Sanders stepped forward. "Ambassador, with all due respect, you seem to be missing the point."

Franklin sighed. "You're right. I am sorry. This whole being the spokesperson for America is harder than I thought. I'm glad they hurt no one on our side. The entire thing makes little sense. I mean, we've had no attacks on Americans in months. Not even a late-night mugging."

The sudden turn toward empathy only amplified Sherman's suspicion. He watched for eye movement. Furtive glances one way or another can give away the real focus of attention. Franklin kept his eyes glued to the floor as if deep in thought. If it was a ruse, then the ambassador was slow-playing a masterful piece of acting.

"Come downstairs," Franklin continued. "I'll make some coffee, and you can walk me through what happened."

The kitchen was next to the living room. It was one giant, house-sized open floor plan. Sherman wandered about the cavernous space as Franklin hit some buttons on a fancy espresso machine. It beeped and hissed for a few minutes before pouring out three cups of oily brown liquid. He handed them over with reverence.

Sherman took a sniff and smiled. It had been days since a legit coffee crossed his taste buds and as many days since he had a full night's sleep. The brew was potent, with none of the astringency of a cheap roast. Franklin eyed him smelling the cup.

"I have it flown in from Italy. Pompous of me, I know, but I can't give it up."

"To each their own," replied Sherman. The whole thing was too much for him. Coffee was coffee most of the time. Even when it tasted like a cup brewed with a two-year-old filter and some grinds scraped off the ground, it did not justify a plane ride.

"So, Major, give me the details?"

Sanders took a sip and gave the ambassador a hardened stare. "I'm sure you've seen it before. We called in our arrival. The embassy provided a vehicle, and we headed to the guest house."

Franklin nodded along with the basics.

"About a half-mile from the building, the local police stopped us. It did not look out of the ordinary. They checked our passports and realized we never officially entered the country."

"Thorough for locals."

"After that, things went south quickly. They drew their weapons. We fired first."

"Major, I apologize for this question, but did you give them any reason to fire?"

"None," replied Sanders. His tone was flat and deep.

"Maybe it was a misunderstanding. There have been reports of drinking on the job."

"I'd like to think there were some extenuating circum-stances, but no, they were sober. Then there is the question of how they knew."

The insinuation landed softly at first. Franklin bobbed his head along with the idea for a moment or two. Maybe it was the early hour or his lack of coffee, but it took him a few heartbeats to grasp the intent of the statement. His mood soured upon arriving at the conclusion.

"You're saying someone on my staff is working for the other side?"

"That is my hypothesis," concluded Sanders.

Franklin's ire rose as his nostrils flared. "I have a hard time believing any of this."

"It's not so far-fetched, Mr. Ambassador."

"Where is this coming from? There has been no hint of treason in your reports. Don't blow smoke at me."

Sanders took a seat on a plastic chair that seemed to defy gravity and comfort. "You already know about the attack on the drone base. Everything we did or found is in the report. *Hisab's* involvement was proven. So, on that account, you were correct."

Franklin's smug smile crept out into the open for a moment before retreating.

"I briefed everyone on our activities in Havre," Sanders continued.

"Yes, the neo-colonialists."

"Correct, but there were certain facts withheld. Facts that shed light on the events earlier tonight."

Deep creases formed on the ambassador's brow as he considered an army officer withholding information from his superiors.

"I understand your consternation, Mr. Ambassador, I do. So, let me fill in the blanks. The farmers of Havre received military-grade weapons. We believe these weapons were smuggled across the border and used by the attackers."

Franklin cut in, "Are you saying these white supremacists were working with *Hisab*?"

"Indirectly. The weapons in question were used in the attack on the drone base and then delivered to Havre in exchange for transportation south."

"Delivered by whom, and why leave this out?"

"Men wearing the triangular logo of your former company."

There was a tinge of shock on Franklin's face, one that Sanders found genuine.

Sanders barreled forward with the story. "We believe they took part in the attack and are in possession of the last stolen CPU. They were helped across the border by a smuggler named Kutu. That same smuggler took the weapons north through the refugee camp."

"Wait... the refugee camp?" Franklin said, but Sanders cut him off.

"We captured Kutu only to have him killed by one Hugo Martel, brother of Danton Martel, the leader of Havre. You met with Hugo Martel at the Akosombo Dam."

"I did?"

"Yes, about an hour before Hugo was taken into custody by JSOC. After questioning, he was transferred to the CIA. Someone with authority changed his destination. They took him to a facility owned by Layer Three. Within an hour, he was dead—murdered by someone working for the company. After learning of his death, we called your embassy to arrange our arrival, and I think you know the rest."

The avalanche of information had pushed Franklin into a sleek leather chair that cost more than a car. He looked shaken and withdrawn.

"You... you think I had something to do with it?"

Sanders did not reply, nor did he release his gaze from the ambassador.

"You're accusing me of treason. This is unbelievable. I had nothing to do with it. I mean, I am completely divested from Layer Three. I don't sit on the board or even own stock anymore. And I barely even spoke to this Hugo character, whoever he is or was. What was it? A twenty-second conversation. Seriously?"

Franklin took a deep breath and rubbed his temples.

"Wait… wait a minute. You said they smuggled the guns through the refugee camp. How did you find that out?"

"A source. The same source that recognized one of the police gunmen tonight."

A gnarled chuckle tumbled out from Franklin's throat. "Charlotte McMillan."

Sherman stood up in surprise at the mention of her name. They had kept her out of all the reports. No one outside of the major's contact at Langley knew she was with them.

"How do you know that name?" he demanded.

The ambassador turned toward him. "We were working together. Word of something rotten going on at the camp had reached my office. I have known Charlotte for years. I met her back at… well, a long time ago."

"Crap," muttered Sherman. Her hesitancy suddenly made complete sense to him. She must have known Franklin was not involved, which was why she took such pains to change the narrative. It also meant she was actively working for the CIA and not just some influencer—a genuine spook.

"Exactly my thoughts," sighed Franklin. "Major, I understand it looks bad for me. My ties to Layer Three and advocacy against *Hisab* paint a rather negative picture, but believe me, I had nothing to do with the attack. Ask Charlotte; she can corroborate my story. Shit, I even reported her missing."

Sherman dialed Gournsey's number.

"Cap," answered the sergeant with an unsure tone.

"Put Charlotte on."

Sounds of a muffled transfer bounced around for a moment before he heard her voice.

"Frank, what's the matter?"

"Why didn't you tell me?"

She sighed.

"Franklin told us you were working together."

"It's true. I am sorry, Frank. Really, I am. These things aren't meant to come out into the open."

"You knew we were pursuing him as a suspect."

"Yes, but I kept thinking you'd find the damn CPU and nothing would come of the insinuations."

"You should have said something. Anything."

"I know. I just couldn't."

Sherman shook his head and ended the call. His chest tightened with anger, shame, or maybe both. He did not mind the cloak-and-dagger bullshit; that came with the territory. What set his teeth on edge was a betrayal of trust. She had information that might have saved lives, yet she withheld it.

"See," said Franklin. Relief filled his voice. "I told you, I had nothing to do with this. We were trying to prevent something."

A faint buzzing sound tugged at Sherman's attention, and he rubbed the bridge of his nose, hoping to drive away the emotions surging in his chest. Sanders started a modest apology, knowing that a bigger one would be due when Franklin found out the major had informed the general of his suspicions. Even then, words might not bring back his career.

Then Sherman's earpiece hissed to life with Lopez's voice. "Cap. Behind you!"

It was too late. A pistol cracked, and he felt the pressure of the bullet passing through the air.

Chapter Twenty-Seven

The first bullet ruined Ambassador Franklin's overpriced haircut and ended his life. His body fell forward off the leather chair and landed with a thud on the hardwood floor. Coffee pooled near a broken cup. Blood splatter mixed with the brown liquid, forming little speckles on top like tiny, melted chocolate chips.

Sherman dove for cover. The act was instinctual—an impulse so basic and buried deep within his brain that it required no intentional thought. His body just moved as if his muscles knew before his conscious mind. He landed behind a couch, but not before feeling the impact of two rounds against his back.

As he slid across the slick floor, several thoughts passed in quick succession. First came the overwhelming urge to panic. He stifled it down, just like all the other times. Next came the realization that his toes still wiggled. It was a good sign that he might live. The third thought pertained to the shots themselves—multiple, and in quick succession from a mid-caliber pistol. They came from behind and above him, from someone with enough knowledge to sneak in through a back entrance. There was no way Lopez missed someone coming through the front door.

That all happened in the space of a second or two. Enough time elapsed for Sanders to do the same. Only he was not wearing a vest. Bullet number one missed wide right. Number two grazed his bicep. Number three hit hard just below the shoulder blade near his armpit. The major grunted with pain and crawled under a coffee table cut from a three-hundred-year-old cedar. Sanders reasoned the thing was thick enough to stop a pistol round.

Sherman drew his sidearm and fired blindly over the couch in the direction his mind had calculated. It was not ideal or particularly effective, but it was all he could do at that moment. Searing pain shot up and down his back. He had trouble breathing. Some action felt better than nothing.

Then came a massive boom. A metallic snap echoed around the room like a supersonic pinball. Even the cavernous space could not absorb the energy of the .50 caliber shockwave. The towering glass window overlooking the front yard shattered in a fifteen-foot-tall cascade of glass. A wave of broken pieces crashed against the ground and spread out like a tsunami. The shooting stopped. Sherman peeked out and glimpsed the shooter turning to flee. He recognized the face.

Even in the chaos, it was hard to miss Agent Clay King, with his oversized mustache flapping around. He wore dark gym clothes as if he had just woken up and rolled out of bed. The slim profile body armor hung, half-secured by one strap of Velcro, with the other unused. He had hurried over.

The deceit collapsed upon him like a barbell with too much weight. Questions raged in his mind, hotter than any forest fire. The basics of how, why, and when bounced back and forth. All the while, he struggled to breathe, to overcome the pain sliding up and down his back. Sliding his fingers under his vest, Sherman felt nothing warm or sticky. He was not bleeding. That was something. Looking over at Sanders, he could tell the major was not so lucky.

"Captain!" yelled Lopez into the radio.

Sherman kept crawling toward the major. "I'm here," he groaned.

"The shooter headed out back, but the marine is on his way in. Should I take the shot?"

"Negative. He's on our side."

"You sure?"

"Yeah, but get a medevac in the air. Sanders got hit."

"Damnit," came the reply.

Corporal Olley burst through the front door with an M16 in hand. He covered the top landing of the stairs where King had opened fire. Satisfied no one was there, he moved toward the body of Ambassador Franklin. Sweat streamed down his face.

"Friendly," yelled Sherman from behind the couch.

"Captain Sherman?"

"Yup," he replied, raising his hands above the couch before slowly standing up.

"What the hell happened?" asked Olley in a trembling voice.

Sherman did not answer. He moved over to Sanders and pushed the heavy coffee table away. Three bullets cratered into the heavily glazed surface, harsh blemishes on the otherwise glassy top. The major was lying underneath in a small pool of blood, but the cedar plank had prevented any further damage.

"You see who it was?" he asked almost immediately.

His face was paler than usual, but Sherman did not think shock was setting in. Not yet, at least. He cut open the major's shirt and started to triage the wound while he talked.

"Agent Clay King."

Sanders winced. "Shit. It felt wrong from minute one."

Turning the major onto his side, Sherman checked to see if the bullet had come out. One hole in the front. One hole in the back. A clean shot. At least that was good news.

"I just called him," Olley admitted.

Sherman looked back at the corporal, who was just standing there watching. "Who?"

"Agent King. I called him as you arrived. It was protocol. I'm sorry... I had no idea."

"I hope not," snapped Sherman.

Sanders was kinder, or maybe it was the blood loss. "Don't sweat it, Corporal. None of us figured it out."

"Do you have any Xstats?" asked Sherman. The device was an oversized syringe filled with tiny sponges that expanded in wounds to stop bleeding. Normally, he carried three, but they didn't fit in the pockets of his fancy pants. He vowed never to wear anything without a cargo pocket again.

"Yeah, in the guardhouse."

"Now's good," yelled Sherman, and Olley took off running.

The corporal returned two minutes later with the first aid kit. Sherman ripped it from his hands and started treating Sanders. He worked quickly and with the precision of someone who had seen too many gunshot wounds to be clumsy. The radio crackled to life as he was wrapping gauze over the wound.

"Cap, we have two fast movers approaching the compound."

Sherman looked over at Olley. "Did you radio for help?"

"Of course."

"How long is the response time?"

"Ten minutes, maybe more."

Stress and adrenaline distort time, but Sherman was sure that it had only been five minutes since King stopped shooting. He keyed the radio.

"How much time has passed?"

"Six minutes," replied Lopez.

"Those aren't friendly. Fire at will."

Olley snapped out of his funk at the sound of impending combat. "I have more rifles in the guardhouse."

"Out with you then."

The corporal was already sprinting out the door before Sherman finished the sentence. It only took him a minute to come back with two more M16A4s and a handful of magazines.

"Does this place have a panic room?" asked Sherman.

The marine nodded and pointed toward a hallway under the stairs. "Yeah, at the end of the hall."

Sherman grabbed one rifle and all the ammo. He press-checked the bolt to confirm if a round was chambered. It was. The magazines went into whatever pockets would hold them. He looked like some jerk with four oversized smartphones jammed into his pants.

"Take the major into the panic room. Lock the door until I say otherwise. If you do not hear from me, wait until you hear another marine."

Corporal Olley said something to the effect that he could fight too, but the look on Sherman's face kept those words well down his throat. In the distance, they could hear car doors slam. Round two was starting, and it was two against many.

Nestled among the rebar and half-finished concrete walls, Lopez watched two SUVs arrive at the front gate. In the black-and-white glow of the thermal scope, he could see six distinct shapes. Tiny, pixelated blobs moved around the cars and toward the metal barrier. Bright flashes lit up the screen. Sparks flew as the men cut through the gate.

"Cap, you have six unknowns breaching the front gate."

"Thin the herd. We are retreating down the hallway under the stairs."

"Copy that."

The shot against King had been instinctual—a bundle of neurons and nerves combining to create an almost instantaneous reaction. Over a mile was always a hard shot. Over a mile in the dark with a thermal scope only added complexity. Even with top-end military gear, the image was small and blurry—a fuzzy white shape against a smudged gray background. Not exactly precision.

Unfortunately for the men out front of the mansion, Lopez had plenty of time to line up his next shots. Gauging the wind and drop, he placed the crosshairs above and to the right of the first target. On the exhale, he pulled the trigger and acquired the next small white blob.

The first round from the Barrett .50 caliber struck whoever was holding the blowtorch. They were a stationary target and the biggest threat to the men inside the house. There were other ways of getting in, but it would cause delays, and time was not on the attackers' side. They needed to get out before the Marines arrived and ruined their night.

The round hit with enough force to lodge the corpse into the spaces between the bars of the gate—a bloody pulp jammed between thick metal cylinders. Bullet number two arrived a long second later. Someone unlucky enough to be standing out in the open took one and a half ounces of steel straight to the chest. It threw the person—at that range, Lopez could not tell the gender—straight back against the SUV. The dent was deeper than a mule kick.

With two operators down, the rest of the team circled behind the first SUV. They did not panic or scatter. No one ran for the hills. Instead, they gathered by the engine block and plotted their next move. Lopez could see they had skills and experience. There was no doubt in his mind—they were mercenaries.

"Two down," Lopez radioed.

Inside the house, Sherman was holding the angle toward the front door. The interior was bathed in a warm glow despite the grisly scene. Outside was dark, and he couldn't see much past the gigantic windows surrounding the front door. It was a distinct disadvantage. They could see in, but he could not see out.

"Olley," he barked. "Can you turn off these damn lights?"

Inside the panic room, the corporal flipped open a control unit and hit some buttons on a touchscreen display. The house slid slowly into darkness.

"Good. Now turn on the exterior lights."

The corporal hit some more buttons, and the front lawn burned with harsh fluorescence. The reversal gave Sherman the advantage of surprise, even though he lacked numerical superiority. Edges, no matter how small, could still cut deep.

Lopez kept his scope on the SUV, waiting for whatever decision was being made. Running was the smart move, but he didn't think they were getting paid for their survival. Bodies brought cash. Completed missions brought cash. Getting out alive didn't mean shit to the powers that be.

"They running?" asked Sherman.

"Negative."

"Good. Don't let them."

The boom of two more shots rolling across the sandy expanse was Lopez's reply. He smashed both SUV engines. Steam hissed out of the fist-sized holes in the side. Blurry white pixels dotted the thermal scope.

"Calvary is still six minutes out," announced Olley through the panic room's intercom.

"Six minutes," relayed Sherman. "They'll make a play soon. Status on medivac?"

"Bird is in the air but holding for the marines. How is he?"

"Stable for now."

"Wait, I see movement," said Lopez.

Tiny flashes of white appeared above the hood of the SUV. The mercenaries were repositioning and getting ready. Then something flew over the car in the direction Lopez was hiding. A massive flash of white filled the screen, and he blinked hard to avoid the screen's saturation. He reversed the color pattern so that black was hot, but it was no use. The flares were completely obscuring his view.

"They flared me. I can't see shit."

"How fast can you run a mile?" asked Sherman with a mordant sense of humor.

"No faster than the marines."

"Take some shots."

"Will do."

More flares lit up around the guardhouse. Lopez fired where he remembered the gate being. He emptied the magazine and loaded another. In the house, Sherman could feel the impact of the rounds against the thin steel skin. It screeched like nails on a chalkboard and sent a shiver up the back of his neck.

"Five minutes," came Olley's voice.

"Be quiet," he ordered.

Five minutes or fifty. It did not matter if they were dead. He needed all his senses, and a countdown over the intercom was not helping. He was still holding in the small hallway under the staircase that led upstairs from the primary room. The stairs protruded from the wall without visual support, as if they were just glued on. It left a gap between each tread of about four inches. The space was enough for Sherman to shoot through at the front door. He flipped the fire selector to single fire and waited.

Crunching of shattered glass announced their arrival. They came from the far right, avoiding the well-illuminated space that Sherman could see. No safe way existed to enter a building with armed men inside. Tactics, however, reduced the risks. Sherman knew all of them. He had used them on four continents and taught them on six. Everything he knew about the attackers told him they were not amateurs. That meant only one thing—flashbangs.

His thought materialized around the same time a stun grenade sailed through the open door. Sherman swiveled around the corner, covering his eyes and ears to dampen the effects. The loud bang and bright flash were designed to disorient anyone in the vicinity. Confused targets were easier to shoot.

The namesake bang exploded in the living room, and he swiveled back around the corner with the rifle leveled at the front door. Within a breath, two men stormed through the opening, looking for targets. Both men wore heavy Class IV body armor. Sherman recognized the brand as a high-end aftermarket type. The NATO standard 5.56mm round chambered in his rifle would not penetrate the chest plates. Unfortunate, but not unexpected. He dropped the front sight of the M16 and fired.

Mercenary number one fell to the ground, screaming in agony as his hip bone splintered. He went down, firing wildly into the pitch-black room. The second man took another step forward before a round shattered his femur and severed his femoral artery. The wound was mortal, and the man clutched helplessly at his leg as blood soaked through his pants.

Sherman continued to hold his angle on the door, but he knew the tactics would change. Their numbers were cut in half. Given the same situation, he would have switched to explosives. He did not have to wait long to see it happen.

Grenades rolled in while the first mercenary was still howling on the ground. Deep, thunderous booms rocked the house. Shrapnel hissed through the air and sizzled as it became embedded in the wooden floor and walls. Sherman peeked around the corner as more explosives rolled across the living room floor. This time, the grenades went a little further, forcing him to dive toward the panic room. More explosions filled the space with thousands of tiny but lethal fragments. A piece tore through his pants and nicked the back of his thigh, causing a thin trickle of blood to ooze down the back of his leg.

Footsteps thumped on the hardwood as the remaining two men entered the house. Sherman could do nothing to prevent it. He was too far down the hallway to shoot toward the front door. Retreat was his only option.

The hallway was about twenty feet long. Two doors on the right led to some office space and a bathroom. At the end of the hall was the panic room. There was not enough time for Olley to let him in. Sherman picked the bathroom. Dying next to a toilet was not particularly noble, but metal bathtubs had stopped bullets.

His mental clock had the Marines arriving in two minutes. One hundred and twenty seconds, plus the time it took them to come charging through the front door. Call it three minutes total. He had survived for fifteen years, but those few minutes felt like a lifetime.

The hallway was darker than the living room—a black rectangle devoid of light. Sherman could feel the cold granite floor seeping through his pants, and his knees burned from the hard surface. Bracing himself against the doorjamb, he leaned out just enough to get an angle down the hall. The rifle was too long, so he had switched to his pistol. Panic rose in the back of his mind, but he focused all his attention on each breath in and out. His chest expanded with rhythmic ease, and the dread faded.

A silhouette poked around the corner. The faded edges of a helmet were visible against a faint glow coming from the living room. Then the rest of the shape followed. Suddenly, the hall roared to life with rifle fire. Flashes from the muzzle illuminated the entire space, and Sherman could see the face of the man firing the weapon. Almost like a switch being flipped, he could see all the tiny details: the look of fear stamped on the man's forehead, the fancy chrome door handles, the shine of the hardwood floors. All the space collapsed around him as bullets zipped down the corridor. He pulled back into the bathroom.

Amid the firing came an even louder crack. Lopez was on the long gun again. The flares outside had petered out, and he could just make out the thinnest of heat signatures in the main room. His third bullet squeezed through the space between the stairs and caught one of the remaining mercenaries in the hip. It spun him through the air like an Olympic figure skater doing a triple axel.

Surprised by the shots, the man in the hallway turned to see his friend practically cut in half. Sherman seized the slight distraction and leaned back out. He put three bullets in each leg as the mercenary fell backward with an aching yelp. Down, but not out. The guy fired a few more rounds before his gun ran out of ammo. Taking a prisoner occurred to Sherman, but he let the idea come and go quicker than a summer breeze. The culprit was clear. Point-blank, he fired once more at the figure lying on the ground.

"All clear," he radioed loud enough for Olley to hear.

"Good timing," replied Lopez. "The Marines are pulling up now."

"Open up, Corporal," ordered Sherman.

The reinforced door swung open, and Sherman could see the two men hunched in a corner with guns in hand.

"Cutting it close," muttered Sanders.

Blood was trickling down into his boot, and Sherman groaned when he stood up. "I had everything under control."

"Give me your phone; mine got trashed."

He handed the device to Sanders without question. The major dialed a number and sighed while it rang.

"General," he said as someone finally answered. "We have a problem. Ambassador Franklin is dead."

The yelling was loud enough to hear across the room. It continued for several moments before Sanders got in a reply.

"We know who did it: DSS Agent Clay King."

More yelling ensued.

"Yes, sir. That Agent King."

Several cones of light bounced around the room as the marines entered. The man with the shattered hip whimpered as they approached.

"Friendlies down the hall," shouted Sherman.

"Corporal, you down there?" came a voice, unconvinced by Sherman's outburst.

"Yes, sir," yelled Olley. "All clear." He turned the lights back on in the house.

A man not much older than Sherman strolled down the hallway like he owned it. He was two inches shorter but three inches wider and had deep brown skin. The rank on his shoulder indicated he was a first sergeant, the leader of the marines stationed at the embassy.

"Captain Sherman," he said, extending a hand that could crush walnuts. "I'm First Sergeant Garcia. Right mess you've made."

The two shook hands, and Sherman looked around at the pockmarked walls and blood-streaked floor.

"Good help is hard to find."

Garcia laughed. "Want to fill me in?"

"Sure, but Major Sanders needs to get on the medivac now."

The sergeant motioned, and two marines arrived to help carry Sanders out, but the major was having none of it.

"I got shot in the shoulder, not my damn legs," he barked as they helped him outside.

"You're bleeding too," added Garcia.

The back of Sherman's right pant leg was red from thigh to ankle. Pain crept past the adrenaline and settled in for the long haul.

"Get a corpsman in here," Garcia ordered and waited until one arrived.

Sherman stood still as they cut apart his pant leg and

started working on the shrapnel wound. Once it was bound, he took a seat on the couch. By that time, Lopez had arrived too.

"Nice shooting," said Sherman.

"Anytime."

Garcia looked grimly in their direction.

"Right," said Sherman. "You want to know what the hell is going on."

"Would it help if I said please?"

"No, but I won't stop you."

Garcia laughed again.

"Let me cut to the ending: Agent King killed the ambassador."

Betrayal affects people differently. Some lash out with anger. Others turn inward and blame themselves. Almost always, it includes surprise, except with First Sergeant Garcia.

"Never liked that *puto*," he replied with an even expression.

"I see you've met."

"Sure. I had to work with the racist asshole, but he always seemed off, like he was too good for the job or the country. He was one of those people who thinks he deserves a better lot in life."

"That was my take," Sherman replied.

A decade earlier, Sherman had come to a similar realization. It was early in the war, yet after Bush Jr. had declared it won. Saddam was gone, but the Americans were still puppeteers of a kingdom they never wanted. Sherman and his team lived in the Green Zone, a reverse apartheid where those in power kept to a small ring of wealth and weapons while everyone else stayed away. The country was falling apart, slipping deeper into a sectarian bloodbath that never ended.

Somewhere during it all, Lieutenant Sherman met Agent King. He didn't remember the exact timing, but it was at the embassy's Fourth of July party—a big affair back then, with lots of booze, food, and fireworks. The illegal kind, but in a country without laws, no one cared.

Amid hobnobbing businessmen and diplomats snorting cocaine in the bathroom, Sherman went searching for a glass of whiskey. It seemed an easy enough task; the place was awash in beer flown in from the States earlier that day. Turned out it was not. He wandered through the party like a Catholic in Riyadh—out of place and time and space. People were falling over themselves to sign the next enormous deal or solve the crisis beyond the concrete blast walls, or simply because they had drunk too much. He stopped in the Map Room, where King and a few other randoms were sitting around a two-hundred-dollar bottle of bourbon, talking about the nuances of country music. Sherman knew nothing of music, let alone the country genre, but he knew bourbon.

King held sway over the conversation like a sultan in his harem. Most of the topics were mundane, but his political leanings had remained unchanged since his family fled Reconstruction-era Mississippi and the liberalization they so feared. Sherman did not particularly care either way; to each their own. But there was a veneer of narrow-mindedness that covered his words.

Overriding the puritanical politics was an aura of self-aggrandizement, as if King knew more than everyone else. Had it not been for the whiskey and his own general feeling that he could conquer the world, Sherman would have left the room. Youth has a way of hiding the truth that only age reveals.

Months passed, and King kept producing bottles of bourbon while Sherman kept drinking them. He tolerated the talk and privileged babble. Even the realpolitik did not bother him. Much of the war was restricted and fought in a limited fashion. Sherman sympathized with a grand vision of victory, even though his disillusionment with the endgame grew by the day.

Nothing back then struck him as particularly threatening. Pretentious? Sure. Petty? Absolutely. Treasonous? Not really. Sherman drifted in and out of their circle for a few more months, and that was the end. He rotated out to Afghanistan, and King sailed for some other posting.

"We called up our local counterparts," added Garcia. "But I don't think it will help much."

"He'll go to ground. A place where a white guy doesn't raise questions."

"Resort area?"

"Maybe." Sherman was looking off into the distance, and Garcia could see that their conversation had moved beyond the present.

"You can move your team to the embassy. We have space, and anyway, you should see the Navy doc."

It was a reasonable offer, but Sherman hesitated. Although he had no reason to believe anyone else there was involved, it came with inherent risk. King killed the ambassador in the man's own house. He accepted the timeless adage of keeping your friends close and your enemies closer.

"Works for me. Do you have something secure for the survivor?"

The first sergeant smiled wide and thin. "Not officially, but yeah, I have a spot for him."

"Good. Make sure he doesn't bleed out before I talk to him."

Garcia nodded and moved off to supervise the grisly task of bagging Franklin's body, even the bits scattered across the floor. The process was tedious, and Sherman watched with absentminded disinterest. Gore no longer had the same stomach-churning power. People were made of many pieces, and Sherman had encountered almost all of them in unnatural circumstances, never meant to be seen. The beautiful surprise of human anatomy had long ago lost its mystery.

He borrowed a phone from Lopez and dialed Gournsey's number. The sergeant answered with some hesitation. There were three numbers in his phone, and that was the last one he expected to get a call from.

"Grab the gear and head to the embassy," ordered Sherman.

"Copy that. How did it go?"

"He's dead."

Gournsey paused for a moment before replying, "Us or them?"

"Agent King is behind it all."

"Shit," exclaimed the sergeant.

"Yeah."

"You whole?"

"Mostly. Sanders took one through the shoulder. He's stable but cranky."

"Shit."

"Yeah."

"I'll see you at the embassy."

"Don't stop for anyone," ordered Sherman.

"Understood."

Sherman handed the phone back and surveyed the living room one last time. Under the bright lights, it looked surreal, as if *someone had* staged it all. Broken glass covered the entry like a tiny transparent puzzle. The viscous streaks of red running across the floor resembled strokes from an impossibly large paintbrush. Only the bodies were unmistakably real, contorted with pain and fear.

"What a mess," he muttered to himself.

Chapter Twenty-Eight

"I see you've got a souvenir."

Charlotte was gazing at the back of Sherman's leg through the stream of water from the shower. Tiny bits of blood streaked down despite the stitches.

"So, we've done away with the decorum of privacy," he replied. It was not the first time she had walked in unannounced and uninvited.

"Oh, Frank, we're long past that, don't you think?"

"We're long past something."

She giggled a little, but it was constrained by the circumstances. "I suppose that's true with each passing day, but that's not why I came here."

"I assumed it wasn't to sneak a peek. You've seen it all before."

"True," she said with a sigh that left Sherman further confused about her motives. "I want to apologize."

He turned off the water and attempted to dry off, but the humidity left a sticky film on his skin. At least the towels were nice. Tax dollars well spent.

"Don't let me stop you."

"You know how these things work," she began. "I can't just divulge government secrets."

"Just?" he retorted, still naked save for the towel.

"You didn't—shit… still don't—have that clearance level."

"And the major?"

She lowered her head with a pained look. "How is he doing?"

"Other than the extra hole? He'll be riding a desk for a while, which, for him, is the worst of the two outcomes."

"I still couldn't tell you. Either of you."

"Were you always in the fold?" asked Sherman.

"You remember when we met?"

He did and would never forget. A sweltering bar made of plywood and lost hope. Somewhere south of Erbil and north of Baghdad. A place swelling with expats, mercenaries, and militias. Most were aid workers and soldiers of fortune: ex-military folk working for the highest bidder, contractors for the government who'd seen it expedient to outsource the dying. And the do-gooders that followed. There was not much difference between the two. Both were in search of the next adrenaline rush. What side of the gun they stood on was the only distinction. Finally, there were the locals: militiamen fighting for God or country or both. Their fervency came in different strengths, but the truest believers would not set foot in the place. Those that did were mostly Kurds, and a few lapsed Muslims unconcerned with their reputation.

Operations in the north were picking up steam, and Sherman's team was knocking down doors almost every night. He was the only active-duty soldier in the bar that night, not that anyone could tell the difference. It had started a few hours earlier: a simple mission. Some Chechen fighting for the pious side. Except his taste for vodka was stronger than any religious conviction. Sherman was there to kill him, but the guy never showed up. Charlotte did instead.

All the heads in the bar turned when she walked through the solid wooden door. A dozen sets of eyes drilled right through her clothes, and she didn't give a damn. She strode right up to the bar and took the empty seat next to Sherman. A fistful of tequila slid across the linoleum-covered top without her having to say a word. His nose was happily buried in a glass of bourbon when he glanced over. Trouble was his first and only thought.

They spent the night talking—her life story and an abridged version of his own. Charlotte was a year past a reporting gig for AP that brought her to Iraq. That lasted until she couldn't take the inaction anymore. She turned in her two weeks' notice and started working for a local NGO the next day. Sherman kept his story vague, just the rough framing of a life. She smiled at the indistinct edges but said nothing. Maybe it was part of the allure; maybe not.

"How could I forget?" he said.

"You were there to kill a Chechen," she replied.

Surprise edged into the corners of his eyes. "That answers one of my questions then. Were you there to clean up the mess?"

"So to speak."

Sherman thought of their relationship that followed and asked, "And the rest of it?"

"Oh, that had nothing to do with orders."

Suspicion overtook surprise.

"Does the deception bother you?" she asked.

"Depends on what else you left out."

"The cat is out of the bag."

Sherman scoffed. "The cat is dead."

She ran her hands through her long black hair. "Maybe."

"I've learned that there is always more with you. What else did you leave out?" he demanded.

"There were whispers of something big. Nothing concrete or actionable. Just the faintest scent of rot. Franklin, for all his arrogance, smelled it. He was the one who reached out. Few people knew of the op."

Sherman slid on some underwear and pants but stopped at the shirt. He chuckled at the sudden realization of what Charlotte had done.

"You opened those crates on purpose."

She nodded. "I did."

"Knowing what would happen."

"I knew something would happen, but I didn't expect *Hisab* or Mr. Kutu to show up."

"Yet, that was the risk of being bait."

"True," she said.

Sherman didn't know if he was shocked or not. "Big risk."

"We knew a team was rotating in-country."

He turned to pull on his shirt. "You knew I was coming?"

"No, I wasn't told who," she answered before looking at his back. "Jeez, those bruises are nasty. Wait, did you get shot?"

Sherman let out a hollow laugh. "Yeah. Twice. The leg was shrapnel from a grenade, so I guess that doesn't count."

Her face filled with empathy. "Sorry."

"Comes with the territory. Something you almost found out."

"Yeah, thanks for that."

"What if we hadn't gone looking?"

"Franklin made sure you did. He arranged the call to Sanders."

"Did his friend know too?"

"No. It was a favor redeemed. Nothing more."

He laced his boots and stood up. "You're quite the spook."

"We've each got our strengths. I heard you took out an entire team of mercenaries."

"Not entirely. Come on. Follow me."

They walked down the brightly lit hallway of the marine barracks, a tall corridor with white walls and white doors. It sat at the edge of the compound, set back from the other two embassy buildings. All shared a similar stone and steel facade, but the barracks was shorter and less obtrusive. They passed the bar stocked with beer and Fanta, the rec room with all the trappings of a frat house, and the TV room with a flatscreen large enough to crush a horse. Sherman came to a stop at a small unmarked door hidden down a circuitous side passage. He hit a buzzer and looked up at a tiny camera barely protruding from the ceiling.

"What is this?" asked Charlotte.

"You'll see," he answered as the door unlocked.

Down two flights of metal stairs, Charlotte got her answer.

The bare basement held three steel cages, each no bigger than the standard prison cell—six by six metal containers with bullet-resistant glass doors. The last part was a precaution against suicide, a lesson learned over the long years of the War on Terror.

Corporal Olley was sitting in a chair in the corner, flipping through a fishing magazine. He nodded as they approached.

"He's stable but won't be walking soon."

"If your team hadn't shown up, he'd be dead."

Olley watched for cues to see if Sherman was serious. He found plenty and decided silence was the best response upon hearing a potential war crime.

Charlotte stood in front of the glass door and gazed at the mercenary lying on the floor. The cell was empty save for the wounded man. The corpsman had stripped him down to his underwear and a shirt. Even in the heat of West Africa, the basement hovered just above sixty degrees. The mercenary was shivering, and shock was close at hand as his core temperature plummeted.

"What's your name?" she asked, taking the lead as Sherman stood off to the side.

The man could do little more than raise his head without howling in pain. He looked at her disdainfully, his eyes filled with ire and fear.

"Does it matter?"

"It does to me," replied Charlotte. Her voice was sweet and silky—somewhere between a mother and a lover.

"Nathan Heyns."

"Well, Nathan, I'm sorry to be meeting under these circumstances."

"You're not, so cut the bullshit." His voice was tense and carried no discernible accent.

Charlotte tilted her head to one side with an inquisitive stare. "Where's home?" she asked. "You sound like a California boy, but the name is what? Dutch or German?"

"Dutch."

"Central Valley then."

Nathan chuckled softly. "You're good, I'll give you that.

Building rapport and trust. It doesn't matter. I already told you that."

Sherman's phone buzzed with a text from Sanders. It contained the service record for one Lieutenant Nathan Heyns. It looked like a facsimile of his own experience, just a decade younger. A local boy joins up after high school. Army Ranger. Multiple tours. Iraq and Afghanistan. Gave it his all. Good marks on leadership. Solid reviews from his superiors. When his stint was done, he headed home. Except home hadn't changed—still the dusty shithole he left six years before. No future. No job. Plenty of skills, but few that translated into a resume. He tried to re-up, but some old injury came back to haunt him. The Army said no thanks. He disappeared off the grid after that.

"Tell me, Nathan," continued Charlotte. "Will you help us?"

"Why? I'm looking at a long stint in prison if your friend around the corner doesn't put a bullet in me first. How will helping you change any of that?"

"It might not, Lieutenant," answered Sherman as he stepped into view. "But we want to hear your story before I chamber that round."

"That rank doesn't mean shit anymore."

"Look, we both know I would have aimed higher if you weren't wearing that armor. And we both know you would be dead without it. Let's skip the song and dance. You were there to kill us; I accept that. It is the job. What I want to know is who sent you and why?"

Nathan sighed. He appreciated the honesty. "What's your name?"

"Captain Sherman."

"SEAL? No, not with that beard. Not Green Beret and too dirty to be a Marine. Delta then."

"Call me the Coast Guard for all I care; just name your price."

"No prison," Nathan began, before adding, "and no bullet."

"Deal," replied Sherman without hesitation.

"And I want it in writing."

"Not gonna happen. In fact, none of this is happening. You don't exist. We have no one in our custody. The corporal over there is just taking a break and doing some light reading. The video isn't rolling. Our conversation is not being recorded. Do you understand?"

"Persona non esset," replied the lieutenant.

A non-existent person. The Latin made Sherman smile. It encapsulated Nathan's position nicely. In another life, he would have bought the man a beer, maybe even have been friends. They had seen the same tragedies and lived the same jarring misadventures.

"Exactly."

"Then I have your word? No prison. No bullet."

"If you help. Then, yes, you have my word."

Nathan struggled to his elbows and winced with pain as his core activated muscles down his leg. "Fine. Where should I start?"

"The beginning is always a good place."

"About a month ago, someone showed up on my porch offering me an envelope full of cash for some protection work. I had no job, no money, so I said yes. They flew me out here a week later."

"The delivery person. Describe them."

"Some corporate suit. They all look the same."

Sherman motioned for him to continue.

"Once we landed, it was mostly guard duty. A few warehouses, some apartments, and an old house in the forest. That was it until tonight."

"I'll need locations, except for the old house. That one I know."

Nathan bit his tongue for not putting it all together sooner. "You took it out?"

"No. The SEALs did most of the heavy lifting."

"Your modesty is touching."

"And tonight?" Sherman reminded him.

"They told us to gear up. We were on standby in case the primary got into trouble."

"So, you had no idea American soldiers were there?"

"You picked us apart in the forest. I mean, the guys were on edge; we didn't care who was there."

"How many in total?"

"I can't say. We usually worked in small groups. Maybe thirty all in."

Sherman started doing the math: a dozen at the old mansion, plus the four underground, six more at the ambassador's house. Ten or fewer remained.

"Okay, so you got the call and came racing in blind?"

"Basically. We showed up and breached. Two guys got vaporized almost instantly. Superb shot, by the way. Maybe seven or eight hundred yards?"

"Seventeen hundred."

Nathan was at a loss for words as he calculated the distance. "That explains a lot," he finally said.

"Who was the primary?" asked Sherman.

"Never met him."

"So, you were guarding someone you never met?"

"Just a description: white male, five-foot-nine, one-seventy, handlebar mustache."

A fair portrait of Agent King, thought Sherman, although he looked pudgier than one hundred seventy pounds.

"What was the plan after the plan?"

"Exfil on the beach and head back to the apartment."

"And the other locations?"

Nathan rattled off the description and relative location of several more buildings, including two warehouses, two apartments, and one office building. If Sherman's mental map was correct, they scattered them across town. Divide and conquer was the expedient choice, but not the safe one. With ten or so mercenaries left, the odds were not in his favor.

"Alright, if I see you again, you're a free man. Corporal Olley will deal with you if I don't come back."

"Wait," Nathan protested.

"Your deal is with me, not them. If I get killed, the deal dies with me."

"That's the end of a terrible beginning. Good luck then."

Sherman turned to Charlotte as he walked toward the stairs. "Stick around. If he cares to add any other details, I want to know about it. And make sure this stays off the record. I don't want it to go wrong if someone does the right thing."

Gournsey and Lopez were waiting in the rec room. Both men were ready to go. They looked at him expectantly, waiting for the order.

"Alright then. Let's go and knock down some doors."

"Your gear is in the car," said Gournsey.

"Lopez is driving."

The corporal smiled. He was a car guy and loved driving things he did not have to repair. "We got the armored one this time."

"Good thinking," replied Sherman.

The three of them walked out to the white Land Cruiser. Armor came at the price of blending in; it was a trade-off Sherman willingly accepted.

Lopez fired up the throaty V8 and asked, "What's first?"

"Warehouses," answered Sherman. "The apartment seems too obvious."

"North Industrial Area?" asked Lopez.

"Sounds good. He has a good head start, so it could be any of them. And listen, I want him breathing long enough to ask some questions."

"Understood," replied the men in unison.

They drove in silence across the vastness of the capital. Horns blared in the morning heat, and smartly dressed people crossed the road with little warning. Street merchants hawked their goods, and the few kids not in school tried to sell water or snacks. It was a typical Ghanaian morning. Despite the noise, the chaos of the road was subdued. It convulsed with its own rules and priorities.

Crossing over a canal of water clogged with trash, they saw the industrial area Nathan mentioned. A few modern steel-frame warehouses mingled with old cinder block store-rooms. It was a mixed bag of the old and the new. Car sale-rooms were next to banks, which overlooked brick factories and butchers. The area was turning over as more commer-cial businesses used the larger spaces. Still, it was a warren of large and small buildings all mashed together in a two-mile strip. Not far in the distance was a police training center.

"We should be close," said Lopez.

"He said after the church with the blue sign."

The corporal slowed as they scanned dozens of overlap-ping signs and billboards. Finally, he pointed to a small cross outlined in dark navy blue. A six-foot-tall concrete wall ran next to the road past the church. Beyond the barrier was a beige two-story building clad in corrugated metal. The roof undulated with triangular peaks, resembling a series of playing cards leaning against each other.

A small open-air kitchen was located just outside a red gate leading into the compound. Several women were busy preparing *fufu* and *banku* for the inevitable lunch rush. The gate was half open, and Lopez pulled up to it. Upon seeing the typical Western SUV, one woman shouted to a youngish boy in a blue polo shirt, who politely opened the gate all the way.

"Cap?" asked Lopez.

"Go ahead. I don't want to scare these ladies."

They pulled forward, and the boy returned the gate ajar. The size of the place looked deceptively small from the road. Up close, they could see it stretched back for a few hundred yards and contained many sections, each with its own entrance. A dozen workers loaded an assortment of goods into vans and trucks. They shifted from one business to the next as the need arose—a decentralized moving crew.

"He said, 'Which one?'" wondered Lopez.

"Near the end."

No one seemed to notice or care as they rolled slowly onward. The activity, so prevalent near the gate, petered out toward the end of the building. A few doors were open, and a few locals were walking about, but most spaces were unoccupied. Sherman looked at the locks as they inched forward.

"That one," he said, pointing toward two doors leading into one bay of the building. A massive, gleaming padlock secured the door opening outward—the kind of thing that screamed security. He could only assume there was one on the inside of the other door. "That's a three-hundred-dollar lock. I don't see the locals spending that kind of cash on protection."

Lopez stopped one door down next to an empty section of the warehouse.

Gournsey eyed the hardware. "It'll take time to get through it. The damn thing is resistant to cutting, grinding, prying, and drilling. Shit, pretty much everything a normal crook would have."

"I don't plan on going through the main door," said Sherman.

Gournsey smiled and grabbed a few long strips of shaped charges. The explosives used a metal backing to direct the energy of the blast toward the target. Even a paltry amount could cut through a concrete wall.

The three soldiers quietly exited the SUV and entered the vacant space next door. Some old wooden pallets and a fair amount of trash lay strewn on the dusty floor. No one had used it in some time—a selling point for the mercenaries who leased the adjacent unit.

"Towards the back?" asked the sergeant.

Sherman nodded, and Gournsey started outlining the shape of a door with the explosive strips. They stuck easily to the metal wall. He connected everything to a small detonator. All three stacked up against the wall and covered their ears. Sherman gave the sergeant a squeeze, and he pressed the button. The boom was loud but paled compared to most military hardware—more akin to a jackhammer than a bomb.

A rush of smoke and the smell of charred metal filled their nostrils as they rushed through the newly created door. Gournsey went first, using his bulk to push the unconnected metal to the ground.

They were inside the space within seconds. Sherman

braced for gunfire, but nothing came. Silence shrouded the cavernous space, and he could hear each footstep the team took. Light streaming in from the windows near the roof revealed dozens of crates stacked in neat piles. Other than that, the place was empty.

"Hey, Cap," called out Lopez. "Check it out."

Sherman walked over to the crate the corporal had pried open. Six new SCAR assault rifles were still in boxes straight from the factory.

"Take photos of the serial numbers," he ordered. "Maybe the data crunchers can figure out who bought them."

"They aren't skimping on the toys. Got some M249s over here," added Gournsey.

"Some deep pockets are bankrolling these guys," Sherman surmised.

"Or someone with access," suggested Gournsey.

"True. Why have just one insider when you can have many?"

"All good," said Lopez, putting away the camera.

"Let's go before the police show up."

"Are we leaving the gear?" asked Gournsey.

"Yeah. Leave it for the locals."

Retracing their steps, they carefully exited the abandoned unit. Lopez swung a fast U-turn and raced out of the compound as the sound of sirens wailed in the distance. Sherman dialed the major and informed him of their first miss.

"¿Número dos?" asked Lopez.

Sherman nodded in agreement while he sent the pictures to Sanders for analysis.

Chapter Twenty-Nine

Warehouse number two was at the western edge of town, near a vast swathe of salt ponds that connected to the ocean. Viewed from above, they were splendid grayish-blue dots surrounded by strips of vibrant green. Asphalt gave way to dirt, and the potholes got deeper as they edged further out from the city center. The density and congestion thinned. Fewer people were on the street, and noise levels dropped off.

"What were they guarding out here?" wondered Lopez.

Modest but neat homes lined the streets. It was a quiet, almost sleepy neighborhood less than a mile from the beach. Construction was rampant, and price tags were high.

"Take this until the road ends," instructed Sherman. "He described it as an old concrete plant."

Following his directions, Lopez drove, and they could see the dirt road ending next to some marshland. A building faded by age stood sagging on the other side of a thin metal fence. The corporal stopped behind a row of cars parked down the street. Compared to the hustle and bustle of the industrial area, the neighborhood felt deserted. Almost no one was in sight.

"How do you want to handle this one?" asked Lopez.

The fence and gate looked more ornamental than functional to Sherman. "Just ram it. We can sweep and clear from the front. Gournsey, grab a breaching charge just in case."

Swerving back onto the road, Lopez gunned the engine and launched the SUV through the black metal gate. The thin chain holding both sides together snapped under the force like the thin plastic loop holding on a price tag. They skidded to a stop a few feet from the front door. Were they driving an MRAP or Bradley, Sherman would have gone right into the building, but they weren't in Iraq.

The factory looked like a giant carport—a big flat roof with no sides and one office attached to the edge. Some translucent plastic sheeting hung around the open area to give some semblance of privacy. It was a very nondescript place to hide something. There was enough money in the area that a bunch of foreigners did not stick out.

Everyone exited the vehicle within seconds, their eyes focused on every angle and shooting lane. Sherman pointed left, and Lopez went to sweep the carport. He and Gournsey bounded up to the office door. Despite all the preparation, there was no need for a breaching charge; the door didn't even have a handle or lock. The two factory-cut holes were still there, untouched since the day they were made.

Having taken point, Sherman kicked in the door, which swung open against the wall with a dry thud. It took only a moment to realize it was another dry hole. Gournsey rotated toward Lopez, who was slicing through the plastic sheeting with his knife. Sherman entered the carport a few seconds later. A similar scene of emptiness greeted his eyes.

"Déjà vu," said Gournsey, standing in the middle of the space.

The carport was clean—too clean, to the point that it seemed out of place. There was no red dirt scattered across the floor, no trash, and no ubiquitous black bags stuck in the corners. Only an odd oil stain in the center stood out.

Lopez poked through a few boxes stacked neatly in a corner. It was the only evidence that anyone had used the space.

"Smells like chemicals in here," noted Gournsey.

"Paint," corrected Lopez.

Sherman turned to examine one box. It contained a few buckets of paint and a fancy-looking sprayer. Lopez held up each container—green, red, white, yellow, and a very dark blue.

"Car paint," concluded the corporal.

Another box held stencils—ten letters in total. Sherman flipped through, rearranging them in his head like Scrabble tiles. An old memory surfaced: he was playing against his grandma. She sat hunched over her tiles, deep in concentration. He was still young, a kid of ten or eleven. She held nothing back and beat him by two hundred points—that was from a woman who did the Sunday crossword like it was a word search on a kid's menu.

Two words jumped out at him. "Clever," he admitted. "Ambulance and police."

"That would make things easier to move around," added Gournsey.

Sherman dialed the major and listened to the gruff answer.

"Dry hole," he began. "But we think they're driving emergency vehicles."

"Keep on it," Sanders responded. "The joint chiefs are getting an embolism over Franklin's death."

"Where does that leave us?"

"On a short leash."

"Any benefits?" asked Sherman. High-profile damage usually lit a fire under someone's ass.

"Sat coverage and a Reaper overhead in ninety."

"And the cons?"

"SEAL Team Eight will take operational command when they land."

"How long?"

"Two hours, if the weather holds."

Sherman glanced outside at the clouds building like a dappled wall in the distance. "Understood," he replied before ending the call.

Curiosity creased the faces of Gournsey and Lopez. They had been in politically complex situations before, but a dead ambassador topped the bizarre list.

"We lose operational freedom in two hours," Sherman summed up.

"¿Número tres?"

"Or you could have Charlotte shoot the merc in his other leg and see what information oozes out," suggested Gournsey.

The sergeant's solution appealed to Sherman on a base level where violence was the *lingua franca.* Despite his penchant for savagery, he felt Nathan was, overall, a decent person. Causing him more pain would probably not uncover more actionable intelligence. He got the sense that the lieutenant had given them all he knew.

"The next place is close enough. After that, we can apply more pressure if the need arises."

The last location was due north, away from the ocean. Buildings grew even further apart as they drove, and Sherman resisted the urge to second-guess himself. A foreigner might stick out more, but there were fewer people to notice or care. Within fifteen minutes, they pulled over a quarter-mile short of something Nathan described as a depot.

As promised, it was across the road from something called Christ's Chicken. It was a brightly colored building with a hand-painted sign in slanted lettering—one of many places to eat, having more tables outside than inside.

Gournsey's stomach rumbled at the sight of food. "You still owe us a steak dinner," he mentioned offhandedly.

"Do I?" wondered Sherman. He vaguely recalled the offer but was too busy looking opposite the restaurant to dredge up the memory.

The depot, if it could be called that, looked more like a rundown used car lot. A short concrete wall topped with barbed wire created a perimeter around a single central structure. Ten cars in various stages of disrepair dotted the lot. Some had wheels, some had engines, others had neither.

An old man with wisps of gray hair was sitting outside, slowly cleaning some engine part with a rag. He looked local enough to Sherman. Doubts about the location blossomed in his mind, but so did something else: a kernel of speculation.

"Should we hit it?" asked Lopez.

"Hold," answered Sherman.

Traffic was sparse and intermittent. A semi-truck roared

by on the main road, followed by a gaggle of cars waiting for a chance to pass. Smoke from the restaurant kitchen rose into the air. No pedestrians were in sight, and the man kept cleaning the same part.

"Cap?" asked Gournsey. The sergeant sensed a change in Sherman's mood.

"Let's wait."

"You see something?"

"No."

"And that's bad?"

"Maybe."

Gournsey nodded and gave Lopez a gentle pat on the shoulder. Years earlier, he had learned to trust his captain's gut. Some people had an ear for the unheard and unsaid. Sherman was one of those people.

A car pulled up in front of the chicken restaurant and sat idling. Sherman could not see the driver or passengers through the tinted windows. The old man kept cleaning the same part. His eyes darted around the road and strayed from the object often.

Several minutes passed. The car stayed put. The man kept cleaning. Then a police car pulled in front of the depot. Things changed quickly. The old man dropped the car part in the dirt and ran over to a garage door. He opened it and jumped into the driver's seat of a white van stenciled with the letters "AMBULANCE" on the back and side. The police car pulled up past the gate while the idling sedan flipped a U-turn and took position behind it.

"Here we go," said Sherman, his eyes still peeled to the unfolding scene.

The ambulance pulled out of the compound and stayed between the two cars—a convoy of sorts. The three vehicles slid onto the major road during a lull in traffic and headed west.

"Don't spook them."

Lopez nodded and followed only after several more cars passed. Less than a mile separated the Land Cruiser from the convoy. Gournsey slid forward to get a better view. Sherman called the major.

"Update?" asked Sanders.

"We are following a convoy: three vehicles—one police car, one ambulance, and one unmarked sedan."

"Location?"

"Two miles west of Accra, heading toward Cape Coast."

"Copy. The drone arrived early. I will task it in your direction."

"Understood. Out."

"Cap, do you think this is real?" asked Lopez.

"It could be a decoy," admitted Sherman.

"And if it is?" asked Gournsey.

"We'll be ruined," Sherman concluded.

The sergeant smiled. "Good times then."

"Where do you think they're headed?" Lopez wondered.

Sherman was considering the same question. The obvious embarkation point for smuggling out the CPU was Accra. King changed that equation by shooting the ambassador. He would assume the docks were being watched. They needed a different way out. "Takoradi has a port."

"The travel brochure said it was the principal port," Lopez confirmed.

"You read a brochure?" joked Sherman.

"I read," countered Lopez.

"They could head across the border," added Gournsey.

"True, but I think the risks are too great."

"Well, riddle me this," the sergeant continued. "How are they going to get this thing onboard a ship without inspection? They look at all containers these days."

"How big is this CPU?" asked Lopez.

"A TV box," answered Sherman.

"Easy, they just wheel it on."

"You sneaky bastard," exclaimed Gournsey as he realized what Lopez had in mind.

Sherman got the gist. "Under the gurney in the ambulance."

"Easiest way to get stuff past border guards."

"Assuming they are going to Takoradi," said Gournsey.

"Assuming that is King," added Sherman.

Chapter Thirty

A small white crosshair tracked the ambulance as it slipped into the city limits of Takoradi some four hours later. Sherman watched a live stream from the drone circling above. They had leapfrogged ahead when the convoy of mercenaries stopped to refuel outside of Cape Coast. It was a gamble, but one worth taking. With live coverage, they no longer needed to remain in sight.

From a twenty-thousand-foot vantage point, he traced King's route. The men entered from the east through the sister city of Sekondi on the central road, which took them through the northern heart of the city. They passed a technical institute, restaurants in the name of God, and more churches than a rural Mississippi town. Turning onto Liberation Road, they headed toward the central market. From above, it resembled a dartboard, with the market as the bullseye. Stretching out around it was a vibrant old neighborhood filled with thousands of people going about their day. The convoy slowed as traffic thickened like sludgy porridge, moving only a few feet at a time.

Fruit sellers, flip-flop peddlers, girls with water sachets, and all manner of hawkers crisscrossed the street. To the side were businesses selling everything under the sun, their wares spilling out onto the street for all to see: beer, soda, knock-off Nikes, pots, pans, palm oil, plastic buckets, brooms, and more crowded the sidewalk. It was the abundance of a growing city—colorful and chaotic.

Sherman sat in the shade of a red umbrella, soaking in a cool sea breeze. The salt and humidity invigorated his tired face. Sleep felt like a distant memory, so hazy and old that it did not take on a solid form.

"They are approaching the market. About seven minutes out," he radioed.

Atop a large metal storage building, Lopez loaded the silenced rifle resting across his lap. They had bribed and coerced the manager to unlock the ladder leading to the top story. The woman did not agree quietly, and the corporal sensed he was being silently cursed from the office below.

Sherman and Gournsey were on a jetty flanked by docked ships waiting for cargo. Both men had stolen reflective vests and hard hats. They were doing their best to fit in with the rest of the workers. Neither was succeeding, but no one seemed to question their movements; everyone assumed they were important.

They were about midway down the tiny spit of land jutting out into the ocean. Guessing which boat was a crapshoot, so being centrally located made sense. Sherman was sitting behind a laptop with three boats in view. Next to him, in an old gym bag, was an MP5. The safety gear did an excellent job of hiding his tactical vest, but anyone looking hard enough would notice the oddity. Sitting on a bar stool further out, Gournsey watched the three other boats while slowly sipping on an orange Fanta. He too had a bag with a submachine gun hidden under a sweat-stained shirt. Then there was Lopez, high above the port, with everyone in his scope.

The convoy stopped at the front gate, a thick and imposing arch of metal rusted by years of neglect. Sherman watched the screen and waited, hoping his gamble would pay off. Guards came and went. A minute later, the white pixels moved forward down the jetty.

"They just cleared the gate."

"Eyes on," confirmed Lopez.

The police car was unsurprisingly in front, as it projected the most authority. The ambulance followed second, with the sedan bringing up the rear. How they got the third car through was unclear, but Sherman assumed money had exchanged hands.

The convoy rolled past ship number one. It was a smaller fishing boat, and Sherman had eliminated it as a possibility almost immediately. A small boat like that did not have the range King would need to smuggle the CPU to somewhere safe.

Ship number two was an option: a medium-sized cargo hauler loaded with raw materials for export to Asian markets. Such a destination would have been ideal for offloading the stolen equipment. It checked certain boxes of possibility, but the convoy kept going, right past Sherman, who ducked his face behind the laptop.

As soon as they passed, he grabbed the bag, stuffed the laptop underneath the MP5, and started walking toward Gournsey. He did not have to walk far.

The three vehicles stopped in front of the third ship out. Registration listed the home port as Dubai, but Sherman guessed it was from Nigeria or Angola. It was dull, mediocre, old, and easily overlooked—a perfect choice for getting stolen goods out of the country.

Sherman stayed in the shadow of the cranes as he approached. Ahead of him, two men got out of the police car. They were either African or descendants of Africans. A white guy in a police uniform would have stood out. They had shiny AK-47s slung across their chests and dark wrap-around sunglasses. For the average citizen, they projected a menacing presence—one not to be questioned.

"Eyes on two tangos," radioed Gournsey. He was moving in from the front of the vehicles while Sherman moved in from the back.

"Copy. I see them."

The two fake police officers scanned the crowd, the ship, the horizon, and everything in between. They were taking no chances. Finally, one raised his hand, and the doors of the ambulance swung open. Two more mercenaries slid out of the front cab and maneuvered around to the back door. From inside, they removed the gurney. A thick white sheet covered the top. An angular shape stood out despite the cover. The weight made them strain and stagger to one side.

"Cargo is in sight."

"Confirmed," replied Lopez. "I have a visual of some wires sticking out from under the sheet."

"Eyes on King?" asked Sherman.

The agent was not among those already out of the vehicles, but no one had yet exited the sedan. With its heavily tinted windows, seeing anyone inside was impossible.

"Negative," replied first Gournsey, then Lopez.

The cops stayed close to the ambulance, but a few curious onlookers stopped to ask what had happened. They craned their necks and looked in the back, but there was nothing serious. Gournsey grabbed a clipboard and used the distraction to move near the gangway leading up to the ship. The thin ribbon of steel was the only way for passengers to get on or off. Cranes loaded all other cargo.

Sherman held back at the edge of some small shacks running down the middle of the jetty. They served some bureaucratic function, perhaps for inspectors, but he wasn't sure. Whatever their purpose, it made blending in much easier. Dozens of people milled about the buildings in the same hard hats and vests he was wearing.

The sedan was still idling. Whoever was inside had not committed to leaving. They were biding their time. Sherman thought it a prudent move. The bigger bait was out in the open. Most groups would have taken the shot right away and captured the CPU. The SEALs would have gone in already. Yet, something akin to pride was holding him back. Agent King had killed a man right under their noses. That did not get dropped so easily. It was not a bad round of golf forgotten over a twelve-pack. Failure stung more than any slap to the face. It was personal. Sherman knew it, accepted it, and owned it.

The police and the paramedics began moving toward the gangway. Time was running out. Sherman had no intention of allowing them anywhere near the ship, but he wanted King to get out first. He wanted verification. In preparation, he reached into the bag and grabbed the grip of the MP5. For anyone looking closely enough, the act was suspicious, but everyone around him was more focused on the emergency vehicles.

"Sergeant, you have the police. Corporal, you get the paramedics. On my order."

Neither man replied verbally, but they both clicked their radios twice. An understanding was built on static.

The men were forty feet away from the metal ramp, and

the sedan door still had not opened. Thirty. Twenty. Fifteen. The door finally cracked open as Sherman ran out of time. In that sliver of space, that split second of time, he saw enough of a mustache to be convinced of the occupant's identity.

"Now," he ordered.

Gournsey fired first, almost point-blank, into the face of the closest cop. He opted for a pistol. It was quicker to draw and easier to handle than a submachine gun, but not silenced. The sudden pop filtered through the crowd like a tremor. Outright chaos erupted a split second later when he shot the second mercenary in the same spot. People were screaming, running this way and that. It was so loud that no one heard the two heavily muffled rifle rounds strike the paramedics, but their limp, bloody bodies only heightened the panic.

The door to the sedan closed quicker than it opened, and the engine roared to life. Sherman slid out a black polymer gun and emptied the entire magazine into the driver's side door and window, advancing as he fired. As the bolt clicked against nothing, a sinking realization struck his mind. Nothing had happened. The window did not shatter. The door barely dented. An armored car was the only answer.

"Shit," he muttered a second before the sedan roared to life and launched backward into the running crowd.

It struck three of four people with a sickening crunch before wheeling about and speeding toward the exit. Some dock workers dove out of the way. Others were not so lucky. They bounced off the hood and spun in the air before crashing to the ground. A few went under the hood and tires. The sedan treated them like speed bumps in a rental car.

"Hit the tires," Sherman yelled into the radio. He caught Gournsey's eye for a moment and motioned for the sergeant to secure the package. Then he dropped the MP5 and ran after the sedan.

Lopez had already fired two shots at the windshield to little effect, so the suggestion was moot. He knew the situation. Adjusting for the target's momentum, he sent two more rounds downrange. The passenger-side tires exploded upon impact and sent the sedan skidding toward the water. Trying to keep it together, the driver overcorrected and swung back toward the center of the jetty before crashing into the building Lopez was hiding in. The scene unfolded before Sherman as he sprinted hard through the tumultuous crowd.

"Target is under me. No eyes on. I'm heading down."

A figure jumped out and ran toward the dock's exit. They had a fifty-yard head start, and Sherman had no clear shot. He ran up to the car, but it was empty.

"Moving to the exit," he said breathlessly.

Bounding down the stairs like a goat, Lopez exited the building just behind Sherman. The younger soldier caught up to him just before the exit to the port. Both men were breathing hard, fighting against the heavy air and straining to see where King went.

The crowd at the exit was thick. Panic rippled through the air. Judging from his earlier encounters, Sherman knew the agent was not in pristine shape. Age and complacency had rounded out his edges. There was no way King could outrun him for long, even while running for his life. The man was close.

On their left was a road hemmed in by a twelve-foot-high fence. There were no sidewalks, no places to hide. Straight ahead was a warren of old warehouses and storage buildings—rotten and discarded structures. There was no road to the right, only a path blocked by barbed wire gates.

They stopped by an older gentleman in an immaculate three-piece suit sitting on a nearby bench. *"Obruni?"* asked Sherman.

The old man laughed and pointed straight down the road. They nodded and kept running. About forty yards later, the landscape opened up. An empty scar where train tracks had once lain cut across the road. The steel was long gone, except where it was embedded in the asphalt. Dilapidated buildings clung to either side of the old right-of-way. Sherman glanced at the nearest sign. It read "Ghana Carriage and Wagon," a relic of the post-war industry once dominant in the city. Those days were gone. Oil was the new baron of commerce.

Instinct took over. He pointed left, and Lopez took off at a trot into the mud and sagging wooden buildings. The right side remained. A muddy track stretched out ahead. It was empty. Only an abandoned car stood mired in the red earth. Sherman turned back to look at the old man on the bench. He was pointing emphatically at the building.

Sherman pulled on the door to the Carriage and Wagon. To his surprise, it squeaked open, and he stepped inside. A musty odor built up over decades overwhelmed his nose. Old shelving units filled the place, storage for parts long since used. A layer of dirt caked the floor. In the dim light, he could make out several footprints. One looked fresher and more clearly defined than the others—a boot, not so different from his own. It went down the middle aisle. He headed left.

A brief flicker of hesitation came and went, snuffed out by years of experience. Sherman was confident but not cocky. King had the advantage of entering first, but

Sherman already felt at home in the dingy gloom. He moved with the quiet ease of a predator. The H&K pistol in his hands danced back and forth with each potential target. Sherman was methodical; anything else risked certain death.

He cleared the left side all the way to the back door. There were no boot prints on the ground, and he had not heard the front door squeak open again, so King was still inside. Unwilling to say anything out loud, he tapped his radio twice to let Lopez know the target was close. Then he circled toward the right side. He figured King was somewhere in between, hiding behind an old wooden box or pallet. It was a matter of speed. First to fire won.

Halfway down the length of the building, he stopped. The deeply buried core of instinct and response, that ancient part of the brain, buzzed to life. He halted and listened. Somewhere to his right, he heard labored breathing—the rise and fall of a chest unaccustomed to sprinting or the fear of confined spaces. Gently, he reached down and grabbed a hunk of broken concrete lying on the ground. It was heavy but not unthrowable. Sherman tossed it through an opening between shelves. A dry crack echoed throughout the building as the object hit one-hundred-year-old wood.

The noise made King turn in a hasty response. In the space between boxes, Sherman could see an elbow shaking nervously. He placed the front sight of the H&K over the joint and fired. The 230-grain bullet pulverized bone and shredded tendons and tissue. An excruciating howl of pain confirmed his aim.

King's screams filled the space—a mournful wail buttressed by heavy sobs. Sherman slid through the space between shelves and found the agent leaning against a heavy timber supporting the roof. King's right arm lay limp in his lap, and tears rolled down his face. A standard-issue Glock lay a few feet away. Sherman pushed the man down onto his stomach to a cacophony of shrieks. Satisfied there were no other weapons, he sat King back up, whose head lolled to one side, and started pulling out his meager first aid kit.

"I'm in the Ghana Carriage and Wagon building."

"On my way," Lopez responded.

King swatted weakly at Sherman as he applied a tourniquet to stop the bleeding.

"What is that for?" he demanded.

"Making sure you don't bleed out on me."

King gave a meager laugh through the pain. "It doesn't matter anymore."

"Oh, I'd wager there are a few people who'd like to talk with you."

"I'm screwed. I'm a dead man."

"Not yet."

"Frank. Help me. Please."

"Clay, we're beyond pleading. This is your come-to-Jesus moment."

King's eyes drooped, creating sharp valleys in the uneven light. "I may have recently found God, but don't hold that against me."

"Just your treason."

"Oh shit," groaned King, his face growing paler. "Don't lecture me. Your hands are dripping with more blood than a damn butcher."

Sherman gestured around with the pistol, unsure of how to respond. Truth hung from King's words, whether he wanted to admit it or not. He had blood on his hands. There was no doubt about it.

"There ain't language for the things I've seen or done."

"And it's okay because it was for flag and country?" demanded King.

"No, I suppose not, but it changes nothing."

The door squeaked behind them, and Lopez slipped into the warehouse.

"Over here," yelled Sherman.

"He got morphine?" asked King. His arm was as white as snow below the tourniquet. Shock was setting in.

Lopez looked down at the two men sitting on the floor with a pool of blood between them. "Nice shot."

"Thanks," replied Sherman.

King glared back. "I have rights."

"Oh damn, Cap," joked Lopez. "Did you know that? Should I call his lawyer?"

"Make it the president."

"Fuck you both," snarled King.

"I'll make the call when you give me something worth knowing," replied Sherman.

"You're an asshole," spat the agent.

"Tell me something I don't already know."

King hung his head and said nothing.

"Did the sergeant secure the CPU?" asked Sherman.

Lopez nodded. "Yeah, bird is in the air. Thirty minutes out."

Talk of a helicopter stirred King's hope of making it out alive.

"I'll talk if you get me to a doctor and give me some damn morphine."

Sherman nodded toward the corporal, who grabbed a pre-measured syringe from his vest. King flinched as Lopez jabbed it into his arm and pressed hard. While King tried not to look down at his ruined elbow, Sherman fished a phone out of his vest and dialed the major. He placed it between them on speaker. Sanders answered within two rings.

"I have Agent King here with me," said Sherman. "He'd like to cut a deal."

Sanders expressed no surprise. "Mr. King, I hope you have something worth saying."

"I want immunity in writing, a damn doctor, and safe passage."

"Then you really better have something worth saying," Sanders replied.

"Do we have a deal?"

"Yes."

King sighed with relief at the news, even though Major Sanders had no authority to guarantee anything other than his safe passage out of the building.

"One day, they'll see me as a hero. Maybe I'll get one of those giant statues," he began.

"They?" asked Sherman.

The Texan gestured around as if surveying the entire continent. "Africa. The entire thing is going to shit. Corruption. Waste. Poverty. Dictators feeding off their people. This place is sicker than a dog passing peach pits."

"And you will save them?"

"Someone has to. These people cannot do it themselves. Come on. Look around. This country is crumbling, and it is supposed to be one of the good ones."

Sherman resisted the urge to shoot him again for being a prick. Even Lopez shifted uneasily toward his gun.

"Do you have a plan?" asked Sanders.

Clay King sat for a moment and tilted his head to one side as if considering the question and the outcome of answering it. "Order," he replied.

"Care to flesh that out?" demanded Sherman.

"Don't be obstinate, Frank. Y'all know what I'm talking about."

It was true. Sherman had a good guess the bastard was talking about a coup—seizing power to enforce the order of his own design. It was not a fresh idea. Africa was littered with the skeletons of such grandiose plans. They rarely succeeded, especially when wrought by outsiders.

"You want to take power."

"Is there any other way to get it?" asked King rather philosophically. The morphine was in full effect.

"Get to the details," ordered Sanders.

The warmth of the drug crept into the corners of the agent's eyes. "A coup. No one gets to the presidential palace through the ballot box."

"And you were going to start next door in Burkina Faso?" asked Sherman.

King looked at him with a mixture of surprise and displeasure for ruining his telling of the story. "Yes."

"With the help of Danton Martel?"

"With all of Havre. Think about how much better this place would be if the entire country could make something out of nothing."

There was a certain cold, bare logic to King's statement. Lots of people had swallowed the idea over the centuries. They built empires upon the ruins of others. Some were still standing, while others had crumbled under their own crooked weight.

The pieces were falling into place in Sherman's mental puzzle. Only a few odd shapes were missing.

"The attack on the drone base... was that for the money?"

King smiled. "Revolutions don't come cheap."

"That and you had to buy off *Hisab*."

"We came to an arrangement with the strange bedfellows. A little *quid pro quo*."

The picture felt almost complete. Only a single missing fact remained. "An arrangement Franklin threatened to ruin with his push to war?"

A smug, satisfied smile creased King's lip. "You could find a whisper in a whirlwind."

"Easier to get rid of him," concluded Sherman.

"He needed to swallow a bitter pill."

"And the rest of us?"

"Wash off your war paint. We're all playing the same game."

"What about your financing?" asked Sanders, angling for bigger fish.

"Danton took care of that. Passed the money through Hugo."

Sherman could almost hear the major's brow crease with suspicion. The answer rolled off King's tongue too easily, like a small lie dropped in a pool of truth.

"And your little army?"

"Help is easy to find these days. Hell, half of the guys working in Home Depot served."

Another lie, plain as day. Sherman knew it took more than a few discharged soldiers to get Hugo killed in a black site prison. Someone with serious pull was lurking in the background.

"What about Layer Three?"

"What about them?" King responded. His eyes were slack and centered.

"Danton's daughter saw the men after the attack. They were wearing the emblem on their damn clothing."

"Just a ruse, Frank."

"Then who are you scared of? You said you were a dead man."

Even with the morphine pushing away all the pain and ills of conscience, King still recoiled at the thought of his own words. "Just you," he said.

Sherman laughed at the truth, however misspoken it was. "I think you got into business with Layer Three. They helped arm your little band of bigoted neo-colonialists. Maybe for a slice of the resource pie if you succeeded. And now you are worried they might see you as a threat. Maybe even do what they did to Hugo."

King said nothing. Sanders said nothing. The silence said enough.

"Who pulled the strings to get Hugo transferred?" Sherman asked.

"I don't know," answered King with a dejected slump of his shoulders.

"Who knows?"

"Some suit. He was my contact. Did all the recruiting. Paid the bills."

"Does he have a name?"

"In situations like this, it's best practice not to ask a lot of questions," snapped King.

"So, you're telling me you know nothing else?"

"You've got your story. What about that helicopter?"

"Twenty minutes out," said Lopez.

"Major, did you hear enough?" asked Sherman.

"I heard plenty. It's your call," answered Sanders before ending the call.

The phone sat there for a second on the home screen— a plain black background with no hint of personalization or life. Lopez stooped down to grab it and walked out the door.

King's eyes followed the man out. "Your call?" he wondered aloud.

"What did you tell me back in the Green Zone?" asked Sherman. "Don't sign anything by neon?"

King shrugged half-heartedly. It sounded like something he would have said.

"Well, there ain't no neon here," Sherman continued, "but the sun's bright, and you chose the wrong side."

He raised the pistol to King's forehead. Surprise, horror, and fear flashed across his eyes for a moment. He was so sure of himself that he believed Sanders and Sherman to be sincere, as if his actions were separate from theirs and somehow redeemable. His lip curled upward in anger beneath his mustache, contorting one side of his face. Sherman had seen enough. He pulled the trigger, waited a beat for the one-hundred-and-seventy-pound thump on the floor, and walked away.

Chapter Thirty-One

The full-throated growl of jet engines filled the tarmac as the World Health Organization plane taxied to a stop near the private hangar at the Accra airport. It was late, but that was nothing new. In African time, it was on schedule. Charlotte sat on a small bench in the sparse metal building, reading a book—something related to international relations. It was the best way to pass the time. She smiled as Sherman sat down next to her.

"I heard you recovered the last CPU," she said.

"We did."

"And Agent King? Is he alive?" she asked, as if the news were anything but new.

"Ask me a real question."

"Pissant deserved worse."

"Maybe," he said with a shrug. "Maybe not."

"And now?" she wondered. "What's left?"

"Danton Martel."

"You're going back to Havre?"

"Wheels up in thirty minutes."

"Geez. Frank, take some time for yourself. Go and live a little."

Sherman smiled thinly. "This is my life. I guess you're heading back to your own."

She nodded.

"Which one?" he asked. "The newly promoted regional director or the spy?"

"So, you know my little secret," she said coyly. "What are you going to do with it?"

Sherman cocked his head to one side. He hadn't thought to do anything with it. Who she was or why she did it mattered little. Keeping his men safe was the priority, not outing a spy.

"Nothing," he replied.

A bent smile angled across her lips. "After all these years, Frank Sherman, you still have some mystery in you."

"I'm not much of a read," he replied. "The book is short and plain."

Charlotte scoffed and said, "There is nothing vanilla about you. Take care, Frank. This war is far from over." Then she turned and walked up the stairs and into the jet.

Sherman sat long enough to watch the giant blue letters diminish into the distance. He wondered what havoc a woman of her talents would bring to the brutish world they shared.

"Cap, you ready?" said a voice.

Sherman turned and looked over his shoulder to see Sergeant Gournsey. He stood up and walked over to a Blackhawk helicopter wedged behind the hangar walls. The two colonels were finishing up the last round of checks while Lopez stowed the gear inside.

"Captain Sherman," said the pilot. "We've got to get

you a frequent flier card. Think of all the rewards you're missing out on."

"I'll take a cold beer if you have one."

The colonel smiled. "Sorry. I think the engineers swapped out the mini-fridge for the mini-gun."

"And you wonder why your rating is only three stars," he joked.

The pilots laughed and fired up the turbines. The rhythmic thumping of rotor blades filled the air. Sherman flashed a thumbs-up, and the helicopter rose into the blinding early morning heat.

They turned north. The weather was clear, hot, and humid. Colonel Paulson kept the altimeter around two thousand feet as they raced across Ghanaian airspace. The mission was no longer shrouded in some messy cloak of secrecy. Certain details were shared, and some were not, but they had notified the government of their flight. The war across the border was heating up and threatening to spill over. More refugees were arriving at the camp, which was already overflowing with more humanity than it could handle. Ghana had mobilized part of the army and placed them on alert. Tensions in the region had escalated, and some talking heads were calling it a powder keg waiting to blow. Sherman found the analysis overdramatic. *Hisab* did not want a regional conflict that it could not win, and Ghana did not want to be humiliated in a fight with a ragtag bunch of radicals. No one would start a proper shooting war. Everyone was content with words instead of bullets.

An expansive patchwork of green and brown slithered by underneath them. Vast swaths of forest, punctuated by farms and scars of red earth, seemed to continue forever. The landscape made Sherman smile. There was something about the place he enjoyed but couldn't quite explain. Maybe it was the abundance of water after years in the desert, or perhaps it was the people—generous, kind, and polite, so full of life and color. Whatever it was, he liked it.

On the way to Tamale, they skirted the edges of Lake Volta. The water shimmered like giant tendrils covered in silvery scales. Small inlets crisscrossed the landscape below, hiding between hills and filling up valleys. A sudden urge to sit on the beach tugged at Sherman's mind. A lounge chair, a beer, bright white sand, and the ocean breeze called his name. *Maybe*, he thought, *just maybe.*

They refueled close to the city. It was a brief stop: wheels down, fuel in, wheels up. The range of the Blackhawk was less than four hundred miles, so several stops would be necessary. On their previous flight north, they had landed at a small Burkinabe army post. That was long gone, overrun by *Hisab* on their march south. Not much remained of the former state. A few holdouts were still fighting near the southern border, in areas like Havre, which remained distant from the conflict.

Hours passed over land that grew ever more arid. Green and red gave way to brown and beige. Smudges of life slipped beneath the plexiglass windows. The landscape became harsher, more unforgiving, and more recognizable. Sherman saw familiar rocks, dunes, and smooth expanses. He knew what was below without ever stepping foot on the spot. The harsh environs all blended together despite their differences.

"Where's the next stop?" asked Sherman. His mental map had them three hundred miles north of Ghana, which meant they were running out of fuel.

Colonel Carlman pointed a few thousand feet up towards a looming screen of gray clouds. A single blip of black was visible against the pale background. Sherman squinted at the distant object. Barely visible in the midday light was a lone KC-130 tanker plane.

"Only seen this once before," Sherman added.

"It's fine," said Paulson.

"Yeah," remarked Carlman. "As long as you don't chop the boom in half with the rotor blade."

"Right. Then we all die," agreed the pilot.

"And you do this all the time?" asked Sherman.

"Number five for me," said the copilot.

"Six or seven," replied the pilot.

"Out of how many flights?"

"Seven or eight hundred," came the reply.

"Quick mental math says you have terrible odds."

"It's fine," replied Colonel Paulson.

"One hundred percent," added the copilot.

"I hated statistics," groaned Lopez.

"It's all in the eye of the beholder," said Sherman as the helicopter ascended to match the elevation of the plane.

The pilots dropped deep into concentration as the delicate dance between two bodies in motion demanded their utmost attention. Not even a drop of sweat rolled down their faces before it was all done. The helicopter coupled with the boom and gobbled down fuel. Up there, *Hisab* was not a threat. They had no Air Force or anti-aircraft capability, except for a few heavy machine guns.

The tanker went into a holding pattern as they continued onward. It would wait for them on the return flight—if there was a return flight. That all depended on the next few hours. Radio chatter erupted on the comms as the colonels glanced at each other.

"What is it?" asked Sherman. His headset was not tuned to the normal back-and-forth channels.

"SEAL Team Eight is following us."

Sherman's eyes narrowed. A mission like theirs did not need backup unless the intel was all wrong. "Do they give a reason?"

"No, emphatically not."

"ETA?"

"They are about twenty minutes behind. Commander Morris formally asked us to slow down so they can catch up."

"And?"

"Well, that's why we're asking you," said the pilot.

"Slow down," ordered Sherman. "If they want to take the lead, by all means."

"Copy that."

The helicopter slowed its forward motion enough for the other bird to intercept it just outside of Havre. Sherman switched over to the comms network.

"Captain Sherman," came a voice. "This is Commander Morris. With all due respect, we have orders to capture Danton Martel for questioning."

"Commander," he replied. "It sounds like we're on duplicate duty."

"I'm happy to follow your lead, but Danton comes back with us."

"Fine with me."

"Good. See you on the ground."

The commander sounded relieved that Sherman had not put up a fight over jurisdiction. The effort did not seem worth the outcome. They would eventually lose Danton to some acronym organization. It did not bother him, nor did the added personnel on the field.

Instead of playing it safe and landing miles from view, both helicopters came in fast. The trees on the wide boulevard shook violently from the rotor wash swirling downward. They landed a few yards from Danton's front porch, with its one-hundred-year-old façade and long open porch. The SEALs jumped out first and headed straight for the ornate front door. Sherman nodded toward the back. Gournsey and Lopez followed.

Inside the grand home, there was a great racket. People were yelling and screaming, pots and pans clanged against unnatural surfaces, but no one came running out. Dogs barked down the street, and people skittered toward shelters or guns. The town was facing the ultimate unwelcome guests. A decision between fight or flight was forthcoming.

From behind the old mansion, Sherman could hear the door frame splintering under the force of a breaching ram. More screaming poured out of the open windows. Moments later, the back door burst open. From within came a silhouette almost wider than the opening—a deeply tanned face sitting atop a thick barrel chest bereft of clothing. Danton Martel was running hard with only a pair of shorts on.

The three Americans watched the Frenchman charge out like a bull from the rodeo gates. Had it been cold enough, steam would have shot from his nostrils. Instead, sweat poured down his brow in the late summer heat. Danton's eyes narrowed upon seeing Sherman, and he lowered his shoulder as if charging the opposing quarterback. So focused was he on pulverizing the captain that he did not see Gournsey swinging his massive fist.

In a flash, the sergeant slung an uppercut through Danton's chin and into the humid air. All the anger and energy faded as the enormous man's eyes rolled into blackness. He fell to the ground in an inert heap of oversized limbs. Gournsey stood over him like Achilles, looking down at

Hector's body on the sands of Troy. Images of the bloodshed at the CIA base played through his mind, swelling with anger.

Sherman gripped the sergeant's shoulder. "Feel better?" he asked, defusing some tension.

"A little."

"You want to kick him a few times too?"

Gournsey took the question at face value and landed a boot solidly on Danton's unprotected side. It was a hard kick but without real venom. Had he tried, Gournsey would have broken a half-dozen ribs.

"Now I feel better."

Sherman smiled and leaned over the unconscious recipient. "I told you, this continent is no longer for you."

Commander Morris came out the back door and surveyed the scene. "Is he alive?"

"For now," replied Sherman.

Bending down, Morris placed the back of his hand over Danton's nose until he felt a few shallow puffs of hot air. "Well then," he began. "Danton Martel, you are in the custody of the Joint Special Operations Command. You have been designated an enemy combatant and, well, you are screwed."

He motioned, and two of the other SEALs dragged Danton back towards the idling Blackhawk.

"Captain," he said with a nod. "Nothing like a little cooperation."

"Glad we could help."

"Stay sharp," added Morris with a wave goodbye.

"Always."

Turbines whined and blades thumped as the helicopter rose into the air, momentarily suspended above the swaying trees. Then it turned and headed back towards the tanker circling in the southern sky. Gournsey and Lopez moved back towards their own ride home, while Sherman lingered in the late afternoon sun.

"*Francois, where are they taking him?*" came a question in French.

Sherman turned to see Eloise leaning against the back door with her arms crossed. She was wearing another simple dress, but the cut was shorter, and her slender legs seemed to glisten in the light. A look of distress stretched from the corners of her mouth.

"Call me Frank," he replied in English.

"Well then, Frank?" she asked. Her English was impeccable.

"For questioning," he answered. "Depending on his level of cooperation, he'll be handed over to the local authorities after that."

Her face darkened. "What authorities? *Hisab* has all but won."

Sherman understood her hesitation. Handing Danton over to the jihadists would be a certain death sentence.

"Ghanaian authorities. In connection with your uncle's death."

"Hugo?" she asked, with no surprise in her tone.

"Afraid so."

"What is that English saying... live by the knife, die by the knife?"

"Something like that," he replied with a grin.

Some locals were gathering in the distance, unsure of what had transpired or how to react.

"Should I be concerned?" he asked.

Eloise looked across the dirt street at faces she had known all her life—a community of spirits held together by a common goal, or so her father had told her while she was growing up.

"No," she said remorsefully. "I don't think so."

Sherman watched her eyes scan all that she knew. "You know, this doesn't have to be your life."

"This is my home," she replied.

"Their world is like an old tattoo fading in the sun but still clinging to the skin."

Eloise hung her head and sighed. Havre was home—the only one she had ever known. It was in her blood. The red earth baked hard like clay, the lakes teeming with fish, the sand dunes growing closer each year, the whispering acacia trees, and the calls of egrets. All of it, but not everything. Hers was not a choice but an outcome of birth—a relationship built on a lie. That great yarn her father had spun culminated in the rebirth of French dominion over Africa. Her life dangled from a sham, a fable too far-fetched for even Danton to believe.

"I don't want to be a scar on this land," she finally said.

"Then don't," replied Sherman.

"It sounds so simple coming from you."

"I'm not what you would call a role model, but simplicity I can do."

She scoffed and turned back inside.

"Look, I don't pretend to know how this place has shaped you, but I know a fair amount about leaving home. If you don't want to be here, there is nothing stopping you from getting on that helicopter."

A thin smile creased her lips, pulling them upward ever so slightly. "You can't be serious."

"It's a wide world out there. Sometimes finding home takes a journey. Hell, maybe it's here, but you won't know until you look."

She laughed at the thought of all those places. "You know, I've never seen the ocean."

"And I've been daydreaming about the beach."

"What about my father and this place?"

"That's a question I am not equipped to answer, but it sounds like that is his legacy, not yours."

Eloise nodded, running her hands through her cinnamon-colored hair. "He thinks he's the toughest man God ever strung a gut through."

"Your father?"

"Yes, but what a coward he is."

The radio hissed in his ear—a subtle reminder from Gournsey about time—but still, Sherman said nothing. His own father was no chicken, but he had his henhouse ways.

"Do you think we are alike?" she asked.

Sherman raised his eyebrows in confusion. "You and Danton?"

She waved her hands lyrically. "You know, parents and their children. Are you like your father?"

Sherman's father was a major in the United States Army. A decorated sniper. A military man. A family man. An angry man. A drinking man. An old-fashioned man who was hard on his son and his wife. A man whose only descriptions of his feelings were "fine" or "good." The comparison between Sherman and his father did not sit well with him.

"Yes and no," he admitted.

"Is that good or bad?"

"I can't say."

"So, what can you do with that knowledge?"

"Be yourself."

Eloise stood with the thought for a few seconds. Her

eyes darted around the dusty town with its history, eclectic architecture, and indefensible reason for existence.

"Tell me more about this daydream of yours."

Sherman smiled warmly—the first smile in weeks that felt tied to some genuine emotion. "Come on, I'll show you."

She grabbed a small bag. They walked back to the helicopter as the bracing wind whipped dust down the empty boulevard. Gournsey gave Sherman a look that landed somewhere between surprised and unperturbed before handing Eloise a headset for the upcoming flight. Colonel Paulson looked over his shoulder to confirm the addition. Sherman nodded with an easy affirmation. Rising above Havre, the town suddenly looked small and thuggish against the encroaching desert—a receding bastion of bygone hope.

Perpetua: Chapter One

No one drove by the house for hours. The only thing visible through the dirt-stained windshield was a blank canvas of asphalt and concrete. Nothing entered. Nothing left. Horace Filby knew because he kept diligent tallies in a small spiral-bound notebook. It stayed in his front pocket with a mechanical pencil. He never wrote with ink, always graphite. Such a habit meant he always wore shirts with pockets. A modest collection of the collared variety—mostly beige or grey—inhabited his closet. He was particular in such matters. That singular attentiveness carried over to his meticulous notes on the comings and goings in the neighborhood. Make, model, and color. Descriptions of the drivers and passengers. All the details went down in a neat, slanted script… except, that day's entry was blank.

The house in question lay at the end of a compact, tree-rimmed cul-de-sac. Wide without being grand. A post-war addition when such excess came without question. The street was one of a handful that existed on the far edge of town, which was predominantly working class with a smattering of small businesses and a seasonal tourism industry. Most people called it quaint, but that was just a polite way of saying average.

Horace thought the home's location was a poor choice for someone on the run. It offered only one paved exit and the back of the property edged onto farm fields. The homes were small and lumped together as if personal space was unnecessary. It went against the whole notion of the suburbs. Neighborhoods like that bred either friendship or nosiness. Neither trait was ideal for those laying low. In his experience, such people favored rural communities at the edge of population densities. Places where locals don't ask questions or invite those sharing a property line over to a barbeque. Then again, the woman he sought fell far from average.

His employers gave few details when Horace took the job, but that was typical. Although his service suite was broad, finding people was his specialty. The harder to find, the bigger the fee. His current client was paying five times the going rate. It was enough to take the rest of the year off if Horace had been the type to take vacations. Instead, he favored work over play. It suited his reclusive personality, and he was content to spend most days alone in a cheap car watching for his target.

Over time, his file on the woman had grown in height. The cheap manilla folder bulged open at a forty-five-degree angle. Unable to close it, he used a pistol as a paperweight. It was a Glock 22 with no extra frills or additions. Horace craved the conformity of the weapon. Over sixty percent of police officers carried one. It helped convey authenticity when the occasion called for wearing a uniform.

Leafing through the stack of pages, Horace pulled out a well-worn photo. The woman looking back was in her early thirties, slim with a fair number of curves. Horace took her to be attractive by societal norms. Her smiling face was topped with an unruly crop of chestnut brown hair that Horace ignored. He focused on the eyes and the mouth. The geometry of the face was more important to him than hair or eye color. Those things could change easier than a favorite brand of toilet paper. The face, however, took a lot of money to alter—he was one to know, having gone under the surgeon's knife.

It happened after a haphazard job in which the police came close to catching him. He shed the old name easily enough, but getting over an unfamiliar face took time. The woman had no such operation, at least to the best of his knowledge. Bank and credit card statements for her alias did not show the monetary resources. Besides, it didn't fit her pattern.

The file traced her from Chicago to Texas and then to California. Each stop after the Windy City was substantial. She settled down and created a life in small towns. Usually, the woman found work at a local bar. She had a body type that most of the local clientele enjoyed seeing on the serving side of their beer. Her last move from California coincided with a violent episode. Horace understood why she ran from that unwanted spotlight. He also understood the appeal of Stalworth. The town carried a certain level of anonymity or blandness that made hiding easier. That part of the country also carried a rugged individualist streak that favored reinvention, be it personal or professional. It still didn't explain the cul-de-sac choice, but he chalked that up to a constricted rental market.

On or about hour six of his surveillance, Horace felt almost certain she had pulled up stakes and left. Prior to his arrival on the quiet and sterile street, he visited the local watering holes. Only five called the town home, and it didn't take long to find out where she worked. The owner of one bar prattled on about the woman, smitten with parts of her. The man admitted to Horace that he had not seen or heard from her in several days and that, given her recent disappearance, he might have to let her go. Horace smiled politely, paid the bill for his tonic water, and drove directly over to the neighborhood.

The barkeep had divulged other facts that supported Horace's hypothesis. The late nineties Jeep she drove to work was not in the driveway. She had looked edgy in the preceding week and requested her paycheck in cash. Credit card receipts from his contact at Equifax showed she made a large fuel purchase one hundred miles north only one day prior. Horace might have bypassed the house altogether and tried to cut her off towards the Canadian border, but he was too meticulous to leave such a 'T' uncrossed.

After seven hours parked down the street in an old silver Lincoln bought with cash to avoid a rental car record, he walked up the driveway. It was concrete and short. A few faded oil stains marred the otherwise clean gray surface. Grass crept up to the edge, but it was more brown than green. The woman did not have a sense for landscaping or did not care enough to put in the effort.

The house was a solid but lackluster structure. Architectural features were all but ignored. Storm shutters were the only consolation, but those were purely decorative. Cheap plastic curtains in the front window clung tightly together, and the interior was devoid of artificial light. Even in the summer sun, the place felt cold and lonely—abandoned.

Horace circled around the grayish-blue siding towards the back door. He wore an ocean-blue polo shirt emblazoned with the local power company's logo. It concealed the

Glock tucked into his belt. A clipboard and hat rounded out his disguise. Long years had taught him most people ignored a man in uniform meandering through a neighbor's yard.

The back door was metal, originally painted white, now scuffed by time. As useful as a fire break but having no ascetic purpose. People could enter and leave, but it had no character. He tried the doorknob but it was locked. Using a small crowbar that he carried for such situations, Horace pried it open. The old wood frame, more rotten than solid, gave way with a concerted push. A damp crunch met his ears as the lumber disintegrated. Horace glanced inside before slipping on a pair of black latex gloves. He left nothing to chance when committing a crime—a lesson learned the hard way.

Inside, there was scarcely a noise. No hum of an air conditioner despite the summer heat. No music or television noises. Only the faint clanking of an ancient beige refrigerator was audible. He opened the latter and was unsurprised to find it bare except for a box of baking soda and a few condiments. The air was stale but not musty... the woman was not long gone. A few days, but not more than a week. Odors turn after a week. The pantry and cupboards were devoid of contents too. Only one plate and an old plastic cup remained on the shelves. Cheap remnants of an outdoor picnic—a second-hand store purchase.

Beyond the kitchen lay the living room, all bare and lifeless and un-vacuumed. The lack of furniture shrank the space. It appeared small and gloomy. A cable cord protruded limply from the wall like a long rope of black licorice. Two slight indents on the carpet indicated the TV used to sit on the floor.

The bedrooms were upstairs and Horace slowly

ascended the steps, listening for anything out of the ordinary. The house was a simple two-bedroom with a common layout. One room to the right, one to the left, with a bathroom in between. He poked his head in and opened the medicine cabinet mounted over the sink. A lone toothbrush and a sample-sized tube of Crest remained. The sight of such personal items caused his eyebrows to rise, but those things could be bought anywhere. No actual loss in leaving them behind. The shower curtain still hung from plastic rings over the tub and Horace ran his hand across the interior surface. It was drier than Palm Springs. He moved towards the larger of the two bedrooms.

It looked no different from any other rental. Cheap off-white paint, crappy brown carpet, and blinds that were impossible to clean and always got tangled. Horace walked around the room once, then twice. Looking at the floor, he found it peculiar that there were no marks. No furniture had been removed as if none had existed. The woman usually settled in for years, so the lack of fixtures after nine months felt odd. He opened the closet, which held nothing but a hanger. No scuff marks adorned the walls. None of the inevitable wear and tear that rental homes endure.

He moved onto the second bedroom, facing the back of the house. It too had the same cheap paint, carpet, and blinds, but seemed more worn. The coarse brown fabric revealed slight indentations. Nothing substantial, but something akin to furniture. With a delicate touch, he parted the blinds and looked over the vast emptiness behind the house. Something grew out there in the fields but he cared little about the details. Perhaps wheat or barley. Then he remembered he was in Idaho and assumed it must be potatoes. Either way, the intricacies of farming did not pique his interest. He was a city man whose proclivities could only be satiated in large urban areas.

Lost in that mundane thought, Horace took out his phone and dialed a number given to him at the start of the job. He had called it twice before. Three rings rolled by before someone answered.

Two thousand miles away in a curving steel-clad building overlooking the Potomac River, James Abney drummed his fingers against his rosewood desk. Slim and modern, it sat on stainless-steel legs that formed two squares underneath the large rectangular top. It reminded him of the provost's desk at Harvard, only more expensive. The cost of a mid-range car in his case. Not that he sweated the money. Quite the opposite.

A shrill ringtone emanated from inside. He opened a drawer and removed a cheap flip phone. It came from a rundown bodega a few miles from the capitol. A place that had no cameras and only accepted cash. No record of the sale existed, which suited Abney fine.

"What news do you have?"

"She's not here. I'm moving north," replied Horace.

Abney's eyes narrowed. Years had gone into the search, not to mention the hundreds of thousands of dollars. Finding the woman meant a lot to him, but even more to his client. Not just any client. His benefactor. The reason for his success. A man Abney might call his father if he had allowed such a thing.

"Keep at it and remember I'm paying good money for this," Abney growled.

"Of course," Horace replied with an audible sneer.

Abney closed the burner phone and slid it back into the desk drawer, which closed with a soft click. He continued drumming his fingers against the smooth copper-colored top as the quiet action helped him think.

Filby came highly recommended by friends whose problems resembled his own. Despite his reputation, the man was not generating much success. The latest lead carried promise. He'd seen the image—it was her. Older and thinner, but still the same woman. Days had passed with nothing. Then the call came, and still nothing. A seed of doubt grew in his mind, calling into question Filby's abilities. He considered telling his client, but no news equaled failure and Abney did not fail. He built a business on success, results, and getting things done that others could not or would not do. No, the call could wait a little longer.

Horace placed the phone back in his pocket and took a deep breath. Clients were clients and money was money, but something about his current meal ticket chafed against his better judgement. He did not like the man or his attitude. He pictured the guy in an over-priced suit, the tailored kind, sitting in some leather armchair in a wood-paneled room. Smoke would waft by from the cigars and hollow laughter would fill the space. An asshole, if he cared to be so succinct.

Horace shook back his disgust and sniffed. Lingering on the stale air was the faint trace of perfume. He sniffed again, this time more thoughtfully. It was a woman's scent. He wondered how long essential oils hung in the air, but the question drifted to the back of his mind. The rear bedroom must have been hers. It made sense. The woman was no slouch. She had disappeared three times. Repetition bred experience, but it also created complacency. Too much success led to sloppiness and slip-ups. The local newspaper took her photo, which ended up online. The algorithms did the rest. His arrival was inevitable.

He turned to open the tiny built-in closet with scuffed wood doors. It was too late. They were already open. Standing in the small, shadowy interior was the woman from the photo. Her eyes were wide but focused and almost shiny in the gloom. Horace went for the Glock concealed beneath his shirt. It didn't matter. The scratched-up revolver in the woman's hands fired first. Knocked over by the force of the heavy grain bullet, Horace gazed at the white popcorn ceiling as it slowly faded to black.

The woman stood over the body for a moment, willing her hands to stop shaking. There was no doubt in her mind the man on the ground was dead. She hit center mass and the wound was fatal. A professional would have fired once more, just to be sure, but the woman was not a professional, not at that.

She reached down, grabbed the Glock, an extra magazine, and the phone before stuffing them into a plain green backpack. She searched for a wallet but found nothing. On the way out the back door, she stopped long enough to send a quick text from her own phone. Then she disappeared into the barley field.

Grab your copy...
vinci-books.com/perpetua

About the Author

Joel Austin grew up in rural California under the leafy oak trees and holds an M.A. in History and International Relations. He lives in Colorado with his wife and daughter.